PRAISE FOR THE CALLING

"*The Calling* is a powerful, gripping and terrifying novel, the sort that possesses your whole life while you're reading it; it'll stalk you through the day, and inform your dreams. Swartwood has delivered a novel that will become a classic."

— TIM LEBBON, *NEW YORK TIMES* BESTSELLING AUTHOR OF *THE SILENCE*

"Robert Swartwood's *The Calling* is a diabolical rocket sled of a psychological thriller. Told through the vivid, almost druggy point of view of a young man on the edge, tangled in a web of tragedy and surreal horror, Swartwood's novel gets under the skin and stays there. Highly recommended."

— JAY BONANSINGA, *NEW YORK TIMES* BESTSELLING AUTHOR ~~ ~~~~~ ~~~~ KING

NOR

"Small town horro

— HELLNOTES

THE CALLING

ROBERT SWARTWOOD

RMS PRESS

Copyright © 2011 Robert Swartwood

Cover design copyright © 2019 Damonza

This is a work of fiction. Names, characters, places and incidents are either products of the author's imagination or used fictitiously. Any resemblance to actual events, locales, or persons, living or dead, is entirely coincidental. All rights reserved. No part of this publication can be reproduced or transmitted in any form or by any means, electronic or mechanical, without permission in writing from Robert Swartwood.

ISBN-13: 978-1-945819-17-9
ISBN-10: 1-945819-17-0

www.robertswartwood.com

AUTHOR'S NOTE

While many of the places and locations mentioned within this novel are real, the towns of Lanton, Pennsylvania, and Bridgton, New York, and their inhabitants, exist wholly in the author's imagination, and any resemblance between the people who live there and people who live in the real world is coincidental and unintended.

For my parents

Who in the rainbow can show the line where the violet tint ends and the orange tint begins? Distinctly we see the difference of the colors, but when exactly does the one first blindingly enter into the other? So with sanity and insanity.

—Herman Melville,
Billy Budd

PROLOGUE

LIFE ISN'T FAIR.

It's an old adage, a tired cliché, but you know this to be true. You've known it all your life, ever since you were a boy.

Like when you were forced to eat all your Brussels sprouts before being allowed to leave the dinner table. Or when you twisted your ankle on the first day of middle school practice and couldn't play soccer for the rest of the season. Or when you asked Lydia Mynell out and she said no and then avoided you for the next two weeks, which you later admitted was a pretty impressive feat as your lockers stood side by side.

Life isn't fair, but who said it would be?

Your parents certainly didn't.

Not your father, an intelligent, hardworking man who has been laid off three times from jobs at which he excelled. A college graduate, he now works as an assistant grocery store manager at the local Giant, earning much less than he did at all of his previous jobs.

Not your mother, a smart, compassionate woman who teaches children with special needs. You were thirteen when she was diagnosed with breast cancer. You were fourteen when she began her treatments, when she lost her hair and over the course of five months went through at least a dozen different wigs.

Your parents are a testament to the fact that life isn't fair, yet they've never complained. Even when your father worked at a temp agency to help make sure the bills were paid on time, even when your mother lay in what everyone believed was her deathbed, they never said boo.

They always stayed positive, no matter what happened. Always smiling. Always holding hands. Always telling you they loved you.

It's because of them you began to understand it doesn't matter if life isn't fair. No matter what it throws at you, how many curveballs, it's your job, your purpose, to do your best. To never complain. To always put one step in front of the other and keep walking.

Then one morning, the day after your high school graduation, you wake to a faint distant buzzing noise. You open your eyes, roll over in bed, and look at your alarm clock. It's eleven-thirty. The distant buzzing is coming from your parents' room. You've heard it for as long as you can remember, and it's okay, because soon the buzzing will be turned off.

You roll back over, reposition the pillow, and close your eyes.

And still the buzzing continues: a repetitive *bwaamp-bwaamp-bwaamp-bwaamp* that has begun to drill into the side of your brain.

You sit up, propping your elbow on the bed, and yell for someone to turn it off. You wait a few moments for a reply, maybe even silence, but all that answers you is the buzzing.

You yell again, louder this time, and glance back at your own alarm clock. This early morning insanity has been going on now for five minutes. It feels like an hour. Grumbling under your breath, you throw off the sheets and get out of bed.

Opening your door, you yell for your father. No answer, so you yell for your mother. No answer still, none except that annoying low *bwaamp-bwaamp-bwaamp-bwaamp*, which is much louder now that you've stepped into the hallway. You call out one final time, but when still no answer comes, you start to make your way toward their bedroom.

Their door is closed. You knock, once, and call their names. Once again, no answer comes, and for the first time in the couple of minutes you've been awake, you begin to worry.

Placing your hand on the doorknob, you notice you are shaking.

When you open the door the first thing that hits you is the smell. Like a massive fist, it knocks you back just a couple of steps, and for a moment you aren't even aware of what you're staring at: you aren't aware of the two bodies on the bed, of all the blood.

Your stomach tightens. The house begins to spin. Putting your hands to your mouth, you back away. You realize you've stopped breathing and in your throat bile is rising, and you look around the hallway, at once feeling frightened and alone.

A dream, you tell yourself, this is just a nightmare, and any moment now you will wake up, you will open your eyes to the sound of a distant buzzing coming from your parents' room—the same very buzzing now crying out inches from their dried blood and cold flesh.

Bile is still in your throat, but you're able to keep it down, you're able to start breathing again. Lightheaded, disoriented, you turn away and head toward your room, the only thing you still know and trust.

And you see it.

On your door, you see the thing that will no doubt haunt

you for the rest of your life. You see it and you know that this is no dream, that this is no simple nightmare. All this is real, all this is reality, and you are left standing there staring, trembling while your parents' bodies lie motionless behind you.

Only later does the nightmare begin.

CHAPTER ONE

THE CHURCH PARKING lot was deserted. I parked in the handicapped space closest to the entrance. The trailing police cruiser
parked in the handicapped space beside me, and for a moment
I expected the officer behind the wheel to shake his head,
motion for me to back up and park in a regular spot. But when
I looked over at him he had already shut off his car and had
this morning's paper open in front of him.

Pastor James Young was waiting for me at the entrance. A
man in his early fifties, with light brown eyes and a round,
pleasant face, he wore chinos and a red polo shirt and shook
my hand the moment I stepped inside.

"Christopher," he said solemnly, "how are you doing?"

"Honestly?"

He nodded.

"Honestly, I'm exhausted."

It was June 6, 2003, and my parents had already been dead
for a week.

Without a word Pastor James Young led me toward his
office. The hallway was long and deserted, its carpet shaded
midnight blue with a design of blood red diamonds scattered

throughout. Just as we entered the lobby, I glanced up at the support beam in the ceiling and saw a body hanging from a noose.

"Christopher?" The pastor was a few paces ahead, looking back at me with a frown. "Is everything all right?"

I blinked and the body and the noose were gone. It was just a normal support beam, thick and wooden, its weathered look clashing with the flawless white paint.

"Ever wonder the truth?"

"It's just a story," I said, because I knew it was just a story, some ghost story a kid no doubt made up one day during service because he was bored. But ever since I was young I'd heard the stories, the rumors, the myths of that crossbeam.

Staring up at the ceiling, Pastor James Young said, "The way I heard it, when this place was built fifty years ago, a local man came late one night and hung himself there. Supposedly he had done something awful, something he thought was unforgivable, and figured killing himself like that was the only way."

I wondered briefly how many times the pastor had told this story. For as long as he'd been here, he was no doubt asked about the beam. Did the story change slightly every time he told it—did he add something new? Or did he have the thing memorized and got so bored with the telling after so long that it was like saying one of the many Bible verses they make children learn in Sunday school?

"The only way for what?" I asked.

"Forgiveness. Redemption, maybe." He shrugged. "Who really knows?"

We continued walking again, down another hallway, and seconds later we were in his office, Pastor James Young behind his large oak desk, me in one of the two chairs facing him.

"Now," he said, "what is it I can help you with?"

"To be honest, I'm not really sure you can help me at all."

He forced a smile. "I can always try."

Despite the church's size—its attendance for both morning services was close to one thousand on any given Sunday—his office was tiny. Besides the desk, which took up a good quarter of the room, there were three filing cabinets huddled in one corner, and a large bookcase that covered nearly an entire wall. Books mostly on theology filled the shelves. A bonsai tree sat on a table behind his desk, and while it was positioned to receive sunlight from one of the two open windows, it looked as if a few of its tiny branches had begun to wither.

"How much do you know about what happened last week?"

He looked down at his desk, moved a stack of papers from one side to the other, and sighed. "Just that your parents were murdered. That you found their bodies. That the police first suspected you of doing it but then cleared you."

"That's it?"

He nodded.

So that sounded about right. Those were the key facts, the essential information, that was put in the papers. Not about what was painted on my bedroom door. Not about how it was supposedly a calling card from the killer saying I was next.

"I'm going away for a little," I said. "For a week or a month, I don't know how long. Steve ... well, he wanted me to talk to a psychiatrist before I left. Wanted to make sure I'm okay in the head."

The frown appeared on the pastor's face again. "So then why did Police Chief Carpenter ask that I speak with you?"

"Because I told him I'd rather see you instead."

"Why?"

I glanced away, toward the wall that had random pictures of different sizes scattered all over a large cork board. Many were of Pastor James Young and his family—his wife and two sons—while others showed him together with various church families. One of those church families was my parents. Taken at what looked like a church picnic, the pastor standing between my father and mother, all three of them with their arms around their shoulders, smiling at the camera.

"Christopher? Why did you want to see me instead?"

I leaned forward in my seat. Opened my mouth but didn't say anything.

"Are feeling okay?" James Young asked. "You look pale. Do you want something to drink? I can get you a bottle of water. Or—" His eyes shifted to something on his desk. "How about a lollipop?"

It was then that I noticed the jar of lollipops on his desk. Together they created the color of the rainbow. I remembered it was one of Pastor Young's trademarks, to always have a lollipop or two in his suit jacket every Sunday morning. Oftentimes a child might start acting up, begin crying, and while he was in the lobby he would hold out a lollipop and say, "Hey now, no need to be sad." It was the same thing he'd said to me the day I was baptized. I had been five years old. I was nervous, having to go out in front of a full congregation of strangers, and began crying. And James Young, the good pastor that he was, pulled out a red lollipop, leaned down, and with a smile said, "Hey now, Christopher, no need to be sad."

It had been true then, but now, thirteen years later, my life had been turned upside down. Family that I'd hardly even known existed was now part of my life, and I would soon be traveling with them to New York to hide away from what could only be called a sociopath.

"What's that?" I said, pointing past the jar of rainbow-colored lollipops at something else on his desk. "You're not recording this, are you?"

He gave me a peculiar look, then glanced down at the tape recorder resting beside his telephone. He placed a hand on it, shaking his head. "No, of course not. Before you came I was listening to a tape Matt Hatfield sent me yesterday. They had a speaker over at Trinity last weekend he wanted me to hear. The man travels around the country with his—"

"Do demons exist?"

A breeze came through the windows, causing the bonsai tree to shiver.

Pastor James Young said, "I'm sorry?"

"Demons," I said. "Do they exist?"

"That's why you wanted to see me? To ask me about"—he cleared his throat—"demons?"

"Actually, I'd originally wanted to discuss the indifference of God. You know, that whole why-does-bad-stuff-happen-to-good-people debate."

"And you don't want to discuss that anymore?"

"Not really. Pardon my French, but I figure if we discuss that, you'd give me one long line of bullshit, and I really don't have the patience for that right now."

"So instead you'd rather ask me about demons."

"That's right."

"Any particular reason why?"

"Just curious."

He was silent for a moment, just watching me, before speaking. "Why, yes, of course they exist."

"Can you prove it?"

"They're mentioned in the Bible."

"No, I mean something more substantial."

"I baptized you when you were very young. If you don't mind me asking, Christopher, are you still a believer?"

"That doesn't pertain to my question."

"But it does. Because if you believe that God exists, then you believe that Satan exists. And if you believe that they exist, you must also believe that angels and demons exist."

"But how do you *know*?"

He opened his mouth, started to speak, stopped. Seemed to think for a few seconds, before saying, "Faith."

I shook my head. "That's not good enough."

"Okay, then what about ghosts? Do you believe that ghosts exist?"

I didn't say anything.

"You know it's funny, but people around the world are more apt to believe in the existence of ghosts than they are in demons. Maybe that's because through the ages people have come to think of demons as little red creatures with horns and tails and pitchforks. But they're nothing like that. They ... they're just like angels in a way, but no longer good."

He leaned forward in his chair, setting his hands on the desktop.

"Some people also believe that when you die, you become either an angel or a demon. This is untrue. Angels and demons, they're completely different species than us. They were here close to the beginning of time and they'll be here toward the end of time, but we humans ... our existence lasts only in a blink of God's eye."

He paused.

"Christopher, I'd really like to help you, but I can't do that unless you tell me what's going on. Why are you asking about demons?"

I glanced at the wall of pictures again. "Last week," I started to say, but then faltered, lost my voice. I cleared my throat and tried again. "Last week, after what happened, I remembered a dream I had about a year ago. In the dream I was walking around a massive store, like a Walmart, and it was completely deserted. Eventually I needed to take a piss so I went into the bathroom. It was really bright inside and silent, so much so that when the door shut it echoed."

My eyes had focused on the picture of my parents.

"So then I'm standing there at the urinal, just minding my

own business, when someone comes out of one of the stalls. He doesn't flush the toilet or anything, he just opens the door and comes out. And ... and somehow I'm seeing all this, like from a third person point of view. I see myself standing at the urinal, and I see this man walking from the stalls toward the sinks. To get there, he needs to pass me, and I don't really think too much about it, because why would I? But it's right when he passes me, his shoes echoing off the floor, that he suddenly steps forward, wraps his hands around my neck, and starts choking me."

I blinked, looked back at the pastor.

"And at that same moment I woke up and I ... I couldn't breathe. It was like someone was standing right over me, trying to choke the life out of me. I couldn't move. I tried waving my arms around but I just couldn't move. And it was still dark in my room but I could have sworn I saw someone leaning over me, right there in front of me with his hands around my neck. And ... well, I eventually managed to fall off the bed. Once I hit the floor I could breathe again. And I looked around, trying to catch my breath, and in every corner I expected to see someone there, someone ... you know, the person who had just tried choking me. It was still early in the morning, both my parents were asleep, so I went back to bed. But I couldn't sleep. I just lay there and watched the corners, figuring that the moment I closed my eyes, the shadows would move and the person hiding there would come back out and finish the job."

I paused, cleared my throat, and said, "You know, I think I could go for a bottle of water after all."

Pastor James Young swiveled on his chair and opened a mini-fridge underneath the table behind his desk. He pulled out a bottle of Deer Park and handed it to me.

I uncapped it and took a few sips of the water, then wiped my mouth and set the bottle aside.

"Okay," Pastor James Young said after a moment, when it

was clear I wasn't going to speak. "So you think … it was a demon that tried attacking you?"

"I didn't. I thought it was just one of those dreams that was really real. Like when you dream you're playing baseball and the ball comes right at your head and you jerk up out of sleep the moment it almost hits you. But I told my parents about it the next day, and my mom"—glancing once again at the corkboard—"*she* put the idea in my head. She said that I was being oppressed."

"Do you think you were being oppressed?"

"I don't know. But after last week, after … after finding my parents like I did, I've been thinking a lot about that dream. Because you know how you asked me earlier how I'm feeling? I'm exhausted, yeah, but ever since last week, I've felt just like I did that morning a year ago. Just lying in bed and watching for one of the shadows in the corner to move. Because I know what this guy is waiting for, the bastard who killed my parents."

The pastor looked even more uncomfortable than before. He glanced down at his desk, started to move that stack of papers but then thought better of it, took a deep breath. "What do you think he's waiting for?"

"He's waiting for me to close my eyes. He's waiting for me to go back to sleep so he can finish what he started."

CHAPTER TWO

HERE IS how the police reconstructed the last couple hours of my parents' lives:

After the Lanton High School graduation Friday night, after hearing their only son's name announced and then watching him receive his diploma, after tracking him down through the sea of students and parents afterward so they could give him a hug, so they could get a few pictures of him in his maroon gown and mortarboard, they told him they were very proud of him and then got ignored when their son spotted some friends and said he had to leave, that he'd see them later.

Somewhere then in the gymnasium lobby they met up with Jack and Celia Murphy, whose older daughter, Melanie, I had dated for nearly two years. We had since broken up, but over those two years the Murphys had become close friends with my parents. So my parents met them there and engaged in some small talk, before deciding to meet them at Friendly's along the highway. There they ordered ice cream sundaes and the men talked hunting while the women talked books. According to their waitress, whom the police only identified as Bethany, they spent nearly two hours at their table, taking their time with their desserts, getting their water glasses refilled every half hour. Then, around ten o'clock, my father and Jack Murphy argued over who was going to pay the check. Neither of them agreed to split it. They actually ended up playing a game of Rock, Paper, Scissors, and then got into a heated debated on whether it was one two three go, or one two and then go on three.

"It was kind of cute," Bethany told police. "They sort of acted like brothers."

In the end, my father came out victorious, his rock beating Jack Murphy's scissors.

At ten-fifteen, in the Friendly's parking lot, my parents and the Murphys said their goodbyes. My mother and Celia Murphy hugged, my father and Jack Murphy shook hands, Jack promising that he was going to beat my father next time, and then my parents left. They stopped at a gas station on the way home, my father filling up the tank of his Volvo, then going inside to purchase a quart of milk and a fresh loaf of bread. This the police confirmed from credit card receipts and the gas station surveillance video and the night clerk. My parents drove directly home, where they arrived at somewhere between ten-forty and ten-fifty. This was confirmed by Bud Donnelly, a forty-two-year-old investment banker who lived next door with his wife. He had just gotten back from taking his cocker spaniel for a walk when my parents pulled into the driveway.

He said to them, "So Chris finally graduated, huh? Congratulations."

"Don't congratulate us yet," my mother said.

Bud said, "What do you mean?"

My father said, "She means once Christopher finally graduates college, *then* it's time for congratulations."

The three of them apparently got quite a chuckle out of that.

Once inside the house, it becomes only speculation. As

their only child, who'd lived in that house for eighteen years, I can pretty much assume my dad took off his tie, unbuttoned the top two buttons of his shirt, and sank into his recliner to watch the news. My mother probably took off her heels, her earrings and necklace, before sitting at the dining room table and grading papers until eleven-thirty rolled around and my father called her in to watch the opening monologue of *The Tonight Show*. Depending on who the first guest was, they turned off the TV and headed upstairs, where they undressed, brushed their teeth, and got into bed.

I arrived home at about five-thirty in the morning. It was still dark outside. I came in the backdoor, took off my shoes, and went upstairs where I literally passed out on the bed and did not wake back up until six hours later, when the repetitive blaring of my parents' alarm clock yanked me from my sleep.

I thought about this when I returned home that Friday afternoon. It was the first time I'd seen the place since last week. I'd been staying at a Motel 6, under constant police protection. The house was still a crime scene, but since I was going away for a while, Steve said he'd allow me back in the house for a few hours to pack. Driving through my neighborhood, I tried spotting changes in the houses, in the trees, in the cars parked in driveways or along the street, but everything looked the same. Then I pulled up in front of the house I'd grown up in and looked at the two-story as if for the first time. It looked the same, yet it didn't. The grass needed mowing, sure, and the conspicuous yellow and black crime scene tape strung up around the property would have to go, but besides that … it still didn't look right.

There were two cars already parked in the driveway. One was a black Ford Explorer, the other a township police cruiser. Standing between them, their arms crossed, Steve Carpenter and Dean Myers seemed to be deep in conversation.

I got out of my car and started up the drive toward them.

Both men had noticed me pull up, had glanced my way, then went back to their conversation. It was as I neared that my uncle uncrossed his arms and extended his hand toward the police chief. He said, "Steve, thank you for all your help. I really appreciate it." Then he was walking toward me, saying, "Chris, how did everything go?"

"Good."

He nodded and said, "Great, I'm glad to hear it." He glanced past me at where my tailing cruiser had parked across the street. "I think Mom's resting right now, so we should hopefully be back around two o'clock. Okay?"

I told him it was. Then we just stood there for a moment, neither one of us saying anything. I stared at my uncle, who stared back at me. He stood just under six-feet, his black hair shaved into a crew cut, a trimmed mustache hovering just above his upper lip. I didn't know much about him except that he was thirty-seven, unmarried, and had spent some time in the military. Now he worked as a deputy in New York. He and my grandmother had come down Monday, for the funeral on Wednesday. I hadn't seen or heard from either of them since I was six years old, the last time I visited New York with my parents. Something happened the next year, something that involved my father's father, and that was why all communication had been cut. To be honest, until Sunday night when my uncle had been contacted and then called me, I didn't even remember they existed.

"All right, Chris," he said, "we'll see you then."

I watched him get into his Explorer, then watched him as he backed out of the driveway. I waited until he'd turned the corner, until he'd disappeared behind houses and trees, before turning back toward Steve.

"Well?" he said as I approached. "How did everything go?"

I told him the same thing I'd told my uncle, not wanting to impart the real reason I went to see Pastor James Young.

"Good," Steve said, but his voice somehow betrayed him, making it clear he didn't believe things were very good at all.

He wore his gray uniform today, his silver badge catching some of the sun. An older man, large but not overweight, he was widely known for his gentle nature, for his fairness and patience. But I remembered the rage in his eyes for the first two days, when he had been convinced I'd murdered my parents. It remained constant until I'd gone through all the lines of questioning, until I'd passed the polygraph test, until the forensic lab came back and confirmed that my DNA was nowhere to be found in my parents' room. Until two of my friends hesitantly stepped forward to admit that I'd been drinking and smoking pot with them at a party until about five a.m. Friday night.

"Is everything cleaned up in there?" I asked finally. Meaning, was the mark in blood taken off my door?

Steve shook his head. "Not everything. Some things we still had to keep there in case we need to come back to it." Meaning, yes it was.

A light breeze picked up, rustling the leaves in the massive oak in the front yard.

"Believe me, Chris," Steve said, "this is the best route right now. We just ... I can't afford to keep twenty-four hour protection on you anymore. I'm sorry."

"No, you have nothing to apologize for." I glanced at the cruiser parked across the street, the police officer inside who'd somehow gotten stuck babysitting me. "I understand how things are."

"Trust me. You'll be safe up there in Bridgton. Your uncle will be able to keep an eye on you. Nothing's going to happen to you. I promise."

I didn't say anything to this. I didn't tell him that he shouldn't make promises he wasn't certain he could keep, not when a week had gone by and the police had no leads at all on who had murdered my parents. No evidence found inside the house. No apparent motive for the crime. No apparent entry point. It was like the killer had been hiding in the shadows of their bedroom the entire time, waiting for them to close their eyes, before stepping out and cutting their throats.

Steve said, "I know there's some tension between you and your grandmother and uncle. I sensed it at the funeral. Hell, I sensed it a few minutes ago. But whatever happened in the past, things change. People change. You'll all get over whatever happened too, I know you will. It just takes time."

A car drove down the street. For a moment I thought it was somebody with the news, somebody doing a drive-by to see if anything had changed here, and now wouldn't they get a nice surprise to find that the victims' son was standing right in his own front yard with the chief of police? But it was Darren Bannister in his blue Buick Rivera, the old man only glancing at us as he drove toward his home three houses down.

I said, "Do you even know what happened eleven years ago? When I was seven, why my dad cut off all ties with his family?"

Steve shook his head.

"My grandfather tried to kill me. When I was seven years old, he came down here and kidnapped me and tried to kill me."

Steve opened his mouth, started to speak, then must have thought better of it. He waited a moment, letting that sink in, before saying, "Like I told you, Chris, it just takes time. Everything will work out. We're going to catch this guy. I mean, hey, look at what happened to Kevin Parker and his wife. That worked out for the best, right?"

Kevin Parker, a local bestselling author, had lost his wife nearly eight months ago. Some thought she had just run off, but as it turned out she had been kidnapped. A few days ago she had been found again, somewhere in the Adirondacks, but from what I could tell the Lanton Police Department had had no hand in the rescue.

I said, "So you're certain it wasn't Grant?"

Steve sighed. "Again, yes, we are certain Grant Evans had nothing to do with your parents' murder."

"You talked with him?"

"Chris—"

"He has an alibi and everything?"

"Chris, believe it or not, we know what we're doing. And for the final time, Grant is not a suspect. I know you two had your disagreements in the past, but trust me, he's clean."

Our "disagreements" was me beating the shit out of him a month ago in the cafeteria, for seemingly no reason at all.

"Anyway," Steve said, stepping forward and patting me on the shoulder, "you take care of yourself. I'll be in contact with your uncle daily. Hopefully in another week or two you'll be back here and everything will have cooled down."

He shook my hand, smiled once more, then got into his car. Just like with my uncle, I watched him as he backed out of the driveway and pulled away. Then, in the sudden silence, which somehow overpowered the typical summer sounds of birds chirping and busy traffic out on Rockwell Road, I heard the distant growl of a lawnmower. Also there were kids playing somewhere close, probably in someone's backyard. I tried imagining what they were doing; playing tag, maybe, or swimming in a pool. It didn't really matter. All that mattered was that life went on just as it always did. People live, people die, and still the world turns. It all seems so obvious, so standard, until someone close to you dies, and you notice the world hasn't stopped. Then the realization hits you that when you die, the world won't even hesitate, because it doesn't care at all.

CHAPTER THREE

I WAS a half hour into packing—going slowly, taking my time in a room that had become alien to me—when the doorbell rang. I paused, thoughts of who it might be racing through my mind: Steve, my uncle, a reporter … or my parents, waiting dead at the door like the son in W. W. Jacobs's "The Monkey's Paw." I shook the image from my mind—

my parents standing side by side, staring ahead with no eyes

—and hurried downstairs. When I opened the door, the officer who'd been waiting in his cruiser across the street stood staring at me.

"I'm sorry, Mr. Myers, but there's a gentleman here who says he's your neighbor down the street. A Darren Bannister?"

Before I could even open my mouth to ask who he meant —from all I could see it was just the two of us here on the porch—he stepped aside. Behind him, cowering like a lost kitten, was one of the oldest men in the world.

"Hello there, Christopher."

I nodded to him, then told the officer he was fine. Once the man had left, walking across the lawn toward his car, I forced a smile.

"So, Mr. Bannister. How are you?"

Short, hair whiter than snow, he was dressed in baggy jeans and a yellow short-sleeved shirt. He wore thin glasses that looked as if they'd been made during the Depression. He'd lived three houses down from me all my life. His wife had died years ago, and ever since then he'd been living alone. When I was younger, I made twenty dollars mowing his lawn or shoveling his driveway, depending on the season. In his hands now was a brown paper-wrapped package.

"Oh, I'm just fine." He had a thick Irish accent and a rustiness in his voice from smoking all his life. He smiled, showing the yellow teeth he had left. Then, just as quickly, his expression became somber. "I was at me daughter's house all last week. Just got back Wednesday. Heard about your parents. I'm sorry, Christopher, really. They both were fine people."

I thanked him. "What can I do for you, Mr. Bannister?"

"Here you are." He held the package out to me. "Yours."

"Mine?"

He nodded. "Had it for ... oh, five years, I'd say. Your granddaddy mailed it to me. Said I was to give you it when ... when something bad happened. And I'd say what happened was quite bad indeed."

"My *grandfather*?"

Darren Bannister simply nodded, not taken aback by my sudden incredulity.

I stared at the package in his hands. It was a mail parcel, which looked just as old as Bannister himself. I said, "What's in there?"

"Don't know exactly. Your granddaddy wouldn't tell me. Just said that I was to—"

I grabbed the package, held it up to my ear as if to listen for the ticking of a bomb. There was nothing, so I weighed it in my hands. It felt like a book.

"How did you know my grandfather?"

Now that his hands were free, the old man didn't seem to know what to do with them. Finally he put them in his pockets, shrugged and said, "I met him the couple of times he came down here to visit you and your folks. Then ... you know, after he went away, he wrote me every once in a while. Asking how you and your family were doing."

"And you never thought that was odd?"

"Course I did, Christopher," he said, actually sounding cross. "But his letters seemed so sincere, I just couldn't ignore them. So I wrote him back, told him I'd try to keep him updated, but I never did after that one time. Then I received that in the post and didn't know what to think. Your granddaddy said I was to give it to you if anything happened. Said if I knew I was going to die or get real sick, I should find someone else to give it to you. Figured I'd ask me daughter, if that was the case. Sounds queer, I know, but that's all I can tell you."

I kept staring down at the package in my hands. Eventually I blinked, looked up at the old man, and said, "I'm sorry."

"For what?"

"I shouldn't have snapped at you like that. I apologize."

He held up a dry gnarled hand, shaking his head. "Don't you worry about it, Christopher. You've already been through so much, you don't need to apologize about nothing. I just wanted to make sure you got this. I tried dropping it off yesterday but nobody was here. Then I was passing by here earlier and saw you so ..." He forced a smile and spread his hands, palms out, as if to say, *And here we are.*

"Thank you," I said. "I appreciate it."

He may have nodded, or forced another smile, or stuck his tongue out at me. I have no idea. I just continued standing there, staring down at the package, and the next thing I knew the old man had turned away and was walking down the porch steps. I watched him for a moment before I stepped back inside my own house and shut the door. I walked directly toward the couch and sat down with the package in my lap.

I didn't want to open it. Whatever was inside, I didn't want to know. It felt like I had Pandora's Box in my hands, that if I opened it I would unleash a whole new evil into the world.

Come on, I thought. *You can do this. Evil doesn't exist. There's nothing hiding in the shadows.*

The packing material was old and worn, like thin cardboard; I didn't even need scissors. Once it was opened, I hesitated a moment, then looked inside. A book, just as it had felt like. I pulled it out and set it on the coffee table, then glanced inside the package to see if there was anything else. Nothing, so I tossed it aside and picked up the book.

It was thick, maybe four, five hundred pages long. The cover was brown and bare. Nothing was printed on its spine. I opened the first page to find an inscription. It was done in pen. I assumed it was my grandfather's hand.

Christopher, this is the fruit of my labor. I am sorry for what happened. Hopefully someday you will understand. Read Job 42 for guidance. Your life depends on it. I love you.

I read it twice then turned to the next page. I recognized it immediately. Not just from the title, but from the text as well. *Genesis*—the first book of the Bible. The entire text was in the same hand as the inscription.

I flipped through the pages. They were all the same, all written in pen by my grandfather's own hand. All the books of the Old Testament.

"Well, I guess the jury's no longer out," I said. "He was a fucking nutcase."

I tossed the book on the couch and then headed back upstairs to finish packing.

Fifteen minutes before my uncle and grandmother came to the house, I sat in front of the computer and tried to compose an e-mail to Melanie. She was in Europe somewhere, having left the day after graduation. Before going to college in the fall she wanted to visit another continent, wanted to spend her summer doing something more engaging than visiting Ocean City, Maryland, for the week. So she was over there now, doing whatever it was she was doing, and she had sent me an e-mail a few days ago, which surprised me, a simple note saying how very sorry she was for what happened and that she hoped I was doing well.

Now here I sat, wanting to reply to her but not being able to think of anything good enough to write.

After ten minutes of just staring at the screen, I closed the box.

The computer asked me, SAVE CHANGES TO E-MAIL?

I clicked NO.

Two o'clock arrived, but my uncle and grandmother did not. I wasn't worried. I knew my grandmother had trouble walking, that the trip down here had been exhausting for her. She was sixty-eight and needed the help of a cane to get around. Her skin was pale, sprinkled by a few freckles and moles on her face and arms. She had spent most of her life in the Restaurant Industry, which was another way of saying she'd been a waitress. It wouldn't surprise me if she had taken an extra half hour with her nap and was slow getting around.

I packed two suitcases, which now rested in the trunk of my car. There was no extra room in Dean's Explorer, not with everything he'd packed to bring down, or else I'd ride up with him. The idea hadn't occurred to Steve until earlier this week, when he first met my uncle. Had he known ahead of time, Dean joked to the police chief, he would have brought a U-Haul.

I sat on the porch steps, trying to ignore the officer in the cruiser. He hardly seemed to notice me anyway. Couldn't be fun at all assigned to babysit an eighteen-year-old. Even if that eighteen-year-old *was* being stalked by a murderer.

When I checked my watch and saw it was only two-twenty, I got up and went to the door, unlocked it and stepped inside. I stood at the bottom of the stairs and stared up. On my trips in and out of my room, I had kept glancing at my parents' bedroom door. It was closed. After I'd turned ten or eleven or twelve, I never once stepped foot inside their room, only briefly saw inside if the door was open when I walked past. I'd never had any desire to go inside, knowing that that was their private place, just like my room was my own private place. But today, as I kept passing their closed door, I kept wondering what was behind it.

I started up the steps, taking them slower than usual. The eighth step creaked, just as it always did. Then I was on the landing, staring at their door. I remembered the last time I opened it, the repetitive buzzing coming from behind. I remembered what I saw and felt.

The first thing I noticed when I opened the door was that the sheets had been taken off the bed. The center of the mattress was stained dark with blood. I took a few hesitant steps inside, feeling like an intruder.

There wasn't much to the room. No pictures or paintings on the wall besides the blue floral border a few inches below the ceiling. Two windows, two closets, the strong scent of lemon disinfectant, and hardly anything else.

I took another step forward, still uncertain what I was looking for, when I noticed the dresser. It sat against the wall next to the door. It was huge, made out of oak. The bottom half was drawers, the top half a large mirror. On both sides were three shelves each, and just by glancing at them I realized the left was my father's, the right my mother's. This was where they stored their mementos, their little keepsakes, that told just who they were.

I went to my mother's side first.

On the top shelf were books. Hardcovers that didn't look familiar to me at all, except one with the title *Peace Like a River*. I remembered it was one of my mom's favorites, because she'd tried getting me to read it more than once. Along with these were dozens of cards. Hesitantly I took them down, began flipping through each one. They were birthday cards, anniversary cards, Mother's Day cards. Some were from my dad, but all the rest were from me, ever since I was old enough to scribble my name. I could tell by the handwriting which cards had been written when I was very young; these were the ones with little notes attached. Misspelled lines like *Your the bestest mommy in the hole wide world* and *If I found a genies bodle I'd give you it so you could have ALL the wishes* soon shortened to lines that read *I hope you have a good b-day* and *Have a good one*. And, in the last two years, I hadn't even included any notes, but just signed my name with an obligatory and unfelt *Love*.

I put them back on the shelf, suddenly feeling empty inside. I turned my attention to the second shelf, which held a small necklace tree with some of her jewelry hanging. Beside it sat a piece of crystal that was shaped like a swan. And beside the crystal swan was a ceramic umbrella, sitting upside down so its ceramic pole was erect. I picked it up. It was light green, the color of freshly grown grass. It was small and rested easily in the palm of my hand. It was clear that the pole had been glued together with the umbrella. My mom had found me the glue the day I came home crying. I'd been in fourth grade, had made it in Art, and on the bus it had snapped off. I wanted to give it to her and was angry because now it was ruined. But she told me it was okay, that everything can be fixed, and helped me glue it back together. I gave it to her then, and she gave me a hug and a kiss on the cheek.

I set it back where it was, turning my attention to the third shelf. Bottles of perfume rested there, nothing else.

On the mantle in front of the mirror itself were pictures. They were all of me. A few showed me when I was in middle school, one with me in my basketball jersey, another with me and Mel, dressed in our best, before some formal. Only one showed me with my parents. It rested in the center of the others. In the picture I stood in the middle, my father on my right, my mother on my left. I couldn't tell where the picture was taken, but people were in the background and it had been inside. It reminded me of the picture back on the corkboard in James Young's office, except in this one only two of the three were genuinely smiling back at the camera. Those, of course, were my parents, their smiles real and wide. My own smile was crooked, clearly forced, and I was staring off at something over the cameraman's shoulder.

I turned my attention to my father's side of the dresser. Instead of hardcovers, he had five paperbacks on the top shelf, all by the same author. My eyes drifted over two titles—*Cat's Cradle, Breakfast of Champions*—and then lowered to what sat on the next shelf. It was a small stuffed plush of one of the Looney Tunes. The Tasmanian Devil, his hands held out at his sides, his mouth open wide showing all his teeth. I remembered winning it at some carnival when I was a freshman, by tossing a ping-pong ball into a goldfish bowl. When I brought it home, he had been in the kitchen doing some work at the table, and I had said, "Hey Dad, guess what I won for you." It had been behind my back, and when I brought it around, his face actually lit up with a smile. He thanked me, told me it made his day since he'd been swamped with work, and I had nodded and said sure, no problem at all. But the truth was he had just been in the right place at the right time. Had Mom been there in the kitchen instead, I would have given it to her. Had neither of them been there, I probably would have taken it along with me up to my room, or else tossed it in the trash.

I reached forward, intending to simply touch the brown stuffed animal, when the doorbell rang. I jumped and stepped back. Looked about the room once more, my eyes purposefully skipping over the blood on the mattress, and then hurried downstairs.

I didn't realize until I reached the landing that the picture of me and my parents was still in my hands. I folded it up, stuck it in my pocket.

When I opened the door, Dean stared back at me. His face was expressionless at first, but then he smiled. "Sorry," he said. "A little behind schedule, I know. But I talked to Officer Armstrong"—he jerked a thumb back at the street—"and he's going to follow us until we get to Manheim. Ready?"

For an instant, an image flashed in my mind: a body lying in what I somehow knew was a hospital bed.

I blinked, shaking it away.

"Whoa there," Dean said. He sounded more upbeat than I'd heard him all week. "You all right? You look like you, I don't know, like you just saw a ghost or something."

I forced a smile and stepped outside, pulling the door shut behind me. "No," I said, turning the key in the lock. "Just a little lightheaded. No ghosts here."

And it was true; I hadn't seen any ghosts.

Not then.

CHAPTER FOUR

As far as towns go, Bridgton isn't much of one. Compared to Elmira, which sits ten miles south and is part of the tri-county area of Chemung, it's not even a dot on the map. It shares nothing commercial with Elmira—no Sunoco or Exxon stations, no Denny's or Howard Johnson's, no McDonald's or Burger King, no K-Mart or Sears. Elmira has three hospitals, two colleges, one giant mall, about sixty churches, and nearly twenty schools. It even has an airport. Its population runs close to forty thousand people, while Bridgton has only two hundred people or so to call its own.

Nestled into the tree-strewn hills of the Allegheny Plateau, Bridgton should really be described as somebody's failed attempt at a town. Bisecting Route 13—which begins in Elmira and continues up half the state, through Ithaca and Cortland and then farther north—is the road that leads into the heart of Bridgton. It's called Mizner Road, though everyone agrees it should have just been named Main Street. Sitting on either side of the road is a large stone church of questionable affiliation, a diner named Luanne's, a Salvation Army thrift-clothing store, and a mechanic shop. There's even a general store, where the locals can purchase anything from bread and milk to condoms and beer, as well as postage stamps during the day, as a window in the back serves as the town's post office. Not much else, unless you want to count Harvey's Tavern and Fellman's Used Cars, both of which sit along Route 13, about a mile from Mizner Road—Harvey's, of course, another place to buy beer, as well as a dimmed and quiet atmosphere to play pool and darts and drink alone.

Houses of all types are scattered throughout the hills and fields beyond Bridgton's "Main Street"—homes ranging from three-stories down to one-story, and even double-wide trailers with the occasional unkempt patches of lawn and empty Rolling Rock and Miller Lite cans littering the backyard. Some have dogs chained up outside, while others just have chains. Some have tire swings hanging off the branches of maple and hickory trees, while others just have tires in the grass. Some have their cars and pickups parked in the spots they call driveways, while others just have them parked beside one tree or another, easy targets for birdshit and rust. Various NASCAR flags hang off porch overhangs, signaling the numbers of favorite drivers.

Bridgton has no schools, so its kids have to go to either Horseheads or Elmira for their education. It has no law enforcement either, and instead relies on the Chemung County Sheriff's Department to provide an occasional deputy to keep the peace. My uncle, who was born and raised in Bridgton, is one of a few deputies assigned to this particular zone of the county.

If one were to know his way around the back roads off Route 13, and go maybe half a mile up the hill, one would find Keller's Bait and Tackle, Bridgton's only reputable business besides the ones on Mizner Road. It sells anything from fishing rods, to lures, to line, to even vests and boxes. A handwritten sign out front announces its ongoing special of two dozen night crawlers for three bucks.

A quarter mile away, on Half Creek Road which leads farther up the hill, is a two-story house with weather-worn shingles and peeling paint. Once, long ago, someone decided to turn the bottom floor into a used bookstore. A green sign outside, as weathered as the roof, reads SHEPHERD'S BOOKS. Another, smaller sign reading CLOSED, perpetually hangs below this. Its parking lot is gravel and always deserted, as the store itself never opens.

Less than a half mile farther up Half Creek Road is Calvary Church. It's a tiny, whitewashed building that has everything but a steeple. It sits off to the left of the road in a wide clearing. Behind it, through a wall of pine trees and following a narrow foot-beaten path to an obscure and cramped clearing, rests a small stone house that once was the center of a lot of pain in the town's history. Now it sits alone, idle, allowing nature to give it a slow and steady decay.

Continuing past the house, another narrow trail leads a little farther up the hill, past spruces and hemlocks, beeches and birches, to another clearing that overlooks the valley in which most of the town rests. Mobile homes have been situated around each other. All the locals call it The Hill—the T always capitalized, as if to give the area its due respect. There are less than twenty trailers in all, owned mostly by folks in their sixties and seventies who retreat to Florida in the winter to escape the snow. A squat cinderblock building, called the Rec House, sits at the entrance to this trailer park, a short in-ground pool with no water beside it.

Of course, when I first came to Bridgton, I knew none of this. All I knew was that it was where my grandmother and uncle lived, and where I would now be staying until the police managed to track down my parents' killer. I wasn't aware that unlike most small towns that try to hide themselves from the rest of the world, Bridgton was a sleeping giant.

The overall trip from Lanton to Bridgton was supposed to take four hours. For us, it took five. Driving in my Cavalier, I followed my uncle down PA 72 through Manheim, up to Lebanon, until we eventually got onto Interstate 81. There it was continuous driving through the Appalachian Mountains. Green rolling hills on either side of the highway, an occasional town or city peeking up from a valley that could be glimpsed only for a couple of minutes as we were doing seventy or so miles an hour. Up past Wilkes-Barre, past Scranton, farther north until we exited Pennsylvania and entered New York. Once past Binghamton, my uncle merged onto NY 17, which we took all the way to Elmira.

Because of my grandmother's constant need to stretch her legs every hour, we stopped at whatever rest area was closest for a couple of minutes. Then, in Great Bend, we stopped at a gas station for snacks. I went inside with my uncle, while my grandmother stood beside the Explorer. He bought some bottled water, a bag of pretzels, and then, at the counter, eyed up the cigarettes. He must have noticed me looking, because a grin broke out over his normally hard face and he said, "Gave them up three times already. This is my fourth. Been two months, and I keep telling myself this is it." He ended up buying a pack of Pep-O-Mint LifeSavers instead.

By the time we finished with 17 and merged onto Route 13, it was close to eight o'clock. The sky was clear and purple, the sun nearing the ragged horizon. Then, ten minutes later, we arrived to Bridgton and the start of a new chapter in my life.

My grandmother's trailer was some luxury model very similar to everyone else's on The Hill. In a very cramped space it included a bedroom, a bathroom, a kitchen and living room. Outside my grandmother's trailer was a wooden swing. It was set up so it faced down into the valley. This was where my grandmother and I sat that Friday evening around eight-thirty, watching the fading glow of the sun.

"Isn't this nice, Christopher?" Her voice was deep and pleasant, almost somber. She didn't wait for me to answer before saying, "I'm glad you came. I wish it could have been under different circumstances, but I'm glad you're here. It's been so long since I've seen you last."

I didn't say anything. There were questions I wanted to ask, questions I'd been holding back since I first saw her this week. Questions like where she'd been for the past ten years, did she ever think of me, did she even care.

My uncle had already left us, driving to his apartment in Horseheads. He wanted to get a few hours of sleep before starting his midnight shift. He had only one bedroom, or else I'd be staying with him. Instead I was being put up in one of the extra trailers The Hill's owner kept around. Dean had called him, explained the situation, and the man was more than happy to let me stay there. It was much smaller than my grandmother's trailer, much more cramped, with only a bed and a shower. Behind an overpowering scent of Lysol was the faint odor of mold and must. I had set my things down and walked the short distance up to my grandmother's, where she told me she just put a frozen pizza in the oven. She suggested we wait on the swing, and now here we'd been sitting for almost ten minutes.

Somewhere behind us, in one of the trailers, a window was open. The sound of *Wheel of Fortune* could faintly be heard.

Beside me, my grandmother made a noise. It was the kind

of noise a person makes when she's thinking of something happy, something fun, and starts to laugh but then stops.

"You probably don't remember," she said, "because it was so long ago, but one Christmas your parents brought you up here to visit. This was when we lived in our old house. You were six, I think. Your grandpa told you Santa Claus was coming to see you, and you got all excited, and your face was just so precious. Your smile, I mean."

I watched her as she spoke, noticed how her jaw worked and how her eyes stared down at the grass, as if back in time.

"So Christmas Eve came, and there was this knock at the door. You started running around trying to find your grandpa because you knew, you just *knew*, it was Santa. Your father answered the door, and sure enough, there he was. His suit wasn't the best quality, not like the kind you see those men wearing at the mall, but it was red and the old man inside had white hair and a long beard.

"Well, you just couldn't believe it. Like your grandpa said, Santa Claus was here. He came into the house and sat down, and you got right up on his knee. He asked whether you'd been a good boy, and you told him yes you were, that you were a very good boy. Then he asked what you wanted for Christmas. And everything you asked for, Christopher, he pulled right out of his bag."

She smiled.

"I can still remember that costume. Your grandpa's beard kept coming off, and he kept putting it back in place, but you never said anything. Your father and uncle had to leave the room, they were laughing so hard. And your mother, she just smiled and kept taking pictures. Then when he had given you all your presents, he left, and five minutes later your grandfather *without* his suit came in. He said he had to go into town for some milk, and when you told him he'd missed Santa, he acted so upset. He asked you to tell him everything that happened, and you did. You told him everything.

"And watching you, I wondered if you knew. As if the entire time when your grandpa came in with that red suit and beard on, you knew it was him, but didn't say anything. You just went along like it really was Santa Claus, because you wanted to make him happy. You wanted to make him think that he was actually doing something you'd love him for."

She looked at me.

"Did you?" Her voice had become a whisper. "Did you know the entire time?"

I remembered what Steve had told me earlier that day, how time changes things, that people get over stuff. And as much as the memory meant to her, as much as the whole thing seemed so important, I shrugged with an I-can't-remember expression on my face.

She stared at me for a moment, then smiled. "It doesn't matter anyway, I guess. Just something I thought about, no big thing. But Christopher, I've only been in love twice my whole life. Once when I was just a small girl, and it was really nothing more than a hopeless crush on a man twice my age. The other was your grandpa, and it was true love because he was also in love with me. And when two people are in love with each other, they share a special bond that nobody else can touch. So believe me when I tell you, your grandpa did love you. I don't care what everybody says he did, you were his only grandchild and he loved you more than anything. You have to believe that."

I smiled but said nothing. I couldn't tell her what she wanted to hear, because I didn't want to lie to her. And as much as I wanted to believe it, to believe my grandfather had actually been sane and loved me, I simply couldn't.

Much later that night, Mrs. Roberts—my grandmother's good friend who lived two trailers up the drive—stopped by. Nancy, she wanted me to call her, but I wouldn't. She was seventy-something, a few years older than Grandma, and it didn't feel right calling a stranger much older than myself by her first name.

"Christopher," she said, shaking my hand, "it's very nice to meet you."

She smiled and adjusted the dark glasses on her face. She had a severe form of meningitis, my grandmother had told me, which caused photosensitivity to her eyes. Lately the condition had worsened and the antibiotics she normally took had begun failing, so her doctor suggested she keep her glasses on all day and even at night.

It was almost ten o'clock, and I was ready to head back to my trailer. The pizza had been good though a little burnt, and the discussion minimal. For the past hour we'd just been watching whatever few stations Grandma's little Magnavox—with rabbit ears antenna, both stretched wide—picked up. I'd wanted to leave sooner, but didn't want to hurt my grandmother's feelings. Now I had my way out.

I gave my grandmother a hug, told her I'd see her in the morning, and wished both ladies goodnight. Then I was out the screen door and headed down the dirt drive. My pace was fast but then quickly slowed, until I was standing still. Around me, the night was alive with insects, the wind, the sporadic traffic down on 13 that could faintly be heard up here. Many of The Hill's residents had gone to bed, because there was hardly any noise coming from any of the trailer homes. In fact, only a few had lights on inside.

For a moment I felt as if this might work out after all. That I could stay up here while Steve and the rest of the police force conducted their investigation and then captured the son of a bitch that killed my parents. For a moment, I actually felt safe.

Then I had the feeling I was being watched.

My body suddenly tense, I turned my head slowly, first to the right, then to the left.

A tall figure stood off in the darkness, right in front of an RV parked across the lane. The figure held a cigarette; I could see the red tip clearly, first at the figure's side, then lifted up to the figure's face.

I don't know why, especially because it was so dark, but I forced a smile, gave a quick wave.

The figure didn't return either. It just stood there another moment, taking one last drag, before dropping the butt to the ground, then turning and opening the door of the RV, the hinges on the screen door rusted so badly that in the dark silence of night it sounded like they were screaming in agony.

CHAPTER FIVE

EARLY THAT MORNING it had begun to rain. I lay awake in bed—which was nothing more than a moldy mattress covered with fresh white linens—for close to an hour, staring at the picture of my parents that I had fastened to the ceiling. Above me, the rain tapped out an irregular but consistent beat on the aluminum roofing, until about nine o'clock, when it stopped completely. Then I waited another half hour before taking a quick shower and dressing into jeans and a T-shirt.

I was out the door and headed toward Grandma's trailer, my sneakers squishing in the wet grass and mud, when I first saw Joey Cunningham.

He was a small black kid, standing no higher than five feet tall. He wore a dark blue windbreaker, the sleeves pulled up, his hands stuffed in the pockets of his khaki shorts as he walked down the drive. His sneakers were gray but nondescript, something bought from a warehouse or bargain store. The glasses on his plain face were thick and goggle-like, and as we passed each other, he looked up at me and smiled.

I nodded at him but that was it, and a second later he was

behind me. His smile stayed in my mind, though; it was like one of those smiles friends give each other, not strangers. Like this kid somehow knew me.

The idea was unsettling and I decided to forget him completely, when behind me I heard him say, "Did you ever wonder if the animals in the Garden of Eden could t-t-talk?"

I paused, my right foot unwillingly stuck in a puddle.

"I mean, before Eve who else did Adam have t-to t-t-talk to? God was there, I guess, but don't you think it'd be cool if the animals t-talked?"

Slowly, hesitantly, I took my foot out of the muddy water and turned.

"Excuse me?"

He smiled and stepped forward, extending his hand. "My name's Joey. What's yours?"

"Chris."

"Nice t-t-to meet you, Chris." His handshake was firm and strong, surprising for his age and size.

I asked him if he lived around here.

Joey shook his head. "Nah, not around here. Actually, I don't live anywhere. Me and my dad travel around a lot. He speaks at churches." He pointed past my grandmother's trailer at an RV sitting along the drive on that side—what some of the locals called Lane B. Parked beside it was a blue Geo Metro. "That's ours."

I nodded, thinking briefly of the figure smoking last night. Joey looked to be ten, maybe eleven years old. But the way he spoke, the way he presented himself, he seemed much older.

Joey asked, "So do you live around here?"

I told him no, that I was just visiting.

"Oh yeah? Family or friends?"

"Family." The word felt strange to say.

"Cool," he said, nodding, but that was it.

Silence fell between us. It should have felt awkward but for some reason it didn't. We were just two strangers, standing underneath an overcast sky, while down in the valley some thin fog had settled.

Finally I motioned toward Grandma's and said, "Well, I should get going."

"Right. But you didn't answer my question. Do you think the animals could t-talk?"

I shrugged. "I really don't know. What do you think?"

Joey seemed to ponder his own question for a few seconds, before saying, "You know, I'm not sure either. But I think it'd be awesome if they did. I'll see you around."

He turned and started down the drive, past the various trailers spread out around The Hill. For some reason I expected him to look back and wave, but he didn't. He just kept walking.

I spent a few hours in my grandmother's trailer, having what she called brunch but which was really just overcooked hamburgers and Tostitos tortilla chips. We played some cards, watched some TV, and then she apologized for not being much fun and suggested I check out the Rec House. She said the last time she was inside it was filled with video games and whatnot, stuff I would probably like. I told her I was content right where I was, though in truth I was bored out of my mind.

Around four o'clock, when Mrs. Roberts stopped by, I stayed for some chitchat and then told them I was going for a walk. Grandma reminded me that we were having dinner with my uncle, and after nodding and saying goodbye, I went outside. The sky was clear for the most part, the grass and drive, except for an occasional puddle, all nicely dried. I started toward the trailer I was staying in when I glanced back toward

Half Creek Road, at the cinderblock building sitting beside the trailer park's entrance.

"What the hell," I muttered, and started up the drive.

The only entrance I could find not locked was a screen door located next to an old RC Cola machine. All the buttons were lit up out of order. Opening and closing the door created such a racket that some little dog started barking not too far away.

The place was dark and cold, the smell of dust everywhere. I tried the switch just inside the door but no light came on. Enough of the sun shone through the dirty windows that I wasn't walking blind as I made my way around. There were two metal card tables, one with a broken leg. A wide couch that looked retro enough to be from the '70s, propped in front of an ancient television set. On top of the TV was an original Nintendo console, its gray cover cracked; resting on top of it, two games that I hadn't played in years: *Contra* and *Duck Hunt*. Across the room were three tables: ping-pong, foosball, and pool. The last table's green surface was marked all over by unforgiving cues.

Hanging scattered across the ceiling were white paper plates. Written on each in different colored markers were names and locations and short messages. I stopped and read a few, realized they were past visitors to The Hill who'd left these as a kind of memorial to their time spent. One written in wide purple letters read

We had a GREEEAAAT time! THANKS!!!
The Trout Family
Darvills, Virginia, '93

while another in blue and yellow read

The best barbeque EVER hands down
Can't wait to come back next summer!
Bob & Sue Willie
Luttrell, Tennessee

All over the walls was a variety of junk, from a chalkboard to framed pictures, to tennis rackets and what looked to be a stuffed armadillo. I walked up to the wall that had Polaroids tacked all over, displaying different activities from organized softball to badminton, to a pig roast and what looked like a marshmallow eating contest. I glanced at these only briefly, trying to catch glimpses of my grandmother or Mrs. Roberts, before deciding to head back out. I turned to leave, not watching where I was going, and stumbled into a card table that had various toys scattered on top. A bright yellow remote control car, balanced on the end, fell off, landing headfirst on the concrete. I didn't even attempt to check and see if it was okay; I said, "Whoops," under my breath and headed for the door.

"Hey, you break it, you buy it."

The voice startled me so badly I actually jumped. A soft giggling followed right after, and I turned around, searching the back of the Rec House for the three seconds it took me to spot her. The building was obviously built with greatness in mind—there was a small kitchen, a stock room, and even a single bathroom pushed against the far side. A large opening was in the wall, right above a counter, looking into the kitchen. She sat behind that, a solid shaft of sunlight shining directly toward her. Dust motes floated freely in the glow. For a moment I wondered just what the hell she was doing there, when I noticed the paperback in her right hand. Her left hand was hiding her mouth, before she quickly composed herself.

"You scared me," I said, half because it was true, half because I couldn't think of anything else to say.

"*I* scared you?" She snorted. "This from the guy who wakes the dead opening a simple screen door."

I opened my mouth, tried to speak, but found that I couldn't. I was stuck. Which was weird, because I *never* got stuck.

"It was ... difficult."

She nodded, like she understood exactly what I meant. "Yeah, I'm sure it was."

There was an awkward silence, so I asked, "What are you reading?"

She held the book up so I could see the cover. "*Billy Budd* by Herman Melville."

I made a face. "Good God, why?"

"It's on the Summer Reading List for a class I want to take next year. Have you read it?"

"I skimmed a paragraph or two."

"Let me guess, you thought it was boring."

"Not really. I just preferred the SparkNotes version more." I approached her and held out my hand. "I'm Chris, by the way."

"I'm Sarah," she said, shaking my hand. Hers was cold and soft, the fingernails unpainted. "And just because you know my name now, don't go thinking you're off the hook. Remember, you break it, you buy it."

For a moment my grin faltered. Was she really serious? Who cared for it anyway? It was just a piece of junk in a building full of junk. Then she grinned again and I knew she was joking, and I couldn't help myself, I started laughing. The first time I'd laughed in a long time.

Her Name was Sarah Porter and she was sixteen years old. Sixteen and a half, really, as she made a point of mentioning that her birthday was in November. Her face was heart-shaped, her skin smooth and white, her nose small. The lighting wasn't the best where we were inside, but as I later found out her eyes were blue—gentian as my mother the gardener would have liked to say. Her hair was strawberry blond, its length down to her shoulders; every once in a while a lock would fall in her face, causing her to push it back behind her ear. She never stood up from behind the counter, so I could only see her T-shirt, which was pink and had some kind of obscure design printed on the front.

I'll say this here and now: she was attractive, there was no doubt about that, and any guy in his right mind would have been a fool not to fall for her, but for me I just didn't feel that way. Who knows, maybe it had to do with my parents, or Mel, or the fact a murderer was supposedly after me, but as I stood there talking with her, I didn't see her in the back of my mind as someone I could potentially be with. Even that bulk of men's brains that controls lust—and I'm sure a scientific study has been done somewhere, explaining that particular part takes up ninety-nine percent—wasn't swayed. Not once did I find myself glancing at her chest, or even wondering what one of her breasts might feel like cupped in my hand. Or the feel of her thighs, her butt, even her tongue inside my mouth. She was just this girl who had scared me, who had proved herself just as sarcastic as me, if not more, and I had no problems talking to her. And it wasn't flirting, either; it was just talk.

We talked for maybe an hour, and it's impossible to recount everything that was said, because it was mainly about nothing. Just one topic after another that changed suddenly to another that didn't seem to have any correlation with the first but obviously did. Sarah had this thing she said she asked everyone new she came in contact with; it was three simple questions that supposedly told everything about you. The first was what CD you last listened to; second, who's your favorite actor; and third, what's your favorite movie of all time. They were tough questions, except for the CD one, so I asked her to give hers first.

"Easy," she said. "Coldplay's *A Rush of Blood to the Head*, Julia Roberts, and *Pretty Woman*, without a doubt."

"Okay," I said slowly. I had been hoping for more time. "In my car, the last thing I listened to was Alice in Chains. Their unplugged album. My favorite actor is … well, if I have to pick one, I'd have to say Bruce Campbell."

She said, "Who?" frowning like I'd just told her I was the offspring of an alien race.

"Bruce Campbell," I repeated, then started to list off the movies and television shows he'd starred in, when I realized it wouldn't be worth it. So in the end I shrugged and said, "I work at Blockbuster, what I can tell you. I see a *lot* of movies."

"Good," she said. "So then you shouldn't have a problem telling me your favorite movie of all time."

"*Citizen Kane*."

Her face went blank. "You're kidding, right? Please tell me you're kidding."

"No way. Orson Welles was a genius. That film's amazing, nearly flawless. Way ahead of its time."

"Oh my gosh." Her voice had gone toneless. "You just said film."

Grinning, I said, "Fine. For the less cultured, movie."

"Okay then, how about this? Favorite chick flick." She smirked. "If, of course, you're willing to impart such private information."

"*Casablanca*," I said, without a beat, and she groaned and rolled her eyes, muttered, "How old are you anyway? *Fifty?*"

"Eighteen. But everyone says I'm very mature for my age." I gave a too-wide grin, then leaned forward and whispered, "Except, between you and me, I can be as immature as the next guy."

"Oh really." She didn't look convinced. "What's the most immature thing you've ever done?"

For an instant I thought about Mel, and what I'd forced her to do three months ago.

I slowly stepped back, shaking my head. "There's way too many to pick just one, I'm sorry to say."

Then, somehow, we began talking about TV, then school, then somehow *water polo*, before starting up on fast food—the pros and cons of Taco Bell. She found out that Lily Myers was my grandmother, mentioned how nice of a lady she was, and told me about her dad, who drove truck, and her brother, who was a senior and would be graduating in another week. I noticed her mother had been absent from the list of family members but decided not to mention it.

Twenty minutes later, after discussing the worst hypothetical pizza toppings of all time (hers was onions and asparagus, mine Spam and black licorice), I wasn't thinking straight and just came out and asked her if she'd want to hang out sometime.

"Not like a date or anything," I said, suddenly self-conscious. "But I'm visiting for a while, and there's really nothing else to do, so …"

She made a smile which looked somewhat forced, and said, "Sure." Then the smile faded, and her face became hard for the first time. She stared up at me, appeared like she was going to say something, but then only sighed and closed her eyes. She slowly stood up. She *had* to, because of the extra weight she was carrying. Her belly, which had been hidden behind the counter this entire time, pressed against her T-shirt. For another instant I thought of Mel, and then Sarah opened her eyes. Something had changed in them—the fun, happy look there now gone. When she spoke, her words had become dull, almost lifeless.

"Unless, that is, you're having second thoughts."

And her hands moved to her belly, where they stayed, as if wanting to protect the fetus from my response.

———

Luanne's, as my grandmother told me, is one of those special diners out in the middle of nowhere that's become almost legend. It's so well known, people from all over Chemung County come to get something as simple as a grilled BLT and fries, and supposedly college students from Cornell trek down at least once a semester, to order Luanne's famous waffle and ice cream. "As big as a tire," Grandma said, on the drive down, "and topped with six scoops of ice cream."

The place—like much of Bridgton—was small and tiny, but it was clean. Besides a long Formica-topped counter where a few lonely old men sat drinking coffee, there were twenty red-leather upholstered booths, ten on each side of the main doors. Despite its supposed notoriety, it wasn't completely packed that Saturday night. There were a few spots open at the counter, and two open booths, one of which we took in the far corner. We looked at our menus, ordered drinks, and five minutes later, my uncle arrived.

He entered in his gray deputy's uniform and talked, shook hands, or just said hello to at least a half dozen people before making his way to our booth. Grandma and I sat opposite each other, so he slid in beside me. He said hello to both of us, apologized for being late, then grabbed a menu.

"I talked to Steve earlier today," he said to me, as he glanced over the specials. I noticed that his posture, his face, even his voice, were much different than they had been back in Lanton. He looked less restricted now, not as uncomfortable.

"How are things down there?"

"About the same."

That's where the topic died, and for the next minute or so

there was silence. After we ordered from an older waitress with orange hair named Doris, Grandma, smiling, reached across the table and patted my hand.

"Christopher met Sarah today," she said.

"Really." There was something in Dean's voice I didn't like, the tone stressing a point he wanted me to hear. "Nice girl."

"She's a very nice girl."

"Yeah, Mom," Dean said. "Too bad she's pregnant and doesn't even know who the father is."

"Dean, please. Keep your voice down. All I said was—"

"Yeah, I know what you said. Let's just drop it, okay?"

I was beginning to regret even mentioning my meeting Sarah to Grandma. It was on impulse, really, having not much else to talk about, and when she asked me if I'd done anything interesting the rest of the day, I just came out with it.

"So will you be joining us tomorrow at church?" Grandma asked Dean.

He glanced at me. "You're going?"

Grandma said, "Of course he's going. Why wouldn't he?"

"I'm sure Chris can answer for himself, Mom."

"Besides, that nice man is speaking. You know, the one who's staying on The Hill with his son. I forget his name."

"Cunningham." Dean's voice was indifferent. He seemed to have quickly become interested with something across the diner. "Moses Cunningham."

"That's right. Christopher, you really should meet him. He's a very nice man."

I nodded but remained silent. I didn't like the tension that had suddenly developed.

"Still," Grandma said to Dean, a slight whine in her voice, "won't you at least consider coming? Please?"

Dean looked back at her, forced a smile. "Sure, Mom," he said, like any good son wanting to please his mother. "I'll consider it."

Twenty minutes later, after tense and token conversation, Grandma talked me into ordering dessert. Before, I'd been skeptical about Luanne's famous waffle and ice cream, but when it came the Belgian was thick and golden and just as big as the plate. And instead of six scoops of vanilla, there were seven.

CHAPTER SIX

Sunday morning service at Bridgton Calvary Church started at ten a.m. Grandma made us pancakes and eggs and, with Mrs. Roberts in my car, we arrived at the church a quarter till. The parking lot was already filled, just a few spaces left, so after dropping them off at the door, I parked the car. Then I stood outside and stared at the building. It wasn't large—quite tiny, in fact—yet still it intimidated me.

Besides meeting with James Young and going to a wedding six months prior to my parents' murder (it had been one of my mom's friends who'd gotten married, one of her friends who hadn't even come to the funeral), this would be my first time stepping foot inside a church in nearly two years. When exactly I made the unconscious decision to stop going I couldn't say; I don't think anyone who once had gone to church every Sunday can determine the specific date when they stopped. For most people—at least in my experience—it doesn't happen abruptly, but over the course of months, where first one week is missed, then another week maybe a month later, until it becomes two consecutive weeks missed and so on.

I do know it was sometime after I turned sixteen, right after my parents had loaned me an extra few hundred dollars to buy my Cavalier, because before then my parents drove me every Sunday. We'd sit together during the service and then have breakfast afterward, at one of the nearby restaurants. Then, when I stopped going, they never said anything but would always ask if I'd meet them for breakfast. And somehow I actually agreed until I stopped showing up to that, too.

It was the morning I first skipped breakfast that my father knocked on my bedroom door. I'd been out late the night before. Curfew was midnight but my parents never really enforced it; I could come home at three o'clock in the morning, as I'd done early that Sunday, and they never would have known because both would already be asleep.

I was lying in bed, hung over from a busy night partying. I really shouldn't have driven home—and how I managed it without getting in an accident or pulled over is a miracle in itself—but I'd rolled in a few hours before the sun rose, ready only for my bed and sleep. I knew I didn't have to get up early; I hadn't been to church in months, and my parents hadn't said a word to me.

My father knocked.

I rolled over in bed, saw he hadn't opened the door, and asked him what he wanted.

He never stepped foot inside my bedroom, just poked his head in and said, "You missed breakfast." He was dressed like he always was on Sunday mornings—dark khakis and a button-down shirt. No tie. He told me once God didn't require a tie when going to church; He only required you actually went.

My eyes half-open, I glanced at the alarm clock beside my bed. It was nearly one in the afternoon. This didn't surprise me —I actually figured it was later—but still I acted surprised. "Oh jeez," I said, yawning. "I guess I overslept. I'm sorry. I won't miss it next week."

"Are you sure?" There was something in his voice that gave me pause, something that said he was asking about more than just breakfast.

I yawned again, my head still on the pillow. I didn't trust myself sitting upright—at least not yet—and wasn't about to try in front of my dad. "Yeah," I said, and then frowned. "Why?"

But my father only shook his head. "No reason. I'm just curious. But Christopher, are you sure there's nothing you want to tell me? Remember, I'm your father. You shouldn't be afraid to come to me about anything."

He knows, I thought. *I must have hit something on the way home. Or maybe I threw up in the driveway or on the porch. He knows and he's trying to let me confess on my own, instead of having to force it out of me.*

"No," I said. "There's nothing. Why?"

My father, the majority of his body still standing in the hallway, shrugged. "I'm your father. It's my job to ask." He paused, appeared as if he might say something else, before he smiled and nodded his head. "I love you, son."

He waited a few seconds for a reply—a simple *I love you, Dad* would have sufficed, of course it would have—but I only nodded and told him, "Yeah, thanks."

If something changed in his face, I never noticed it. Most likely because I was still hung over and didn't feel like making conversation in the first place. But still I doubt anything did change, because just like me my father refused to show emotion. It was the one trait of his I knew I possessed.

Without a word my father leaned back and closed the door.

I stared at the door for a long time, the past couple of minutes catching up to me. I hardly remembered a thing about the conversation; it would only come later that the memory would solidify itself in my mind. When it did I would think about my father's face, his solemn impassive face after I hadn't returned his *I love you*. And the real reason he'd poked his head inside my room that day.

Now, standing in front of Bridgton Calvary Church, I thought of that morning when my father made his last attempt to understand his son. He had never wanted to smother me but never wanted to give me too much distance, either. He'd wanted to be the perfect father, just as nearly every father wants to be. The only problem, I realized as I started up the three steps to the door, was that the only way a father can be perfect is with a perfect son.

The doors opened into a small bright foyer, where probably thirty people stood talking. Two tables were set up: one with two coffee pots and Styrofoam cups and bagels on top, another with pamphlets on what looked like missionary work. Three small coat racks, only a few hooks used now for light jackets. In each corner some kind of green plant. At the back of the room were two large wooden doors, which led into the chapel.

I found Grandma talking to a fat man with a full beard. His tie was bright red. "Christopher," she said, "this is Henry Porter."

"Nice to meet you, Christopher," the man said, shaking my hand. His pinkie finger was missing. "I've heard a lot about you."

I thanked him for letting me use his trailer.

He shook his head. "No problem at all. Stay as long as you'd like."

The last name should have tipped me off, but it was from his blue eyes that I realized he was Sarah's dad. I wondered why she hadn't mentioned it before, then wondered, since she was his daughter, did Sarah know the real reason I was here?

Henry Porter's smile faded. "I'm sorry to hear about your folks, too. It's a real shame."

I nodded, told him thank you.

Grandma began talking to him then, asking him something about the water pressure on The Hill, but already my attention had drifted. I glanced around the foyer, surprised not everyone was dressed in suits and dresses. A few of the men had on ties, and a few of the women wore blouses, but for the most part everyone was dressed casually. It made me think about what my father always said about not wearing a tie.

Someone tapped my shoulder.

I turned, recognized the black kid from yesterday, and said, "Hey."

He stared up at me, his eyes magnified through his thick lenses. "Joey," he said.

"Yeah, Joey, I remember."

"No you don't."

It was true, I didn't.

He said, "Did you ever wonder how t-tall the T-T-Tower of Babel was? I mean, do you think it got as big as the Sears T-Tower?"

Like yesterday, I didn't know what to say. Now that he'd reintroduced himself, I remembered our encounter very well, and I remembered the question he'd asked me then.

"I've never been to Shinar myself," Joey said. "Actually, I've never been anywhere outside America. But I've heard from some p-p-people what the land's like out there."

From inside the chapel, piano music began playing. Everyone in the foyer, amid the murmur of their hushed conversations, started heading toward the two open doors.

"My dad's speaking," Joey said. "I t-told him about you."

Told him about me? Told him what?

"Christopher?"

My grandmother stood at the chapel doors, her weight resting on her wooden cane.

"I'll t-t-talk to you later." Joey smiled at me one last time, then weaved his way through the people toward the church's entrance. An older lady with white puffy hair dropped her napkin that she was using to carry a bagel, and at once he picked it up for her, before continuing on.

I watched him for only a moment, wondering why he wasn't staying to listen to his dad speak, then turned and joined the rest of the stragglers into the chapel.

Grandma and I sat with Mrs. Roberts in a pew two rows behind Sarah Porter and her father—just the two of them, her brother and mom nowhere in sight. They were the old kind of wooden pews, though someone not too long ago had donated enough money to have both the seats and backs cushioned. We filed in and left a space on the end, in case Dean decided to show. Grandma believed there was a chance he might; I was more realistic but kept it to myself.

The church was mostly full—maybe one hundred people, many families with children, some older couples. After singing a few hymns and listening to special music from Lindsey Bowyer—an eleven-year-old with an amazing voice, who sang "My One and Only God"—Reverend Peart stood up in front of the large wooden cross hanging on the wall behind him. He was a short pale man, who wore horn-rimmed glasses and a cheap gray suit. He said a short prayer, made some announcements, then introduced their guest speaker for the next two weeks.

Moses Cunningham was nothing like I'd expected after meeting his son. He was tall and broad-shouldered. His hair was short. He wore dark slacks and a white shirt with a gray tie.

Because Joey wore glasses, I figured he would too. But the man stood up in front of the congregation and read from his Bible without glasses and without trouble.

He read from James chapter 2, verses 14 through 26. I didn't have a Bible of my own and read off my grandmother's. The passage dealt with faith and works, and how both must go hand in hand.

Moses had a strong, confident speaking voice, which reminded me a lot of James Young. He knew when to add emphasis, when to pause in his reading or speaking to make his words more meaningful. Toward the end, when he began talking about Abraham and how he offered up Isaac to God to show how his works perfected his faith, Moses's eyes shifted and he stared right at me. It was only for a second, maybe two, and then he blinked and, bowing his head, said, "Let us pray."

CHAPTER SEVEN

AFTER A LUNCH of tomato soup and grilled cheese (my grandmother, God love her, kept her cooking consistent with making the sandwiches a little burnt), I left Grandma's and headed down the drive toward my trailer. The sky was clear, the sun was bright, and a soft breeze pushed its way through The Hill. Off in the distance I heard the faint sound of traffic down on 13.

Sitting in front of the trailer, in a dirty lawn chair that had been knocked over, was Joey Cunningham. He was cleaning his glasses, and when I walked up, he had to squint at me until he put them back on his face.

He said, "Hey, Chris," his small voice cheerful. "How's it going?"

Truthfully, I wasn't surprised to see him.

I forced a smile. "What's up, Joey?"

"I'm just waiting for John. You know, his dad owns the trailer park. He's t-taking me down to the Beckett House." He grinned. "It's haunted."

"Haunted, huh?"

"You don't have to believe me. That's fine."

I didn't know what to say. It was like this kid had some kind of power over me that kept making me speechless. He'd looked so happy, like nothing was going to get him down, but now his smile was gone and he stared at his sneakers.

"Look," I said, but before I could get anything else out, he stood and pointed up the drive at the Rec House.

"Can you come with me? I wanna show you something."

Two things worked for Joey in that cinderblock building full of junk. First was that he managed to open the screen door with hardly any sound or trouble at all. Second was that when he flicked the light switch, the fluorescents in the ceiling came on at once.

"You heard about Mrs. Porter, right?"

He started through the building, past the table and the bright yellow car sitting upside down on the floor. I followed him, at first glancing back at where Sarah had been hiding yesterday. The spot behind the counter was empty. Then Joey came to the corner of the building, standing in front of a framed picture of a woman in her late thirties. Below it were smaller pictures, of a family that looked happy and strong. Sarah standing with her father and mother and brother, smiling and staring back at the camera with the most innocent eyes.

"She died in a car accident," Joey said. His voice had become a whisper. He tapped the smaller frame with an old newspaper clipping inside; when his finger came away it left a fingerprint in the dust. "This is the obituary. You should read it when you get the chance."

Before I could ask him why, he turned and walked to a narrow chalkboard hanging on the wall, right behind the ancient TV. In bold letters across the top was printed SURVIVORS OF THE BECKETT HOUSE. Below it, in either yellow or white chalk, were maybe two dozen names. Joey pointed to the space beneath the last one.

"That's where my name's gonna go."

The idea of spending the night in a supposed haunted house wasn't something I could see Joey doing. I didn't know him well, of course, but he just didn't seem like the kind of person to buy into all that stuff, let alone actually go along and try to be a part of it.

"Why, Joey?" I asked. "Why do you want to do this?"

He looked up at me. "Do you really care?"

Once again, I didn't know what to say.

"I never knew my mom," he whispered, staring back at the chalkboard. "She died when I was born. When I was like three or four my dad quit his job and started going around speaking at a bunch of different churches. We've been doing that ever since. I never went to school, my dad taught me everything, so I never really had any friends. I meet people everywhere I go, and they act like my friends, but they're not.

"In another week my dad's done speaking here and ... and we'll be moving on. And what will we leave behind? Those plates up there? No one's signed them in a long time. But this, this board right here, after I spend the night tonight my name will be added. It'll be there forever."

He shrugged and gave me a weak smile.

"It might sound weird, but it's just a way to ... be remembered. I mean, in another month, who's really going to remember me and my dad?"

I hadn't realized it, but this was a different Joey Cunningham than the one I'd met yesterday, or even talked to this morning. His happy, outgoing look on life had deteriorated into this small sad child. Also, his stutter was gone. Not that it meant anything, really, but he spoke fluently, without any trouble at all. It just didn't seem like the kid who had problems with his hard Ts and Ps. No, somehow he had matured, had become much older than his limited years.

I said, "I'll remember you, Joey," and even now I'm not sure what made me say it. "I'll remember you and your—"

"There you are, Joe. Sorry I'm late."

Standing in the doorway—he too managed to open the screen door without noise or trouble—was eighteen-year-old John Porter. He was a skinny kid, his hair long and brown, all over the place like he'd just woken up. He wore shorts and a black tank top, grinning like a stoner. He noticed the lights, frowned, then punched the switch beside him.

"What the hell?" he muttered. His voice was deep, sounding almost forced. "You guys think electricity grows on trees?"

"Hey, John, how's it going?" Joey's demeanor had suddenly changed and he was again the cheery, nothing's-going-to-get-me-down kid I remembered. "This is Chris Myers."

We walked up to John, and when we reached the door he stuck out his hand. "Nice to meet you, man."

Joey said, "John, did you ever wonder what Jesus did with the gold, frankincense and myrrh the magi gave him?"

John looked at me. "Dude, what the fuck's a magi?"

I couldn't help it—I busted up laughing.

We filed outside and down the drive, toward the field beside the trailer park. John strode on ahead like he owned the place. I thought of something and caught up with Joey, tapping him on the shoulder. He glanced back at me.

"How'd you know my last name?"

"What do you mean?"

"My last name. I never told you what it was."

He frowned for a moment, then smiled. "Come on, you don't even remembering t-t-talking yesterday. Yeah you told me. You told me you're Chris Myers from Lanton, P-P-Pennsylvania."

He turned away, shouted at John to slow down, and hurried up ahead.

I slowed, hesitated. My trailer was ten yards away, and I started toward it. I'd had enough of this for one day.

"Come on, Chris, hurry up!" Joey shouted. They were waiting for me. I sighed. I knew I'd regret it later, but I turned and jogged after them.

In the small field beside the trailer park was a scattered number of picnic tables, their surfaces weather-worn and covered in spots of gray birdshit. There were also two metal poles standing erect out of the shaggy grass, about ten feet apart, what I assumed had once been used to hang a volleyball net back in the day. John took us past these, toward a wall of lush pine trees that protected The Hill from the valley beyond. At a spot just before the trees you could see where the grass had been trampled to death. Now it was just dirt, the beginning of the trail that led down through the hemlocks and birches and other trees toward the Beckett House.

The slope descended gradually. You had to watch where you stepped or you might stumble over some small rocks or tree vines sticking out of the dirt. John led the way. Somewhere along the path he lit up a cigarette; an occasional puff of smoke drifted up toward the canopy of leaves above us.

"How much farther?" I asked. We'd been walking for two minutes already.

John didn't answer. He just kept walking. I started to call up again, to ask the same question, when I saw the trees thinning out up ahead.

Seconds later we entered a small clearing, and John said, "That's it," almost proudly, nodding at what rested in the middle of the long grass and weeds. "That's the Beckett House."

When Joey had said haunted house, I'd pictured something out of a Hitchcock film: like Norman Bates' house in *Psycho* or Manderley in *Rebecca*. Your overly large house with big shutters and drapes that sometimes move, because there's something dead inside peeking out. The porch would be a dilapidated mess, with boards missing and invisible nails sticking out just waiting for careless feet and hands. There might even be a swing hanging from two rusted chains, swaying slowly back and forth even though there's no wind.

But the Beckett House was nothing like that.

More like a shack than a house, the building was only one story and made completely out of stone. Maybe only fifteen feet high, the entire structure was blackened, as if it had survived a fire. The roof had been thatched but was mostly gone, except for one spot that was covered in generations of dead leaves. No door, except a wide space nearly ten feet tall where a door might have once been. Some white looping graffiti, near the corner of the house, announced that Ted loved Sandy.

I said, my voice flat, "That's supposed to be haunted?"

John offered me one of his Marlboros. I shook my head and he lit another for himself. He took a long and satisfying drag, nodding his head earnestly.

Joey said, "Doesn't look t-t-too scary t-to me."

"Yeah, well, maybe not at first. But wait until you hear this." John picked up a stick from the ground, pointed it at the house. "A long time ago—like fifty or a hundred years, something like that—this guy used to live there. Name was Devin Beckett, a real whack-job, and he never came out of his house. A real, ah … what's it called … recluse. Anyway, one night he just snaps. Goes into town and starts killing people. Killed, I don't know, like thirty or forty people. Used a machete too, sliced them up real good."

For an instant images flooded my mind: my parents in bed, their cut up bodies and all the blood.

John took another long drag of his cigarette. He tapped the stick on the ground and turned back to us, a frown on his face.

"Actually wait, that might be wrong. It's been a while since I last told this story. Maybe he was going around the state killing people, I forget. But all I know for sure is the police tracked him down back to this house. His hideout, if you wanna call it that."

John turned and walked toward the house. Joey and I followed.

Inside there was nothing except some discarded bottles of Bud Light and cigarette butts. No tables, no chairs, no bed; only an open hole in the wall which must have once been the fireplace … and which now, I noticed, contained a few used condoms. The walls were more darkened than the outside. The floor was a mixture of wood and stone, with what looked like a few scratch marks here and there. The scent of alcohol and piss was faint.

John snubbed his cigarette out on the floor with the heel of his sneaker. He grabbed the stick with both hands, lifted it over his head, and rested it across his shoulders.

"So then there's this standoff. Something like ten or twelve hours. And this guy, he doesn't want to come out. He yells at them, tells them there's no fucking way he's giving up, and he shoots whoever tries to come near. So these cops, they tell him they're gonna burn the place down, thinking that's the only way they'll get him out, right? Wrong. The sad son of a bitch never comes out, so they torch the place with him in it."

There was silence then. Above us, past the small patch of roofing that was supported by a thick charcoaled piece of wood, a breeze blew through the tops of the trees. A few birds hid somewhere in the branches, chirping aimlessly.

"That's it?" Joey sounded disappointed. "That's all that happened?"

John dropped the stick and held up a finger. "But here's the really freaky thing. Beckett's body? They never found it."

"Bullshit," I said.

"Dude, I swear to you, it's the truth. Never found his body. Burned this place out, had the whole thing surrounded, and they couldn't find his body." He grinned again. "But you know, Joe, legend has it that late at night, when the wind's quiet, you can still hear him screaming to death. You can even smell his roasting flesh. The legend says that the reason his body was never found is because he's still here, burning forever for his sins."

Joey didn't look frightened at all. In fact, he looked bored. He asked, "Did you see anything when you stayed?"

"Me? Nah, I didn't see a thing. Really, it wasn't so bad. Just cold. Course, I stayed here during the fall, but fuck, make sure you got a sleeping bag and you'll be fine."

"How long do I have to stay?"

"I'll bring you down around midnight, then come and get you before school tomorrow. So, what, around seven hours, give or take."

"School?" I said. "It's the first week of June."

"Tell me about it, dude." John gave an overdramatic sigh. "Fucking blizzard back around Christmas used up all our snow days *and* some. We got pushed back an extra week."

"That sucks," Joey said.

"So yeah, sorry to jet, but I need to be getting back." John clapped me on the shoulder. "Chris, nice meeting you, man. And Joe, I'll come get you tonight, okay?"

"Sure."

Then John was gone.

I glanced around the house one last time, still skeptical about the story, when I noticed Joey staring at me.

"It started here," he whispered. "It makes sense it should end here too."

Again, a different voice and tone from the kid's mouth. Older somehow, more mature. And shouldn't there have been a stutter on that last word?

I frowned and cocked my head. "What was that?"

"Can you feel it, Chris?"

"Feel what?"

Joey stared a moment longer before shaking his head. "Never mind," he muttered, and headed outside.

I stood then by myself in the Beckett House, and for an instant I *did* feel something, a kind of chill race through my body. Was that what he'd meant? After a few seconds I decided it didn't matter and started to leave, before glancing down at the wood and stone floor, before noticing the few scratch marks there. It hadn't been part of John's story, but I immediately saw a child there on the ground, trying to crawl away, screaming and crying and scratching at the floor. I saw its fingernails cracking and bleeding and tearing apart before the child was pulled back into darkness.

CHAPTER EIGHT

BY FOUR O'CLOCK that Sunday afternoon I'd arrived at the conclusion that coming to Bridgton was a mistake. If my parents' killer did somehow find out where I'd gone, and he came up here planning to finish whatever job he started, he wouldn't have any trouble at all. Steve had said coming here was the best route right now, that my deputy uncle could keep a constant eye on me, but so far I'd only seen him once, and that was at Luanne's. I felt like a stranger on The Hill, knew that the rest of the old folks were probably whispering to each other, asking who I was, wondering why Lily Myers had never mentioned anything about a grandson before. I just needed to get away for a while, I needed something to pass the time, so I headed to Half Creek Road, paused, then made a right and started walking.

Ten minutes later, after walking past Bridgton Calvary Church and four rundown houses, one with a series of wind chimes running the length of the porch, another with a tree stump in its front yard, a weatherworn ceramic gnome standing atop keeping a constant vigil, I came around a slight bend and spotted Shepherd's Books. The small parking lot beside it was empty, the wooden CLOSED sign rocking slightly back and forth in the breeze.

An old man sat in the shade of the porch. He stared out at the road, smoking a cigar, his feet up on the paint-flaked railing.

"Excuse me," I said. "What are your hours?"

He glanced at me, puffed smoke, and with only the corner of his mouth muttered, "My what?"

"Your hours. When do you open?"

"Open?" He coughed a raspy chuckle. "Kid, you ain't from around here, are you."

I shook my head.

"Well then, I'll let you in on a little secret." He took his muddy boots off the railing and dropped them on the porch. Leaned forward and said, "I ain't ever open."

"Okay. And why's that?"

"To keep punks like you off my property." He puffed more smoke and then squinted at me, his eyebrows white and bushy. "Where'd you come from anyway?"

I said, "My mother's vagina," and started to turn away to head back up Half Creek Road.

The old man sputtered after me, saying, "You little smart ass. You better hurry up and get off my property or else I'll call the Sheriff and have you arrested for trespassing."

I turned back and nodded. "You do that. Have them send out Dean Myers."

"Deputy Myers? Why him?"

"He's my uncle."

The old man cocked his head, squinted back at me. Then his dry face grinned as he clapped his hands. "Goddamn, he is, ain't he. Now I'm starting to see the resemblance. Well why didn't you just say that before?" He stood up, grimacing at the action, and motioned me up onto the porch. "I'm Lewis Shepherd, the owner of this fine establishment."

His hand was small and calloused, and now, standing just a foot away from him, I noticed the mounds of dandruff on the shoulders of his dark shirt. When he turned, his bird's nest of gray hair was full of it. He opened the door and waved me inside, and I followed him into the house. It was dark and cold, reeking of dust and stale paper. There were rows and rows of books, both tattered hardcover and paperback, on large wooden shelves or in brown unmarked boxes. A counter sat off to the side, an old-fashioned register on top.

"Got anything in mind?" His cigar, half-smoked, was still in his mouth.

"Not really."

"Well, if you find something you want, just go ahead and take it. Not like any of these books are going anywhere anyhow."

I asked him why he never opened.

He shrugged, said, "Just fell out of the love, I guess," and started toward the back, where steps led upstairs. "You can let yourself out when you're done." At the landing he turned back and surveyed his dusty inventory. "Hell, take two or three if you want. I ain't gonna miss 'em."

I walked up to a box of paperbacks. They were all thin, less than two hundred pages each. Looked to be dime mysteries. "Are you sure you don't want me to pay?"

But the old man had already started up the steps, taking them slowly, his heavy boots clapping them one at a time. Then the sound of the door slamming shut.

When I returned a half hour later—with a battered paperback copy of *Billy Budd*—I found Sarah sitting in the same lawn chair Joey had occupied earlier that day. She wore black capris and a large white T-shirt, her strawberry blond hair pulled back into a ponytail. On the ground between her Keds was a plastic cooler.

She said, "Hey," but that was all. Her voice was barely a whisper.

"Hey," I said, surprised to see her. "What's up?"

"I um … remember what you said yesterday, about hanging out? I was thinking maybe … I made some sandwiches." She glanced down at the white and green Igloo. "They're Fluffernutters. And there's some juice boxes and pretzels and …"

While she was the same Sarah Porter I'd met and talked with yesterday, she wasn't. Something about her had changed. As she sat there, her hands folded in her lap, I glanced at the bulge of her belly, and I knew that was the reason. Except it wasn't me who was put off by the reality of what now lived inside her. It was Sarah who was making this hard on herself, acting as if she was some kind of outcast.

"Sure," I said. "That sounds great. But … where do you want to go?"

And when she looked up I saw the doubt in her eyes, the worry that I wasn't being serious. But then, when she realized my sincerity, she smiled. "Harris Hill Park," she said. "My favorite place in the world."

Her directions were flawless. She took us through Horseheads, past the Arnot Mall and Elmira-Corning Regional Airport, past all the stores and restaurants, then onto Big Flats Road that took us up the mountainside. It was about six o'clock when we arrived at what Sarah called the Lookout. Up on the side of Harris Hill Park (*The Soaring Capital of the World*, according to a large sign off the side of the road), we parked beside a picnic area and walked to a few benches looking down at the valley.

"My mom used to bring me up here when I was little," Sarah said.

We sat on a black metal bench, the Igloo between us. A few benches down, an elderly couple sat with their arms around each other. A long wooden split-rail fence ran the entire length of the Lookout, keeping anyone from stumbling off the drop. Behind us was a playground, with slides and swings and a large contraption shaped like a plane. A few teenagers sat there smoking, while a few others juggled a hacky sack.

"She used to tell me it was the highest place in the world. I don't think I ever really believed her. But ... but it was our place, you know? She'd bring me here and sometimes we'd watch the gliders. But mostly we just talked."

I asked, "She doesn't come up here with you anymore?" without thinking. Then, a moment later, remembering what Joey had told me earlier: "Shit, I'm sorry. I didn't—"

Sarah shook her head. "No, that's okay. It's not your fault." Then she frowned at me, asked how I'd known. I told her about Joey and she grinned. "I love that kid. He's so cute."

I didn't know what to say to that. I glanced out into the valley, watched a jet as it made its approach to the airport.

Beside me, Sarah sighed. When I glanced over, she was staring at the ground and shaking her head. I asked her what was wrong.

"Just my mom," she said. "She died the first week of September, two years ago. Right before 9/11. I remember actually crying about it that Tuesday, right after those planes crashed. I don't know why, it's not like I knew anybody who died there. But I was crying and my dad walked in. He thought it was about my mom. I told him it wasn't, then wondered to myself *why* it wasn't. And my dad said, 'Thank God your mom died when she did. She'd be more of a wreck than you right now.' And ... we just started laughing. It was so weird, the way we could actually laugh about something like that. But it wasn't really laughing, you know? We were just … getting our grief out. And I've always remembered it, because it's true. My mom *would* have been a complete wreck. She was the kind of person who got sad when she saw dead deer lying on the side of the road. And I actually thought that it was good she died when she did, so she wouldn't have had to see all that terrible stuff. Does that … does that make me a bad person?"

I told her no, not at all.

Sarah shrugged. "Yeah, I know you're right. Still it worried me for a while. But do you know what *does* make me a bad person? The drunk who hit her when she was jogging—I wanted him to suffer. She died instantly, and he was taken to the hospital where he died an hour later. I'd heard that his entire chest was messed up, and he was in a lot of pain. And later, when I was thinking and crying about it, I wished that he'd just kept on living a couple extra hours. You know? Just so that he could be in all that pain."

She'd gone back to staring at the ground while she spoke. Now she glanced at me and said, "I'm sorry. You don't want to hear any of this. It's just … I feel so open with you for some reason. It's kind of weird." And she laughed briefly, a nervous sort of giggle.

I smiled and shook my head, told her that it was fine.

Sarah wiped at her eyes. "So what about you? How long are you visiting?"

"I'm not sure exactly. Could be a week, could be a month."

"Are you by yourself, or did your folks come up too?"

"You mean your dad didn't tell you?"

"Tell me what?"

"My parents," I said, and at once it hit me how hard it would be to say the rest. "They … they're dead."

"Oh, I'm so sorry." She reached across the cooler and touched my arm. "How long ago did it happen?"

"Just last week." My voice had become a whisper. I was

staring off at single dandelion beside the fence, shivering in the breeze. "They were murdered."

"Oh my gosh," Sarah said. Her voice too had become a whisper. "Did they … catch the person who did it?"

I shook my head. "That's why I'm here. The police think the killer's after me, so … I'm kind of hiding out."

"But aren't you scared?"

I continued watching the lone shivering dandelion. I thought about that morning I woke to the annoying low buzzing. It was just eight days ago but still it felt like a long time, a very long time, and looking at Sarah, I told her the truth.

"I'm terrified."

For a moment neither one of us said anything. Behind us, on the playground, the teens all started laughing.

Finally Sarah said, "When my mom died, I blamed God at first. I guess it's just a natural reaction. Do you blame God for what happened?"

I stared out at the sun that had about another hour or two before it set. I shook my head slowly and whispered, "I don't believe in God."

A long silence fell between us. A few rows down, the elderly couple decided they'd had enough of the view for the evening. The old man placed a brown fedora on his head and held out his hand to help his wife up. When she stood, she pecked him on the cheek and then they started off toward their Cadillac.

I watched them walk, the man with his arm around his wife's shoulders, and thought about my parents. About how they would never get to do the same thing. How they would never grow old together, would never watch another sunset. How my mother would never again peck my father's cheek, and how he would never again put his arm around her as they walked. And how, if they had the chance, they would never again tell me how much they loved me and then wait for me to tell them the same.

"So what ever happened to your granddad?"

We'd been sitting there for almost twenty minutes already, the conversation back on par with yesterday's. Just random, nothing stuff like our favorite old school TGIF shows—hers was *Family Matters* ("I'll actually admit I've always thought Urkel was funny"), mine *Perfect Strangers*—and what bubblegum flavors were the all-time best—she couldn't decide between mango strawberry and watermelon cherry. The Igloo was open, and we'd both had one sandwich each.

After taking a swallow from one of the four juice boxes, I said, "What do you mean?"

"I've lived across from the trailer park my whole life, and I've sort of known Lily for about as long. I never found out the whole story, but I heard something about your granddad going to jail. And the way Lily always talked about him, he was innocent and it never should have happened."

I squeezed the tiny juice box as hard as I could. "Actually, they put him in a mental institution. He was insane."

"I'm almost afraid to ask, but what did he do?"

"He tried to kill me."

She let this sink in for a moment, then shook her head and muttered, "Holy crap." That was all. Nothing else, and from those two words I realized something.

Ever since the day my grandfather tried to kill me I'd always expected the worst. So when I found my parents dead, I was shocked and I was horrified and I was scared. But I wasn't surprised. Maybe it was a small voice in my head that told me a day like this was eventually going to come, and that I'd been waiting for it ever since.

"I don't remember much about it," I said, staring back at that lone shivering dandelion. "I was in the second grade when he came and took me out of class. And we just got into his car and … we drove."

I remembered the crazy way he rushed into the classroom. My teacher, Mrs. Jackson, had been up front talking about something, answering one of the students' questions, and then all of a sudden the door opened and in he ran. He ignored Mrs. Jackson when she asked him just what he thought he was doing, and came straight to my desk, told me we had to go right this moment and then started dragging me. I hadn't been scared. I actually thought it was kind of fun, leaving class like that. On the way out, I'd even waved goodbye to my friends.

"The police eventually tracked us down. We were on the highway. My grandfather pulled over and just broke down crying. And I sat there watching him, all confused. I asked him what was wrong, and he told me he was sorry and that he loved me, that he wished things could have been different. Then when the cops opened the door and took him out, he looked right back at me and told me to know when to stop."

"To what?"

"To stop. To know when to stop. I don't know. Like I said, he was insane."

"But you said he tried to kill you."

"I'm pretty sure that was his intention. After the cops took him away, they found a gun underneath the driver's seat."

Sarah sat back, speechless. I didn't blame her. She had probably thought her life was messed up more than anyone else she knew, what with her mother and her … her baby.

Too bad she's pregnant and doesn't even know who the father is.

And right then I almost did a very stupid thing. The thought of the baby and what my uncle said were too fresh in my mind, and I began formulating a question. I'd even opened my mouth to ask it when Sarah's eyes widened and she gasped. She reached out, grabbed my hand, and placed it on her belly.

"Do you feel that?"

I didn't feel anything at first. I started to pull my hand away when I did feel something, slightly, a small movement from inside her.

"It's kicking." Her face was bright with a smile. "My baby's kicking."

I didn't know what to say. Suddenly the dour atmosphere had changed and it was thanks to the life inside Sarah. All our worries, all our thoughts and fears had taken a step back and now it was just the two of us, experiencing one of life's miracles in its simplest way.

She laughed, and I laughed, and at that moment I didn't think about my parents or my grandfather or the sociopath stalking me. All I thought about was Sarah and her baby, and the joy she now shared with me. It felt good.

Much later that night, after playing several games of dominos and cards with my grandmother and Mrs. Roberts, I sat in my trailer reading *Billy Budd*. Or at least trying to read it. I couldn't seem to focus and was just rereading the first two pages when there was a knock at the door.

It was Joey. "Ready?"

"Ready? Ready for what?"

He shook his head. "Boy, your memory isn't t-t-too good, is it? Don't you remember the Beckett House? You said you'd come down with me and John."

"I did?"

Light shined on Joey's face from the side, then swung over into mine. I had to hold the paperback up and turn my head before the light moved away and I heard John Porter's deep voice.

"So, Joe, you ready or what?"

"Sure I'm ready," Joey said. "But I don't think Chris is coming anymore."

The light shined back in my face. "That so?"

"Would you turn that stupid thing off?"

The flashlight clicked off.

John said, "Whoa wait, Joe. Where's your sleeping bag?"

Joey stared back at me, shook his head. "I won't need one."

"All right, dude, suit yourself." John lit up one of his Marlboros. "Let's go. The sooner we get you down there, the sooner I can get my ass in bed. I haven't slept since Friday."

Joey stared back at me a moment longer. Then he nodded and they turned and started down the drive, toward the field and the line of pine trees. I returned to my cramped bed and sat back right where the light was positioned.

I tried reading again, but after a minute closed the book. I kept thinking about Joey. About the way he stared up at me before leaving with John.

"What's the big deal anyway?" I whispered.

A minute passed, and I tried reading some more. It didn't work. I was no longer even seeing the words. All I saw was Joey's face, and his dark, deep-set eyes. Before I knew it I set the book aside, grabbed my sneakers, and headed outside. The evening was cool, the sky clear and shining with stars.

"What the fuck am I doing?" I asked myself.

By the time I reached the Beckett House, John was heading back up the trail. But Joey was there. Of course he was.

He was waiting for me.

CHAPTER NINE

EVEN AT NIGHT the Beckett House wasn't intimidating. Because of the clear sky, the moon shone light into the small clearing, but it wasn't much. The surrounding trees created moving shadows everywhere, as the wind rustled their tops back and forth. Crickets hid chirping in the branches and tall grass.

Joey sat in the house's doorway, his arms resting on his pulled-up knees. When he saw me he slowly stood up, wiping at his eyes. He was crying.

"Joey, what's wrong?"

"Nothing."

He was lying, but I decided to ignore it. "Why am I here?"

"Your p-p-parents were murdered."

"No, I mean why am I *here*? Standing here with you in front of this stupid house?" I paused. "Wait. How'd you know about my parents?"

"Can you t-tell me about them? About your mom and your dad?"

I stared at him in the darkness and saw another person. Like when we'd been at the Rec House and he told me about his mother and how he didn't have anyone except his dad. I'd felt sorry for him then, but here right now I didn't know what to feel.

"What do you want to know about them?"

"Just something that sticks out. Something that made you love them."

The crickets continued chirping around us, the wind continued to rustle the tops of the trees.

"No," I said. "No, Joey, I don't see the point."

"I just want to know if it's worth it."

"If what's worth it?"

He stared at me, and for a moment I didn't think he was going to say anything else. Then he took a deep breath and said, "Chris, the Lord has a plan for each of—"

"Don't," I said. "I don't want to hear it."

"But the Lord—"

"Fuck the Lord. He doesn't give a shit about me, and I sure as hell don't give a shit about him. Sorry to break it to you, Joey, but you have to get out of that bubble you've been living in. You have to grow up and start seeing that this whole Lord thing is just a waste of time. That's how life is."

"You have no idea how life is."

"Don't I? I'm sorry, but wasn't it my parents who were murdered?"

"Chris," Joey said softly, "did you ever wonder what would have happened if Adam and Eve had said—"

"No. Whatever the fuck it is, I never wondered. I don't care about stupid shit like that. It means nothing to me."

"But—"

"Goodnight, Joey." Deciding to walk away now rather than risk saying something I'd really regret. Starting to turn, starting to walk away, but then finding myself saying, "Don't let the ghost get you," before turning my back completely and heading up the trail.

It was a few minutes after midnight when I returned to my trailer. I didn't know why exactly, but I was pissed off. I grabbed the copy of *Billy Budd* off the bed and chucked it at the wall. I sat down on the bed, grabbed the picture of my parents, and stared at it for ten minutes. I'd done the same thing last night, ignoring the asshole in the middle and concentrating on my mom and dad, on how happy they looked at that particular moment in time.

Finally I turned off the light and went to bed. But I couldn't sleep. I just stared at the ceiling and thought about Joey. About what I'd said to him and how I said it. About the look of disappointment in his eyes.

Tomorrow, I told myself. Tomorrow I would talk to him and apologize, try to make things right.

I rolled over and stared at the wall. Even in the dark I could see where some of the mildew had formed. I decided to concentrate on that until I drifted off, but after a few minutes I realized it wasn't working. So I rolled back over.

And froze.

A dark figure stood just a few feet away from me.

This is him! my mind screamed. *You didn't believe he was after you but he is and now he's here, he's here to kill you, SO DO SOMETHING!*

But I couldn't do anything. I was paralyzed. And it took a few disjointed seconds before I realized that the figure now standing in front of me *wasn't* my parents' murderer, was in fact the farthest thing from that sick bastard. Instead it was a small boy with thick glasses and whose body trembled like he was freezing, as he stared up at the ceiling with dark, terrified eyes.

"Joey?" I whispered. But he didn't seem to hear me, didn't even seem to acknowledge the fact that he was in my trailer at all. Then I realized he wasn't there to begin with, that it was just a faint image of Joey and not the real thing.

My mind raced. I didn't know what to think. Joey's mouth now began moving and I realized he was talking, but there was no sound, I couldn't hear his voice.

Of course you can't hear his voice, my mind said, freaking out now about a completely different matter. *You can't hear his voice because* he's not really there!

Then Joey's mouth stopped moving. He simply stared up. Suddenly his eyes got even wider and before I knew it his mouth opened again. At first I thought he was saying something but then I understood he wasn't, he couldn't possibly be saying anything because now he was *screaming*.

I blinked and he was gone. A second later I realized my paralysis was gone too, so I jumped out of bed and ran to the door, went outside and stepped onto the cool moist grass. I just stood there, in my boxers and T-shirt, listening to the night.

Moments passed and I began wondering why I was standing out here at all, why I wasn't in bed where I should be. Of course what I'd seen was only my imagination, my over-worked mind telling me I needed sleep.

I heard it then, off in the distance, from behind the wall of pines down the hill toward the church. Behind the wind and the insects and the distant sound of a tractor-trailer passing by on 13. Behind everything else in the world at that single moment in time.

Very faint but very real too, the sound of a little boy crying out for help.

CHAPTER TEN

NIGHT HAD TURNED TO DAY. They had five portable flood-
lights and had placed them around the Beckett House. A
handful of deputies and volunteer firemen combed the area
with flashlights. Inside the burnt-out structure came occasional
flashes as pictures were taken. That was where I'd seen
the blood.

Through the trees you could see the deputy and blue-
lighters' vehicles. Three-thirty in the morning, only two of the
cruisers still had their roof-lights flashing. Sheriff Douglas
talked with the fire chief by the path that led from Calvary
Church—as it turned out there was a smaller, narrower trail in
that direction. John Porter stood with his dad and answered a
deputy's questions. Dean stood next to me, dressed in his
uniform. Every couple of minutes the radio Velcroed to his
shoulder squawked, as did nearly everyone else's around the
area. For the first time I noticed he wore a pin just above his
name badge: PISTOL EXPERT.

"This isn't good," he murmured. He popped another Life-
Saver in his mouth unconsciously, began chewing it. (When
he'd first arrived on scene and came up and asked if I was all

right, his breath smelled of peppermint.) He sighed, shaking his head. "This isn't good at all."

He was staring right at the Beckett House. I watched him for a few moments, then glanced over at where Moses Cunningham stood in sweatpants and undershirt. He too stared at the Beckett House, but his arms weren't crossed like my uncle's, and his back wasn't as straight. His broad shoulders were hunched and his dark face was screwed into a look of fear and frustration. Earlier, when he talked to the Sheriff, there had been tears in his eyes, but now they had stopped.

On the other side of the small clearing John Porter stood with his father and the young deputy. John had his hands in his pockets and looked like he was half-asleep. Henry, his face masked behind his beard, stood with his back to his son. He refused to look at John, and he refused to watch the activity surrounding the Beckett House, so he mostly kept his gaze focused on the ground.

I was wearing shorts and sneakers now, not like before when I'd run down here in my underwear and found the house deserted except for the splatter of blood on the ground. Only I hadn't noticed that the first time, but later, when I came back with John.

We'd been out here for over an hour now. Inside the house more flashes went off.

Sheriff Douglas said some parting words to the fire chief and made her way toward me and Dean.

She said to me, "Long night, huh?"

I nodded.

"I hate to ask you this, Chris, but would you mind telling me again what happened when you came down here the first time? As John was leaving, I mean."

I'd given my statement twice already and was too exhausted to do it again. But I knew they needed to know exactly what I saw and heard and felt to get a precise idea of what happened here, so maybe, just maybe, they could find Joey.

"I knew Joey wanted to talk to me about something. But when I came down I realized he just wanted to witness to me, and it kind of pissed me off. He was just ... he was annoying me, so I more or less told him off and went back to The Hill."

"You didn't see or hear anything unusual?"

I told her I didn't. Then I said, "So I couldn't sleep, and I was just lying there in the dark. And I ... I heard him cry out. It was faint, but I could tell something was wrong so I ran down here. But by the time I made it he was already gone."

Of course I didn't mention the fact that I'd seen something that looked like Joey in my trailer moments before I rushed outside and *then* heard him screaming. Or that as I ran down the trail I knew, just *knew*, that Joey was gone and maybe already dead.

"Then?" Sheriff Douglas was being very patient, understanding, and I knew she was a mother. She probably had kids of her own, maybe two if not three, and I understood the burden now on her shoulders, how as a mother she knew what Moses Cunningham was feeling and wanted to end that pain and worry as quickly as possible.

"Then I ran back and got John. Banged on the front door until Mr. Porter answered. When I told him what happened he got John and the two of us came down here. Mr. Porter, well, I guess he called you."

I didn't want to mention how John had reacted when he first saw the blood. Just a few spots on the ground, but it was definitely blood and it was definitely fresh and there was no doubt in either of our minds who it belonged to. John had cried out *Oh fuck!* and his face had paled and for a moment I thought he was going to faint.

"And you saw nothing when you came down here the second time? No footprints in the grass, nothing out of place?"

I shook my head.

She sighed and nodded, but said nothing else. Behind her, the deputies and volunteers still continued to scour the area. The photographer inside the house was done with his pictures, so there were no more flashes. Back in the church parking lot still came those flashing lights. Besides the faint voices of the men and the occasional crackle of static from everyone's radios, there was silence in the trees.

I glanced again at Moses Cunningham. He stood facing the Beckett House. His shoulders were still hunched forward, but now his eyes were closed.

Beside me, Dean said, "What?" which brought my attention back to him and the sheriff. I noticed Douglas was staring at me. She was biting her lower lip, deciding on something. Finally she nodded.

"Listen," she began, "it would probably be best if Chris—"

The commotion started in the trees behind the house. First someone shouted, "Over here!" and then all the flashlights began bobbing that way. Sheriff Douglas turned and started immediately in that direction. Dean didn't hesitate either; he followed right behind.

I glanced at Moses once more. Even though there was now activity going on—the voices louder, the sound of grass being trampled and sticks snapping—he remained in his spot, his eyes closed. John and Henry Porter remained where they'd been standing for almost an hour, only the deputy who'd been with them had left. Henry's attention was now fully on his son, whispering angrily.

I doubted I'd be able to see anything but I started forward anyway. Passing the house and stepping through some trees, I stopped a few feet away from the crowd. There were too many people, and I wasn't about to push through. It didn't matter though. Dean had seen. He shoved his way out of the crowd and was heading back toward the house when I grabbed his arm.

"What is it?"

"I need to talk to Mr. Cunningham."

"What did they find?"

He'd been staring ahead, intent on his mission, but now he looked at me, and I saw it in his eyes, the hesitation to whether he should tell me, and the dread that he would now have to tell Joey's father.

"They found Joey's glasses." His voice was clipped, hurried. He paused, swallowed, stared straight back at me. "There's blood all over them."

CHAPTER ELEVEN

When I was eight years old a kid in the class below me got sick and died. His name was Tyler Madden and he had leukemia. Our mothers were friends, so somehow I knew him, but we weren't close. When he died, the school held a memorial service in his honor. I remember the pastor—it was James Young, no doubt with lollipops in his suit jacket—allowing his friends and classmates to stand up and say something nice about him. I hadn't said anything and just sat there listening the entire time.

That wasn't my first encounter with death. I didn't begin questioning it at that age. Already both my grandparents on my mother's side had died—my grandfather seven years before my grandmother—so I knew what death was, why they were no longer around.

But then with someone my age—even younger—I began pondering my own mortality.

Driving with my father a week after the funeral, I asked him about Tyler.

"Did he know he was going to die?"

My father looked at me, seemed to choose his words carefully, and said, "I think so, yes."

I thought about this, wondering why I didn't know when I was going to die. "Do you know when you're going to die?"

"No, Christopher. You have to understand, Tyler was very sick. He had a disease that was killing him. But me, Mommy, and you, and almost everyone else—we don't know when we're going to die. That's just the way it is for most people. It's all in God's hands and we simply have no idea."

I asked, "So if it's in God's hands, why couldn't God make Tyler better? Why did He let Tyler die?"

And my father, never wanting to lie to me, said, "I don't know."

I thought about this the morning after Joey's disappearance, as I lay in my trailer, staring at the ceiling. According to my watch it was almost three o'clock in the afternoon. I'd gotten maybe eight hours of sleep and had already been up for two hours just lying there thinking.

I thought about Tyler Madden and how sometimes people know they're going to die.

I wondered if Joey somehow knew what would happen to him.

After I took a shower and got dressed, I went outside where the sky was clear and the day was warm. A white and red-striped deputy's cruiser was parked up beside the Rec House. At first I thought it was my uncle, but as I walked toward my grandmother's trailer I realized it was someone else.

Inside, I expected to find Grandma playing cards or dominos with Mrs. Roberts, but she was alone. Sitting at her table, a large box of Cheez-Its open before her. She looked up, startled, when I opened the door, then gave me a weak smile. She asked me how I slept and I lied and told her fine. Next she asked if I was hungry and I told her I wasn't. Then there was a silence and I saw something in her eyes, a sadness that expressed so many different things.

"I'm going back home, aren't I." I didn't even bother making it a question.

She nodded slowly. "Sheriff Douglas ... she mentioned it to Dean, and he agrees. With what's just happened to that poor boy, it's not a good idea to stay."

But what happened to Joey, I wanted to tell her, might not even be related. In fact, I was pretty certain it *wasn't* related. Whoever had abducted Joey, it was a different shadow in the corner. It wasn't mine.

"When?" I asked.

"Sometime tomorrow. Your uncle wants to take you back personally, but he can't do it until then. Also, he wants to get you out before your name gets leaked to the papers."

She went on to explain how Sheriff Douglas was afraid the reporters might force a connection with what happened to me down in Lanton. So far neither John's name nor my own had come up to the press when the official statement was made. They hoped to keep it that way, at least for the time being.

"Christopher," she said then, after a lengthy pause, "I'll miss you."

I looked at her but didn't say anything at first. I noticed there was some crust around her eyes, and it took me a few moments to realize that they were dried tears. I wondered how long she'd cried after she found out her only grandchild would be leaving her so soon after they had been reunited. For some reason beyond my understanding, she really did love me, and it made me sad because I didn't think I could return the same amount of love.

"Yeah," I whispered finally. "I'll miss you too."

Like I'd hoped, Sarah answered the front door. She held her copy of *Billy Budd* at her side, her index finger keeping her place between the pages.

"Hey," she said, stepping out onto the porch and letting the screen door close. "How are you? I heard what happened. It's awful."

"How's your brother?"

"Grounded. My dad's pretty angry. He won't let John leave the house except for school. He's not even allowed to work on his Firebird."

I opened my mouth but wasn't able to speak. There were so many words in my head right at that moment I just couldn't pick which ones to say. Sarah watched me closely, her blue eyes nervous. They reminded me of how they'd looked yesterday, when she sat on the lawn chair outside my trailer, and I wondered how often that particular look in her eyes surfaced.

"I'm leaving tomorrow," I managed after a moment. "I just wanted to say goodbye. And, you know, good luck with the baby."

"Thanks," she said.

"It was just—" I didn't know how to continue without sounding cheesy. Then I realized it didn't matter. "It was nice meeting you."

"It was nice meeting you too, Chris."

I tried to smile but couldn't.

"Also ... I kind of lied to you earlier."

She frowned. "What do you mean?"

"When we were up on the Lookout yesterday. I said I don't believe in God. That ... that wasn't true. At least, not completely true."

Still frowning, she said, "Chris, what are you talking about?"

"I just ... I felt bad lying to you. Telling you that I don't believe in God like I did. Because I do believe in God. I believe he's an absent God. An indifferent God. And lying to you made me realize I'd lied to my parents. They thought I was this perfect son who respected everyone, even God. But I wasn't even close. I partied on the weekends. I slept around on my girlfriend. I even got her pregnant and then forced her to have an abortion. And the worst part is my parents died thinking I was someone I'm not."

"Why are you telling me this?"

"Because when it comes down to it, you can't trust on God for anything. My parents trusted Him their entire lives, and you know where it got them? It got them murdered. I trusted Him when I was younger, and you know where it got me? It got me being stalked by a psychopath who wants to kill me too. So just keep that in mind with your baby, Sarah. Because even if you believe in God, He doesn't give a shit. It's just going to be you and that baby, nobody else."

I stepped back, turned away.

"Bye, Sarah," I said, and walked off the porch and across the lawn, toward Half Creek Road. As with Joey, I didn't look back and just kept walking. Where I was headed, I didn't know, but ten minutes later I found myself in front of Shepherd's Books, the old man on the porch taking his muddy boots off the railing and leaning forward.

"And what can I do for you today, young man?"

"Today," I said, "I was hoping you could tell me a story."

CHAPTER TWELVE

WE SAT on the second floor, where the old man lived. It was small, almost quaint, and just as dusty as the downstairs. The scent of mint and whiskey was strong. An old television was set up against the wall, with a few framed pictures placed on top. Lewis Shepherd sat in a worn recliner facing the TV. I sat on a threadbare couch that had had piles of old newspapers and *Life* and *Time* magazines on it, which were now stacked on the floor.

I told him John's version of the Beckett House's history, highlighting what seemed to be the important parts. Then I asked, "Does any of that sound right to you?"

Lewis Shepherd had been staring down at the ugly throw rug almost the entire time. Now he blinked and looked up at me. He shrugged, his face apologetic, and said, "To tell you the truth, I don't remember much. I do remember it was 1953, because I had been fourteen at the time. And I remember Devin Beckett. I guess I'll always remember him. Your friend got it wrong, though. The man wasn't a serial killer running around the state. No, his full title was Reverend Devin Beckett." My mouth must have dropped open, because he chuckled and said, "I know, not quite what you were expecting. But that's who he was. Besides that ... well, like almost everyone else, I've managed to erase what happened from my memory. Because, truth be told, I didn't want to remember."

He paused then, and I thought that was where the conversation was going to end. Then his brow furrowed, as if he was working out an impossible equation. A second later his dry face lit up and his eyes met mine again. Clapping his hands just like he had yesterday, he hoisted himself up out of the recliner and said, "Follow me."

There were three doors in the hallway, two that were already ajar. Those I could see were the bedroom and bathroom, both looking as cluttered as the living room and the downstairs. But it was the third door he brought us to, the third door that was closed. He gripped the knob, hesitated a moment, then turned it. He pushed open the door and instantly the tang of mothballs and old newsprint hit my nose.

After flicking on the light he winked at me. "In case you're wondering, I'm a packrat."

I'd thought the pile of old newspapers and magazines on the couch had been a bit excessive; that was nothing compared to the boxes and boxes that littered the floor and that were stacked against the walls. Except the room was only half-filled with boxes; everywhere else were stacks of newspapers and magazines, so much so that it made it nearly impossible to walk through.

I said, "You're kidding me, right?"

The old man chuckled. "Told you I was a packrat. But it's really not as bad as it looks. I didn't save *every* paper. Only the ones that needed saving."

He stepped farther into the room and began rummaging through one of the first boxes, removing full newspapers, until he grabbed one. I barely glanced at the headline when he handed it to me. I recognized the colored photograph on the front page at once and understood just what Lewis Shepherd meant by papers that needed saving.

ACT OF WAR the headline shouted, but it was the plane hanging in the air less than an inch away from the second standing World Trade Center tower that really caught the reader's attention. Its twin was already coughing black smoke.

"All news is important," he said, taking the paper back from me, "but some news is just more important than the rest. Say, which do you think people remember more—good news or bad news?"

"The bad?"

"Personally I believe people remember the good news more. Can you guess why? It's because while the bad news can tear a person's heart apart, that person eventually forgets. Not because it's a normal reaction, which it isn't, but because they force themselves to forget. Think about it this way—our minds are filled with doors. With everything that happens to us, we put those memories behind different doors. Some are good memories, and we make sure those doors can be opened again. But other memories, the bad memories, we shove right back as far as we can and lock those doors so they'll stay shut forever."

He looked around the room, his old eyes scanning each stack of boxes and newspapers.

"And I don't think that's good for us. Keeping all those bad memories locked inside our heads like that. We need to remember sometimes, no matter how much it hurts. So that's why I've been keeping these, every time something bad happens. Because it's not good to forget. We need to remember. We need to …" He stepped forward, hesitated, then glanced back at me. "It happened so long ago, but I know it's here someplace."

It didn't take him long. He looked through a half dozen boxes or so, then opened up the closet and began rummaging through the boxes in there. Finally he clapped his hands, announced, "Found it!" and stepped out with one of the oldest newspapers I'd ever seen in his hands. He stared down at it for a long time, squinting his eyes as he read the tiny print. His head went through intervals of slight shaking and nodding, until he sighed and looked up at me.

"I hate to say this," he said, handing me the newspaper, "but some of it's coming back to me now."

It was *The Advertiser*, dated Thursday, August 20, 1953. I don't know when the change came in the layout of the majority of newspapers, but by this time they were still using eight thin columns across the page. The column that caught my attention was one of the middle ones, with a black and white picture of what was obviously the Beckett House. The photographer had probably taken the shot early that morning, with hardly any light, because the house seemed even more ominous than ever in the shadows.

The headline read LOCAL MASSACRE SHOCKS TOWN, SIXTEEN DEAD. The article went on to detail how fifteen innocent people lost their lives in Bridgeton. The sixteenth person was Devin Beckett, a reverend of Light Hill Church, who in a seemingly strategic series of events murdered eight adults and abducted seven children, forcing the latter to a stone house in the woods where a standoff with police later ensued. Two hours of directionless negotiations led police to try to force Beckett from the house. As a result the entire house was set on fire, killing Beckett and the children inside. The children's ages ranged from seven months to eleven years old.

William Grieves, a constable for Horseheads, was quoted as saying, "We are not happy with how things ended. However it was apparent that unless that man was stopped, more lives would have been lost. We did the best we could."

Only four families suffered in the massacre, the article said. Each of the families' husbands and wives were murdered in bed, while all the children but the firstborns were drugged, gagged, and taken to the stone house. Why the firstborns of all four families were untouched was a mystery to Constable Grieves, who said, "My only guess is that God had his hand on each of them."

The article went on to talk about Devin Beckett, how he had come to Bridgton early in the year and was only expected to stay until Light Hill found another permanent replacement in the wake of its former reverend, Colin Edelston, going on sabbatical. It ended mid-sentence, a small note informing the reader it continued on page three. I turned the page, turned another page, then looked up.

"It's missing," I said.

"I beg your pardon?"

"The article continues on the third page, but the third page is gone."

Lewis Shepherd frowned. "Are you sure?"

I handed him the paper, which he immediately began rooting through. He flipped two pages, then four, then six, until he glanced back up at me, a deep frown creasing his face.

"Now where the hell did the rest of it go?"

He sighed, shaking his head, and set the newspaper down. "Doesn't matter. I read enough of it to ... to open the door I had locked long ago." Something in his raspy voice cracked, causing him to sound as if he might at any moment begin crying. I realized then he was nothing like the petulant old man he'd seemed the other day. Just like Sarah had a front, so did Lewis Shepherd.

"Listen, I'm sorry," I said, beginning to feel real pity. In my mind, I imagined an endless field of green grass, innumerable wooden doors marking various spaces across the distance. "I didn't mean to—"

"No, it's not your fault. I'm more to blame than you. I ... I should have known better."

Silence fell between us then, and in that room filled with

years upon years of newspapers and magazines and boxes (not to mention silverfish), the silence was thick. The scent of old paper was still strong in the air, invading my sinuses.

I knew I'd asked too much already, that this man had been forced back to a dark time in his past. But still there was more I wanted to know, more I needed to know, and so I asked.

"What made him do it? Did anyone know? What made Beckett just … snap?"

He looked up at me, his old eyes scrutinizing, and shook his head. At first I thought it meant he didn't know, or that he wasn't going to tell me. But then he sighed and said, "Nobody knows, really. Even back then nobody knew for sure. But there was speculation. I suppose no matter what happens, there will always be speculation."

He stared down at where he'd set the paper.

"Thing is, nobody could have foreseen what happened. Reverend Beckett … he was a good man. He was in his early forties and wasn't married, so of course there was talk. A few had … well, his sexuality had come into question. Or at least that's what I remember hearing later, when some of the locals had nothing better to gossip about. But that summer, a month or so before the Massacre, rumors started floating about. Supposedly Reverend Beckett was involved with one of the local girls."

He glanced up at me.

"Supposedly she was a minor."

I took a moment to let this all sink in, then asked, "So was he?"

Lewis Shepherd shrugged. "To be honest, who really knows? God maybe, but after what happened later that month, not many people in Bridgton trusted him all that much anymore. But those rumors, they started, and they hurt Reverend Beckett and his church. From what I can remember, Light Hill was packed every Sunday. Then, once those rumors started, the congregation began dwindling, until there was hardly anybody else left."

"So that's what made him snap," I said, for some reason disappointed by the denouement. I'd expected something more.

The old man stared back at me a moment longer than he probably needed to, before nodding his head slightly. His face looked more worn than it had earlier when he first invited me inside, and his eyes ... they looked so scarred, so lost.

I did that to him, I thought. I asked for the key to unlock that door and now it's too late to shut it again. It's too late to go back.

But the thing was, there was no going forward either. I could think of no other questions to ask. But as I'd suspected, John Porter's story was a touch of truth, a lot of bullshit, and now here was the real deal. But the problem arose that after everything I'd heard, what did it change? Joey was still missing, the Beckett House was still a crime scene, and I was still going back home to Lanton tomorrow afternoon. Nothing had changed, so just why had I even bothered in the first place?

Can you feel it, Chris?

No, I didn't feel it, I didn't feel anything, and that's what was bugging me.

"I'll tell you one thing," Lewis Shepherd said, and when I looked up out of my thoughts I saw him staring back down at *The Advertiser*. His voice was lower than before, and as he spoke I realized he wasn't speaking to me so much as to himself. "It was pure hell for those surviving firstborns. They were boys, all four of them. I was good friends with one, and I remember a month after the Massacre, we were talking together and he ... he suddenly looked up at me. I forget what our conversation was about, but he just looked up at me and I could see it in his eyes, the understanding of what had happened to him. He started to shake his head and started to cry, and he said one word to me. He said, 'Why?' I didn't know what he meant then, and I still don't. Did he mean why was his entire family murdered? Did he mean why only he survived? Or did he mean why did Reverend Beckett place that terrible mark on his bedroom door?"

Something inside me gripped my soul and squeezed it tight.

"What"—I swallowed—"what was on his bedroom door?"

"Not just his door," Lewis Shepherd said sadly, "but all their doors."

At that instant I saw myself the morning I found my parents' bodies—as I backed away from their bedroom and reeled toward my own room.

"In their own parents' blood."

As I ran toward the thing that had been painted on the door in their blood.

"A cross."

A cross.

I intended on telling Dean. Like Lewis Shepherd said before I left the bookstore, not many people nowadays knew what truly happened that summer night fifty years ago. Mostly because those who lived then wanted to forget, but also in not relaying those events, the story itself would die out just like Devin Beckett and those children as they were burned alive in that stone house.

I wondered if my grandmother knew. I had no doubt she did, having lived in Bridgton her whole life. I wondered if she had known any of the children who were taken, if she even remembered Devin Beckett.

When I returned to The Hill, the deputy's cruiser was still parked in its place beside the Rec House. The deputy inside the cruiser had given up his duty and had instead nodded off. I banged on the window where his head leaned and he jumped, his head jerking around wildly until his eyes focused on me.

I waited until he'd rolled down his window before I said, "I just wanted to let you know I'm still alive."

"Right," the deputy said, wiping at the trail of drool on his chin.

It was as I passed Mrs. Roberts' trailer that I heard the flies.

Only a few, but I heard their familiar buzzing and had to pause to determine where the sound was coming from. Then I realized it was coming from underneath the trailer, and for a moment I knew that was where Joey's body lay. Whoever had taken him had killed him and stuffed him among the sun-neglected grass and weeds, where he'd become food for field mice and stray cats and home for maggots.

"Stop it," I whispered, closing my eyes. I knew better. I knew that it wasn't Joey, was instead the corpse of some stray animal or bird. Still the thought lingered, leaving a very unsettling image, and as I continued toward my grandmother's I wondered if Joey would ever be found.

CHAPTER THIRTEEN

EARLY TUESDAY MORNING on June 10, 2003, around seven-fifty a.m., a local woman drove along Route 13. Her name was Ellen Gordon and she had just dropped off her two daughters at Horseheads Elementary. She was headed back home toward Sullivanville, timing it so that the whites she had put in the dryer would be finishing up on her arrival, when she spotted something lying in the grass beside the road. As she would later tell police, she at first thought it was a dog. Only when she was less than fifty yards away, already going forty-five miles per hour, did she realize what it actually was.

The cup of coffee that she always brought with her on her morning drives almost spilled on her lap as she cried out and swerved into the other lane. Thankfully nothing was coming in the other direction, or else she probably would not have been alive to pick up her daughters from school later that day. Moments passed before she again managed to gain control of the wheel and pulled off along the berm. Later she would dutifully tell police how she kept a cell phone in her Caravan only for emergencies, and how she didn't hesitate at all in calling 911.

She waited perhaps five minutes before the first car arrived. By then a trucker—the paper listed his name as Edward Borrow—noticed the same thing as her and had stopped as well. He pulled his tractor-trailer along the opposite side of the road Ellen was parked, got out, and ran to what lay in the grass. He could tell just by looking that the thing was dead, but still he checked for a pulse ... and almost cried out when he felt one. He backed away, almost stumbled, before jogging across the highway to where Ellen waited. He asked her if she was all right. She simply stared past him, tears in her eyes. Her body was shaking. (Two days later, an interview in the *Star-Gazette* informed its loyal readers that Ellen Gordon had continued shaking for the next six hours.)

Once the first police car arrived, things began happening fast. Another car showed up a minute later, followed by an ambulance. A crime scene had begun to materialize along that particular patch of Route 13—what the woman unlucky enough to have driven past that spot called "a nightmare"—but at the time I knew nothing about it. At that time, I was still asleep in the tiny bed of the trailer I had graciously been allowed to stay in.

At that time, I was busy with a nightmare of my own.

I'm standing with Joey in the Beckett House. It's late at night. He's talking to me, trying to tell me something, but I can't hear a single word he says. In fact, I can hear nothing—even outside, through the open ceiling, the trees make no noise from the wind, and there are no insects singing out in the grass.

What is it, Joey? I ask, but of course I have no voice. It seems in this dream all sound is restricted. But still Joey talks to me, trying to relate something that he deems important. And still I stand there and listen, hearing only silence.

I glance over his head, notice four motionless shadows standing behind him. I think of the shadow that's stalking me, that's still waiting for the right moment, and I think, *Are they demons?* I look back down at Joey, wanting to warn him, and notice his eyes are no longer looking into mine. Instead they're staring at something behind me. Before I can even turn to see (and really, with the restriction of sound, what makes me think I can move an inch anyway?), Joey opens his mouth and screams. A second later he bursts into flames.

I lay in bed for almost a half hour, staring at the ceiling after I woke up from watching Joey burn ... and burn ... and burn. (In most dreams, where a horrific event almost always causes a person to snap awake, I was forced to watch him burn no matter how much I wanted to look away.) It made me think of Devin Beckett and those seven children. The youngest a baby, the oldest eleven years old.

They say that when you're in a burning house, you die from the carbon monoxide, not the flames. But for those few that dreadful morning, I knew carbon monoxide would have been a blessing.

For the most part, my things were packed and loaded in my Cavalier. Last night Dean had called while I was eating dinner with Grandma and Mrs. Roberts. He had no news concerning Joey, no news from Steve, and he sounded like he had back in Lanton—worn out, frustrated, lost. I'd made it a point to tell him about the connection between Beckett and my parents' murder, but he didn't stay on long enough.

"Tomorrow around one we'll head back," he said. "I'll see you then."

He hung up and I was left standing there, listening to only silence for however long it took until there was a click and the electronic voice told me what to do if I'd like to make a call. I wondered if my uncle even knew about the cross in blood that had been left on my bedroom door. I didn't see why not. He must have been told to fully understand why Steve thought it was best for me to hide away. Then again, even if he did know, how could he make the connection when he'd probably never even heard the entire story of Devin Beckett in the first place?

And I wondered to myself, had I even heard the entire story?

The spot the deputy's cruiser had been taking up last night was vacant. Its tires were imprinted in the tall grass.

I passed my grandmother's trailer—I could hear the phone inside just beginning to ring—and kept going, up to the Rec House, looking for the cruiser. There were only a few places the car could be, but I couldn't find it anywhere. It was gone.

Heading back down the drive, I heard the buzzing of flies again. Under Mrs. Roberts' trailer, I could even see a few of their black pinpoint bodies hovering about. The image that had crossed my mind last night resurfaced and I knew I had to check for myself.

I took only three steps toward whatever lay in the cold shade when my grandmother's screen door banged open and she called my name.

"Christopher, I was just coming for you." Her eyes were wide, her breathing heavy, and for an instant I thought she was having a heart attack.

"What's wrong?"

She paused, took a breath, and said, "They found Joey."

"Is he alive?"

"Yes, but barely. He was rushed to St. Joseph's. Deputy Toms drove Mr. Cunningham over there almost an hour ago." My grandmother paused to catch her breath again. "Dean just called. He's sending a car to pick you up. It should be here any minute."

I stared at her, so many possibilities swirling through my head. "Why?"

"Joey," she said, almost breathless. "He's near death. There's not much time."

"Grandma, why is Dean sending a car to pick me up?"

She told me the only possibility I hadn't come up with.

"Joey's asking for you."

Fifteen minutes later I rode shotgun in a Deputy's Blazer speeding down Route 17, heading south. The vehicle's lights flashed and its siren sounded. The cab smelled of coffee and vanilla air freshener. The driver was a young woman named Lacy. She couldn't explain exactly what was happening, because she didn't know all the facts herself. All she knew for certain was that Joey had been found this morning. His pulse had been very weak. He was taken to St. Joseph's Hospital, and when they got him in the ER they found he was badly bruised, many of his ribs broken. Everything else appeared stable, except his heartbeat, which was getting weaker by the second. He was unconscious and spent most of the morning in a bed hooked up to machines.

Then, at about twenty minutes after noon, Joey awoke. Doctors appeared at his bedside immediately. When he spoke his voice was faint. He was told to rest and save his strength, but he kept trying to speak. Sheriff Douglas pushed her way inside and asked him what he knew.

Lacy glanced at me. "He said he'd only talk to you."

We got off at the next exit, made a right at the intersection, and sped down the street.

"Did he say why?"

"No. Just that he'd talk to you and nobody else."

When she pulled into the hospital's entrance, a Chemung County deputy and state policeman were waiting by the glass doors. Once they saw us they hurried forward.

I opened my door and got out.

"His condition hasn't gotten any better," the deputy said. We headed inside, the deputy leading me as the state policeman trailed.

At the elevators Sheriff Douglas waited. She didn't look happy. Her arms were crossed and she was tapping her left toe.

"Third floor," she told me, then pushed the up button. An elevator opened seconds later and we all got inside. As the doors slid shut, she said, "They don't think he has much longer to hold on."

The third floor was animated with people. Half a dozen police officers, a few orderlies and RNs and doctors, even two janitors. When we stepped out of the elevator they all paused in their whispered conversations and turned toward us.

"Come on," Sheriff Douglas said.

A short skinny deputy met us as we passed the nurse's station. He held a small tape recorder. He handed it to the sheriff, who handed it to me.

"Record everything. I don't care what he wants to talk about, I want it on tape. Try to find out as much as you can. I want to know who the bastard is that did this."

As we walked, the crowd parted and I saw Moses Cunningham sitting in a chair against the wall. He was leaning forward, his shoulders hunched, his head in his hands. It looked like he was in prayer.

I stopped and stared down at him. I wanted to say something but didn't know what to say.

Finally he looked up. Stared back at me. Asked, "Did my boy ever say he told me about you?"

I nodded.

"It was before we came to Bridgton," he whispered. Then, nodding slowly: "Before he even met you."

A hand grabbed my arm, spun me around, and there Dean stood in his uniform.

He looked at me hard and asked one word.

"Ready?"

CHAPTER FOURTEEN

I COULDN'T SEE him at first. The fluorescents were off and the only light coming in was from the sun peeking through the closed curtains. The bed rested in the middle of the room. Medical equipment sat around it, wires reaching out onto the bed, and all I saw were sheets until I took a few more steps and noticed him lying there.

Without his glasses his face looked different. Smaller. It looked as if his eyes were shut, but the closer I got the sooner I realized that wasn't the case. Whoever had taken him had bashed his face in pretty good. Only one eye was half-open, the other swollen completely shut.

I sat in the chair beside his bed, between him and the window letting in hardly any light. I turned the recorder on and set it on the edge of the bed.

His head rolled toward me slowly. He stared at me with his one eye. Opened his mouth and tried to speak but then coughed. It went on longer than it should have and finally he was staring at me again. He opened his mouth once more and whispered very faintly, "Turn it off."

"I can't."

"Turn it off."

"Joey, I can't. It needs to stay on."

He only stared back at me. Seconds passed. I reached forward, turned off the recorder, placed it back on the bed.

Joey whispered, "Thank you."

I just nodded.

"Tell me about … your parents."

"What?"

"Please tell me … about your parents."

I wanted to shake my head and tell him my parents had nothing to do with this. I wanted to ask him who the son of a bitch was that took him. But I saw from the desperation in his only good eye that Joey wanted to know, *needed* to know, about my parents.

"My dad was always there for whoever needed help. Whenever someone had a problem they would come and talk to him about it, and he'd somehow make everything better. He wasn't a psychiatrist or anything, but he helped them."

"And … your mom?"

"She was just like my dad. She was selfless. She always put others first, no matter what happened. She never talked bad about anyone either. When everybody else gossiped, she'd leave the room."

"And you?"

I stared at him but said nothing for the longest time. Finally I shook my head. "What is this about?"

Joey wheezed, his small chest rising and falling. He opened his mouth to speak but then began coughing again.

"Do you want some water?"

He shook his head and closed his eye. For an instant it looked as if he was sleeping and I wondered if maybe he was dead. But then his chest rose and fell again. He asked, "Did you ever wonder … what would have happened … had Adam and Eve said no to Satan?"

It was the question he'd begun to ask me back at the Beckett House.

"No, Joey. I haven't."

"You will. I've had dreams of you ... of you running in the rain. Running from a monster. And you are ... you are thinking that question."

"Joey, what are you talking about?"

He wheezed again, then whispered, "He wanted to kill me."

One of the machines next to his bed went beep ... beep ... beep.

"Who wanted to kill you?"

"The angel."

I leaned forward. "What angel?"

"Samael. The angel of death. He wanted ... to kill me."

"Why?"

"So that he could ... stop me."

I shifted in my chair. For an instant I wished the tape recorder was on.

"Why would he want to stop you?" I tried keeping my voice natural and calm.

"He thinks ... I'm the only one ... that can stop him."

"Stop him from what?"

"Thirty-four people."

"Thirty-four people. What about thirty-four people?"

"They are all ... gonna die."

That machine beside his bed kept going beep ... beep ... beep.

"Who, Joey? Who are they?"

He moved slightly in the bed, as if trying to get up, and I quickly held up my hand for him to stay put, to not move a single muscle. He shook his head as he continued his light wheezing.

"I don't know."

"But you know that these thirty-four people are going to die?"

Slowly, so very slowly, he nodded. "Samael gave me ... a choice. To pick one ... and save the others. But I didn't choose. I couldn't, even though ... even though I wanted to."

"Why do you think this, Joey? About these thirty-four people dying?"

"God. He speaks to me."

"And he told you they were going to die?"

Again he nodded.

"But you don't know who these people are."

"No."

"Listen, Joey, I—" But I only shook my head. I had nothing to say.

Joey wheezed again, his chest rising and falling, and whispered, "Samael hates me ... because he knows ... I can stop him. That is why ... he wants me dead. But he's wrong."

That machine kept going beep ... beep ... beep.

"Chris ... do you hear me?"

"Listen, Joey. I need to know who did this to you. Can you describe him? Was it just one person or were there a bunch of people?"

"I already ... told you. The angel ... took me."

"The angel," I said.

Joey nodded. "Samael."

"And he's the angel of death."

Again Joey nodded, closing his eye.

I sighed and hung my head. "Joey, please, you have to be serious here. Why won't you talk to anyone else? Why me?"

He opened his eye. Looked at me. Breathed in, breathed out, and whispered, "Because Samael ... is wrong. Someone else ... can stop him ... too."

Beep ... beep ... beep.

"That is why ... you are here."

"Why I'm here."

"It was no accident … what happened … to your parents."

"My parents. What do you know about my parents?"

He said nothing, only wheezed.

"How did you know they were murdered?"

"I just did."

"Do you know who killed them?"

"Yes."

I leaned even closer to the bed. "Tell me. Tell me who."

"I can't."

I wanted to stand and grab his neck, squeeze until there was nothing left to squeeze.

"Don't do this, Joey. Please don't. If you know who killed them, you need to tell me."

"I'm sorry … but I can't. I can only tell you … three things."

"If it's not who killed my parents, I don't want to hear it."

"First, talk to … my father. He'll explain … about me. He will also … give you … a present … from me. Use it … when it's … time."

"A present? Joey, what are you—"

"Second … so you can believe … stop … Jack Murphy."

"Jack Murphy? What about him? Is he the one who killed my parents? Does *he* know who did it?"

"And third …"

"What about Jack? Goddamn it, Joey, tell me. What does he have to do with this?"

"Third … read Job 42."

"Job 42?"

Joey whispered, "Samael … doesn't know … about you yet. He knows … you are here. But he doesn't … know why."

"And why am I here?"

He took another deep breath, his chest rising, as he stared

back at me with his one good eye. "They are … yawning now … Christopher."

"What are?"

Suddenly the machines surrounding his bed began beeping madly. The door opened. A man in a white coat entered, followed by three nurses and another doctor.

I stood and leaned over the bed, got as close to Joey's battered face as I could. Somebody grabbed my arm, tried pulling me away, but I fought them, just continued standing there, staring at him.

I shouted, "What are?"

Joey's eye was drifting shut. His chest rose and fell very slowly. More hands grabbed me.

"Churchyards," he whispered.

And died.

CHAPTER FIFTEEN

DINNER THAT NIGHT was spaghetti and meatballs. The mixed scent of tomato sauce and garlic bread was thick in my grandmother's trailer where we ate in silence. Grandma didn't even attempt to make small talk. She was aware of what happened today and knew that if I wanted to talk about it, I'd do it on my own time.

The TV was off, which was something new, and made the silence and tension between the two of us even stronger. The windows were open allowing in the noises from outside, the crickets and the wind and the distant sound of traffic down on 13. The curtains were open to my right, and through the screen I could see the large RV with the blue Metro parked beside it.

"Christopher, would you like some more?"

Grandma's plate was cleared and she was sliding out from behind the table.

I'd hardly touched my own plate. I shook my head.

As she went to the stove to fix herself more, I glanced back out the screen at Moses Cunningham's RV.

First, talk to my father.

I wasn't sure what bothered me more about today. Standing

there over Joey as he spoke his last word and watching his only good eye grow blank and glaze over. Or coming out of his room into the hallway and seeing his father sitting there looking back at me, giving me a look as if to say this wasn't a surprise to him at all and he knew exactly what his son had just said before he died.

He'll explain about me.

Sheriff Douglas was pissed, as was my uncle and everyone else. They wanted information which I couldn't provide, and it didn't help that I'd stopped the tape recorder, even if they could clearly hear Joey's voice telling me to turn it off. *What did he tell you?* they wanted to know, but I couldn't tell them the truth, I knew they wouldn't believe me—even I was having a hard time believing it myself. Then again, I wondered as I stood there under their scrutinizing gazes, what if they did believe me? This last was an even scarier thought, and so I lied and told them he had just wanted to witness to me one final time, that was all, he was some kind of Jesus freak and that was it.

Whether they believed me or not, I didn't know, nor did I care. Right now I had more important things to worry about.

As my grandmother set her plate on the table and began to slide back into the booth again, Mrs. Roberts tapped on the screen door. "Mind some company?" she asked.

Grandma started to say something, about how it probably wasn't the best time, but I shook my head and told her it was okay, that I was going to go back to my trailer anyway, thanks so much for the great dinner.

When I stepped outside, I glanced toward the Rec House, at the spot where the deputy's cruiser had once been. It was still vacant. I briefly wondered if they were having any luck in finding Joey's abductor. Then I started down the drive, toward my trailer, as if that was really where I was headed.

I knew better.

A minute later I stood beside Moses Cunningham's RV. I waited by the door, debating whether I actually wanted to go through with this or not. Then before I even had a chance to turn and walk away, the door opened. Moses stood there staring back at me, his dark face hard and set.

"Hello, Christopher," he said. His voice didn't sound the same as it had two days ago in church; now it sounded faint, nervous, almost strained. He opened the door. "You might as well come inside. We have a lot to talk about."

The interior of the RV was small and tight, much like my grandmother's own trailer. Behind the two front seats were a couch and chair. A table rested against the refrigerator, which stood directly across from the sink and stove. Back farther were the bathroom and bedroom, but neither of those rooms concerned me as I sat on the couch. I could only imagine all the places Moses and Joey had driven in this thing, all the trailer parks just like this one they'd stayed in for a night or two before moving on.

Except now it was just Moses.

Would always be Moses.

He pulled a fifth of Captain Morgan's from a cabinet above the sink, then two small glasses from another cabinet. They were from *Sesame Street*, one showing Big Bird, the other Ernie. When Moses turned and handed me the Ernie glass, he noted the look I was giving him and asked, "You don't drink?"

"No, it's not that," I said. "I just never thought I'd be drinking with a preacher is all."

He smiled as he poured. "If it eases your conscience any, I consider myself more of a teacher than a preacher."

"Why's that?"

"A preacher is somebody who tells you what's true. A teacher is somebody who shows you why it's true."

He finished pouring himself a glass, then placed the bottle on the small table—what probably passed for a coffee table in Winnebago territory—between us. A book lay there face-up. From where I sat it was turned away, forcing me to read the letters of its title and author upside down. Moses must have noticed my eyes scanning the cover, because he said, "Ralph Ellison's *Invisible Man*. Have you ever read it?"

I looked up, startled like a kid caught reading his old man's *Playboy*, and shook my head.

Moses took a sip of his drink. "How old are you, if you don't mind me asking?"

"Eighteen."

He nodded, the number not surprising him at all—and even then it didn't occur to me that he already knew everything there was to know about my life, that these questions were merely asked to loosen me up. "Yeah, I don't think they teach this one in high schools. At least not yet. Damn shame, too, because it's a great book. I actually read it to Joey—excluding some parts—when he was six. After that he managed to go through it twice himself."

"What is it about?"

"Finding one's identity. Ellison wrote it with the Harlem Renaissance in mind, bringing voices to the blacks. But the story itself … it could stand for anyone who doesn't know who they are just yet." He paused, seeming to shrug, and said, "My wife majored in English for two years. Loved the stuff. Made me read most of what she had to in her classes so that we could always have something to talk about. Guess it rubbed off on me."

I smiled but said nothing, just sat there with the glass resting in my lap. Finally I said, "I'm sorry for what happened."

"So am I."

I took a swallow and winced at the burn. "Before I saw him today, you said something to me. You said Joey told you about me even before you both came here. Even before he met me. How is that ... how's that possible?"

Moses stared down at his glass and swirled it around. He took another swallow and said, "Before we get too deep into this, I was wondering if you could answer me something."

"I'll try."

"Do you believe in God?"

I opened my mouth but then shut it. Just sat there, staring down at my drink, at the dark golden liquid.

"I take it from your silence you do."

"Why do you say that?"

"If you didn't believe in God at all, you wouldn't have hesitated."

"No, I do believe in God. I believe he's absent. Indifferent. Lazy. Pick an adjective."

"And you believe God is this way because ..."

"He doesn't do shit."

"Man acts, God reacts."

"Meaning?"

"Meaning God isn't going to save the world on his own. If that were the case, why would he need us? Our purpose here on this earth is to serve him. And when we do that, God rewards us." He downed his glass, set it on the table. "Now what about the devil?"

"What about him?"

"Do you believe in him?"

Not hesitating this time, I said, "My mom thought a demon once tried to kill me."

"How so?"

I told him the story, and when I was finished he said, "Do you think it was a demon?"

"I don't know. What do you think?"

"It could have been. Or you could just have simply had some kind of temporary asphyxiation." Moses leaned forward, produced a pack of smokes from under the table. "Joey never liked it when I smoked. I'd been so good about it for the longest time, but now … well, as you can imagine it's been a pretty stressful week. Would you care for one?"

I shook my head.

"Okay," Moses said after he had his cigarette lit, "before we start, I figure it might be a good idea to tell you a little bit about myself. Just the basics. I was born in Riverdale, Georgia, just outside of Atlanta. My dad was a cokehead, my mom was around so he could beat her and screw her whenever he wanted. He beat me too, sometimes really bad, and one time he even raped me. So I ran away from home. This was about when I was thirteen. I went up to Atlanta and I was living on the streets. I got heavily into drugs. Mostly cocaine, but some heroin too. Actually, it got so bad I would do anything to score a hit. Anything. I'm not proud about most of the things I've done in my life, but I will take responsibility for them. I've mugged people for money. I once nearly beat a man to death. I was way out of control, and by all rights, I should have died out there on those streets."

He leaned forward, stubbed his cigarette out, and lit another one. "But God saved me."

Except it wasn't really God Himself who rescued Moses from the mean streets of Atlanta, but it was through a church, through a reverend who was out late one night and who Moses had attempted to mug. He came up behind the man on the dark street, pulled out his knife, and ordered the man to give him all his money. The man just stood there, not saying a word or moving a muscle, and the next thing Moses knew the two of them were surrounded by hundreds of people.

"I couldn't see their faces, or even their bodies, but I sensed them there. They were like shadows there in the dark, just these

… these figures. So I started to run away, I started to bolt out of there, when the old man told me to stop. He called me back. He said it would be all right. He said I didn't have to run anymore, that I could change my life around. It was the same stuff I'd been hearing from other priests and pastors and reverends for the last three years I'd been on the street, but there was something in his voice right then, something that told me this time it was true. So I stopped running. I turned around. And the hundreds of people surrounding us were gone. It was just me and him, and he held out his hand to me. I just stared at it for the longest time, not knowing what to do, because you want to know something sad? In the sixteen years I'd been alive, never once had I shaken anybody's hand."

The man took Moses into his home. He fed him, clothed him, taught him how to read and write. Then, one night when Moses had decided enough was enough and was ready to run away, to steal everything he could from the man, the man caught him. Moses was in the man's study at the time, rifling through the drawers of the desk, when the man stepped in and turned on the light.

"I expected him to be angry. I expected him to kick me out of his house. But do you know what he did? He actually stepped forward, went to the bookcase, and took down a book from the top shelf. It was one of those trick books, because when he opened it there was a hole inside, containing a thick roll of bills. He pulled the roll out and handed it to me. He said, 'If what I've offered you is not good enough, then there's nothing I can do to help you anymore.' I didn't move from where I was behind the desk. Eventually he set the money down on the table beside the door, closed the book and placed it back on the shelf, then left the room."

In the end Moses almost took the money and ran. But then he really thought about it. For the last five months the man had been taking better care of Moses than anyone ever had before.

He forced Moses to go to church on Sundays, that was true, and he forced him to help clean the church and help out during activities on other days, but he constantly showed Moses respect, acted like they were equals. And the biggest thing to Moses, at least right then, was that first night, after Moses had tried mugging him, the man had actually held out his hand and wouldn't move until Moses accepted it and they shook.

"So to fast forward," Moses said, "I cleaned up my act. I understood God was real, and that He cared about me, and that it was my purpose to serve Him. So I started to work for the church. Eventually I moved up north, to help out another church in Ohio. And it was there that I met my wife, Sabrina. It was there that …"

He paused.

"But maybe I'm getting a little too ahead of myself. First, if you don't mind, may I ask what my boy talked to you about today?"

"You mean you don't know?"

"I'm sure I know most of it."

This wasn't quite the answer I was expecting, though I realized this entire situation had gone far beyond expectations.

When Moses saw that I wasn't going to answer him, he said, "Did he at least tell you who took him?"

I hesitated again. "He said … it was an angel."

"An angel?"

"The angel of death."

"Did he give a name?"

I thought for a moment. "Samael."

Moses said, "Did you tell the police the angel of death abducted my boy?"

"No, of course not. That would have sounded …"

"Crazy, I know." Moses forced a smile. "Now do you see why I asked you about whether or not you believe in God and

Satan? Because everything you've heard from Joey, and every-thing you're about to hear from me, is going to sound crazy to you. But I'm asking you to keep an open mind."

"You're going to explain about him, aren't you?"

"That's why you're here, isn't it?"

"He said that was the first thing I should do. To come to see you so you could explain."

"That's right." He leaned forward, ignored the pack of smokes this time and poured both me and himself another glass. "Now, where should I begin?"

CHAPTER SIXTEEN

As almost any self-respecting parent will tell you, all children are gifts from God. Others might disagree, instead explaining how a child's birth is simply the ongoing development of the evolutionary process. And with apologies to Charles Darwin, those latter few must be out of their minds. Because for any father—or any person, for that matter—who has actually been in the delivery room and watched as a woman has given birth, there is absolutely no way he can doubt the existence of God. Even the most hardheaded atheist will think it once, if not for an instant, as he or she witnesses the miracle of life, before continuing to disbelieve the notion of a higher being. Well, okay, that's all fine and good, but how exactly can two simple cells merge together and, nine months later, produce a living and breathing thing? No, that is why every child is a gift from God, not just a product of millions upon millions of years of evolution.

For Moses and Sabrina Cunningham, their son was not just a gift from God.

He was a miracle.

The reason for this is because after two years of trying for a baby with nothing to show for it, both had gone to the doctor. As it turned out, Moses had a low sperm count and Sabrina's tubes were damaged. How exactly this happened neither Sabrina nor the doctor had any idea ("He said she had no STDs, which usually causes it," Moses said), but obviously something had happened, probably when she was very young. There was absolutely no way, barring a miracle, that the two of them would conceive. Had they ever considered adoption?

Yes, they had in fact considered adoption, but for them it wasn't a realistic option. At least not at the moment. Sabrina worked as a first grade teacher, Moses as a youth pastor, and for some reason the idea of adopting just didn't appeal to them. The process itself was what kept them away. They'd heard horror stories from other couples that couldn't have children and tried adopting, and they just didn't think they could do the same. One couple in particular had come so close to actually getting a baby, until the mother, a day after giving birth, decided she wanted to keep the baby for her own. The couple had been heartbroken, and both Moses and Sabrina didn't want to face the same. They were already heartbroken as it was.

"Then," Moses said, his voice soft, "just one day Sabrina got pregnant. It was about a year after the doctor told us she would never be able to carry, and we'd given up even trying."

Sabrina's period was late, which was odd of course, but not as odd as the morning sickness which immediately followed. Here was a woman Moses had met his first year in Ohio, where he'd come to help build a church, a woman he'd fallen in love with at first sight, and a woman he had promised a life together with love and happiness. And while the love had been there, the happiness had faded away at the news that they would never have children. Except now these strange symptoms were occurring, symptoms that surely couldn't mean what they thought, and so they went to see the doctor again. He was the same doctor who had told them almost a year ago that sorry, no, you both can't have kids, I know it's hard to hear but keep your chins up, there are other people out there worse off than you. Now he ran tests and came back, his head shaking, and gazed at them with the most perplexed look on his face.

"He told us Sabrina was pregnant, and I swear, something broke inside him. I don't know what it was. Maybe it was doubt, because his science had failed him. He just shook his head, and simply said, 'It's a miracle.' "

Yes, it was a miracle; there was no doubt about that in either of their minds. And for the next eight months their lives changed drastically. They'd been in love before but now that love had blossomed even more, had really begun to shine. People who worked with them even commented on their sudden good moods. Moses got a second job working at a movie theater, since there was no way they would be able to support a child without some extra income. They just had enough to get by as it was, not to mention with another mouth to feed and another body to clothe and another person to love. But neither of them minded. They were up for the challenge and couldn't wait.

Except happiness is something that should never be taken for granted. When people are happy they don't see things as clearly as they should. They see things in a different light, and not in a light that best represents reality. Had both Moses and Sabrina seen things as they had a year before, maybe they might not have been surprised by what happened next.

"Really, looking back, I wasn't surprised at all. Everything was just so perfect. And the thing is, besides God, nothing's perfect. There's always something that will change, that will falter, that will snap its fingers in front of our faces to wake us up out of the fairy tale we've been living in. For us, it was the day Joey was born. The day Sabrina died."

Her water broke early that morning, a week before the due date. Moses grabbed the bags they had packed and drove her to the hospital. The entire time he held her hand and told her just how much he loved her, how she meant everything to him, and how everything was going to be okay.

Once they arrived and got her inside, she was immediately taken away. Moses had been left filling out more forms than he could handle, and before he finished the last one a doctor and nurse approached him. He knew from the moment the doctor's eyes met his that something was wrong. Some internal switch flicked itself off and his legs lost their strength. He almost fell but managed to hold onto the counter, and just stared back at the doctor. He asked her what it was, and she told him, with only slight hesitation, before saying she was very sorry and then walking away, leaving the nurse to stand by and console him.

Simply put, there had been some kind of complication. Something that had to do with her damaged Fallopian tubes. The baby had made it out but Sabrina had not.

"I didn't really even react until the nurse said something to me. The doctor had just told me my wife was dead and I didn't even blink. But when the nurse asked me if I was okay, I … I just lost it." Moses stared down at his drink. "I started shouting at her, even cursing some. I made quite a scene. The nurse actually looked frightened. The doctor had given me the bad news but I was taking it out on this other woman, calling her a liar right to her face. And she kept repeating the same thing over and over, she kept saying, 'But your baby is alive.' And do you want to hear something terrible? At that instant, I hated that baby more than anything in the world. I hated my son because he'd taken my wife away from me."

In fact, for the first two days, Moses wanted nothing at all to do with Joey. He didn't want to hold him, didn't even want to touch him. He only wanted to be alone. Then finally he went to the maternity ward and stared down at his baby through the glass. His child wasn't difficult to find, as it was the only black infant among a dozen whites, and Moses simply stared. A part of him had hoped for some kind of reaction at seeing the thing that had caused his wife to die, something that might take his hate away or even increase it. But he felt nothing. Then, as if knowing his father was watching, Joey opened his eyes and looked up at Moses.

And at that instant everything changed. All the hatred and disgust Moses had felt toward his child suddenly vanished, was suddenly washed away clean. What shone through was love, an undying love that was somehow even stronger than what Moses had felt for his own wife.

Moses named him Joseph, the name both he and Sabrina had decided on in case they had a boy (their choice for a girl was conveniently Josephine). He took his baby home to a house he knew he wouldn't be able to afford much longer. Not with Sabrina gone, as her job had really been what kept them afloat financially. So Moses had no choice but to sell the house. They moved into a condominium three months after Joey was brought home from the hospital. One bedroom, one bathroom and a kitchen—it was almost like a bachelor pad, only there was a crib in the corner and a child seat at the table, as well as a closet filled with diapers and baby wipes and baby food.

"I believe it's obvious that all women have some maternal instinct. They know when their children are hungry, when they're scared, when they're happy or sad. But most men just don't have that. When I went home from the hospital and sold the house and moved into the apartment, I was doing it with a baby and a responsibility that scared me to death. Sabrina was the one who was supposed to know what to do, not me. But I tried my best and did everything I possibly could, and in the end I think Joey took more care of me than I took care of him."

Moses kept his job at the church, which of course mourned the loss of Sabrina. Even the people at the movie theater were sensitive. Joey went into daycare as much as Moses would allow (which meant as much as he could afford), but the rest of the time he stayed home. On the weekends, if the church didn't require his time, Moses would just sit on the couch—which was pretty much the only piece of furniture in the entire place —and lay there with Joey on his chest. Joey, a pacifier in his mouth (what he would in a year or so call a "nub-nub"), slept peacefully, simply content to listen to his father's constant heartbeat. Even at night, when he awoke crying, Moses would lie down and hold his son's ear to his chest, and within minutes the baby would be asleep again, lost in the world of dreams.

But had Moses known just what kind of world that truly was, he may have stopped doing that nightly ritual right there and then. As it was, he had no idea, and continued doing so. All babies awoke in the middle of the night crying. It was just what babies did. Surely it wasn't anything else.

"Oh God, how I was wrong," Moses murmured. He had finished all of the rum in his glass and now just stared at it. With his thumbnail he scratched at Big Bird's yellow face. Not once had he looked up at me since he started talking. "I was so wrong, but how was I supposed to know it at the time? I couldn't. But still I felt guilty later, when I understood. Before that though ..."

Joey was almost three years old when it first happened. One morning, while Moses was giving him his bath, Joey said, "Maine." He'd been speaking for a little over a year now, and was pretty good with his words. But hearing his son just then Moses thought Joey had said *main* as in the adjective and not *Maine* as in the noun—or, in this case, the state. Moses didn't think much of it at the time—his son, like most babies, would sometimes say random things—and continued giving Joey his bath. But then after a moment, when Joey realized his father didn't quite hear him, he said, "Daddy, we go Maine." Right then it clicked that it wasn't the adjective Joey meant.

"Why do we have to go to Maine?" Moses asked him. No one he knew lived there. No family, no friends, no one. But his son only repeated what he had said before, and when Moses asked one more time why, Joey said, "Seven." And that was it. The issue was dropped at once. Joey went about his business like nothing had happened.

Moses decided to do the same and didn't even think about it again until a week later, when he saw something in *USA Today*. ("I had become accustomed to reading it every morning," he said; "Besides Joey, it was the only family I had.") A bank robbery in Portland, Maine, had gone terribly wrong. It seemed the cops had arrived before the three robbers were able to make it out. Over thirty people were in the bank at the time, both customers and employees. At first the robbers used them as hostages, but then as time went on they started killing them off. Executing them one at a time. When the cops finally got inside, the robbers had killed seven people. The story itself, while tragic, wouldn't really have caught Moses's attention had it not been for the number. The same number Joey mentioned a week before—both seven *and* Maine in the same egregious context.

"But I couldn't say anything to my boy." Moses lit another cigarette. "After the bathtub incident, which I later started calling it, he hadn't even brought up the subject of having us go to Maine, or the number seven. He went on like any normal three-year-old. Besides, what did he know of death, except the fact that his momma was no longer living? Nothing, so I decided to chalk it up as a coincidence and leave it at that."

But then, four months later, it happened again. This time though it wasn't just something small like Joey mentioning it out of the blue while taking his bath, or while Moses strapped him into his car seat to take him to daycare. This time it was late at night and Joey had begun screaming. Moses, hearing this from where he slept across the living room on the couch, jumped straight awake. The shrillness of his child's screams scared him, actually caused gooseflesh to break out over his body. Moses had heard Joey cry before in the middle of the night, but never like this, never with so much intensity. He figured his son had had dreams before, but never nightmares.

This was only the beginning.

"When I got across the room Joey was shaking. Tears were all over his face. He stood up and jumped into my arms. Just kept crying and hugged me real tight, wouldn't let me go. When he finally got settled, I asked him what was wrong. He looked up at me—he didn't need glasses then—and said, 'We go Richmond, Daddy.' I said, 'Richmond? Richmond, Virginia?' He just nodded."

Moses asked him why they should "go Richmond," but Joey shook his head. He only held on tight to his father, and with his son against him Moses felt Joey's body trembling. *He knows*, Moses thought. *He knows but he won't tell me. He's scared. I can see it in his eyes, the fear.* So Moses stood there holding his son, who continued shivering against him, as if he were freezing, while the temperature in the apartment was set at a comfortable seventy degrees. For whatever reason Joey believed they had to go to Richmond, Virginia, and in the back of his mind Moses kept thinking about the morning he was giving Joey his bath, how Joey had told him seven and Maine and then what he had later learned in the newspaper.

For the rest of the day Moses tried to ignore it. Tried to push any thought of it out of his mind. But he couldn't. Last time it had been a week before those three men executed those seven helpless, innocent people. One woman had been pregnant. And now his son was telling him they had to go to a place over four hundred miles away. Moses spent a great deal of time that day and night praying to God. Asking Him for courage and to give him a sign.

"But I had already gotten my sign," Moses said, and now, for the first time in maybe the last half hour, his eyes met mine. They looked very much like Lewis Shepherd's eyes—scarred and lost—that I understood what happened the moment I stepped foot inside this RV. Just as I had back on the second floor of Shepherd's Books, I had somehow produced a key that unlocked that door of terrible memories. Only this door was in Moses Cunningham's head, and though I had no grounds to make this assumption, I assumed everything inside had been told it would eventually see the light of day once more. And now, as promised, it was making an appearance.

"Look," I said, because more than a few moments of silence had passed, giving me the opportunity to jump in with what I felt compelled to say. "You don't have to do this."

"But that's the thing, Christopher. I do. I have to tell you everything so that you can understand what's happening."

"And what's that?"

"You'll find out soon enough. But first I need to tell you the rest. Like I said, I'd already gotten my sign. I knew it then but just didn't want to admit it to myself. The next morning I made arrangements for Joey to get out of daycare for a few days and called off work. Then we packed our things." He paused, swirled nothing around in his glass, and asked, "Would you like some more?"

I noticed my glass was empty. I nodded, held it out, and as Moses poured, I said, "What did you mean by that before? That you knew you'd already gotten your sign but didn't want to admit it."

"You mean that isn't obvious by now?" Moses smiled weakly as he filled his own glass and then capped the bottle. "My son was a prophet from God."

CHAPTER SEVENTEEN

WHEN THEY ARRIVED TO RICHMOND, Moses didn't know
what to do. He kept asking Joey why they had come here, but
his son hardly even acknowledged him. They'd never gone
farther than twenty miles away from home before; coming to
Virginia was not just a vacation, it was an adventure. They
spent their nights in a cheap motel just off the turnpike and
drove around most of the day, Moses hoping that Joey would
see something that might trigger a memory from his
nightmare.

On their third night in Richmond, Moses decided it was a
lost cause. They'd traveled all this way for nothing, and while
they had spent time at some local attractions—St. John's Epis-
copal Church, where Patrick Henry voiced his famous seven
words; the Edgar Allan Poe Museum, housed in Richmond's
oldest home—they had also spent more money than they could
afford to lose. (And here is where I begin to really see Joey as a
child, not even four years old yet, looking around with his wide
eyes at everything he can take in at one time because this is so
much different than home, so much different than the stale

wallpaper and stained carpet.) Tomorrow, Moses told himself, they would head back home and try to forget this nonsense.

Then, lying in bed that night beside him, Joey said one word very softly in his sleep, as Moses stared up at the ceiling and wondered whether God was punishing him for the sins of his past.

"And that one word," Moses told me now, seven years after their failed visit to Virginia, "was fire."

"Fire," I repeated softly. "What fire?"

As it turned out, the next morning a mile east of their motel an International House of Pancakes caught on fire. Most of the people made it out safely, but a few had gotten trapped inside. Five people: four adults and a child. Each of them died.

Moses stood outside the restaurant he and his son had been eating breakfast at for the past two days and watched the firemen work. At his side, Joey stood holding his hand. He didn't seem affected by what was happening at all. He didn't say anything to his father; he didn't even point when part of the building collapsed. He simply stared with what would soon become his trademark: dark solemn eyes.

"And as I stood there, I wanted to look down at him. But for some reason, I couldn't. Because I kept thinking about what he said just that night in his sleep. Somehow he knew. Not completely, but somehow he sensed it. And at that moment, as I watched along with those other bystanders, I understood that we'd been sent here to somehow stop those five people from dying."

Months passed. It began happening more frequently. Joey would get a vision or have a nightmare and he would tell Moses they had to go someplace. Sometimes it was to a small town Moses had never heard of. Other times to a major city a few states away. Joey never knew exactly why they were going there, but he always said a number—and unless he and Moses managed to reach their destination in time and figure out what was wrong, the news the next day would announce the deaths of whatever particular number of people Joey had first mentioned days, sometimes weeks, before.

Moses ended up quitting both of his jobs. He gave up the lease on the condominium. He'd taken some education classes in college and knew he could teach his son the basics. Besides, in only a few short years, Joey had proved himself much more mature and intelligent than Moses had ever thought possible.

They purchased an RV—"Very similar to the one we're sitting in right now"—and started out. Moses had only four thousand dollars to his name, everything that was left of his savings, but he wasn't worried. He knew God would provide. When Joey had a vision that they needed to go to a certain place, Moses would call ahead to one of the local churches and ask them if they needed a guest speaker for the next week or two. And while most churches, as a rule, don't allow outside speakers to come in out of nowhere (especially with no credentials whatsoever), Moses and Joey were almost never turned away.

Months would go by and Joey would have no visions or dreams or signs at all. When that happened Moses found a job that paid under the table, usually working the back of a local diner or restaurant. He always told his employers not to expect him around for very long, so they wouldn't be surprised when one morning he just didn't show up. Whether any of those employers suspected anything suspicious, nothing was ever said and the local law never came around asking questions.

"When Joey had his visions I didn't want to waste any time. I got our things together and we were on our way."

The older Joey got and the more visions he had—"nighmares" he called them until he was five years old—the clearer those visions became. Moses wasn't forced to piece everything together as he had before. Joey knew exactly where they had to go—what town, suburb, sometimes even what street—and how many people were going to be harmed. What Joey never knew was what was going to happen or who would be responsible.

Sometimes they weren't able to succeed in their work—or missions, as Moses had begun calling them. The Oklahoma City Bombing was one of their first major failures. They were called there two weeks before it happened. But Joey couldn't piece it together fast enough. He'd only been five at the time, a month and a half away from his sixth birthday, and he was so innocent and naïve, but he understood that they needed to work quickly. Then suddenly the Alfred P. Murrah Federal Building blew.

"The following month was the worst for my son. Until then we'd only been called to a few different places to save a handful of lives. The largest number was nineteen, when I believe a tractor-trailer whose brakes had failed would have slammed into a K-Mart had we not intervened. But now over one hundred and fifty lives were lost, and Joey felt responsible for each and every one of them. It's no wonder that was when his stuttering began."

Obviously the event had scarred Joey, both emotionally and spiritually, but Moses didn't notice his son's stutter until a few weeks later. Not until he'd begun to recognize the patterns of the speech impediment, how Joey no longer spoke clearly like he had before. The only times Joey's stammer disappeared was when he was "in the zone," as Moses later called it—when Joey was so deep in concentration and attuned with the calling he had been sent that he was in another state of mind.

"It was also around that time that he started watching Westerns," Moses said, his eyes momentarily lifting to a shelf against the wall above the couch. My own eyes shifted that way and I saw, among some books, various videotapes, namely *Once Upon a Time in the West*, *The Magnificent Seven*, and *High Noon*. "I never understood why—to be honest, I don't think I ever truly understood my son—but he loved them. Every time we left for a new place he'd say we were riding off into the backwards sunset. Because in Westerns the good guys are always riding away into the sunset at the end, away from all that bad stuff. But we were doing just the opposite. We were riding toward all that bad stuff head-on."

After the bombing, Joey sobered up to the responsibility that had been placed on his shoulders. At almost six years old, he began to understand his place in life. ("Can you imagine that?" Moses asked. "Most people in their forties *still* don't know their place just yet. Some never do.") Even Moses, who was there every step of the way, couldn't fathom how his son managed it. Never once would Joey talk about his feelings. In fact, he pretty much kept himself closed up, and while Moses would never admit this to anyone else, he was thankful. He didn't want to hear just what his son was feeling or thinking, because Moses didn't think he could handle it. Just having the knowledge that something terrible was going to happen was bad enough. But then also knowing that it could be avoided, and being given the chance to try to make it happen? That, in Moses's opinion, was insanity.

How Joey was able to continue, Moses had no idea. Sometimes he wondered if his son ignored the visions he received, but he never asked. At least once every couple of months Joey would tell him that they had to go to a new place, along with what Moses had begun to think of as the magic number of how many people were going to die. Then they went.

"I could tell it was draining him, but he didn't seem to mind. In fact, he never seemed to mind. There are times when you have to do something because no one else is going to do it. Maybe that's how Joey felt, I don't know. All I know for certain is that it was different for me. For me, the only reason I kept going was because I didn't think I could live with myself if I stopped."

Four years after Oklahoma City they were called to

Jefferson County, Colorado ("What half this country mistakes for Littleton, thanks to our savvy media"). It seemed close to twenty people were going to die. The morning Joey awoke from his latest vision—no longer were they called "nighmares"—his face had been so pained, so full of fear. His son's eyes reminded Moses of the night he first cried out in his sleep, and how he had held onto Moses, shivering like he was freezing. Moses knew at that moment there would be something different about this calling, but he couldn't quite comprehend the importance until after.

They never did make it. Right before Joey was able to piece everything together—he actually managed to run into Eric Harris two days before the shooting—one of the tires on the RV blew. They ran off the road and hit a tree. They were both knocked unconscious. By the time the police and paramedics arrived and brought them to, it was already too late. It was noontime and already the killing spree at Columbine High School had begun.

It was then that Moses understood the role he and Joey were playing. He had no idea why it had taken him this long to figure it out. He'd always assumed God was using them to save these people (so of course it made sense why they never had to worry about money or food or shelter), but he never understood why.

He prayed about it, and after a few weeks he received a vision of his own. He saw the angels of Heaven in all their glory before the Fall. Each held a different responsibility or role in God's plan. But when Satan and his minions fell, those angels with their appointed tasks fell too.

"You see, Satan's always wanted to match wits with God. And since God is the maker and breaker of men, Satan thinks he's up to the challenge too. He tries to take it upon himself to decide when certain people should die and not let their lives run the course God intended. He uses his own angels, I believe, demons that corrupt humanity's life stream so that they die before their appointed time. I think every time Joey had a vision, God had foreseen that the demons would do this and put us in charge of stopping them. It sounds crazy—like I said, a lot of what you needed to hear would sound crazy—but there's no other way to explain it. And even though sometimes the demons think they've succeeded, they've also failed."

"Failed?" I said, though my voice wasn't at its normal level. As he was speaking, Moses's voice had lowered and lowered until he was using a near-whisper, and for this reason alone I had begun to whisper too. "What do you mean by failed?"

"Just look at Columbine. Despite the fact that fifteen people died, that tragedy brought more people to God than you can imagine. Most of those kids died because of their faith. Eric Harris and Dylan Klebold walked right up to them and asked them if they believed in God. Those kids could have easily lied, they could have just shaken their heads no and denied Him. But they didn't. They believed in something and wanted to stand up for it. And because of that they were killed."

He shook his head.

"It's sad really, how tragedy will bring people together. Just look at what happened on September 11th. Joey and I were called to a small town in New Mexico the week before. I didn't understand why until after those planes crashed. The entire town was shocked and saddened, and that Sunday when I spoke the church had its largest turnout ever."

His eyes met mine again. When he spoke, his voice was no longer a whisper. It had gone back to its normal confident tone, the one he used when speaking in front of countless strangers at church. It was the voice he used when trying to sell God. Now he was using it to sell something else.

"By now I'm sure you're asking yourself what all this has to do with Bridgton, New York. Whether you believe in God or not, you have to accept the fact that things happen for a reason. Joey and I were called here because thirty-four people are supposed to die. But the vision Joey received this time wasn't like the others. Something about this one was different, though he wouldn't tell me exactly how, even when I begged him to. All I know is that we were meant to come here to stop something terrible from happening."

He glanced back down at his glass.

"And that we'd meet somebody who was to help us."

Shifting his eyes back up to meet mine.

"Christopher, that somebody is you."

For the longest time I didn't speak. I just sat there, staring down at my glass. Finally I cleared my throat and looked back up at Moses.

"You knew Joey was going to die, didn't you?"

He nodded. "He said it was what needed to be done. I almost considered not coming here. I thought about driving as far south as possible and never looking back. I'd already lost my wife, and I wasn't about to lose my son. But I knew if I did I wouldn't only be failing God, I'd be failing Joey, too. He knew it was his time and he wasn't afraid. He was ready."

"You can't ask me to do this."

"Do what?"

"Just … *this*. It's crazy."

"You have every right to doubt me. It's completely your choice, just like it was Joey's and mine."

"I'm not even sure what you're asking me to do."

"Neither do I. What did Joey tell you?"

I thought for a moment, deciding what I should say, when I remembered something.

"Joey said he knew who killed my parents. Do you know?"

Moses shook his head. "I'm sorry, no."

I stared into his eyes, deciding whether or not I believed him. Finally I said, "So these thirty-four people, when are they supposed to die?"

"I don't know. Joey didn't know either. He was only ever given a location and an initial number, and we had to figure the rest out on our own."

"But this angel that took Joey. Who or what is Samael?"

"I'm not quite sure. But if he tried to kill Joey, then it's safe to assume he's one of the fallen."

"Do you know what he wants?"

Moses shook his head again.

I thought for a few seconds, the past hour catching up with me. Everything was happening so fast and was too much to comprehend all at once. The rational part of my mind told me to leave, to just get the hell out, but the irrational part—the part that had been with Joey and looked into his knowing eyes, saw him in his deathbed and heard the words he spoke; the part that had talked me into going to see James Young to confirm that it was a demon that had tried killing me—knew better.

Moses asked, "Did Joey say he interacted at all with the angel?"

"He said that Samael gave him a choice. To pick one of the thirty-four to die and save the rest. But Joey refused. He told me he believed they could all be saved."

Moses said nothing and only nodded.

"Joey told me"—I swallowed—"that you had a present for me."

At first Moses looked like he didn't know what I was talking about. Then his eyes lit up. He said, "Oh, that's right," and pushed himself out of his chair. He disappeared into the back bedroom and returned with a small package.

"Joey always used comics," he said. "He didn't believe in wrapping paper."

The box had been wrapped in what looked like the Sunday Comics. Colored panels surrounded it. Dennis the Menace peeked out at me.

I tore it open, found that it was a shoebox, some brand I'd never heard of before. I opened it, moved the lid aside to find the inside filled with balled up pieces of newspaper. I reached in, felt what was beneath, and immediately pulled my hand back out.

I said, "I'm not taking that," putting the box on the coffee table between us.

Moses leaned forward and reached inside, extracting the eight-inch butcher knife. The stainless steel blade gleamed in the light.

"I'm not taking that," I repeated, shaking my head as I stared at the knife.

Moses set it down on the table. "At this point, I don't think you have a choice."

"Where did he get it?"

"I don't know. Did my son say why you should have this?"

"Just to use it when it was time."

Moses placed the knife down beside the box. "Before you mentioned that my boy said you should speak to me first. What else did he say?"

"He told me to stop Jack Murphy." Still staring at the knife, now thinking about my parents. "So then I would believe."

"Who's Jack Murphy?"

"A close friend of my family's."

"Anything else?"

"He said I should read Job 42."

"Job 42?"

I nodded.

"Are you sure you didn't hear him wrong?"

"No. Why?"

Moses stared at me a moment longer, then got up and thumbed through a few of the books on the shelf above the couch. He came away with a Bible—which just happened to be leaning against *The Man with No Name* Trilogy—and began to flip through the pages. He did this for a few seconds before stopping and handing it to me.

He said, "Job only has forty-one chapters."

I stared down at the text and saw he was right. At first I didn't understand, but then suddenly it clicked.

Of course Job only had forty-one chapters. Job 42 didn't exist.

At least not in this Bible.

CHAPTER EIGHTEEN

I WROTE my grandmother a note saying I'd gone to Lanton to pick something up and would be back later tonight, that she shouldn't worry. I considered signing my name, but in the end left it as it was.

I knew there'd be questions when I returned. Not just from my grandmother, but from my uncle and maybe even Sheriff Douglas. All wanting to know what was so important for me to drive four hours both ways by myself—and without telling anyone where I was going, either. I had no clue what I would tell them but figured I had the time to come up with something on the trip.

It was six-thirty in the morning. The sun had begun to rise an hour ago. Dew coated the grass and reflected some of the early light. In the trees all around The Hill, it seemed nearly every bird in New York was either chirping or squawking good morning to each other.

I started my car and then walked up the drive to my grandmother's. I hoped she wasn't yet awake and was glad to see the trailer dark and quiet. I pinched the note on the screen door and made sure it stuck.

Heading back to my car, I glanced over at Moses Cunningham's RV. I wondered what the man was doing. Was he sleeping? If he was, were his dreams filled with angels and demons, or something more pleasant, like times spent with his wife and son?

In truth I wanted nothing to do with the man. His story was crazy enough, but the scary thing about it was that I'd actually begun to believe him. Too many things were starting to add up, too many pieces of an ever-growing puzzle beginning to take shape.

Both Joey and his father believed I was somehow going to help them. Last night I decided I would. Joey told me to read Job 42, a chapter my grandfather placed in his own version of the Bible, and I assumed whatever was written there would help. My only concern now was getting the Bible and bringing it back to Moses, so it would be out of my hands.

Besides, I was curious to see what the man who had once tried to kill me had to say.

Except for some construction near Hazleton, the traffic was light and I made it back without trouble. By then it was almost eleven o'clock and Lanton looked no different than it had when I left it four days before. Even the gas prices at the Sheetz hadn't gone up a penny or more.

When I pulled into the driveway I just sat there. I stared up at the house—that yellow and black crime scene tape was still strung around the property—and remembered what I'd found in my parents' room almost two weeks ago. The blood, their lifeless bodies, the buzzing of the alarm clock ... and then the cross that had been marked on my door.

I was being foolish. Scared of ghosts that couldn't hurt me, and yet despite the fact I knew it was all in my head, I didn't want to go inside. I thought about what waited in there and how Moses needed it for whatever mission God had sent him and Joey on, and I considered forgetting the entire thing. There was nothing keeping me from not returning to Bridgton. Dean was going to bring me back home anyway—both he and Sheriff Douglas had thought it would be best—but that never happened.

Instead they'd found Joey, and now the kid was dead and for some strange reason I felt as if I owed him something.

I wasted no time when I got inside. I noticed there were five messages on the answering machine. I didn't want to bother with them and left the light blinking. It would be another distraction, and right now all I had to worry about was getting the Bible so I could head back to Bridgton.

I walked into the living room and immediately spotted the Bible. It was still on the couch, right where I'd left it. I stared at it for a long time, trying to decide whether the book had somehow changed in appearance.

With caution I stepped forward and then sat on the couch, continued staring at the Bible. I didn't want to read it. Just like the day Darren Bannister had dropped it off, I didn't want to know what was inside the package. But still I'd opened it.

"Quit wasting time," I said. I grabbed the book, opened it, and reread the inscription on the first page.

Christopher, this is the fruit of my labor. I am sorry for what happened. Hopefully someday you will understand. Read Job 42 for guidance. Your life depends upon it. I love you.

I thumbed slowly through the pages, amazed at the care he'd taken in rewriting the entire Old Testament by hand. I wondered briefly which version he copied it from, if he kept everything the same, or if maybe he omitted certain scenes and added dialogue. Finally I came to the Book of Job and began thumbing even slower.

Before I knew it I had found Job 42. I read the first line.

Christopher, if you are reading this, something bad has happened to either one of your parents, if not both.

Before I could read another word, the book fell from my hands. It hit one of the couch cushions and bounced off, landed on the floor with its spine sticking up. I noticed one of the pages was sticking out farther than it should have been. Somehow it had ripped during the fall. Then I noticed my hands, which were still held out before me. They were shaking.

I wanted to pick the book back up and read what else was written, while at the same time I wanted to burn it. Whatever it was, it played some role in something I did not yet want to accept, and reading it now would somehow signal my acceptance. And while I didn't want that, I also didn't want to *not* know either.

I stared at the book for another couple of seconds, unsure of what I was waiting for. Finally I reached down to pick it up. Just as my fingers touched the cover, there was a loud knock at the door. I grabbed the book, snatched it to my chest, and turned just as Steve Carpenter entered the living room. He wore his gray uniform, his silver badge not so shiny now that he was inside. His face was red, his eyes now looking almost like they had two weeks ago, when he first believed I'd murdered my parents.

"What the hell are you doing here?" he said.

"It's nice to see you too, Steve."

"Your uncle called me an hour ago. Said you were coming back here by yourself to pick something up. I told him that couldn't be true, that you weren't stupid enough to do something like that, especially after the mess that just happened in Bridgton. But I told my men to keep an eye out for you anyway, and five minutes ago Fred Walker gives me a call and tells me he saw you driving down Norfolk Road. So I'll ask you again. What the hell are you doing here?"

"Just like Dean said, I needed to pick something up."

"What—that book?"

"I figured I could use some relaxing summer reading."

"Goddamn it, Chris," he said, his voice now a growl, "what the hell's wrong with you?"

I decided it best not to answer that, and instead asked if he'd had any luck finding my parents' killer.

This caused the look of malice to disappear from his eyes. They shifted from mine for just an instant before returning. He shook his head. "No, we haven't come up with anything yet."

I nodded, the news not surprising me at all. For a moment I thought about mentioning how there was a boy who'd claimed he knew who killed my parents but refused to tell me, no matter how much I begged him. How instead he had whispered he could only tell me three things. Thinking of this now, I glanced down at the Bible in my hands. Reading Job 42 was step three in Joey's instructions. I'd already completed the first step and figured what the hell.

I asked Steve if he knew where Jack Murphy was right now.

"Jack Murphy?" He frowned, looking almost suspicious. "Why do you ask that?"

I opened my mouth but said nothing, my well of bullshit having suddenly run dry. It isn't easy keeping your lies straight when you've got so many, but I doubted telling Steve the truth would do much good anyhow. How would I even begin to explain about Joey and his father?

"I just really need to speak with him. It's important."

He looked uneasy but said, "He's probably at home. I'll call him for you if you'd like."

I started to say yes to this but then shook my head. "No, it's probably best you don't. It ah … it's kind of complicated." Looking around the room, trying to find the best way out, I realized there wasn't one and said, "But hey, why don't you drive me out there? Maybe I can explain on the way."

He gave me another questioning look before he said, "All right then, Chris. As long as I can keep an eye on you. My car's outside."

———

Jack Murphy worked as a dairy farmer. You wouldn't think it if you saw him. He was thin and wore glasses and looked more like a teacher, which he actually was. He'd taught math for eight years before finding a farm for sale and deciding to buy it. He'd been running it ever since.

The day before my parents' funeral, while his wife Karen got things prepared inside my house for the wake, he stopped by to talk to me. We went out back, behind the garage, where he lit a cigarette. "The wife would kill me if she knew I was still smoking these," he said, then offered me one. I declined and waited, wondering what all this was about. Jack took a long drag, then another, before sighing. "You might not believe this, but when you were dating Melanie I thought of you as a son. Hell, I still do. I don't know what happened between you and my daughter, and to be honest, I'm not sure I want to know. That's your business. But ... shit, I don't know just how to say this. If there's anything you ever need, anything at all, don't be afraid to ask. Got it?"

I hadn't known what to say and only nodded. I just stood there, thinking about everything I had done with his daughter, everything I had done *to* his daughter, and here he was now, trying to be my friend. He was a good man, this Jack Murphy, who I had at one time actually believed would someday become my father-in-law. But after everything that had happened, after how badly it ended between me and Mel, I made the decision that I would never ask for his help.

That I wasn't worthy of it, that I didn't deserve it at all. I promised myself I would never ask him for anything, not even an opinion, not even a sip of water if I was dying of thirst.

But now, a little more than a week later, I planned to break that promise. What it was I'd ask him I didn't know, but I knew when the time came I'd think of something. If not, I'd improvise.

Jack Murphy's farm was located on the eastern edge of Lanton Township, in large rolling fields about fifteen miles from my house. It took us twenty minutes to get there, Steve taking his time because he thought that the slower he drove, the sooner I'd tell him what was going on. Too bad for him, I kept my mouth shut and enjoyed the ride.

The farmhouse sat a quarter mile off Lewiston Road. The drive was paved and ended beside the first of two barns where Jack kept his cows. There was about a fifty-yard gap between the barn and the house, with a stone walkway leading up to the porch steps. I remembered driving out there at night to meet Mel, lying out in the fields and staring up at the stars. She'd hated the fact her dad stopped being a teacher, had instead decided to become a farmer. She was popular at school, sure, but still the fact she was a farmer's daughter was a title that had become solely hers, and which she absolutely loathed.

When Steve parked and we got out, he glanced around and frowned. "That's strange."

"What is?"

"Every other time I'm out here, his dogs always come running."

It was true. There were two dogs that constantly ran the Murphy property, a German shepherd and a Husky. Their names were Ben and Jerry. They were Patty's dogs, little nine-year-old Patty who I had once thought of as a little sister, a girl who would always want me to partake in her knock-knock jokes, who would always say, "I really like you a lot, Chris, even more than *Mel*," saying her sister's name as if it was diseased.

We stood on either side of the cruiser, both our doors shut. The sky was clear, the day was warm, and the smell of hay and cow dung was thick in the air. It was a familiar smell that I'd somehow forgotten, the months erasing the memory of the odor from my mind.

Steve rested his hands on the hood and stared at me. "All right, Chris. Now that we're here, what's going on?"

"Where do you think he is?"

"How the hell should I know? His truck's parked over there. It doesn't look like Karen's home though. At least I don't see her car anywhere."

Jack Murphy's Dodge Ram was parked beside the barn. The wide double doors were opened; I could hear the cows shuffling and mooing in their stalls. I wondered briefly why none of them were out in the field when I turned to face the house.

That's when I felt it.

A sudden sense of wrongness, like a pang of ice shooting through my soul. It pulled me forward, and before I even knew I'd begun walking, I heard Steve behind me.

"Hey, where do you think you're going?"

The house was three stories, its first two stories stone, its third story covered in white siding. Its trim and shutters were sky blue. It almost looked as if it'd been built during the Civil War era. A large oak tree stood a short distance from the house, a tire swing hanging from one of its high branches. On the second floor were two windows that faced front. The chill pulling me forward was coming from the open window on the left, which I knew was Patty's bedroom.

I was almost to the porch, my sneakers crunching the gravel on the walkway, when I heard her faint voice coming from that window.

"*No ... Daddy, stop ... please.*"

So soft, so small, yet I sensed the fear there, the urgency, and before I realized it I'd begun sprinting up the steps. The front door was open, the only thing keeping the outside world away a screen door. I crashed through this and then I was inside, the fragrant scent of apple cider hitting my nostrils, while behind me Steve called for me to stop.

I noticed a collection of things as I ran toward the stairs— the antique pots on the floor, the two dogs tied up in the kitchen, the framed pictures in the hallway of Jack Murphy and his wife and daughters—but none of it mattered to me, because now inside I heard her voice more clearly, I heard her moans and her gasps and her pleading.

I took the steps two at a time. Blood pounded in my ears. When I reached the second floor I went straight for the closed door, opened it and walked right in.

He had her on the bed. She was naked but he still wore his briefs. Her arms were being held up above her head and she seemed to be struggling with her legs, which he kept in place with his knees. He outweighed her by more than one hundred pounds, him being at least forty while she wasn't yet even ten years old.

He looked back at me. His face was naked without his glasses, his lustful wild eyes now filled with confusion and bewilderment.

"What," he started to say, but that was it.

Everything was silent in that single instant. Even Patty had stopped her whimpering and pleading. Downstairs, one of the dogs started barking. Then behind me, the sound of heavy footsteps on the stairs. Seconds later, Steve grabbed my shoulder.

He meant to pull me back, meant to ask me just what the hell I was thinking. But then he stopped. He saw what I saw.

He whispered, "My God."

Two police cruisers showed up five minutes after Steve made the call. Jack Murphy was read his rights and placed in the back of one of the cars.

Patty Murphy was taken in the other cruiser to her grandparents' place across town. She was silent the entire time, tears dried on her small face. She had seen me, had looked right at me, but didn't say anything, didn't even wave. The guy who had played along with her knock-knock jokes, the guy who she said she liked a lot, even more than her own sister, was now somehow a stranger to her.

I stood on the lawn in front of the house, beside the tire swing. It was an actual tire, a worn Goodyear. Ben and Jerry had been untied. They hadn't seen me in a couple months and had come up to me right away, wanting to be petted, but when it became clear they were being ignored they started to roam the property, oblivious to what was taking place.

Steve waited until the car with Jack Murphy left, then came and stood beside me. He crossed his meaty arms and sighed. "He's not saying a word. Guess he's going to wait until he gets his lawyer. But I'll tell you what—he's going away for a long time. We ... well, I really shouldn't be telling you this, but we found pornography on his computer in the den. Child pornography. It was actually on the screen when one of my men passed the room, so he went and did a quick search. There are thousands of files." He shook his head. "And as it turns out, Karen is away. Down in West Virginia for the week."

In other words, Mel was off touring Europe for the summer, Karen was down south on one of her retreats, where she met a group of other artists that shared their love for pottery in the same way she did. Meaning that Jack Murphy had been left alone with his nine-year-old daughter for at least a week. Jack Murphy, who had been addicted to child pornography all this time but had never let the desire take control of him until today.

"Christ," Steve said. "Things come in threes, don't they? First your parents, then the Youngs, and now this."

I looked at him. "The Youngs?"

"Your uncle didn't tell you? I thought I'd mentioned it to him. Shannon Young was driving with the boys Monday afternoon. They went through an intersection and a truck ran the light. Smashed right into them. Killed them instantly."

"What about Pastor Young?"

"He wasn't in the car. But he's been a wreck ever since. Real shame, that. Real shame, all of this."

The dogs raced past us, Ben nipping after Jerry's tail.

Steve cleared this throat. "Now, Chris, I'm going to ask you something. I'm not sure if I want to hear the answer, but I'm still going to ask because I feel I have to. How did you know?"

I waited a moment, then another, then said, "I didn't." I still smelled the mixture of lavender and sweat from Patty Murphy's bedroom, like it had somehow gotten into my clothes, saturated my skin. "Let's just leave it at that."

Steve seemed to allow my words to soak in, because he stood there for a while, stock-still. Eventually he nodded. "All right then. I guess I can live with that. That's fine by me."

I thought about Joey and what he told me to do about Jack Murphy. The rational part of my mind had needed this to be nothing, to be just one big mistake so it could call Joey a liar and throw everything Moses had told me back in his face. Now I saw that couldn't happen, because Joey had been right and I had no reason not to believe.

But unlike Steve, it wasn't fine by me.

Just before Scranton, I stopped at a Sunoco station to fill up and take a piss.

By then it was already three o'clock. I'd gotten a late start dealing with Steve and trying to persuade him to let me go back to Bridgton by myself. He was still shook up after the whole Jack Murphy incident and seemed to sense that something else was going on but kept his suspicions to himself.

There were only four available pumps, as two were out of order. Cars were waiting, so after filling up and paying inside, I moved my Cavalier to the side lot and parked between the building and an old red Celica. The bathrooms were outside here—one men's, one women's.

I tried the men's door but it was locked and someone inside shouted, "Almost done," so I stood back and waited. I glanced at the bare picnic tables on the grass, then at my own car. I tried not to think about my grandfather's Bible inside on the passenger seat. While before I'd been curious to see what was written, now I wanted nothing more than to get it out of my life.

From inside the bathroom I heard the cranking noise of the paper towel dispenser, barely audible over the busy afternoon traffic on the highway.

I had about another two hours of driving left. I wondered what my excuse would be for leaving when the red Celica parked beside my car caught my attention.

Only two doors, its paint was faded and peeling, and the rear windshield had been shattered or taken out. What replaced it now was a sheet of heavy plastic kept in place by duct tape.

Something's in the trunk.

I had no idea what it was but the same chill raced through my body like it did back at the farmhouse. I was drawn to it, needing to know what was inside, but before I could even take a step forward the men's door opened and a small Hispanic man walked out. He barely looked at me as he stepped off the curb and walked around to the Celica. He took one glance at the highway as he opened the door, and as he did his eyes widened just a bit.

I glanced over as well. At first I couldn't connect what he was looking at, and then I saw it. A Pennsylvania State Police cruiser had just pulled in and was waiting in line at the pumps. When I looked back, the Hispanic man had already gotten into the Celica. The engine coughed to life and the car slowly backed up, its brakes squealing. It then started forward with some hesitation before pulling out onto the highway.

"Hey," I said, but it was barely the shout I'd intended, and I watched the car go, my body motionless, thinking *there's something in that trunk* and wondering just what the hell I was supposed to do about it.

Then it was gone, lost in the continuous line of traffic, and I turned away, entered the men's room. By the time I got back in my car and started off toward Bridgton again, the thought of that Celica and what was in the trunk was the furthest thing from my mind.

CHAPTER NINETEEN

WHEN I RETURNED to The Hill around five that afternoon, my grandmother sat by herself on the swing beside her trailer. It was still positioned facing down into the valley. I parked, left the Bible in my car, and walked up to her.

Her cane rested between her legs, her hands on her lap. She stared out at the ragged horizon, her small face set, her eyes squinted. Even though I stood right there, she refused to look at me. I opened my mouth but didn't say anything. I couldn't think of anything worthwhile to say. I looked toward Moses's RV, but the Metro was gone.

"He's not there." Her voice was soft and low. "He left about an hour ago. He came over and asked me if you were back yet. I told him I had no idea. I told him I thought I knew my grandson, but I guess I don't. No grandson of mine in his right mind would run off and leave his grandmother scared to death like that."

"I'm sorry," I said, but it sounded weak even to my own ears.

"Your uncle's not happy. He doesn't understand either. Just what could possess you to go all the way back home, Christopher? And why did that man know more about where you were than us? He's just a stranger. We're family."

"That's right," I said. "We are family. But what about a month ago? What about last year? Were we family then? Until my parents died, did you ever wonder about me? Did you even care?"

She stared back at me, giving me an expression I would have expected to see had I just slapped her across the face.

I opened my mouth, meaning to apologize. But the shock in my grandmother's face turned to anger and I wanted nothing more to do with her, so I just walked away. Five steps to the drive, where I meant to turn toward my trailer, but then I saw Sarah coming out of the Rec House. She carried a paperback in her hand. She was headed toward Half Creek Road.

I started up the drive. Sarah had just looked both ways and was crossing the road, and as I passed the Rec House I called her name.

She turned around on the other side. Shielded the sun from her eyes with the paperback. I stood where I was on my side of the road and stared back at her, uncertain now what I wanted to say or do.

Finally I came up with two words.

"I'm sorry."

"What?" She frowned. "Why?"

"For before. I shouldn't have said those things to you."

"And why's that? You were being honest. That's nothing to apologize for."

A pickup truck came up the road, lumber stacked in the back. Sarah gave a quick wave to the driver as he passed us. I waited until it was gone before crossing the road.

"Because I made you upset," I said. "I'm sorry for that."

She started walking toward her house. "I told you, there's nothing to be sorry about. You did the one thing almost nobody else in your position would have done."

"And what's that?"

"You were honest. Why should you be sorry?"

The garage door was open. Inside John Porter was busy working on his Firebird. "Perry Mason" blared on the stereo, Ozzy Osbourne singing about kids riding painted horses.

Sarah started walking but then stopped. She glanced at the garage before looking back at me.

"In fact, I'm going to be honest with you. Remember that day you met me in the Rec House? Did you even wonder why I was in there? I go there every time my dad and brother are home. Because since my mom died, they've both started hating each other. There's no reason for it. Did you know my dad lost his pinkie finger while he was working when we were kids? John used to call him Pinkie behind his back. Now he calls him that to his face."

She pushed a stray lock of hair behind her ear.

"My mom was the glue that held our family together, and now without her it's falling apart and I can't put up with it anymore. Don't you get it? That's why I was there that day, because I was hiding from the silence that comes from both of them. It scares me."

She shook her head.

"And you, Chris, you scare me, too. But not in a bad way. It's just … I want to be your friend, but I know it wouldn't work out. Because right now I've got no friends. All those people that call themselves my friends at school are fakes. I'm an outcast, that's all I am, and I'm afraid if I get close to you I'll somehow drive you away. Either that or pull you down with me."

She kept her gaze level and steady.

"I mean, don't you get it yet? Don't you see who and what I am? Look back across the road. That's a *trailer park*, for Christ's sake. And do you know what that makes me, just because my dad—who's *also* a truck driver—owns that trailer park?"

She paused, willing me to answer, but I didn't.

"Trailer trash," Sarah said. "That's what I am, Chris. No matter what I do, I'll always be trailer trash. No matter if I played the clarinet in school, or got good grades, or tried out for the debate team, or"—she held the paperback up—"read classic literature just for fun. Nothing I do can change my place in life. Believe me, I've tried, and it was never going to happen. I am what I am. And then this trailer trash girl got herself knocked up. Isn't that just the perfect ending to my crappy life story?"

She waited, letting that last question hang out there between us, and when she realized I wasn't going to say anything, she turned and started up the steps. Opened the front door and disappeared inside.

It was a couple of seconds before I realized John now stood in the doorway of the garage. One of his Marlboros hung in his mouth. He nodded at me to come over.

"Don't worry," he said, once we stood facing each other. Behind him, in the garage, Ozzy now sang about seeing the man around the corner waiting. "I don't give a shit what all that was about. I know you're a decent guy and my sister's crazy, so whatever. But how you holding up after Sunday night?"

"Not bad. How about you? I thought you were grounded."

He was inhaling when I said this; now he laughed, coughing out smoke. "Yeah, right—grounded. I guess you could say that. I'm only grounded when my old man's home, and he left like an hour ago. He'll be gone tomorrow night too, which is sweet, 'cause me and a few of my buddies are crashing this pre-graduation party." He paused, gave me a look, and said, "Hey, you wanna come?"

Dean stopped by The Hill around seven o'clock that night. I was exhausted from my day trip and was taking a nap when he knocked at my trailer door. When I answered he looked at me, his face hard, and said, "Get your shoes on."

Ten minutes later we were at Luanne's. The place had its diehard regulars, as I recognized most of the men at the counter from my last visit. We even sat at the same booth, only this time Grandma wasn't with us. As it turned out she wasn't up for dinner tonight, and though Dean never gave a reason, I knew why.

He waited until we'd ordered our food before he got down to it.

"All right, Chris, what the hell's going on?"

"What do you mean?"

"Don't bullshit me. First that Cunningham kid gets abducted. Then when he's found he refuses to speak with anyone but you. Now he's dead and the sheriff's got men working round the clock trying to find the bastard that took him. And the worst part is we don't have any leads. But what really piqued my interest was when Mom told me you went over to Moses Cunningham's place last night. Then this morning you take off back to Lanton. Why?"

"I left something there I needed."

"Really. Like what?"

"You wouldn't believe me if I told you."

"Try me."

I held his stare and wondered what he thought was going on. He probably had some crazy idea concocted in his mind, nowhere near the truth. Telling him now would throw a wrench in whatever machinery he had going, but when all was said and done I really had no choice.

"I went back to pick up a book your father sent me a long time ago. It's the entire Old Testament handwritten by him word for word."

Dean stared back at me, his brow furrowing just a bit. "What?"

"I left it in my trailer if you don't believe me. You can look for yourself when we get back."

"No, that's okay. But you're right—I don't believe you. Why would he do something like that?"

"Well, let's see," I said, and raised my index finger. "One, he was crazy. Do we really need to know anything else?"

Dean's face reddened. His hands balled into fists. Images of him lashing out and punching me raced through my head. But he only sat there and whispered, "My father—your grandfather —may have been a lot of things, but if anything, he was not crazy."

"Yeah, okay. Then why did he try to kill me? Why was he locked away in that mental institution? The last time I checked, they just don't put you away for the hell of it."

Something broke in my uncle's face—it seemed to soften a little, as he shook his head slowly.

"I can't explain what happened, Chris, because I don't know the whole story. But I knew that man my entire life. He raised both me and your dad real well, and what they say he did just isn't something he'd do. He was a good man, a damned fine man, and things really changed after he went away. For a while the Myers name had a stigma to it that I thought we would never live down. And your dad ... he cut off all contact with us. He turned his back just like that, and you know, I can't say I blame him. A lot of weird stuff happened, but I swear to you, your grandfather was not crazy."

The conviction in both his eyes and voice asserted the fact that Dean believed it was true. No matter what may have happened, my grandfather was sane in his son's eyes.

"Okay," I said. "So where is he now? Is he still alive?"

"No. He's been dead almost four years."

I thought of my father and how he'd cut off all contact.

When did he find this out? The night it happened? A week later? A month?

"How?"

For the first time I saw the hesitation in my uncle's eyes as he looked away.

"Suicide," he whispered.

Moses still wasn't home by the time we got back to The Hill. Dean stopped his Explorer right in front of my trailer, put it in park, and then pulled out a pack of Winstons from the glove box. He placed one in his mouth, lit it, then blew the smoke out his window.

"I thought you gave them up."

"So did I."

My uncle kept his attention forward, as if he didn't want to look at me. I undid my seatbelt and got out, was about to shut my door when Dean said my name.

"You know, despite what may have happened in the past, we're still family. Just because we haven't seen or talked to each other in over ten years doesn't mean we're not. Both Mom and I care and love you very much. Just remember that."

He flicked his cigarette out the window and drove away.

I waited another hour before Moses returned. By then it was almost nine-thirty. As I met Moses at his RV, I saw Mrs. Roberts at the table in my grandmother's trailer. They were probably playing cards or dominos. Grandma glanced out the window for a moment, saw me, then quickly looked away.

Moses had the Metro's passenger door open. He was bent

over and picking something up off the seat. When he turned, he held a stack of newspapers in his arms.

"What are those for?" I asked, for some reason thinking of Lewis Shepherd's collection.

"All the papers in the tri-county area. Every place Joey and I went to we got all the morning and evening papers. Sometimes we'd find clues while rooting though them." He noticed the Bible in my hands. "Is that it?"

I nodded, told him he wasn't here when I got back or else I would have given it to him then.

"I had to go to the hospital. They're ready to release Joey's body. I'd love to take him back to Ohio and have him buried beside his momma, but I can't leave. So I'm having him cremated. At least then I can always keep him with me."

I held my grandfather's Bible out to him. "Here, take it. Whatever Job 42 says, it's the only help I can give you."

"You haven't read it?"

"No."

"Why not?"

"I just … I think it's best if I don't know what it says. I hardly knew my grandfather, and the little I do know isn't good."

Cradling the newspapers in one arm, he took the Bible from me. "How was your trip? Did you end up talking with Jack Murphy?"

Images of today flashed through my mind: little Patty's near-violation, Jack Murphy's lustful wild eyes, that cold knowing feeling I'd had when I turned toward the farmhouse.

"Not really."

"Not really," Moses said. "What does that mean?"

"Look, I don't want to talk about it."

"All right. I understand. And thank you for getting this for me. But are you sure you don't want to read it?"

I thought about sitting beside Joey on his deathbed, how he

told me to read Job 42, and I knew deep down it was what I had to do; even Moses knew it. But I just couldn't. The puzzle was growing bigger piece by piece, and I didn't want to see what the finished product would become.

"No," I said. "I don't."

He stared back at me another moment, then nodded. "You know, Christopher, whether you believe in God or not, you can only run from Him for so long. In the end you'll tire and have no choice but to face Him."

"Take care of yourself," I said and walked away.

CHAPTER TWENTY

FOR BREAKFAST my grandmother made French toast and bacon. The coffee she brewed was bitter, the eggs were undercooked, and there was no syrup. But I didn't complain. I'd been surprised when she woke me a half hour earlier and didn't want to jinx whatever was happening between us now, even though we'd barely spoken a word to each other besides a simple good morning.

To drown out our silence, her small Magnavox gave us the local NBC affiliate morning news. I didn't give it my full attention until a picture of a red Celica, with clear plastic duct taped over its rear windshield, flashed across the screen.

My face must have paled, because Grandma tilted her head and squinted her eyes. "Christopher, are you all right?"

The remote lay on the table between us, beside the stack of UNO cards. I picked it up and increased the volume.

A female newscaster was saying, "… when police pulled over the car just outside of Binghamton late last night. Carmen Alexander, a resident of Reading, Pennsylvania, called 911 when she realized he had kidnapped their five-year-old son yesterday afternoon."

The picture cut to a headshot of the man who had walked out of the men's restroom yesterday. Only in this picture the Hispanic man's eyes were darker and his black hair was messed up.

The reporter went on to say how Juan Alexander was being charged with kidnapping and grand theft auto. How police had not yet decided whether any more charges would be filed, as the five-year-old unidentified boy was gagged and tied up in the trunk of the car. How Mr. Alexander claimed he wasn't aware of a hole in the muffler that caused his son to inhale exhaust fumes for almost four straight hours.

The reporter finished by saying, "When police found the boy, he was unconscious and his pulse weak. He was rushed to Binghamton General Hospital where he's in stable condition at this time."

The picture then cut to the two news anchors. They both stared back into the camera, their eyes full of empathy. The male newscaster shook his head, started to say what a shame, but I turned off the TV.

"Christopher, what is it?"

I didn't realize it until then, but my hand holding the remote was shaking.

"I'll be right back," I said.

I slid out of the booth and left the trailer and seconds later stood in front of Moses's RV. I knocked only once—banged, really—before he answered.

"Christopher?"

"There's something wrong with me and whatever it is I want it to stop."

I said the entire sentence in one breath and then had to pause, staring back at Moses. He frowned at me.

"What are you talking about?"

I thought for a moment, tried putting it into words, but couldn't come up with anything simple enough. So I just rushed through what happened yesterday. The feeling I'd had when we stopped at Jack Murphy's place, then what I found inside. And the other feeling at the Sunoco station near Scranton, about something inside the Celica's trunk.

"I knew it, too, something was there, but I didn't do anything about it and now the kid might die."

"Okay," Moses said, "so what do you think is wrong with you?"

"Just … *this*. Those feelings I got, what the fuck were they?"

"Christopher, don't act stupid. You know exactly what they were."

"But how—"

"I don't know. Maybe … maybe Joey somehow passed it on to you."

I stood there, wanting to say more but not sure what else to say. I glanced past him into the RV, noticed my grandfather's Bible on the coffee table. When I looked back up at Moses, I couldn't seem to meet his eyes.

"Did you read Job 42?"

"Yes."

"What … what did it say?"

Moses stepped back and picked up the book, came back to the screen door and opened it. He held the Bible out to me. "You should read it. After all, it's essentially a letter to you."

Reluctant, I took the Bible from him. Held it with both hands. It felt heavier than it did before, though I knew that couldn't be possible.

I whispered, "I'm afraid of what it says."

Moses nodded slowly. "You should be."

I sat on the tiny hard bed in my trailer and stared at the picture of me and my parents. I stared for a long time, wondering what I'd tell each of them if I had the chance. But I knew just staring at the picture was putting off the inevitable. I'd wasted an hour already just sitting here, so I set the picture aside and picked up my grandfather's Bible. Opened it and flipped through to Job 42.

I stared at the first word—my name—for a very long time.

Then I began to read.

Christopher, if you are reading this, something bad has happened to either one of your parents, if not both. And I'm sure you may be asking yourself why you should even waste your time, because the past you have been told about me is certainly one filled with darkness and doubt. Perhaps you even remember the day I picked you up from school; perhaps you even resent me for my actions. What you do not know, however, is what I was feeling inside myself that day, or even why I came to get you in the first place. But before I begin with what I need to tell you, I want you to know that you are my only grandchild and I love you dearly. I always have and always will. And because of this, I fear your life may now be in danger.

I do not know exactly where to begin. I have been at this institution for nearly five years. I know I must get this message to you somehow, but writing a letter is simply out of the question, as the people in charge here read everything outgoing. Then again, you may never get this, which will mean all the effort I have put into this book is for nothing. I had to come up with some way of getting this to you without suspicion, and while rewriting the entire Old Testament by hand is odd and may certainly seem like a large waste of time, believe me when I tell you I had no other option.

While you may not believe the following (which I have come to think of as a kind of ghost story), a part of me fears that if whoever I put in charge of keeping hold of this book does his or her job, and you are truly reading this, something terrible has happened to both my son and his wife. And if this is the case and your parents are dead, then your own life is in serious trouble now as well. Why do I say this? Because a long time ago, back before I was even born, my father and three men—in their late teens at the time—did something I believe will forever haunt our bloodlines.

This happened back a little before the turn of the century. In 1897 my father had just turned seventeen. He lived in a small town in southern New York now called Bridgton. Cabins and houses and a general store—the same one that's still there on Mizner Road, I believe—were built around an area outside Elmira and slowly expanded. Nearly everybody knew each other and got along well and had no real reason to worry, except maybe about how much wood and supplies they needed for winter.

However, this was not always the case. There was a man— some called him a giant—who lived in a stone house in the woods. Nobody knew a great deal about him except the fact that he was a hermit. He kept to himself, and for everybody else that was just fine.

Then one August morning a young girl went missing. Her parents, friends, and neighbors searched everywhere but to no avail. What they found instead were pieces of her clothing spotted with blood. Some hunters, later hearing what happened to the girl, remembered spotting a black bear roaming the woods, and it was immediately assumed she had fallen victim.

Another month passed before a second girl went missing. The local constable and his men did not search long before the bear was blamed. The town already knew the bear had claimed one life, and now another, and they all agreed it needed to be stopped. A hunting party was formed of different men throughout town to go after the beast. Only two days passed before they found the black bear and shot it dead. It was brought back into town for everybody to see. *They all believed the worst was over, when in reality it had just begun.*

Christopher, what you need to understand is that even though these people may have seemed like simple folk, they were not naïve. They were God-fearing for the most part, and distrusted strangers. According to my father's journal, which he wrote concerning what took place—and which I found years later after his vicious murder —despite the bear, there was talk that the giant who lived by himself in the woods was somehow responsible. After enough of this talk circulated, the local constable went with two of his men to confront the giant. They returned empty-handed. When questioned what happened, the men claimed the giant was just lonely and that everyone should stop worrying about him before things got unruly.

A series of disappearances followed in the space of three months. First a young boy of five years; second a girl, almost sixteen. Then twins, a boy and a girl, both three years old. Something had to be done. The town was scared. Some who could afford to even moved away into Elmira. There was talk of forming a posse and going up into the woods where the giant lived. But the constable talked the men down, assuring them that the hermit was in no way responsible. Whether he knew the truth or not I cannot say. What he and his men found when they first went up to the house nobody knows. But from what my father wrote, the constable believed the giant was innocent. And in a way, perhaps he was.

For my father and his three friends, it was initially only talk. Then the day came when one of my father's friend's sisters went missing. After this they knew something needed to be done. They were young, and angry that this was happening, and wanted to make things right. They knew the giant needed to be stopped and made themselves believe they were the only ones who could do it.

Early the next morning Benjamin Myers—my father, your great-grandfather—went with Clive Bidwell, Paul Alcott, and Daniel Weiss up to the stone house in the woods. They were prepared, each carrying a rifle and knife of their own. "We were scared," my father wrote, "but none of us intended to show it; thankfully, none of us did."

When they arrived to the house the giant was gone. The house itself was small, its interior consisting of a wooden table and chair, a fireplace and a long bed against one wall. Nothing to suggest the giant had kidnapped children. As they stood looking like young men in a militia, the four of them realized they were being foolish. Clearly they had overreacted. They decided they should return to town before the giant returned home. But then, before they left, one of them noticed the sundress peeking beneath the bed.

My father wrote: "Clive began weeping before us all. We did nothing more than watch. It was clearly his sister's dress, which caused us to wonder how we would feel if it had been one of our sisters or brothers instead." While the Bidwell boy cried and the three of them stood in silence, the giant returned home. "I cannot recall which surprised us more," my father wrote, "the fact that he had come home or that he truly was a giant." The enormous size of the man did not stop Clive Bidwell, however; without hesitation he charged the giant with his knife. The giant, perhaps confused by the strangers in his home, was not prepared for the attack. Clive stabbed him repeatedly in the gut.

The rest, Christopher, I cannot tell without creating a fiction of my own. Up until that point my father's narrative was precise, but after that it became jumbled into what I can only speculate was caused by his emotions overtaking him. What I can gather is that despite being stabbed, the giant managed to throw Clive Bidwell back and attempted to advance. But someone else—my father did not say who; perhaps he was too guilty to name himself—took aim and fired, striking the giant in the throat. When he fell to the ground, all four of the boys attacked at once. They were impetuous. Using whatever weapons they had on their persons, they butchered the giant like a pack of dogs.

How long it took before they went back into town I do not

know. But when they did return, they returned heroes. The constable was not happy with the way the four had handled themselves, but everyone was so relieved the horror was over that in the end it did not matter. The stone house was open for anyone to see. It reeked of death and blood and was full of flies because my father and his three friends had strung up the giant's body from the ceiling. The constable wanted to take it down, but this was quickly met with disapproval, as everyone wanted a chance to see the monster.

The body did not hang there for long, however. The day before it was to be taken down, all four of the boys returned to the stone house. They wanted to admire what they had accomplished together, how they had stopped the evil that had plagued their town. Except when they arrived the giant's body was not alone.

From my father's journal: "There is no denying that it was a man. He wore a long dark robe and had medium-length auburn hair. His back was to us when we arrived, but as he stood in the doorway he turned around to face us. He appeared to be middle aged and was quite striking, yet his face was cold and his eyes were blacker than even the night itself.

"Dan inquired of the man who he was, as none of us recognized him. He gave us only a cold stare, without a word of response. He made us all uneasy. I suggested we leave and come back later, when the man finally did speak. Very slowly, and in a voice that did not sound quite natural, he said, 'That was my only follower and you have killed him. Not only will each of you pay for what you have done, but your blood as well, for as long as it exists.'"

And then, Christopher, my father writes that both the man and the strung-up giant disappeared. One second they were both there, the next my father blinked and they were gone. The four of them had no idea what to think, though they all admitted to being scared. They promised themselves to never speak of what happened and went back into town, to their families, to their friends, and to their lives. When the constable came and asked what happened to the body, they denied knowing, because in truth they had no clue.

Thirty years passed. My father and his friends still lived in Bridgton, as none of them ever found any reason to leave. They had watched the town grow just as they had watched themselves grow, and had decided to call the place home. It was peaceful where they were, and they took pleasure in the lives they had made. They all had wives, children, a happy and content life. Their past was something that only haunted them in their sleep. The idea of that strange experience back in the stone house—which is still standing, mind you, no one ever found the courage to tear it down—was far from their minds.

I was sixteen at the time, my sister Katherine twelve. We lived in a house near the highway that is now called Route 13. Sometimes in the winter you could go out in the backyard and see the center of Bridgton through the trees. Everything was fine, almost perfect. Except then a young interim reverend named Devin Beckett went insane. There were rumors that it had something to do with a young girl who he was involved with, but no one really knew for certain and it was probably nothing more than mere gossip anyway. But one night he went into the houses of four families, murdered the parents, and took the youngest children. He left the firstborns—who all happened to be males—alive in bed. On each of their bedroom doors he left a cross, painted in the blood of their parents. He took the youngest back to the stone house where the giant once lived before four brave boys killed him. It was there Devin Beckett kept the children, completely bound, as he went to the next house to kill the parents and kidnap the youngest. It was terrible, something that haunts me even now. How could anyone possibly sleep through such a thing?

My father and his three friends: Clive Bidwell, Paul Alcott, and Daniel Weiss. They were the fathers of the families who were slaughtered that night. Their youngest children taken to the house where Beckett kept them until the police arrived. The house was burned and they all died, every single one of them. By then the only survivors of the terror were the four firstborn sons, who during all this time were at home, either still asleep or awakened by county deputies. I was one of the sons who was awakened.

I wish I could describe to you everything that took place days after the Massacre, as the old locals probably still call it, but I neither have the time nor the energy. In fact, it took more out of me telling you this than I planned, as I have had to step away and come back to it four times already. But I hope you understand the reason I did so, why I felt the need to let you know, especially if something awful has happened to your parents.

Since the Massacre, I and the three other survivors went our separate ways. Our fathers had been friends, though we as boys only knew each other fairly well. The only survivor I was close to was Gerald Alcott. He was two years younger and went to live with some nearby neighbors since he had no other family left of his own.

I went away and joined the army. I spent a few years in the service before returning to Bridgton. Time had changed the town and the people who lived there (there was a new diner on Mizner Road, and Bud Keller opened a fishing store), but some things were still the same. Gerald still lived in town. The house where I once lived was still standing, though now it was taken over by a new family. They were not local, instead a couple from New England, and I sometimes wonder if they even knew what happened inside its walls years before. The few belongings I had taken from the house were still with the young woman I had been courting before I left. And it was this woman who I had returned to Bridgton for, and who had waited for me all this time. That woman, Christopher, was Lily Thorsen, your grandmother.

We married soon after and continued living in town. Despite its terrible history, this was where I had grown up and, like my own father, I had come to call it home. Your grandmother got pregnant and we had your father. Four years later we had your uncle. My past seemed to no longer matter, as I began a family of my own. *Gerald kept in touch, but the other two boys, James Bidwell and Richard Weiss, moved on. I heard rumors that James moved out to Oklahoma, where he got a respectable job and made a family. Then supposedly he went crazy and killed his family before killing himself. I did not believe it until I saw the article with my own eyes. A note he left claimed he saw his father.*

It was difficult to believe. I had known the man when he was young and he seemed peaceful enough, quite sane. It made no sense to me, until a month later when I started going through the boxes left over from before I went into the army. It was in one of those boxes that I found my father's journals, and it was in one of those journals that I began to understand just what happened to my parents and sister, and the rest of the families, and why.

What I can tell you and what you have probably already inferred is that it began with my father and his three friends killing the giant. Though it was agreed upon that the missing children had been sacrificed, none could say to whom, except maybe the Devil himself. And I believe that is who the man was the day my father and his three friends returned to see the dead giant, though the man claiming that the giant was his only follower does not make sense. At least it did not then. But it would help explain how he and the giant's body disappeared, and make a connection between the four murdered families. And it would explain why almost sixty years after my birth, my dead father came to visit me one early evening when I had finished mowing the lawn.

We were living in a house you visited once before during Christmas. If I remember correctly you were five, maybe six years old. One minute I was putting the John Deere away, the next I turned around to find my father standing directly behind me. He appeared just as I remembered him, wearing the same pajamas he had had on the night he was murdered. Only something was different about him. His eyes were completely black, and immediately I remembered what my father had written in his journal. I stayed completely still; I did not even blink. I had no idea what to say or do. It was as if time had ceased all motion at that moment. Everything became silent and went still and the only people left in the world were my father and myself. When he spoke, his voice was not his own.

"Hello, Stephen. How have you been, my son?" I did not answer him. I knew this was not my father and was instead the Devil, who had promised revenge long ago. He said, "You must love your son and his wife very much. And your grandchild. What is his name?" I refused to answer. "It doesn't matter, really. In the end, they will all suffer." Finally I did find the courage to speak; I asked him if he was the Devil. His already grim face seemed to grow even grimmer, and he said, "I am not. My name is Samael." When I asked him what he wanted, he said, "What I want makes no difference and does not concern you. What concerns you, however, is the choice I am willing to offer. Something will happen to your son and his family, something that will kill them all. But I am willing to offer you a choice." Hesitantly, I asked what the choice was. "Simply to spare the living from the dead. You can choose your son and his wife and sacrifice your grandchild. Or you can choose your grandchild to live instead." I took a deep breath and asked Samael if this was the same choice he gave James Bidwell. He actually looked both surprised and pleased. He told me, "That is none of your concern. Your only concern now is the choice I have given you." I asked what would happen if I made no choice and was told that then all three lives—your father, your mother, and you—would perish painfully.

Since I have been in this place I have done much reading, much more than I would ever have thought possible. I have read the great classics—Homer, Virgil, Chaucer, Milton, Shakespeare, Dickens—and I have dipped into reading works by many great philosophers, such as Aristotle, Voltaire, Descartes, and Kant. There is one work in particular written by an English philosopher named Charles Westis who dealt much with life and death and the idea of human will. He said, "In every man's life there comes a time when churchyards yawn and his fate becomes dependent upon a single choice." If that were true, I would have thought marrying Lily Thorsen would decide my fate. But that evening with Samael posing as my dead father, I knew that this choice right then was it, when churchyards yawned so to speak.

I have done research on Samael. According to Jewish mythology, he is one of the angels of death. I did not know this then, but what would it matter even if I did? I suppose now that if you are indeed reading this, Christopher, then what Samael told me came true. It was a difficult decision to make, one that haunts me even now, but in the back of my mind I kept seeing you at the house when you visited, the innocence in your eyes not yet infected by the world. In a way, it probably would have been better to make the other choice, but I simply could not, because deep down inside I knew you had to live.

After I told Samael my decision he simply vanished, leaving me with the knowledge of what I had done. Later that week the pressure and guilt became too much. I couldn't stand it anymore, knowing that I had damned my son and daughter-in-law. That was why I came to Pennsylvania. That was why I took you out of school and tried to get away. Why the gun? Because if Samael came back I intended to stop him whichever way I could, even though a part of me knew bullets would prove useless. Truthfully, I did not know what I was doing. I did not know when the time would come for your parents to die and you to be left all alone. The only thing I knew was that no matter what happened, since I was your grandfather, and since my father was your great-grandfather, it would happen to you someday too. The more I thought about that, the more I questioned whether I had done the right thing. Because putting death on one side and making an irrevocable choice like the one I had on the other, I was not sure which was the lesser of two evils.

The state police ended up stopping me. I doubt you can even remember what happened. It does not matter anyhow. There was *much confusion, much shouting, and you had begun to cry. I did my best to comfort you. Naturally I did not tell them the truth about why I took you away. I did not tell them how I made a deal with the Devil for your life. Nor did I tell them that I wanted to somehow make you understand.*

I hope you do not think me crazy, Christopher. I am sure to everyone else I am nothing more than a madman. Even your father refuses to speak to me, for I have tried many times to contact him letting him know about Samael. I cannot say I blame him, especially with my own knowledge that I am responsible for his eventual death. But perhaps I am crazy; perhaps what happened was all in my mind. Then if this is so, how can you explain what happened to James Bidwell and Richard Weiss? Just last year in my research I found that Richard went into a daycare and killed thirteen children and employees before taking his own life. I can only imagine Samael coming to him as his dead father. I am not certain of his choices, but I have a good idea which he made. His wife and two sons, at this present moment, are still alive.

I wish I could tell you this in person. I wish I could see how you have grown up, what kind of man you have become. I am certain I would be proud of whoever you are. At this moment as I write you are in your eleventh year, and I wonder just how many more you will have left. Not before you die, but instead before the time comes when churchyards yawn and you will have to make that choice. So why did I want you to see this and know? Because when the time comes I want you to be prepared and not taken aback like the others before you.

Again, I do not know the entire story, or else I would do my best to tell you. I only know as much as I do and I hope that is enough. If you decide to disbelieve me, that is your decision. But I want you to understand at least one thing: I did what I did because I love you. I made that choice without hesitation because I knew you were special and worth it. So please, do what you think is best. Again, I love you.

CHAPTER TWENTY-ONE

THE CREMATORIUM WAS LOCATED in the far corner of Elmira Cemetery. Hidden by pine trees and bushes, the red brick building had only two long windows facing front, with a steel door between them. Its tall narrow chimney—located behind the building—was coughing dark smoke when we first arrived, and for an instant I wondered if that was from Joey.

Moses went inside alone. By then the smoke had stopped its ascent to the clear afternoon sky.

I stood leaning against the parked Metro and stared out across the cemetery. I couldn't help but remember the day my parents were buried, how I'd looked out over the vast array of tombstones and thought about how meaningless life really was. People lived their entire lives, working nearly every day, and when they died what else did they have to show for it but a stone tablet with their name engraved six feet above their decomposing bodies? It was sad, the revelation that crept into my mind during my parents' funeral, and while I knew it was mostly true I also realized what else my parents had left behind, and it saddened me even more.

The door opened and closed behind me. Footsteps

approached. When I turned I saw Moses walking slowly with his head down. In his hands was a silver box.

I opened my mouth to speak—maybe ask him if he was okay—but decided not to say anything. We just stood there on either side of the car, silent. Finally he cradled the box in the crook of his arm, reached into his pocket, and tossed me his keys.

"You're going to have to drive," he said, not looking at me. "I don't think I can right now."

Once inside the car, I asked, "Where to?"

"I don't care. Just drive."

Not familiar at all with the area, I figured just driving wouldn't be a problem. I maneuvered us out of the cemetery and then onto the main road.

After a couple minutes of silence, of Moses just sitting there staring down at the silver box in his lap, I cleared my throat.

"Aren't you going to ask me?"

His eyes still downcast, he said, "Ask you what?"

"If I read it. What my grandfather wrote."

"Did you?"

"You know I did."

"Do you believe it?"

I kept my eyes on the cars ahead of me, unsure whether I wanted to answer him.

"Well?"

"Yes," I said. "I ... I think so."

Silence was his only reply. It was all I needed to know that my answer was good enough for him.

"So now what?"

"Hmm?"

"The thirty-four people. How do we save them?"

"Oh," Moses said, and I knew he was off in a world of his own, probably trying to keep memories of him and Joey away from one of those doors in his mind. "Well, thirty-four is a relatively big number. Our best bet is to try to find a place where that many people or more are going to be."

"But that could be anywhere. In a store, in a movie theater, at a park. Even in a McDonald's."

Moses said, "I know," but that was it. He continued staring down at his lap.

There was a question then that came to mind, but one I wasn't sure I wanted to ask. The real clincher in Job 42 for me was my grandfather's mention of Samael, the angel Joey said had taken and tried to kill him.

"Moses," I said, as we stopped at a traffic light.

"Hmm?"

"What about Samael? How … how do we stop him?"

The light turned green. Traffic pulled ahead. Beside me, Moses was silent. I glanced over at him to make sure he was still with me. The box still rested in his lap, but his eyes were no longer downcast. Instead he was staring out his window, and when he spoke, his voice was small and soft.

"I have no idea."

Sarah sat in the same lawn chair outside my trailer she'd been sitting in the day we went on our picnic—only this time there wasn't a cooler between her Keds.

I said, "Hey," surprised to see her.

"Hi." She managed a smile and stood up slowly. I almost stepped forward to help her but knew she'd get angry, so I stayed put. Then, once she was standing, she glanced down the drive toward the Rec House. "I thought you said you were going back home."

"I thought I was."

She nodded but didn't say anything, seemed to avoid my eyes. "Mind taking a walk?"

We walked in the field behind the trailer park, the one with the deserted picnic tables and pair of volleyball poles. Neither of us spoke but only seemed to enjoy the nice day and soft breeze. Finally Sarah stopped and sat at a table that didn't look like it had been a complete target for birds. I lowered myself on the other side.

"If it's all right with you," she said, "I want to start over."

I just nodded.

The smile on her face only lasted a few seconds. Then she tilted her head and frowned at me. "What's wrong?"

"What do you mean?"

"Something's bothering you. What is it?"

I wanted to tell her everything. I wanted to tell her about Joey and Moses and what my grandfather wrote. I wanted to tell her the real reason I was helping Moses. Not because of the thirty-four lives or whatever Samael had planned, but because my own life was in danger and I was scared and wanted to live. It was selfish, but I was a selfish person. Probably even more so now than before my parents died, even though I tried fooling myself that I'd changed. I wasn't like Joey or Moses. I couldn't just put my life on the line for other people, especially strangers.

"Nothing," I said. "It's just been a weird week."

She nodded, her blue eyes questioning, and I wondered just how much she believed. Then she surprised me by asking, "Can you tell me about your girlfriend?"

I hesitated. "What do you want to know?"

"Just anything, I guess."

I wasn't sure if this was her way of making conversation, but if so I didn't mind. Even if she considered herself trailer trash, I didn't. I still saw her as the girl I'd met in the Rec House, the one reading Herman Melville just for fun. Her favorite movie *Pretty Woman*, her favorite actress Julia Roberts, the most recent CD in her player one of Coldplay's. The girl who couldn't decide between mango strawberry and water-melon cherry as her favorite bubblegum flavor.

"There really isn't much to tell. Her name was Melanie. We dated off and on for two years. And then ... she got pregnant."

"She didn't want the baby?"

I actually had to think about it for a moment. "I never really asked her. I just knew I didn't want to be a father. I mean, I'm eighteen years old. I was planning on going to college in the fall. We both were. We just ... we couldn't be parents."

A part of me thought I should feel uncomfortable talking about Mel like this, but for some reason I didn't. Maybe I was just relieved to get everything out in the open. I hadn't told anyone what happened between us until today.

We were both silent for the longest time. Then finally she took a deep breath and began speaking in a soft whisper.

"His name was Justin. I never found out where he lives, and even if he told me I'm not sure I could believe him anyway. He usually passed through here and spent a few nights in his van twice a year. I remember looking at his license plate one year and seeing it was from Maryland, then the next year—I swear to God—New Jersey. My dad even gave him a special rate for it. He seemed nice enough and respectful and would even help out when it was needed.

"He was twenty-five, which isn't too old, but I'm only sixteen and ... well, he was always nice to me. That's really the thing. He was always nice. He always made me feel special, even the few times I saw him. He'd been coming almost every summer for about five years, I think. Anyway, I never really had a boyfriend, and he was just so handsome and things had been so crappy ever since my mom died that I ... I needed someone. And he was there. Every night I would come over and see him and we'd just talk and sometimes smoke pot and then ... then one night we started fooling around and one thing led to another."

"Did he rape you?" The words left my mouth before I even had a chance to stop them.

She shook her head. "No, he didn't. I mean, I guess it could be considered statutory rape, but I … I wanted him to. I wanted to feel even more special and he did that for me."

I asked her if she knew where he was now.

"I don't know. I never did find out where he comes from or what he does. Heck, he's probably married with kids or something, and was trying to get into my pants from the beginning. It wouldn't surprise me."

"Does he know?"

"He left the day after it happened, and two weeks after that I found out I was pregnant. He hasn't been back since and I don't think he will any time soon."

"Your dad doesn't know it was him, does he?"

She shook her head again, this time very slowly. Her eyes were now focused on the line of trees. "He flipped out at first, which I guess was what I expected. But he's managed to come to terms with it. Even John has. For some reason they just don't get along anymore, they're constantly fighting, but when it comes to me and this baby they actually cool down. It's almost like this baby keeps them civil."

A question came to my lips, but I forced it away. It was a question I couldn't ask, one I would never ask.

And so we sat there on the picnic table, staring across at each other, neither of us saying a word but communicating just the same. I told her with my eyes that I didn't judge her and with her eyes she told me she didn't judge me, and as trite as that sounds, I knew at that moment we would be friends forever.

I'd told John Porter yesterday I couldn't go with him and his friends to crash that pre-graduation party, that it was cool of him to offer but thanks anyway. Then, for some reason, I mentioned it to Moses and got the surprise of my life when he said I should go.

"Are you sure?" I'd stopped over at his RV after my grandmother made dinner. It was almost seven o'clock. "I mean, wouldn't that be a bad idea?"

"Not at all. Right now we have no leads anyhow. Besides, the interaction will be good. You'll get a sense of who these kids are, and maybe even get an idea of what will happen. Who knows, you might even get another feeling."

The prospect didn't thrill me but I realized he had a point, so about two hours later I crossed Half Creek Road and found John and four of his friends in the garage. They had started the party early, as they sat listening to Jane's Addiction and passing around a joint. John noticed me first, said, "Chris, I thought you said you couldn't make it," and offered me a hit.

John made quick introductions. There was Rich, a tall kid wearing a Yankee's baseball cap, his ear stuck to a cell phone; Chad, who was really tanned and had spots of acne on his face; Sean, whose long brown hair he kept in a ponytail; and Tyler, the shortest of them all, who stood about five feet five inches but made up for it by obviously lifting weights every minute he could, as his biceps looked bigger than my own thighs. All of them except Sean wore faded jeans and T-shirts. Sean had on a pair of frayed khaki shorts.

"And this," John said, motioning to the car parked in the middle of the garage, "is my baby. Found her in the junkyard three years ago when she was just a pile of shit, but look at her now."

"She still is a pile of shit," Sean muttered. John made a face and gave him the finger, before leaning down to the car's hood

and cooing, "Don't listen to him, honey, he's just jealous."
Everyone sniggered.

I'd already noticed the Firebird while walking past the
garage, but I'd never gotten a close look until now. Under the
lights I saw just how much work John had put into it. The dark
cherry finish made it look as if it had just gotten off the
assembly line. In my mind I saw him working nights and weekends, finding used parts, ordering new ones, spending a few
hours here, a few hours there, until all the time and effort paid
off into one beauty of a car.

"Wanna hear about it?" John asked me, a bright grin on his
face (which was probably more from the weed), and Tyler
muttered, "Aw shit, not again." John spun around, both middle
fingers blazing, and said, "Shut your traps, motherfuckers."
Then he turned back to me and placed his hand gently on the
hood, grinning again.

"Sure," I said.

"Her name's Bambi. She's a '76 Pontiac Firebird Trans Am.
Her engine's a 455 with a V-8 I managed to take from a beat-
up Bonneville. Four-speed manual, with two hundred horse-
power at thirty-five hundred RPMs. Original vinyl bucket
seats, and this baby right here—"

He began to caress the shake-hood scoop, started to say
something else, when Chad interrupted him.

"Blah, blah, blah," he said, rolling his eyes. He pulled out a
can of Old Milwaukee and popped the top. "You don't even
know if this bitch is gonna run."

John stepped back, crossed his arms over his chest. "I don't
even know why I'm friends with you fuckers." When Tyler said
it was because of the good hash, he said, "Oh yeah, that's right.
But who's up for it, huh? Who wants to do the first three-way
with me and Bambi?"

There didn't look to be any volunteers. Chad handed me a
can of beer. Everyone was silent for a few moments, before first

Sean started laughing, then Chad, then the rest. Even I did, though I wasn't quite sure what was so funny.

"Fuck you all," John muttered, then glanced at me. "Chris, you wanna ride shotgun?"

"Sure," I said, grinning for no apparent reason, and downed my beer.

Minutes later we'd all split up. Tyler, Rich, and Sean piled into Chad's Jeep outside. I got into Bambi the Firebird's passenger seat. The seats were indeed vinyl, though I couldn't imagine them being originals. Then John got in, hesitated before putting in the key. He glanced at me, said, "Here goes everything," and started the engine. It roared to life.

John nodded, a wide smile on his face. I noticed one of his lower teeth was chipped. He put the car in gear, revved the engine once more, and said, "Hope you're ready, dude. It's gonna be one wild night."

CHAPTER TWENTY-TWO

THE PARTY WAS at a house in Breesport, about fifteen minutes away, an overlarge two-story house that sat on a hill overlooking the road. John said it belonged to this girl Denise Rowe, whose parents were away and wouldn't be back until Saturday.

Cars were lined up on both sides of the extended driveway, some parked awkwardly on the lawn itself. John parked beside Chad's Jeep and got out of the car. He immediately started to say something to his four friends when he noticed what had grabbed their attention. A black utility van was parked on the other side of the driveway. Rich said, "Is that—" and Sean nodded his head, answering, "I think so." Then John, walking up beside them, muttered, "What the fuck is he doing here?"

At that moment explosive laughter came from just in front of the house, and someone shouted, "You're all fucking assholes!" Seconds later two kids were heading up the drive toward us. John and his friends moved away from the black van. One of the kids was soaking wet, his hair dripping.

"Howdy, faggots," Chad said. He raised his can of beer in a salute, and the one—they were both dressed in black—

muttered, "Fuck you, you piece of shit." Chad, smiling, glanced back at us. He winked and said, "Clever."

The van's doors slammed shut, the engine coughed to life, and then we were all bathed in the red glow of taillights. When the van backed up, the kid in the passenger seat gave us the finger. Chad raised his beer again, sounded like he was about to say something else, but then the driver attempted to peel out onto the road.

"That was weird," Rich said after a moment. "What the hell were they doing here?"

John shrugged, lighting himself a cigarette. "Who the fuck cares. They should know better anyway."

We turned then, the tense moment or two passing, and started down the driveway. It seemed those kids in the van were forgotten at once, as spirits again were high. Rich started telling a Polish joke he said he read online, and as he talked, I asked Sean what that was all about. When he shrugged, saying it was nothing, I asked him about Denise Rowe.

"Denise? Oh, she's just one of the many stuck-up bitches in our class. Really, none of us were invited to this little shindig of hers, but fuck it. Look at all these cars here already and tell me anybody's gonna give a shit."

The night was cool and cloudy, and the music and talking and laughter coming from both inside the house and around back increased as we neared. There were even some kids out front, standing around with blue plastic cups in their hands. One of them, I realized, was responsible for drenching that one kid in black.

"I hope she has a good fucking table for beer-pong," Chad mumbled. He and Rich both carried twelve packs of Old Milwaukee. Rich, having just finished his lame joke, already had one open. Chad lit a cigarette.

I counted about thirty-some cars and trucks parked everywhere.

"Anyone see Jeremy's Eclipse yet?" Sean asked, and everyone except me started laughing. Sean noticed I was left out of the joke and said, "We pulled one major-ass prank today."

"Hell yeah," Chad said. "There's this guy we've gone to school with for like ever. He's a real prick. We all used to be cool but then he got in with the jock crowd and became a real toolbag, and he always acts like he's about to kick our asses for no fucking reason or anything, just because he thinks he's hot shit. So anyway, I came up with this idea—"

"Bullshit you came up with the idea," Tyler said.

Chad gave him the finger. "Okay, we *all* had this idea to do something real badass, you know? And so we had this vanity plate made up, cost like fifty bucks or something, but fuck was it worth it."

We were almost to the house now. The kids standing out front were passing what at first looked like a cigarette around. Then, seconds later, the breeze picked up and the scent of marijuana drifted our way. The group stopped their conversation; they were now staring at us. I realized John and the rest of his friends were staring back, and, thinking of those two kids who were obviously denied, wondered just how welcome here we really were.

I asked what the vanity plate said, which seemed to break the stares. Tyler grinned and said, "Get this. We made it so it spelled I-L-U-V-C-zero-C-K. Fuck, it was classic. We put it on this morning first period and he fucking didn't even realize it when he left after school. The bastard's probably been driving around with the thing all day!"

We stepped up onto the porch, heading for the front door, when one of the guys on the lawn said, "Hey, it's a five dollar cover."

"So's the rate to fuck your mother," Sean said, giving them the finger, and laughing, we entered the party.

So maybe we weren't invited, but that didn't seem to matter once we were inside. A few glares were directed our way but nothing to make me worry that we'd get in a fight anytime soon, and eventually everyone started splitting off, going their separate ways. Chad asked me if I played beer-pong, and when I told him yes, he grinned and said, "You're my partner then."

We found the basement stairs and headed down. Here there was a widescreen TV, billiard and ping-pong tables. Beer cans already littered the table, as people were lined up throwing the plastic ball back and forth at the cups set up in a triangle. It looked as if three guys were playing the drinking version of Cutthroat, where with every shot they missed, they had to take a drink. A dozen or so others were on the couches talking and watching really nothing on the screen, as someone with a short attention span had control of the remote and kept switching the channel every few seconds.

"If you see anything you like, you tell me," Chad said, indicating three blondes wearing midriffs and short skirts. They stood by the wall watching the beer-pong game. Each of them held a Mike's Hard Lemonade.

"You know them?"

"Well, I know *of* them. But really, they're all just snotty bitches. Almost everyone here ranks in the top of the class, or their parents have a lot of money, so that makes them popular. Or maybe they're jocks. You know how it is, just fucking bullshit. But hey, I wouldn't mind banging a snotty bitch any day, you know what I mean?"

We walked up to the ping-pong table and Chad cleared his throat dramatically.

"All right, you lazy fuckers," he said, "who's ready to get their asses kicked?"

Both Chad and I had won three games straight and were working on our fourth playing two of the snotty blonde bitches —their names were Traci and Kelly, though they actually didn't seem too stuck-up, and Kelly kept flirting with me—when I got the feeling.

By this time someone had come downstairs and made an announcement for everyone to shut the fuck up. When all was pretty much quiet (even the TV, still crawling through channels, got muted), he introduced a kid named Melvin Dumstorf, who he claimed was *the* best goddamned white freestyle rapper in Chemung County. "Come on, Melvin!" he shouted. "Show us your shit!" A beat was put on the stereo, and while at first Melvin didn't look like he was going to do anything—he was a small kid, in jeans and a bright green polo-shirt, the collar up, his blond hair curly and his face now red—he started into something at once. It was kind of hard to keep up at first, but that was probably because I'd had at least six beers and three hits off the joint. Still, the kid sounded too well rehearsed, which I mentioned to Chad, who immediately began chanting, "Re-hearsed! Re-hearsed! Re-hearsed!" to which others started calling out random words, anything from vagina to banana, from vending machine to canoe, and Melvin Dumstorf actually managed to keep up, his lines witty and oftentimes hilarious. But then, after about five minutes of the same irritating beat, the kid's rapping became annoying and the same kid that had announced him before said, "All right, Melvin, now show us your ninja skills!"

Melvin gave him a look, said, "Hell, no," but the kid announcer wouldn't let up. He started chanting, "Nin-ja skills! Nin-ja skills! Nin-ja skills!" getting everyone else to join in. Finally one of the pool cues was handed to Melvin and again he just stood there, like he wasn't going to do anything, until suddenly he started spinning the cue around, the stick going so fast it was almost impossible to see. The crowd exploded into cheering and clapping, and then the stick was taken away and he was given three knives.

Chad nudged me, said, "Eminem here is fucking crazy."

But we watched for a minute or so as Melvin juggled the knives. He put one in his mouth and then balanced the two other knives on his arms, the end of their handles resting in the crook of his elbows. He held them both there, his arms at ninety degree angles, looking like he had his hands up. He turned around slowly, for everyone to see, then dropped his arms. Gravity pulled the knives down, their blades racing for the plush carpet, and Melvin caught them at the last moment, dropped the knife out of his mouth, caught it with his foot, then carefully kicked it into the air, began juggling all three again.

"I swear to God," Chad said, as we turned back to our game, "some circus is missing its clown."

So then we were playing again, and Traci had just sunk the ball in my cup. I had grabbed it and was draining the warm beer inside, when all at once I realized something bad was happening upstairs. I set the empty cup back on the table. I looked around. I felt buzzed, and thought that was the feeling, but knew at the same time it wasn't. It was the same sensation I'd had at Jack Murphy's place; the same one I'd had at the gas station where I'd seen the Celica.

"Chris, you okay, man?" Chad was more buzzed than me, plus a little high, but he still actually seemed good enough to know something was up. He stood there, holding the ping-pong ball out to me because it was my turn. I just stared back at him, my mouth opened, as if asking whether he felt it too.

Then before I even had a chance to say anything, someone came running down the stairs. Nearly everyone glanced up; even Melvin Domstorf stopped his juggling act. Rich had taken two steps at a time and then stopped at the bottom. He scanned the entire basement until he spotted us and waved us over.

"What is it?" Chad asked, over the continuous beat and the few people who were still talking.

"Fucking Jeremy," Rich called, nearly out of breath, and Chad didn't hesitate, he dropped the ball on the table and started forward. I followed. Seconds later we were upstairs and headed toward the front door. The music was still pumping, especially loud in the living room, where the expensive chairs and couch and coffee table had been moved so that the kids had space to dance.

Right before we walked outside we passed the stairs leading to the second floor—and the pang of ice shot through my soul again, trying to direct me up the steps. I hesitated, actually shivered, and glanced up there.

Chad shouted, "Hurry up, Chris," and I kept going forward.

A few people were at the top of the driveway. Rich got into a jog that increased to a sprint. Both Chad and I matched his pace the best we could. Then we were there, standing with John and Tyler and Sean and two other kids I didn't know but who didn't look as if they were at the top of the preppy scale. Even in the dark I saw how flushed John's face had become. Actual tears brimmed in his eyes. At first I didn't understand why until Chad whispered, "Holy fuck," and I looked at the Firebird.

Someone sure went at it hard and without any care at all, except maybe with the hope to get back at John Porter and his friends for what they'd done to him. All the windows were busted out. The tires were slashed. The dark cherry finish had been desecrated by something sharp. There was hardly a space that hadn't been destroyed, except what had been scrawled near the front, right under the shake-hood scoop.

Rich muttered, "That fucking son of a bitch."

John stood motionless, staring down at his baby. I'd tried imagining before just how much time and effort he'd put into this car and couldn't come up with anything then, but now I saw how much it hurt him, how much it shattered him inside. Three years, day and night, all gone.

One of the kids I didn't know shook his head. "Those assholes have got no fucking respect."

I'd assumed that their old friend Jeremy was involved, but obviously there was more, most likely Jeremy's *compadres*, too. I wondered just how much bad blood there was between all of them, how some simple prank could be retaliated with something as terrible and destructible as this.

But the destruction only went so deep. What had been written on the hood went even deeper. Carved in long straight letters, someone had written this:

YOUR MOMMA MIGHT BE DEAD
BUT SHE STILL GIVES GREAT HEAD

For a moment no one spoke. The only sounds were the faint music from the house and the infrequent traffic out on the road. John continued staring down at what was left of Bambi. His face was still flushed. Tears were still in his eyes but he hardly seemed to notice.

Tyler placed his hand on John's shoulder. Didn't say anything.

Finally John acknowledged the tears and wiped his face. He looked at each of us, then turned to the kids I didn't know. "When did they leave?" he asked, his voice low and steady.

"Like five minutes ago. We just got here and saw them finishing up."

"And who did that?" Pointing at the words.

"Who do you think?"

John nodded, more relaxed than I could have imagined,

and turned back to the car. "Chad, get your Jeep started. We're going after the fuckers." Then to the two new kids: "And Frank, about graduation, if we get out of this thing in one piece, I think we should do what we talked about. Really give those assholes something to remember."

Everyone was silent for another moment. An image flashed through my mind the space of a heartbeat, completely unbidden, but before I could even blink Chad had begun moving toward his Jeep, his keys already in hand. John, Rich, and Sean followed. I started to take a step forward, too, but Tyler shook his head and said, "This ain't your fight, dude," and turned and followed his friends.

I watched as they climbed in. John sat in the passenger seat, silent and staring ahead, as Chad backed out and pulled onto the road. I wondered just what was going through his mind. I thought maybe I could sense it but I couldn't. Instead I still had that feeling, that ice in my soul pulling me back to the house.

And so I turned.

Stared at the brightly lit house, at the windows on the second floor. I knew the one on the far right was where I had to go, the only window whose room was dark inside. Whatever was happening, I didn't have much time before it was over.

CHAPTER TWENTY-THREE

SOMEONE HAD SPLIT a beer on the carpet just inside the front door.

A brunette in tight jeans knelt over the puddle with a roll of paper towels, while a lanky redheaded kid with a goatee leaned watching against the wall. Neither of them said a word to each other, but still I knew what was happening between them. I knew their names (the guy Bobby, the girl Ashley), their birthdays (his in August, hers in March), their favorite colors (green, yellow), everything. I knew that Bobby was pissed at Ashley for talking to a guy named Tom a few minutes ago out by the pool. He had stalked off when he saw the two of them, Ashley with her hand on Tom's arm, laughing at something he'd just said. She saw Bobby take off and followed, calling after him to wait up, but he kept going. Through the kitchen, through the living room, past the bathroom where kids were inside doing lines of cocaine. The music accompanied the rage beating in his head. Then he stumbled and dropped his cup of beer. He stared down at it, muttered, "Aw fuck, look what you made me do," and Ashley had taken it as an opportunity. She stopped him, put her hand to his face and told him that there was nothing going on between her and Tom, that they were just friends, that she loved Bobby with all her heart —and how really, in her soul, it was all a lie.

How I knew all of this I had no clue, just as Ashley now finished dabbing up the mess, I had no idea how I knew what she was going to say next.

"See, Bobby," she said, standing up and touching his arm, "everything—"

"Can be fixed," I whispered.

Neither of them had noticed me until then. So far I'd been just another faceless kid at the party, just another horny teenager trying to get lucky before graduation came and this uninhibited life of sex and drugs and alcohol came to an end. But now that I spoke and called attention to myself, I'd invaded their little space, whatever privacy they had, and Bobby didn't look happy about it at all.

"What the fuck did you say?"

For a moment I almost told him. About how I knew their names, how many times they'd made out and had sex in their relationship so far and would until they broke up in the next seventeen days, how many times Ashley threw up a week after eating her meals. About how the only reason I knew what his girlfriend was going to say was because it had been my mom's favorite saying.

"Nothing," I said, shaking my head, and when I turned and started up the steps I heard him mumble something under his breath. He wanted to kick my ass, wanted to shove his foot right up my crack, but then Ashley intervened and told him don't, to just let it go. I ignored them and continued upstairs.

The lights were on in the hallway. The carpet was white, the wallpaper baby blue. Pictures hung between each closed door. The Rowes were a handsome family, Mr. Rowe looking to be in his early fifties, with a strong chin and intelligent eyes, his wife probably in her forties, her face well rounded and her dark hair thick and long. Denise, their only daughter, was obviously either seventeen or eighteen now, but the pictures along the wall showed her throughout the years. One when she was about four years old, standing in a white dress beside a tree; another when she was in middle school, her face a little pudgy as she smiled and flashed braces; another still when she had reached high school, wearing some kind of formal black dress before her prom or homecoming—she'd had lost the pudginess in her face, had lost the braces, and had become a rather attractive girl.

That chill became an ice pick and pierced my soul. I turned toward the source: the only room with its lights out at the end of the hallway, its door closed. I knew without a doubt who it belonged to.

I started forward, realizing that whatever was happening had already begun and I might be too late to stop it, when I heard low moaning and panting coming from the door on my right. I stopped. Thought immediately about Grant Evans and why I'd beat the shit out of him in front of everyone during lunch.

I turned and opened the door.

There were only two of them. The lights were on and he was taking her from behind, and while her moans sounded like she was in pain I could see from the contortions on her face she was in ecstasy. With every hard thrust he gave, her large breasts jiggled back and forth. I didn't share the same connection as I did with the couple downstairs, so I had no idea who they were. But then I noticed the guy was starting to look over at me and I quickly said, "Sorry, wrong room," before closing the door.

I continued on to Denise Rowe's bedroom. A few feet before her door I stopped. I reached for the knob—and once I touched it I saw the girl in my mind, I saw her entire life, and I knew just what I was going to find once I opened the door. A part of me wanted to shout for someone to call an ambulance, to call 911, but I kept telling myself it was impossible for me to know for certain, so I opened the door and stepped inside.

I smelled perfume and flowers and at first I couldn't find the switch on the wall. When I did, three gold-painted lamps came on simultaneously, each in separate corners. I saw her at once on her bed, her body motionless among the array of stuffed Winnie the Poohs and Piglets.

"Denise," I whispered, and started forward.

She lay on her back. Her eyes were closed and her mouth was open. She wasn't dead yet; her chest moved almost imperceptibly, reminding me of Joey in his deathbed. Then, after a few more steps, I saw the brown plastic bottle resting just outside her opened hand—and I knew it was empty and that she didn't have much time.

I quickly backed out of the room and sprinted to the door I'd opened only moments earlier. I banged on it hard, shouted, "Call 911, someone's overdosed!" and ran back to Denise's bedroom.

Her chest still rose and fell, but it was happening now even slower than before. I approached her bed, unsure of what to do next. I thought about the fastest way to make her throw up when I realized she should be awake first, so I sat on the bed and leaned over her, slapping her cheek to try to wake her up.

She only moaned and turned her head away.

Footsteps sounded at the door, and a low harsh voice said, "What the fuck is your problem?" When I looked up I saw it was the guy who'd been railing the blonde. He was obviously some jock, looked like he played football with a chiseled face and gel in his short highlighted hair. He had his jeans on, wore sandals with no socks, and was in the process of buttoning his silk designer shirt when he saw Denise.

"Call 911," I said. "Now."

He stood staring for a just moment longer, his eyes wide,

then seemed to forget about his shirt and disappeared. I heard him shouting something out in the hallway and then my attention was back on Denise. I slapped her face again, not too hard but not too soft, and I tried talking to her, tried getting her to come to. At that moment I had no clue how many Valium had been in the bottle, but I knew it was enough to stop her heart.

"Denise, come on, wake up." I stared down into her face. Her skin was soft and creamy, and the place where I'd slapped her was turning red. Her mouth was still open and I could hear her breathing, but it was faint and seemed to be getting even fainter. "Come on, Denise. Goddamn it, wake up. Wake up!"

She wouldn't respond and just lay there, already lifeless in my arms. I opened my mouth and started to ask her why, when I suddenly knew the answer.

I'd known the instant I stepped into her bedroom.

Her parents were loving but strict, and as all good parents went, they only wanted what was best for their daughter. After all, that was why they'd paid more to have her transferred to Elmira High School, where Mr. Rowe had attended so many years ago and which he believed would be the best place for his daughter. But still, no matter how much and how hard Denise tried, it was never good enough in their eyes. They were the Rowes, one of the wealthiest and most respected families in the county, and their daughter was either going to be a lawyer or a doctor, no ifs ands or buts about it. Denise, while she appreciated her parents' enthusiasm about her future, wanted to be a social worker, a topic she had regrettably brought up one night two years ago and which resulted in her parents flipping out. Later, when she reviewed the events in her mind, she thought they would have reacted better had she told them she'd become pregnant by a heroin junkie.

Five months ago she was accepted into Cornell University, her father's alma mater, and every day they told her how proud they were of her. Despite their varying views in the past and her foolish idea of social work, her parents had forgiven Denise and now thought they knew everything there was to know about their daughter's life—when, like most parents, they hardly knew the truth. And the truth was ever since their spat about her future career choices, she'd begun hating them, wanting to do whatever she could to hurt them. She'd begun to let her grades, which were normally very high, slip on purpose, as she began hanging out with what her parents would no doubt call the wrong crowd. She started going to parties where she drank and smoked pot and had sex. She was having the time of her life, until just last week when she learned that because she failed her History final she would not be graduating and would have to take summer school. She'd been so flustered and desperate she had actually considered asking her teacher, old Mr. Granato with the harelip, if he would pass her if she gave him a blowjob. But in the end she had chickened out and went home, where she cried herself to sleep. So far she had kept it from her parents, even when they hugged her goodbye before leaving for her father's business trip, and she knew what kind of wrath she would be forced to bear once they returned and found out.

So Denise Rowe, believing she had no options left, decided to take the easy way out. Have a large party, invite all the popular kids, then pop an entire bottle of pills while it was happening, and not only would she not have to face her parents, but then she would forever be remembered.

But it wasn't her time just yet and that was why I was here, why I'd been called to this particular room on the second floor of this particular house. I sensed the sadness and desperation in her soul, and I knew that deep down Denise Rowe did not want to die.

Footsteps sounded again at the door. Only this time it wasn't the jock with the sandals and expensive shirt, but a girl wearing a black halter-top and glasses. She paused in the doorway, her eyes finding Denise on the bed, and her hands went immediately to her face. She started screaming, "*Oh God Denise no not Denise my God!*"

"Hey!" I shouted at her, wanting to break her focus on Denise, and when the girl blinked at me, I asked her if anyone had called an ambulance yet. She nodded, her body beginning to shake, and said, "Josh did, yeah. They—they should be here soon."

I turned my attention back to Denise and slapped her face again, told her she had to wake up, told her she couldn't die just yet. And my attention was so trained on waking Denise and trying to keep her alive that when the girl came and sat down on the bed and took her friend's hand, I didn't even notice.

The paramedics arrived ten minutes later. And with the paramedics came the police.

By then news of what happened had spread throughout the party. Maybe a dozen people came upstairs and poked in their heads, some asking if Denise was okay, others clearly blitzed out of their minds and wanting only to see a possible dead girl. One pothead with long dark hair wrapped in a ponytail actually started laughing and said, "Yo, that's fucking awesome," before one of the girls called him a jerk and pushed him out of the room. Mostly all who stayed were Denise's closest friends, one who even said she was a trained lifeguard and knew CPR. But the girl was too tipsy and reeked of dope, and I knew CPR was the last thing Denise needed right now and told her so. She looked disappointed, called me a prick under her breath, and walked to the corner to sulk.

I continued slapping Denise's face. The spot on her cheek now was even redder. I was uncertain if my actions were more harmful than helpful but kept doing them anyway. Once her eyes fluttered and she moaned, said something that sounded like apples, but then she just shifted her body and lay still. One of the girls watching screamed, "She's dead!" which caused others to begin panicking, and I told them all to shut the fuck up.

The dance music continued pumping downstairs. It was faint but the beat could still be felt through the floor. I figured the party was still going on and even though many knew an ambulance was on its way, none of them were smart enough to realize that when an ambulance is called to an overdose scene, the police are dispatched first. This didn't seem to register for anyone until the music abruptly shut off, and someone shouted that the cops were busting the place.

Out of the half dozen girls and two guys standing watch in Denise's room, only two of the girls split. The rest looked nervous but knew they were screwed anyway, and wanted to wait it out with their friend. I tried sending this message to Denise through her soul in hopes it would give her more reason to wake up. But she only continued to lay motionless in my arms, her chest hardly rising and falling at all anymore.

A deputy stepped into the room a minute later. He glanced suspiciously at everyone, then at Denise on the bed, before motioning two medics inside. A man and a woman rushed in, wearing blue jumpsuits and carrying equipment, and the next thing I knew I was pulled off the bed so they could begin working.

The deputy had headed back downstairs. A few others had as well. I stood there a moment watching, then turned toward the door when the female medic spoke.

"Do you know how many she took?"

I shook my head, told her I had no idea. But in my mind I knew there had been eighteen pills in the bottle when she emptied it, though I wasn't about to say that aloud. I could just imagine the stares I'd receive.

I went downstairs into the frenzy of running drunken teenagers. Melvin Dumstorf ran past, the front of his green polo splattered with vomit, and judging by the hurried expression on his face, it didn't look like he was in the mood to do any of his freestyling or ninja skills anytime soon. Through the open front door I saw one of the deputy's cruisers parked in front of the house, the ambulance right behind it. Two more cruisers were up at the end of the extended driveway, blocking any escape. One girl asked me if Denise would be all right. I shrugged and told her I didn't know, but it was a lie.

I knew.

I knew that in the next two minutes the medics would cause her to throw up the Valium. I knew that she would spend the night in the hospital (a floor above the one Joey had been on) and that in the morning she would have to face her parents, who would fly home a day early from their trip. I knew how difficult it would be for her to tell her parents why she tried killing herself, and confessing to them how she would not be graduating on Saturday.

Almost everyone now had concluded that they weren't going to run away. Though a few had taken off through the back, up into the trees, others simply waited for the deputies to come to them. One big kid wearing an Elmira High football jersey, number 79, walked outside the front door with his hands in the air. Between his lips was a fat unlit joint. Someone shouted, "You go, Boomer, you show 'em who's boss." I knew I was sober enough to pass the motions—especially after the rush I'd just had upstairs—but passing the Breathalyzer would be next to impossible. For the first time I thought about John and his friends and wondered just how they were faring.

I went to step outside toward the bright red blue and white

flashing lights when a hand gripped my arm and spun me around.

"Well hello there, nephew," my uncle said. He was dressed in his uniform, the PISTOL EXPERT pin flashing in the light. "Funny seeing you here."

We drove down 13 in silence. We passed Harvey's Tavern, its parking lot moderately filled with pickups and cars, then eventually made a left onto Mizner Road. I knew we had about another five minutes until we reached The Hill. I was beginning to think we could go the entire ride without a single word when Dean spoke.

"She'll live, you know. One of the medics told me they reached her just in time. Another five minutes and she would have been gone for good."

We came up over a rise and our headlights splashed a deer three hundred yards ahead of us, the animal stopping and staring, its glossy eyes reflecting the light, before hurrying into the trees.

"You know, you're the last person I expected to see there tonight." Dean shook his head, seemed to have to force himself not to look at me. "How'd you get there anyway?"

"Does it matter?"

He emitted a low heavy laugh without smiling. "You just don't know when to stop, do you?"

"What can I say? I'm incorrigible."

This time he shot me a glare, one that suggested it'd be best to stop being a smartass. "Mom doesn't know where you went, I'm guessing."

"I didn't tell her."

"Do you realize how she lost it when she found your little

note yesterday? I never thought she'd stop crying. Chris, you have got to stop doing this."

"Doing what?"

He shook his head. "I've been talking to Steve. We both think it's a good idea if you went back to Lanton. To stay for good. Too much bad stuff's been happening up here, and …"

"Yeah? And what?"

"And you seem to be right in the middle of everything."

"That's bullshit."

"Is it? Then explain to me why you and Moses Cunningham are such good friends all of a sudden. Mom tells me she's seen you hanging out in his trailer and going places with him. Am I the only one who finds it odd that after his son gets abducted, the kid refuses to speak to anybody but you? Then after he dies you've got nothing to tell us but yet you're hanging around with his old man?"

I was silent for a long time. Then, "So what do you want me to say?"

"Nothing. I don't want you to say a goddamn thing, because to be honest, I really don't want to know. But I have off on Saturday. I'll take you back to Lanton then. I know you've made the trip already by yourself, but I'd just feel more comfortable if I went too."

Silence again. I couldn't wait to get out of the car. I'd been sitting in it ever since Dean placed me there two hours before. He'd told me to get in, and I waited while nearly everyone else got citations for underage drinking and even arrested for possession. I wondered when I was going to get mine, too, when Dean got in without a word and we started off toward The Hill.

"I would like to know one thing," he said as we passed by a dark and empty-looking Shepherd's Books. "How did you know about Denise?"

"I didn't. It was an accident. I opened the door and found

her there, and knew she needed an ambulance."

"Don't bullshit me, Chris. Steve told me about what happened back home, at that guy's farm. He said you … that you almost sensed what was about to happen."

"And you believe him?"

He glanced at me once more, as we slowed down to make the left into the trailer park. "Let me tell you a story. Back about twenty-five years ago, I had just graduated high school. I was dating this girl then, her name was Susie, and we were in love. She was going to college close by—nearly all our friends were, even my best friend Tom—and she wanted me to come along too, said it'd be the perfect place for me. But I wasn't sure. Instead I followed after my old man and joined the army. I asked Susie if she'd wait for me and she said she would.

"I spent five years in the service. I tried writing Susie as much as possible. Occasionally I'd get a letter from her, or she'd answer when I called. But pretty soon her letters didn't come as often, until they didn't come at all, and every time I called she wasn't there. Not until I got back to Bridgton did I find out she was already engaged to somebody else. And the ironic thing about it is she was engaged to Tom. The guy who got us together in the first place. My best friend."

He stopped the cruiser in front of my trailer. Cut the lights but kept the engine running.

Dean, staring ahead through his bug-splattered windshield, said, "You'll have to fend for yourself tomorrow morning. Mom always has breakfast with some of the girls up here on The Hill on Fridays down in Elmira." He glanced at me. "But the point of my story is that I learned early on you can't trust anybody. I think everyone learns that eventually, some just take longer than others. But after living your life and coming into contact with people who only care for themselves, you begin to realize the only way to survive is having faith in yourself and nobody else."

He shook his head.

"But you, Chris ... the sad thing is, I don't even know who you are. The little I do know is what Steve told me last week. Like how you were suspended for fighting and should have been arrested, but the kid didn't press charges."

"You don't know the whole story."

"It doesn't matter. What matters is I can't trust you. Tonight just proves it. I should cite you for drinking and God knows what else—I can smell the weed on your clothes—but I think you saved that girl's life tonight, so I'm going to let it go. But by Saturday you'll be back in Lanton and out of our lives. Hopefully we'll keep in touch."

He sighed and shrugged.

"So do I believe what Steve told me? There are times when I think I can, but then I always have to remember that unless I'm there to actually experience it myself, I can't be certain. That's why I never go with Mom to church anymore. I just don't have the faith to believe in God. But Steve ... he sounded like he believed it."

Dean had been staring forward at the field beyond the drive hiding in darkness. Now he looked at me.

"And in case you're wondering, I'm not going to tell Mom about tonight. She might ask where you were, and if I were you I'd tell her you were with Moses Cunningham. At least maybe she can believe that. I know she does try her best to trust people. And I know she trusts you." He paused, nodded once. "Goodnight, Chris."

I got out of the car, shut the door, and waited until he turned back on his lights. I watched him as he drove down the drive and circled around the trailer park. When his taillights disappeared down Half Creek Road, I headed toward my trailer. It didn't take long before I was inside and in bed. And it didn't take much longer before I was asleep and had the dream.

CHAPTER TWENTY-FOUR

I'm standing in a narrow hallway. The pictures on the wall show me and my family, but I can tell from the white carpet and blue wallpaper that this is Denise Rowe's house. A cold pang slices through my soul, and I turn around, notice her closed bedroom door. Behind it, a faint but familiar sound: *bwaamp-bwaamp-bwaamp-bwaamp.*

Joey suddenly appears not ten feet away. He's wearing the clothes he had on the night he stayed in the Beckett House: plain shorts and T-shirt, his nondescript sneakers. His hands are behind his back. He faces the wall, staring at a framed picture.

"Joey?" I say, my voice faint and echoing. Then, as any naïve dreamer is apt to do, I begin, "I thought you were—"

"You should read it when you get the chance," he says, his voice not only an echo in the hallway but also an echo from the past. Slowly, and in a very stiff way, he looks at me. His eyes are gone. In the empty sockets, deep darkness stares back. "Really," he says, pointing with a hand that has now become a skeletal claw, "you should read this."

Then he's gone and I have only a moment to step forward

to see the picture. Only it's not a picture. It's a section of a newspaper hiding behind thin glass. A black and white photograph of a woman rests in the corner, surrounded by text. I recognize her immediately as Sarah's mother.

Another icy pang stabs my soul, and I turn back toward the door at the end of the hall. Behind it, my parents' alarm clock has gone silent. I start forward but immediately stop when I hear heavy breathing coming from behind a closed door to my right. It's a mixture of moaning and panting, and before I can stop myself, I open the door.

Like before, he's taking her from behind, only this time the girl is someone I know. I watch as he grips onto her shoulder with one hand, his other hand holding her waist. Her hanging breasts aren't large but still they sway back and forth as he thrusts. Her eyes are closed as her face writhes in pleasure, but as she begins to cry out in orgasm they snap open. She looks straight up at me.

She screams, "*Promise me, Chris! Promise me!*"

I grab the door and slam it shut. I expect to hear her continued screams from behind, but there is only silence. I continue down the hall.

Something lies right in front of the door: a large bundle in the dimness. I can't tell what it is until I'm standing less than three feet away. It's a bloody bed sheet—my parents' bloody bed sheet. Something moves around inside the bundle. The movement is slight but it's still there. I lean down and reach out, even though I want nothing to do with it. If I could have it my way, I'd kick it aside and continue on to what's behind the closed door—where I know something terrible is happening, where I need to be—but this is a dream, and just like in most dreams where we fool ourselves into thinking we have control, I'm forced to unwrap the bed sheet.

A fetus rests inside. It's a living fetus covered in blood, and even though it's impossible—I *know* it's impossible—the fetus stares up at me.

Why did you kill me? the fetus's black eyes ask.

Blinking, the fetus is gone. Blinking, the bloody bed sheet is gone. Blinking, the only thing in front of me now is the closed bedroom door.

I step forward, grab the knob, turn it.

The door opens inward. Inside, Mrs. Roberts lies in bed. She's sleeping, so her dark glasses are off her face, resting on the wooden stand beside her bed, along with a clock and a large print trade paperback of Danielle Steele. Her one wrinkled hand is on her chest. A soft and steady snore comes from her open mouth.

I wonder what I'm doing here, why the icy pang has brought me to this room, when I see the fly.

It crawls freely from her mouth, onto her dried lip, then down her chin. It seems to be alone until, seconds later, others follow. More appear, from behind the curtains and pillows, from behind the clothes and under the bed. They fill the room with a buzzing roar so loud that I wonder how the woman can possibly continue sleeping.

Then, as if on cue, she awakens.

Her eyes open and her mouth widens even more as she sees and feels the flies. At once they attack. Those that aren't already swarming her body come at her hard and fast, until she's covered and then covered again. She tries to scream but her mouth quickly becomes blocked. She tries coughing but only manages to swallow more flies.

I stand in the doorway watching, my entire body frozen. Mrs. Roberts stares back at me, her eyes the only thing not yet covered. They scream at me, her eyes, they scream for help, and as much as I wish I could I still can't move.

Then both her eyes disappear as even more flies land and begin driving their way into her sockets.

I awoke with a start. For one disconcerting moment, I didn't know where I was. Then the present caught up with me and I lay back down in bed. My hair was damp with sweat, my neck sore. I did my best to slow my heavy breathing.

I lay there for a few minutes, staring at the ceiling. My head pounded some from my hangover. Sunlight streamed behind the closed windows and curtain, enough so that the cramped trailer had begun to overheat. I glanced at my watch, saw it was almost nine o'clock.

I sat up, yawning, wishing for a glass of cold water. I thought about what all had happened in my dream. I remembered everything.

And suddenly I had a feeling.

Not *the* feeling, but another feeling which was almost the same, though this was more of a hunch.

I stood and grabbed a pair of shorts, a T-shirt, my socks and sneakers. When I walked outside seconds later, a cool breeze hit me at once. The sky was clear, the sun bright. Off in the distance, behind the faint traffic on 13, I heard the sound of a lawnmower.

And flies.

Lots of flies.

I started up the drive. As I passed my grandmother's, I noticed a note taped to her door that in big curved letters read

Christopher,
   The girls and I went to Alice's for breakfast. We should be back around ten.
   Love, Grandma

but I ignored it and kept walking. Moments later I stood in front of Mrs. Robert's trailer. I figured she was one of "the girls" and was gone, but something told me that wasn't the case. The flies were even louder now, their low buzzing drone coming from within.

I took a step forward to knock on the door—why I did this I don't know, logic said nobody was home—when I noticed the curtains.

The curtains were moving.

Closing my eyes, I saw my dream and pictured exactly what was happening inside, and before I knew it I had pulled open the door.

I stood there then, my body tense and ready, waiting for something to happen.

For a single instant nothing did.

Then all at once the low drone erupted into a chorus of chaos, as thousands of flies escaped from inside, and I couldn't help myself, I threw up.

I don't know who called 911, but by the time the police arrived already a dozen elderly folk had scattered themselves along the drive to watch. Even Henry Porter, who hadn't gone into work today, made his way across Half Creek Road to see what had happened. Everyone stayed far enough back so they wouldn't be forced to smell the stench of the old woman's decayed body that had been cooking for days in her trailer, but still the breeze occasionally tossed it from one direction to another.

After the police came the fire department. It took them awhile to navigate the bright yellow truck down the drive, but once it was parked the men inside weren't quite sure how to get rid of all the flies that hadn't already flown away.

I watched with Moses beside Grandma's trailer. Neither of us said a word. I'd already spoken with a deputy and explained how I'd been walking toward the Rec House when I heard the buzzing. I was worried about Mrs. Roberts, as she was one of my grandmother's closest friends. So after knocking with no answer, I got nervous and tried the door. The rest was pretty much evident.

"I just saw her yesterday, too," Moses said softly. "She asked me how I was holding up after what happened to Joey. She was such a nice lady, it's a shame this had to happen. I just hope she knew the Lord well enough."

Up at Mrs. Robert's, a fireman decked out in gear entered the trailer. Two deputies had attempted already but hadn't made it more than a few seconds before running back outside coughing and cursing the flies. One had even dry-heaved. Standing there watching, my arms crossed, I heard Moses's words but at first they meant nothing. Then, as a fly flew into my face and I knocked it away, I began to play with another piece of the puzzle.

I frowned and looked at him. I'd brushed my teeth after vomiting, gargled Listerine three times; my mouth still tingled of cool mint. I said, "You saw her yesterday?"

He nodded, still staring ahead. "She stopped by the RV for a couple of minutes. Said she couldn't stay long but wanted to see how I was doing."

I stared at him, my mouth slightly open. As I tried processing the last half hour, I glanced at the trailer once more, the propped open screen door scattered with flies, before looking back at Moses.

"But that's impossible. The stench alone proves she's been dead more than a few days. There's no way you—"

It hit both of us then. Our eyes widened just a little as we stared at each other. At the same time we looked back at the trailer and realized the truth.

Staring at nothing in particular up the drive, I said, "Moses, do you have your keys handy?"

He told me he did.

"Can I have them?"

He brought them out of his jeans pocket and placed them in my hand. At first I wasn't sure why he had done so, I wasn't even sure why I'd asked for them to begin with. But then the note taped to my grandmother's door caught my attention again, and everything fell into place.

"Let's go," I said, already walking.

Moses followed. "Where are we going?"

I grabbed the note off the door and handed it to him, as we started around the trailer toward Moses's Metro. The car's key was out and ready, and I wondered just how long we had. Grandma said she would be back around ten. Already it was nine-thirty and I didn't know how long it would take to get to Alice's.

Opening the driver's door, I noticed Moses hesitate. "What's wrong?"

"Christopher, I don't know about this. Do you realize just what you're planning to do?"

Actually no, I didn't have a plan, but I at least had an idea and it was enough. We had to stop Samael somehow, and confronting him face to face seemed like the most obvious choice.

"Christopher? Did you hear what I said?"

I blinked and looked up at him, saw the concern and worry in his face. He'd been doing this much longer than me, and the fact that he was scared should have made me reevaluate the situation.

"I heard you. But if Samael really has been posing as Mrs. Roberts all this time and he's at Alice's with my grandmother and her friends, then he doesn't know what's just happened here. Which means we've got the element of surprise on our side."

"That's not all we've got on our side," Moses said. "We also have God."

CHAPTER TWENTY-FIVE

DOWN HALF CREEK ROAD, through Bridgton, onto 13 toward Horseheads, then down 14, the Metro's speedometer climbing to forty to forty-five to fifty, making all the traffic lights, not encountering any cops, maybe Moses was right—maybe we did have God on our side.

"How do you know where we're going?" Moses asked as we sped through a yellow light and I pressed my foot down on the gas.

"I just do."

The fact was after touching my grandmother's note, I'd felt another pang of ice shoot through my soul and I knew exactly where Alice's Family Restaurant was located, and at 9:44 according to the Metro's dashboard clock I pulled into the parking lot, spotted an open space in the front row and didn't hesitate at all in taking it.

Putting the car in park, I undid my seatbelt and went to open my door when Moses grabbed my arm. I glared back at him, my body already shaking, my heart pounding in my ears. He stared back at me with his son's trademark: dark solemn eyes.

"Be careful," he whispered.

I got out and headed for the front entrance. I balled my hands into fists to keep them from shaking so much. I took long, slow breaths to make sure I wouldn't hyperventilate. Last night I'd felt a kind of exhilaration in saving Denise Rowe's life and for a time convinced myself I was unstoppable. I'd thought the same all this morning and on the drive over, but now that I was out of the car and almost inside, I realized I was scared shitless. Just what the hell did I think I was doing? Joey had already confronted Samael and had been put in the hospital for his efforts.

The angel of death … he wanted to kill me.

When I made it to the door I almost turned around, almost headed back to the safety of Moses's Metro. But in my mind I pictured everyone who had suffered because of this demon—my parents and grandfather, Devin Beckett and all the children, Joey and Mrs. Roberts—and I knew I couldn't back out.

I opened the door and stepped into the air-conditioned foyer, realized a second too late that I didn't have the knife Joey had given me, that it was still in the glove box of my Cavalier where I'd stashed it Tuesday night.

"Christopher?"

Grandma stood leaning on her wooden cane, staring back at me with surprise. Two other ladies stood with her, one with glasses and a pinched face, the other with dyed curly hair and what looked like a red bowler hat.

I couldn't see Mrs. Roberts anywhere.

"Christopher, what are you doing here?"

I opened my mouth to reply when the curly-haired woman said, "So this is your grandson, Lily?"

She nodded, still staring at me. "Yes, it is. Visiting from Pennsylvania. But Christopher, what *are* you doing here?"

I smiled and nodded at both women, then said, "We were

driving past and I remembered you were here having breakfast. Thought I'd stop in and say hi."

"We?"

Dean said she already knew about me hanging out with Moses, so I figured it wouldn't hurt to tell the truth. "Me and Mr. Cunningham."

"Oh," she said tonelessly. "I see."

"Christopher, it's very nice to finally meet you."

This was from the woman in the glasses. Her hand was thin and light, and as I shook it I instantly knew her name was Carol and that she only had eight months more to live before she died in a hospital bed without seeing her daughter who was halfway across the country. The sudden revelation made me hesitate, but I managed to smile and told her it was nice to meet her too.

"We're actually leaving," my grandmother said. "Just waiting for Emma and Nancy. They needed to use the restroom."

"Yes," Carol said. "Emma's our driver or else we wouldn't be standing here taking up this waiting space."

Actually, besides the three women and myself, there was nobody else in the foyer. Beyond a dry-erase board with today's specials written up in colored markers and a sign asking patrons to wait to be seated, a young hostess appeared. She went to grab a menu but then realized I was with the ladies and just stood there, crossing something off on her stand.

"You know," I said, glancing past the hostess and over the tables and people to the back, where a red neon sign announced RESTROOMS in cursive script, "I might as well use the men's room while I'm here."

The thought to tell my grandmother's friends it was nice meeting them came to me a second too late, because by then I was already walking past the hostess, to whom I forced a smile, then down the aisle of tables. Past families and friends and strangers all enjoying their breakfasts, completely unaware of the possible confrontation which might soon occur. There was even one family at a large round table, two parents and their three sons. All three of the boys were eating pancakes, and I wanted to tell them to leave right now, to go as far as possible before it was too late. Then before I knew it I'd stepped under the buzzing neon sign and stared at the two doors, both marked accordingly, wondering just how long I'd have to wait until I met the demon head on.

I turned and took four steps so I could see back out across the restaurant. Amid the murmuring din of Friday morning conversations, of silverware clinking against plates and dishes, I realized there was faint muzak playing from invisible speakers above. It was something contemporary, something I couldn't name off the top of my head, and I hated the fact that the soundtrack to my life right now was so peaceful, so calm, while at the moment I was anything but.

I glanced out one of the large plate-glass windows into the parking lot. Spotted the blue Geo Metro in the front row. Moses was still inside, still in the passenger seat. I wondered if he was still praying. I hoped that he was and that he wasn't lying when he said God was on our side, and I even began to think I should pray myself, when the women's restroom door opened behind me.

"Um, young man?"

Her voice was soft and frail, and when I turned around to stare into her eyes I knew that she was Emma and that she wouldn't die of natural causes like Carol, but would instead be suffocated from a pillow stuffed in her face by her own son-in-law. He was the one she'd never wanted her daughter to marry in the first place, the one who she just could never trust, and the one who would need the inheritance he and his wife would be left so he could pay off most of his gambling debts.

I saw it all in an instant and managed to cut the connection by forcing myself to blink the images away. When I did, I noticed the woman was staring at me curiously. She opened her mouth to ask me if I was okay, but I quickly smiled and shook my head.

"Sorry about that," I told her. "Just felt a little lightheaded there for a second."

The answer seemed to satisfy her somewhat, and with a forced smile of her own she started past me. I watched her as she headed back down the aisle toward the entrance—she was a short woman and actually waddled like a penguin. The hostess had just seated a new family who'd come in: a father and mother with a three-year-old daughter, bright pink ribbons keeping her hair in pigtails. The idea of shouting and telling everyone to leave entered my mind again, but before I could even seriously begin to consider the thought, I felt the darkness.

It clouded my mind and chilled my soul, and without any conscious effort I turned to face the sweet old lady who lived just two trailers up from my grandmother.

Her hair was thin and gray, her skin pale. Her dark glasses rested comfortably on her small face. She only stood there for a moment, before grinning—and in the grin I saw her yellow crooked teeth and sensed a maliciousness that wasn't natural.

"I felt you and the black man coming."

The voice sounded the same as it did the first day I met her, only I knew it had been the real Mrs. Roberts then, that I had shaken the hand of a living and breathing human being.

I stared at the dark glasses, as if looking into Samael's eyes, but all I could see was my own reflection. I realized he was waiting for me to speak next, and while I knew it was best to not give in and allow this creature to direct the progress of our interaction, I opened my mouth. But nothing came out, even when I tried.

"That's okay," Samael said, and now behind the light feminine voice I heard something darker. "You needn't say anything. Even the black boy did not say much. He simply screamed … and screamed … and screamed."

The grin widened with each emphasis on the word, and before I knew it I opened my mouth again and blurted the stupidest, most unoriginal thing that came to mind.

"You won't get away with this."

The grin—though impossible—grew even wider. "So it speaks. Tell me, just what to you and the black man hope to accomplish? The boy was gifted and without him you both are nothing. Neither of you have what it takes to stop me."

"Maybe," I said, amazed that I could even find a voice to speak at all. "But you've already slipped up. Who's to say you won't do it again?"

"Slipped up?"

"Mrs. Roberts's body. They already found it. They know she's dead so your cover's blown."

"You certainly speak bold for a young man who is aware of neither his past nor his future."

"I know my past. I know what my great-grandfather and his friends did. And I know someday as revenge you'll try to give me a choice."

The grin morphed into a sneer. "Is that so? Perhaps then I should give you that choice now."

"Like the choice you gave Joey?"

"You think you know everything, do you? Then tell me this —who murdered your parents?"

I forced myself to stare back into the dark glasses. "You did."

The grin returned. "Interesting you think that. But perhaps you put too much trust in what the black man and boy tell you. It's clear now they believe you were sent here for a reason. Perhaps they believed this so strongly they did whatever it took to get you here."

Even now I can't say what made me do it. Besides his words all I heard was my heart beating (even the faint calm muzak was gone) and I kept thinking that at any moment I could die. Then, before I realized it, I reached up and snatched off the dark glasses.

Two black eyes stared back at me.

"It's true what they say," Samael said. "The eyes are the windows to the soul. But for creatures such as myself who have no souls, when we possess a body or create our own shell, what stares through those windows is our true essence. Now let me ask you one question. Do you wish to die?"

I didn't even hesitate. I simply shook my head and whispered no.

The grin grew again, but I hardly noticed this as I stared back into the pitch black eyes. I couldn't look away. And it wasn't until Samael spoke again that I realized I no longer heard my heart pounding in my ears—and wondered briefly if it had stopped.

The demon said, "That is very good to know, Christopher Myers," and someone cleared their throat behind me, and when I turned I saw it was a little girl, no more than eight or nine, staring up at me.

"Excuse me," she said. "I need to get through."

But I couldn't let her pass. I couldn't let her see the darkness in Samael's eyes. I couldn't risk the chance of something terrible happening to her like what happened to Joey.

And suddenly I understood my purpose in this entire puzzle. I realized why I'd been given this gift or curse or whatever it was Joey had given me. I realized it was now my job to stop Samael once and for all.

I turned back then, uncertain whether I would be alive in the next minute but not caring anyway.

Samael was gone, the space empty.

For one wild second I wondered if it had all been my imagination and nothing more.

But the weight of the dark glasses in my hand was proof enough, so I let the girl pass and started back toward the entrance.

———

A maroon Buick Park Avenue sat idling just outside the restaurant. All four ladies waited inside, my grandmother in the passenger seat. The window was down and her arm rested on the door.

The glasses were still in my hand. I dropped them in the trashcan outside the entrance and walked up to the car.

"We're just waiting for Nancy," Grandma said.

I didn't say anything at first. They were all waiting for a woman who'd been dead for at least two days, and I wasn't quite sure how to tell them the truth. How could they possibly understand, especially when they just had breakfast with the deceased?

"Nancy's not coming," I said. I stared into my grandmother's eyes, then into Emma's, then the two women's in the back. And as I spoke I forced myself to believe what I was saying, so that somehow these women would believe it too. "Only the four of you had breakfast this morning. In fact, you haven't seen Nancy since Wednesday. And even then she wasn't doing well."

For an instant doubt crept into my mind. What if they didn't believe? What if I wasn't able to make them believe the way I wanted them to, and they remembered everything that happened this morning up until this very moment?

But I stomped on that doubt and kicked it away and just kept staring back into their eyes, from one woman to the next, using the connection I had with all of them. And as one collective unit, they each closed their eyes at the same time and then reopened them, blinking like they just woke up.

Grandma stared at me. For a moment her face was filled with confusion, and then she smiled. "Well, Christopher, it was nice of you to stop by. I'll see you back home."

The three other ladies voiced their goodbyes and how it was nice meeting me. I told them it was nice to meet them too, then looked directly at Emma.

"Don't go to your daughter's for Thanksgiving," I told her, but it wasn't forced like before, only a suggestion. She made a face and started to say something but I quickly stepped back, waved at them one last time.

After the car drove away, I walked back to the Metro. When I opened the door and got inside, Moses still had his eyes closed.

"I'm assuming it went well," he said.

"What makes you say that?"

He opened his eyes and looked at me. His face was long and his eyes were red and I knew he'd been praying the entire time. "You're still alive."

CHAPTER TWENTY-SIX

"I THINK I know what's going to happen."

"What do you mean?"

"About the thirty-four lives. I think I know how it's going to go down."

We were at Harris Hill Park, at the same spot Sarah had brought me to only a few days before. Moses sat on one of the benches overlooking the valley. I leaned against the split-rail fence, my back to the view. We both knew it wouldn't be wise to return to The Hill just yet. I'd already convinced my grandmother and her friends that they hadn't eaten breakfast with Mrs. Roberts, and I couldn't begin to imagine the shock they'd receive when they found out what had happened to their friend.

"And?" Moses said.

"Last night, after John Porter found his car trashed, he said something to one of his friends about graduation. Something about making everyone remember. And when he did, this ... this image passed through my mind. It was only there for a second, and then it was gone, and I didn't have much time to think about it. But I saw people, hundreds of people, all moving around frantic. They were screaming. It reminded me … well, it reminded me of the footage they showed of Columbine."

Moses stared back at me, his face impassive. "Christopher, do you realize what you're saying?"

"Think about it. How many students graduate at any given public school? Two hundred? Three? There'll be over a thousand people attending. Thirty-four is nothing. And like you said, that may just be the initial number."

Moses had gone from watching me to staring off into space. He had mentioned before how he and Joey had dealt with possible school shootings, and I hoped he'd have an idea now.

"Moses."

He blinked, looked up at me.

"What do you think?"

"I think we should definitely consider the possibility."

I asked him then what we should do.

"According to the paper, New York's former governor Mike Boyd will be speaking at the graduation tomorrow. So there's definitely going to be security. But who's to say a couple of students couldn't sneak in some guns anyway?"

"Should we call the police?"

"And tell them what? Right now all we have is speculation. If we take this to the police, what are they going to think? They'll be more suspicious of us than anyone we try to turn in. They'll want to know why we think what we do, and what are we going to tell them? That my dead son was called here by God and that you now have a feeling?" He shook his head. "No, this is why it's always been difficult, because in the end we've got no one to help us. We've got to do this on our own."

"Then what about John? Can we try talking to him?"

"That's all we can do right now. Joey managed to stop a girl from poisoning a dozen of her classmates just by talking some sense into her. Maybe you can do the same."

A dark shadow had settled itself over the trailer park. I sensed it the moment we returned to The Hill. By then the deputies' cruisers and fire truck were gone. We parked at Moses's, where he went into his RV and I headed back to my trailer ... but then noticed Grandma sitting on her swing.

She was alone, her hands in her lap. She stared forward at the view we'd shared the first day I arrived. She wasn't taking up the entire swing and there was room for me to sit, but after I walked up to her I remained standing.

I softly said her name.

At first she wouldn't look at me. She just kept staring out into the small valley. Her eyes were red. There was some crust on her face, just below her eyes, like the day she'd told me I was going back home.

I said her name again.

Finally she looked up. One of her hands squeezed into a fist, grasping a tissue. When she spoke, she said only one word and it was barely a whisper.

"Nancy."

I sat down beside her.

She took my hand, squeezed it tightly. "I just saw her on Wednesday. My God, Christopher, she was my best friend. And now ... now she's gone. She's dead. And I ... I didn't even have a chance to say goodbye."

At that moment I hated myself for what I'd done to her and her friends back at Alice's. True, I did save them the confusion of what they'd find once they returned home, but it was clear they'd had a good time with the thing they thought was Mrs. Roberts, and I had taken that away. Erased their final moments together like a videotape and dubbed them all with new memories. Thinking this now, I felt sickened as I realized what it was: mental rape.

I wanted to say something to her then, to somehow take away all her sadness and grief, but before I could even open my mouth she whispered, "They said there were flies," and burst into tears.

I watched her as she held the used tissue to her eyes. I didn't know what to do. I didn't know what to say. Then instinct took over and I placed my arm around her shoulders. It felt awkward, and for an instant I wondered if she'd cried this way when she found out the news of my parents. But I quickly shoved the thought from my mind. Instead I held her close, I told her that it was okay, that everything was all right and that she needn't worry.

We sat there for a long time, while above us the wind fashioned clouds into different shapes and sizes like it had done since the beginning of time.

Sarah answered the door after two knocks and, smiling, said, "Hey, Chris."

I smiled at her but said nothing. I'd been hoping John would answer.

"Are you okay?" she asked. "You look exhausted."

"Is John home?"

"He's upstairs. Dad grounded him a second time after last night. Really knocked it hard into his head that he's not supposed to leave the house, and he's been in his room ever since."

For an instant I saw Henry Porter raving at his son, asking him just what he was thinking, and John talking back, calling him Pinkie to his face, and Henry stepping forward and smacking him in the mouth and John, a second later, spitting blood.

Sarah frowned. "You were with him last night, weren't you?"

I nodded.

"What happened? I mean, besides John getting into that fight with Jeremy, what happened at the party? I heard Denise tried to kill herself and—"

"I need to talk to John, Sarah." I tried smiling but couldn't seem to pull it off. "Please. It's important."

She seemed to hesitate again, then stepped back and opened the door. She told me which room was his upstairs and that I shouldn't take too long, as Henry Porter would be home in the next half hour or so and he wouldn't be at all happy to know his son was having company while grounded.

I thanked her and headed up the steps, then down the hall and stopped in front of John's bedroom door. It was closed, with two large black and white stickers placed in the middle, one above the other: the first was Tipper Gore's failed attempt at keeping children's ears safe from questionable music— PARENTAL ADVISORY EXPLICIT CONTENT—while the other simply said I HATE STUPID PEOPLE. I knocked and waited for him to answer, and when he didn't I knocked again.

"I'm busy," John called from the other side. Behind his deep voice, very faint, was the sound of an aerosol can being sprayed. "Go away."

"John, it's Chris. I need to talk to you."

There was a moment when I realized that this wasn't going to work, that I wasn't going to get a chance to speak with him. I wondered just what Moses and I would have to do then.

The door opened. A battered version of John Porter stared out, his right hand behind his back. His left eye was swollen and there was a cut on his forehead—both, I somehow knew, from last night. But there was another cut on his upper lip, which was from this morning and which I wasn't at all surprised to see. He grinned, once again showing off his chipped lower tooth.

"Shit, dude, what the hell are you doing here?" Despite the tiredness in his voice and the fact that he was probably grounded for the next couple of years, he seemed in a good mood.

"I just wanted to stop and see how you were doing."

"Yeah, well, same old shit." He stepped back and motioned me inside. "Here, have a seat."

Once I stepped into the room, I understood John's unusual good mood. I smelled the mixture of marijuana and Brut deodorant, and when I looked at him, he brought the body spray can out from behind his back and tossed it on the bed. One of his two windows was open. On the sill, a curl of smoke drifted up from the roach.

"Want a hit?" he asked.

I shook my head and sat in the chair he'd pulled out for me from beneath his cluttered desk. There was one bookcase, with more videotapes and DVDs than books on the shelves. Posters showing bands like System of a Down and Linkin Park, and half-naked women like Pamela Anderson and Carmen Electra, covered the walls.

John grabbed the joint and sat on the bed. "Sorry about ditching you last night. But you know how that shit goes."

"Don't worry about it. But what happened? You look …"

"Like shit?" It seemed that word had become his new favorite. "Yeah, well, we managed to track them guys down at Jeremy's house. The prick got in some lucky punches, but I got him right in the balls and then kneed him in the jaw. Sean got it the worst though. One of Jeremy's friends—I think it was Ted Schur—nearly broke his arm. He had to go to the emergency room. Good thing the cops showed up when they did, or who the fuck knows what might have happened."

I asked him how much trouble they got in.

"Eh," he said, taking a hit, "not too much, just the usual."

Though I had no idea what the usual consisted of, John Porter and his friends had been given citations for underage drinking and disorderly conduct. When one of Jeremy's friends admitted to what they'd done to John's car, they were cited for not only disorderly conduct but vandalism as well.

"And my dad's pretty pissed, too." His hand went unconsciously to his mouth. "But shit, that's nothing new."

I sat staring at him, uncertain how I wanted to proceed. I thought of Joey and wondered what he'd say or do right now.

John, though now clearly high, noticed me watching him. "So what is it?"

"What do you mean?"

"Come on, Chris, we're boys now. Don't give me any of that bullshit. What is it?"

Now or never, I thought, and though I still had no idea what I wanted to say, I managed to come up with, "It's just I ... I mean, your graduation's tomorrow, right?"

"Yeah, so?" He waited a moment, looking paranoid, before shaking his head. He started to laugh. "What the fuck does that have to do with anything? You're not just trying to fuck with me because I'm lit, are you?"

"I know what you're planning to do."

"You do?" He laughed again. "Who told you? Was it Chad?"

"How can you laugh about something like that?"

"What do you mean? It's gonna be hilarious. We're gonna be legends after tomorrow's over."

My body trembled and my heart pounded and I couldn't help it, I actually jumped up from the chair as I shouted, "But people are going to die!"

Something changed in his face. "Dude, what the fuck are you talking about?"

"You can't do this, John. It's not right."

"The fuck? Just who the fuck do you think you are? You can't tell me what to do."

"But—"

He lurched from the bed, pointing what was left of the roach at his door. "Get the fuck outta my room."

I didn't move.

"I thought you were cool, but now I don't know what the fuck to think anymore. My fuckin' old man tries telling me what to do, and I'll tell you the same thing I tell him. Go to hell."

It was enough. The realization I'd blown my chance hit me hard. There was nothing else for me to say or do to try to change his mind. For a moment I even considered threatening him with calling the police, but feared that would enrage him and his plan even more.

Without a word I left his room and headed downstairs. Sarah sat on the couch, one leg pulled up under her body. The TV was on but she didn't appear to be watching it, as she had her book open before her.

She said, "Was John just yelling at you?"

"Yes, he was."

"What happened?"

"You don't want to know. But Sarah, can you promise me something?"

"What is it?"

"Don't go to graduation tomorrow."

"Are you kidding? John's graduating. I can't miss that."

"Please, don't go. Just stay home. I—"

But I couldn't tell her what I knew, just like I couldn't tell the medics how many pills Denise had taken, or Steve how I knew about Jack Murphy and his daughter. It was a terrible curse Joey had given me, being able to know something but not being able to say what that something was. I wondered just how much longer I could go before I lost my mind. And knowing this, as I stared back at Sarah, a name flashed unbidden through my mind. Jeff Snyder was the name, a quiet boy from school that Sarah had known for two years and had once had a crush on. That crush was now gone, had been for a while, but tomorrow he was speaking and she wanted to see him, wanted to see him up on stage more than her brother getting his diploma.

"Yes, Chris?" Her head was tilted, her blue eyes watching me curiously. "You what?"

"I ... I just don't want you to go."

"But why?"

I'm afraid something bad is going to happen. I'm afraid thirty-four people are going to die, maybe more, and I don't want you there. I don't want you there because I'm afraid one of those thirty-four people will be you.

"Never mind," I said. "Look, I should go. I'll see you later, okay?"

"Well?" Moses said, standing in the shade of the Rec House, a cigarette between his lips.

I shook my head.

"That's okay." He took one final drag and dropped the cigarette on the ground. "I'm sure you did your best."

I wanted to believe him, I really did, but I kept seeing that dark look in John's eyes and hoped I hadn't somehow caused more lives to suffer. "So what now?"

"Now I'm going to take a drive into Elmira."

I asked him if he wanted me to come along.

"Not this time, Christopher. I'll see you tomorrow."

"Tomorrow?"

"Of course. Graduation starts at noon."

Dean called later that night. Grandma and I had just finished dinner and I was helping her with the dishes when the phone rang.

"Chris, I wanted to let you know I might not be able to take you back like we discussed."

At first I wasn't sure what he meant. Take me back? Then, after a moment, I remembered about returning to Lanton tomorrow. Dean had mentioned me returning home on the way back from Denise Rowe's house last night. But with everything that had happened since, of course it slipped my mind.

"Chris, are you there?"

"Yeah. So … should I go back by myself?"

"Like I said before, you've already made the trip alone so I know you can do it again. But I'd just rather I went with you too. I'd feel more comfortable that way, and I know so would Mom. The plan was to start out early tomorrow morning, so after I made sure you were settled I could head right back since I work Sunday. But if graduation goes over too long, we might have to put off heading back to Lanton until Monday."

I sensed an edge to his voice and asked, "Graduation?"

He sighed. "Some nutcase called Elmira High School's principal and said he was going to assassinate Mike Boyd at the graduation tomorrow, so they're tightening security. A guy I know from the city asked me to help out undercover, and since I already owe him a favor I said I would."

As he spoke, I turned my attention out the window to Moses Cunningham's RV.

Dean continued talking in my ear: "So you might as well pack your things. I'll try to give you a call later in the day."

And he hung up.

When I left my grandmother's trailer later around ten o'clock, I intended to see Moses. I wanted to ask him if it was really him who'd called in the assassination threat. So as I stepped out into the cool summer night—the breeze and the insects quiet—I started to turn left to head toward his RV when movement caught my attention up toward Half Creek Road.

I turned at once and saw a shadow entering the Rec House. And even though I knew it was impossible, one name materialized in my mind.

Joey.

I wasted no time in sprinting up the drive. When I got to the screen door and opened it (no racket this time) I paused, now second-guessing myself. Had I really seen anything? Or was it just my overstressed imagination? For all I knew Samael waited inside, that perpetual shadow in the corner, ready to give me the choice I wasn't quite yet prepared to make.

I stepped inside and flicked on the lights.

Thankfully this time the power worked. The six bulbs in the ceiling lit up right away, only one in the corner flickering off and on before it stayed strong. The Rec House's interior looked the same as it did the first time I entered. The gaming tables all sat untouched, the clutter still resting on top of the ping-pong table. Even the yellow remote control car lay upside down on the floor.

"Joey?"

I spoke his name before realizing I'd even opened my mouth, and immediately I felt stupid. I knew better. Of course I knew better. I'd sat beside him when he died. I'd gone with his father to pick up his ashes. But still … hadn't I seen something enter this place?

"Joey, are you there?"

There was no answer.

"I don't know what to do," I told the empty room. "I can't do this by myself. Your dad's trying to help me but I … I'm scared. Can you help? Do you know what's really going to happen?"

The silence continued. I stood there for a very long time, waiting for anything at all. Even if that one bulb began flickering again I would have been satisfied—though how I would have taken it as a sign, I had no clue. Finally I gave up. Nothing was going to happen.

I started back outside, my hand hovering over the light switch, when a soft voice inside my head whispered *you should read it when you get the chance* and I paused. Standing there, I remembered both my dream and the day Joey had brought me here before visiting the Beckett House. I remembered what he'd shown me, how he'd been looking at me with his dark solemn eyes that for a moment I wondered just what was really going on inside his head.

Thinking this now, I turned and looked across the Rec House. Stared at the wall where pictures of the Porter family stared back. In the center was Mrs. Porter's framed obituary.

"All right, Joey," I whispered, starting forward. "What's this all about?"

Five minutes later I found myself in the deserted gravel parking lot of Shepherd's Books. I'd run the entire way down Half Creek Road. A cramp had formed in my side. I stood before the bookstore/house, half bent over as I tried catching my breath. I stared up at the dark empty windows.

He was in there somewhere—there was no doubt in my mind about that—yet I didn't know what to do about it. I considered banging on the door, but there was no guarantee he'd answer. I thought about breaking and entering, of shoving my way inside and running up to the second floor and finding him cowered in a corner, as he realized I'd finally figured it out. But what would I say to him? Would I hit him, slap him around? Maybe I wouldn't do anything because it had been my own stupid fault in the first place. I'd been too naïve and trusting and now there was no turning back.

Besides, I told myself as I started back up the road, it's no use anyway. Had I known earlier in the game maybe it would have made a difference. But now it was too late. Much too late.

CHAPTER TWENTY-SEVEN

IT WAS ALMOST three o'clock in the morning when I heard her outside.

I'd been lying in bed since midnight, after staring at the picture of my parents for nearly an hour. I kept trying to use whatever gift Joey had given me to figure out who had murdered them, but it was no use. I could glimpse into meaningless areas of people's lives—like what their favorite colors were and how often they clipped their toenails—but when it came down to actually seeing something I cared about and needed to know, nothing came.

Finally I set the picture aside and turned off the light. I tried to sleep, but I was too wrapped up in thoughts of Samael and the thirty-four lives and what tomorrow had in store. I kept turning over and over in bed, settling first on my left side, then on my right, then on my stomach, and finally on my back, before doing the positions all over again. I flipped my pillow at least a half dozen times, hoping for the cool side but never satisfied with what I got. I wondered if Moses was asleep. I figured he probably was, as he was used to dealing with these situations, to all the pressure, that getting a good night's rest was second nature.

As I flipped my pillow back over, I heard footsteps outside. I froze. My mind ran through the different possibilities of who it could be—Moses, Grandma, Samael, my parents' murderer, my parents themselves, again in that twisted W. W. Jacobs version—when suddenly the footsteps stopped. Besides my watch ticking next to the bed and the insects outside, there was silence.

Then the footsteps started again. After a moment I realized they were now heading away, so I jumped out of bed and went to the door. I wore only my boxers and T-shirt but didn't care as I stepped outside.

She had only gone a few steps up the drive. When she heard my door opening, she paused. Her back was to me for the longest time, before finally she turned. In the moonlight I saw her pale face and the tears that lined her cheeks.

I whispered, "Sarah?"

She started forward immediately, sobbing, wiping her eyes as she met me and placed her arms around me. She hugged me tight. At first I didn't know what to do and just stood there hesitant, my one arm holding open the screen door while my other arm hung useless at my side. She continued to weep, her body jerking against mine with each individual sob, and instinctively I placed my arm around her and held her, until her sobbing subsided enough so I could lean back and see her face.

"Sarah, what's wrong?"

"I ... I'm sorry, but I ... I had a bad dream."

"That's all right. There's no need to be sorry."

She continued to weep, pressing her face into my shoulder. After a while I got her to settle down and invited her inside. The trailer was cramped enough just for me, but we managed to sit on the bed. She continued to sniff back tears, and I found some tissues and placed them in her hand.

I asked her again what was wrong.

She looked up at me, her blue eyes piercing in the dark. She made a long sigh and began to speak between hiccups.

"It was … a nightmare. But it … it felt so real. I was giving … birth to my baby … but when … when it was born … my baby was … it was dead." Shaking her head, wiping more tears from her eyes. "God, it was … awful. That's the last … thing in the world … I'd want. Anything but … my baby. Anything but … my child."

I wanted to tell her that it was okay, that she needn't worry about anything because it was just a dream. But for some reason I knew I couldn't do that. She would sense my lies faster than my grandmother, and lies were the last thing she needed.

I remembered the question I'd considered asking her yesterday as we sat talking on the picnic table. The question that would never be voiced, no matter what happened. *Have you considered an abortion?* Of course she'd considered it, even if it was for an instant, but now I had a better idea just what kind of answer I would have received had I asked.

The year before there was a girl in my high school who had gotten pregnant, who everyone had called trailer trash behind her back, and I remembered lying awake some nights in bed thinking about her. Thinking about the life she would now have because of a simple mistake. And because of her, I now saw Sarah in a whole different light.

Sarah too was a girl who, in all respects, was trailer trash. But was it destined from the moment she was born, or had she brought it upon herself? At what point in her journey of life had she lost her way and started down this new path? In five years where would she be, considering that nothing happened to her baby and she did her best to raise it on her own? Before, with the girl from school, I had imagined her eventually getting married with the guy from the neighborhood who had impregnated her, so that everything worked out in the end. But I had been fooling myself, because a part of me actually took pity on her. Now, realistically, I wondered what kind of life Sarah would have if she planned to raise the baby on her own, with no help at all from anyone else. Would she have to drop out of high school? If not, if she actually managed to graduate, would she consider taking college courses? There was no real career for a woman like her, except one waiting tables at Luanne's or Harvey's Tavern. She'd live in Bridgton her entire life, maybe date a guy from Horseheads or Elmira or even Ithaca, a guy in his twenties and already working toward becoming an alcoholic.

I started thinking about what would happen next, how the guy might get her pregnant and they'd eventually marry, but before I could I remembered Sarah again, not the girl of endless tragic possibilities but the girl who once saw herself doing so much more than having a baby before she even graduated high school. I realized I knew none of her desires, none of her ambitions in life, because the moment she realized she was pregnant, they had all been tossed out the window.

She sniffed again, wiping her eyes, and looked up at me. "Do you mind ... if I stay here? Just for a little? I don't want ... to be alone."

I nodded and told her of course. I pushed myself back against the wall, so that she would have more room on the bed. She leaned in against me and I put my arm around her, placed her head on my chest. Then we just lay there in silence, the only sounds our slow steady breathing.

Minutes passed, and as I held her, my chin resting on her head, I thought maybe she'd fallen asleep when she softly said my name.

"Yeah," I whispered.

She sniffed once more. "Can you promise me something?"

"What's that?"

"Don't let anything happen to my baby."

Softly I shushed her. "Sarah, it was only a dream. Don't worry about it."

"Promise me, Chris."

An image of her naked, being taken from behind by some faceless guy, came flashing through my mind as I remembered that morning's nightmare. Only I hadn't given it any thought then, because the real Sarah hadn't said that yet, she hadn't asked me to promise her anything.

"Chris?"

"Yeah."

"Please, can you promise me?"

It was the last thing I wanted to do, the very last, but I had no choice. It was meaningless, of course it was, but a promise was a promise and though I'd been a liar I had never been one to go back on my word when I meant it. Though I asked myself just how could I promise the safety of her unborn child? What powers did I hold that could determine whether it grew healthy or died prenatal?

It was crazy, completely insane, but this was what she wanted to hear—what she *needed* to hear—and so I relented and whispered, "I promise."

"Thank you," she said. She took my hand, gave it a tight squeeze.

She was asleep within five minutes, but it would be another hour before I drifted off, afraid of nightmares real and imagined—and not being able to tell the difference between them both.

CHAPTER TWENTY-EIGHT

IN THE MORNING I opened my eyes to find Moses standing over me.

"What time is it?" I asked, yawning.

"Almost nine o'clock."

"How long have you been here?"

"Only a few minutes."

I sat up and rubbed at my eyes. "Why didn't you wake me?"

"I figured right now you need all the rest you can get. Besides, I would have waited outside but your door was half-open. I know it might not mean anything with Samael, but considering what we're up against it'd be best to stay safe at all times. For a second there I—"

But he didn't finish the thought. He didn't have to.

"You best get around," Moses said. "I'll wait outside."

He left and I sat there for another minute, wondering just how long Sarah had stayed before I asked myself whether she had even been there in the first place. Lately I'd been having dreams that felt real and maybe that was just another. But I pinched my T-shirt to my nose and smelled Sarah there, the scent of her hair and skin, and knew it had been real.

I took a quick shower and dressed into jeans and a red polo shirt and then stepped outside. The sky was clear, only a few clouds hanging off near the horizon, and the sun seemed to shine down brighter than ever. Moses sat in the same chair his son had sat in only days before, though it felt like months.

He nodded and smiled at the sky as he stood up. "I think it's a good sign."

"What is?"

"The sky. They'd been calling for rain all week but now look how clear it is. Maybe it's an omen."

We stopped by my grandmother's, Moses waiting outside while I went in to check on her. I hadn't decided yet what excuse I would give her of where I was going, and as it turned out I didn't need one. She was still in bed, snoring quietly, so I wrote her a note that said I went out with Moses and would be back later.

Before I got into Moses's car, I took one glance off The Hill down into the valley where the white church rested, the heart of Bridgton behind it. It was almost nine-thirty on a beautiful Saturday morning and it seemed like no one was up yet, like the entire trailer park was still sound asleep.

Or dead, my mind murmured. *Dead like Mrs. Roberts with flies covering their bodies and crawling into their mouths and noses and ears.*

"Stop it," I whispered, opening the car's passenger door.

"What was that?" Moses asked.

I swallowed. "Should I bring the … Joey's present?"

"What do you think?"

I shook my head and climbed inside.

We had just passed the Rec House and were turning right when I murmured, "Oh, yeah."

Moses glanced at me, took his foot off the gas. "What?"

Too late now, I thought, remembering what I'd seen inside the cinderblock building last night. I told Moses to just keep going. Then we drove down the hill, picking up speed. As Shepherd's Books came around the bend, I pointed.

"You see that place?"

It was there for only a second or two before we drove past.

"The bookstore? Yeah, what about it? It's been closed for the past week, if not longer."

"That's right. And for the past week I've been thinking the man who lives there is Lewis Shepherd, the owner."

Moses said, "But he's not."

"No, he's not. In fact, Lewis Shepherd's been dead nearly two years. He was drunk when driving home and ended up hitting Mrs. Porter while she was jogging. She died instantly. He died a few hours later."

"I heard she was killed in an accident. Where did you find this out?"

"Her obituary posted in the Rec House, as a kind of memorial I guess. Joey mentioned it to me almost a week ago. He told me to read it when I got the chance, but of course I didn't, and it doesn't make sense. I mean, why wouldn't he just have me read it then and there instead of having me wait like this?"

"Maybe because he knew you weren't ready to find out just yet. Or maybe because it wasn't time. I don't know the reason, Christopher, but what's this all about?"

"He's Gerald Alcott. Paul Alcott's son. My grandfather said that he was still living in Bridgton the last time he checked. He'd found out news on James Bidwell and Richard Weiss, but nothing on Gerald. Who knows, maybe he went into hiding, but in the obituary it mentioned Gerald. About how he was the passenger in the truck when Lewis Shepherd hit Mrs. Porter. Shepherd ended up dying, but Gerald walked away with only a broken wrist and a new bookstore left in his name." I shook my head. "Damn it, Moses, he was playing me."

"He told you he was Lewis Shepherd?"

"Shook my hand and everything."

"You know what that means, don't you?"

"Yeah, I do. It means Samael got to him already. They must have made a deal. He probably realized his father's curse and got scared and begged for his life. *Shit!*"

I smacked the dashboard hard, just once, feeling the anger that I'd felt last night while I stared at the dark empty house. It lasted only a few seconds and then I went back to staring out the window again. We had passed through town and were now on 13, headed toward Horseheads.

"Feel any better?"

I said nothing.

"Look, Christopher, I understand where you're coming from, but don't let it get to you. It's in the past. Right now we need to worry about the present. We'll deal with Alcott later."

I heard his words but didn't answer and kept staring out the window. While I knew Moses understood my frustration to an extent, he didn't understand fully. In my mind, I saw Gerald Alcott making a deal with Samael and then trekking down to Lanton. Waiting outside my house until it was well past midnight, late enough where everyone would be asleep, and then breaking in through a door or window, making sure to leave no signs behind. Walking up the stairs, stepping over the eighth step that he somehow knew always creaked, then passing by my room with hardly a thought of me inside. (I, of course, would have just gotten home an hour or so earlier, passed out on my bed from partying.) He probably cut my parents' throats first, to keep them from screaming out, and once the blood poured from each of them, he began going to work. Slicing here, tearing there, until they were nothing more than butchered meat. Then, before leaving, he took their blood and painted a cross on my bedroom door.

It made sense, too, perfect sense, and I couldn't believe I'd been so blinded, so naïve to buy into the man's entire façade.

Then I thought of my brief encounter with Samael and what he told me.

"Moses?"

"Yeah."

Still staring out the window, I asked, "Did you and Joey kill my parents?"

He didn't answer for the longest time. Finally he said, "What do you think?"

"I don't know what to think anymore."

We stopped at a McDonald's just after entering Elmira. Moses used the drive thru and ordered us breakfast. Once we got the food, he parked in an empty space and turned off the engine.

He handed me my Sausage Egg McMuffin, hash brown, and orange juice without a word. Then he unwrapped his own meal and began to eat. Five minutes passed in heavy silence before Moses spoke.

"No, Christopher. Joey and I did not kill your parents."

I glanced at him. "Why didn't you just say that before?"

"I was too shocked you had even considered the possibility. I didn't know what to say."

"It was Samael. He … he put these ideas in my head."

Moses nodded. "He'll do that. You have to be prepared. You have to decide what it is you believe in and stick to it, no matter what." He paused. "Now I think it's time I should be totally honest with you. I could have told you earlier, but I … I didn't think it was a good idea."

My stomach tightening, I said, "What wasn't a good idea?"

Without a word, Moses reached behind him into the small backseat which was littered with newspapers and discarded fast food bags, empty soda cans and water bottles. He rummaged for about a minute until he handed me a folded up piece of paper. I was about to ask him what it was before the words on the front caught my attention.

Below a sketch of a church was written

Trinity Church of God
May 25, 2003
267 Ashmore Road
Lanton, PA 17359

in bold letters. At the bottom of this was a list of names, the first that of Reverend Matthew Hatfield, then—

"What the hell?"

I glanced up at Moses. He stared back at me, nodding slowly.

At the very bottom of the list, underlined, was this: **Special Guest Speaker: Moses Cunningham**.

"Like I said before, Joey told me about you even before you came here. He knew who you were and where you lived and we stopped in Lanton three weeks ago. Joey wanted to see you, to somehow get a sense of who you were. I managed to speak at Trinity that Sunday, the day after your parents were murdered, and then Tuesday we headed up here to New York. Neither of us had gotten a chance to see you, but Joey said it didn't matter, since you'd be coming here soon anyway."

"But my parents," I whispered. "You knew they were going to die."

"Yes, we knew. At least, Joey did. He told me about it but it was only that Friday afternoon and by then it wasn't like we could have changed anything."

"You could have prevented it. You could have saved their lives."

"That's true, we could have. But sometimes you have to let bad things happen for the greater good."

"That's utilitarianism bullshit."

"No, Christopher, that's life."

"But you knew ahead of time. Both of you did. You could have called the police, told them what was going to happen. Maybe they could have stopped it. Maybe then my parents would still be alive."

"Christopher, I know this, believe me I do. But you have to accept the fact that everything happens for a reason. Your parents being murdered happened so that you would come here to Bridgton. It's not fair, I know it's not, but that's how it works."

"How God works, you mean."

He was silent for a long time, staring down at the steering wheel. Finally he said, "It's not about God. I mean, not completely. It's about fate. It's about how the world works and how each and every person in it faces life. We have the freedom to decide what course we want our lives to lead before we die. Every second of every day, we're able to change it any way we want. Sometimes I look back and regret some of the choices I've made. Like coming to Bridgton. I told you, I didn't want to come here, I knew what was going to happen to Joey, but I had no choice. It was something that needed to be done, so I did it. Just like your parents, Christopher. I did nothing to prevent it because it had to happen."

I sat very still and silent. Breathing slowly. Thinking about things. Thinking about my parents. Thinking about Moses and Joey. Thinking about them knowing of my parents' murder before it even happened. Thinking about ...

"The knife," I whispered.

"What was that?"

I looked at him, my jaw set, my hands balled into fists. "Joey's present to me—where did it come from?"

"Christopher—"

"Goddamn it, Moses, tell me."

He closed his eyes, took a deep breath. "The night before we left Lanton, Joey had us drive to a specific point of the Susquehanna River. He went into the water and kept diving until he found what he was looking for. He said"—Moses swallowed—"he said you'd want to have it. Because it had already been used for evil, but when the time came, you would use it for good."

I had to close my eyes, place a hand to my head. The inside of the car had begun to spin. "So that knife …"

"Yes," Moses said. "It was the weapon used to murder your parents."

CHAPTER TWENTY-NINE

"UNBELIEVABLE."

"Henry."

"Ridiculous."

"Henry, please."

"But look at this *line!*" Henry said, waving his arms around. "There's no excuse for this."

Moses and I stood behind Henry and his wife, an old couple that looked to be in their sixties. We were lined up along the sidewalk outside Elmira High School's gymnasium, where the graduation was now taking place because every weatherman in the tri-county area had been promising rain. The line stretched out from the entrance where metal detectors were placed and continued around the building where it disappeared. So far we'd been in the line for twenty minutes.

A uniformed police officer walked up and down the line making the same announcement—"Be prepared to empty all metal objects from your pockets"—while two other officers near the front checked bags and purses and camera cases.

As one of the officers checked Henry's wife's purse, Henry

said, "This is insane! I was just at my granddaughter's gradua-tion last week and we weren't forced to go through this circus."

"This is standard procedure, sir," the officer said. His voice was flat and bored.

"Standard procedure?"

"Mike Boyd is the keynote speaker, sir. This is for his safety."

"His safety? But I didn't even vote for him!"

"Shush now, Henry," the old man's wife said.

Disgusted, Henry shook his head and kept mumbling. He took off his Wilson Golf cap and wiped his brow. Putting it back on, he noticed me watching him, and no doubt needing someone in his corner, he said to me, "Young man, don't you think this is absolutely absurd?"

My hands had been working in and out of fists since we got out of the car. My body was shaking. I couldn't get the thought of Joey's present out of my mind, or the idea that Moses had known all along, or the fact that I had actually held the thing that had caused my parents' death, that I was in fact in posses-sion of it. I'd never hated anyone so much as I hated Moses right then, and hearing Henry's words now, I nodded.

"Yeah," I said, looking at Moses for the first time. "It's fucking unbelievable."

                            ———————

Two women stood inside the entrance. They both held programs and handed them out to everyone who entered. Behind them was a table where another woman in a wheelchair sat, and behind her was a short corridor that led into the gymnasium. A sign on an easel beside the table read YOU WILL NEED TICKETS FOR FLOOR SEATS.

In the hallway itself, people—some teenagers, mostly adults —made their way toward the table or off to either the left or right. There were stairs on both ends farther down that took you up to the second level. After accepting our programs, Moses asked me which way I wanted to go.

"Don't fucking talk to me," I said.

"Christopher—"

"I said don't talk to me."

He took a moment, then started off toward the right. I was going to give it a few seconds before I followed him, but that's when I saw Sarah.

She had appeared down the end of the corridor. Standing with her arms crossed, she wore a bright yellow dress, the hem coming down to just below her knees. On her feet were leather sandals. She was talking to another girl who looked to be about the same age, wearing jeans and a black T-shirt and who looked to be ... well, trailer trash.

"Christopher, what is it?"

Moses was watching me. From the look on his face, I could tell he thought I'd just had a feeling.

"Keep walking, preacher man."

He stared at me for another moment, then turned and started away.

I walked toward the corridor, ignoring the table and the woman, until she said, "Excuse me, do you have a ticket?"

I glanced at her. "Ticket?"

She sighed. "Yes. Every graduating student's family is given two tickets for seats on the floor. Do you have one?" She said this like she'd said it a hundred times already (which she probably had), and when I shook my head, she continued, "Well, then I'm sorry, but you'll have to sit upstairs on the bleachers."

"I just need to talk to a friend of mine," I said. "She's right there."

And I pointed, as if that made any difference, but the woman simply shook her head. "I still can't let you through."

Then she turned her attention to the front doors, waiting for those people lucky enough to possess tickets.

It didn't matter, though. Sarah was done talking with her friend and had walked away, disappeared from sight down the throat of the corridor. I didn't know why, but I felt disappointed. Also, I felt angry, because she'd ignored my warning about not coming here today. But who was I kidding? Had I really thought she was going to take me seriously, a guy she hardly even knew who'd probably spooked her more than anything else?

I turned away, ready to track down Moses, and almost walked straight into my uncle.

Dean wore a light tan jacket, faded jeans and boots. He was sucking on a LifeSaver, and when he spoke I could smell a mixture of cigarettes and peppermint.

"Tell me something. Why am I suddenly filled with this unsettling dread? Is it that you've got no reason being here in the first place? Or is it that I've finally come to the conclusion that you're just bad luck?"

"There's no third option?"

"No, there's no third option."

I shrugged. "Well, then I don't know what to tell you."

Dean gave me his cold hard stare. "Moses Cunningham is here too, isn't he?"

"Who?"

He reached forward, gripped my arm. "What the fuck is going on here?"

I forced myself to stare back at him, to not break eye contact, to ignore his hand squeezing my arm and everything else in the world right at that instant. "What do you mean?"

"You know exactly what I mean. There's something going on between you and Moses Cunningham and I want to know what it is. I've had a background check done on him. He's a ghost. Nothing's come up on him since he moved away from

Ohio six years ago. He has no line of credit. He hasn't paid his taxes in years."

"And since when did you start working for the IRS?"

He squeezed my arm tighter. "Don't screw with me, Chris. What is going on here?"

"You wouldn't believe me even if I told you."

"You've said that before."

"You didn't believe me then."

"And why should I believe you now? All I ever get from you is bullshit anyway. Hell, I could have you and that ... that pastor taken out of here so quick it would make your heads spin."

I continued staring back at him without a word. It was slight, but I'd noticed the hesitation in his voice. A word had been on the tip of his tongue, a word he had caught an instant before it was too late. Nigger, he had wanted to say, he had wanted to call Moses.

"Have us taken out?" I said. "For what reason?"

"Suspicion. They received a threat last night about Mike Boyd. Who's to say that threat didn't come from Moses Cunningham himself?"

"And why would Moses do something like that?"

"I don't know, Chris. You tell me. You're both such great friends all of a sudden."

I said nothing, and neither did he. We simply continued our staring contest, waiting for the other to break.

Finally I said, "Are we done?"

He nodded. "For now. But stay on your toes. I don't know what you're up to, but I'll figure it out. And believe me when I tell you, I can't wait until you're back in Lanton and out of my life."

I should have left it at that. I should have let him have the last word, to let him turn and walk away. But I didn't. Instead I grabbed his hand still gripping my arm, pushed it away, and said, "You know what, Dean? The feeling's mutual."

Then I stopped ignoring everything else in the world and remembered where we were again. From the corner of my eye, I saw people making their way toward the stairs. After another second, I stepped around my uncle and filed in with the crowd. I didn't realize until I reached the stairs that I was shaking.

I found Moses a few minutes later. He sat by himself near the top of the bleachers overlooking the gymnasium. A little farther down, a trio of teenagers wearing all black lounged themselves over three rows; two were wearing headphones and bobbing their heads. It was nearly ten minutes before graduation was to begin and already the place was packed.

The top of the gym was a circular cement track bordered by white four-foot high steel rails. The floor itself was a wooden basketball court. Besides the usual painted lines for the key and three-point arc, there were other thinner lines used for volleyball and badminton and whatever other sports were played during P.E. Wooden bleachers were pulled out and faced each other on both sides of the court. Nearly every space was filled, except for this section which would no doubt soon start filling up fast.

Wires raised both basketball backboards so that they were out of the way. A stage was set up beneath the one backboard, with chairs and a podium and a lectern and a long table with diplomas on top. Above this stage was a long blue banner with the words

CONGRATULATIONS CLASS OF 2003

in bulky white letters. The school's band all sat clustered off to the left of the stage, and above the murmuring din of people talking, an occasional trombone or clarinet or cymbal could be heard. Rows of chairs were lined up facing front, down the entire court with a walkway in between. The first twenty rows were empty, while the rest were filled with whoever had been fortunate enough to acquire tickets.

It took me a while to spot Sarah and her father. They were near the back, a few seats in. Sarah sat reading her program (or *Billy Budd*), while Henry Porter chatted with someone behind them.

Directly across from the stage, down the walkway toward the other end of the gym, were two open exit doors. Sunlight streamed in onto the court. Though I didn't have the best position, I could see that was where all the graduating students waited. A sea of blue-robed teenagers stood talking outside.

There were only three uniformed officers spread throughout the gymnasium, at least from what I could see—two on the floor, one walking the track.

Moses didn't look up when I sat down beside him. He had his program open, seeming to read while his eyes scanned the crowd.

"Everything okay?" he asked, not looking at me.

I didn't answer.

He sighed. "Christopher, I know you're upset with me, but right now you can't let your emotions overtake you."

"Thank you for the insight, Dr. Phil. I sincerely appreciate it."

Minutes later the band started playing. The crowd quieted as they found their seats. Parents got their cameras ready. Four rows down, the one kid in black who wasn't wearing headphones nudged his two friends, who took theirs off. I glanced at Moses and saw his eyes were closed. I knew he was praying, and for the first time in a long while I felt like praying too.

Graduation had begun.

CHAPTER THIRTY

NEW YORK's former governor Mike Boyd never got a chance to make his keynote speech. Jeffery Snyder was halfway through his salutatorian address a half hour into the ceremony when there was a scream. More screams followed. Commotion began on the floor, and moments later someone shouted, "*Stop, drop your weapons!*" and then there were three consecutive gunshots followed by silence.

It all happened within the space of two minutes.

And in those two minutes, a familiar feeling passed through me and I saw and felt everything. How this happened, even now I can't explain, but I saw and felt everything because, somehow, I was there.

I'm sitting next to Moses in the bleachers, watching the crowd, and when that cold pang slices through my soul, I close my eyes—

BLINK

—and when I open them again I'm no longer next to

Moses, I'm no longer even in the bleachers. Instead I'm standing on stage, in front of everyone. A mass of students in blue robes sits in the seats before me, their parents and grandparents and other relatives sitting in the seats behind them. Many of their eyes are trained on the student standing at the lectern to my left, not seven feet away. It's Jeffery Snyder, the second in his graduating class of two hundred and fifty one, and right now he's in the middle of his speech. His voice is low and monotone, and he keeps clearing his throat and looking down at the note cards scattered in front of him.

I look around, at the teachers and principals and administrators and even Mike Boyd in the chairs on the stage behind the lectern, at the band on the platform, at the people in the bleachers. None seem to notice me. Even one of the police officers, standing near the stage, hasn't looked my way. I'm here but I'm not here, I realize, as I take a step forward and glance toward where I found Moses sitting earlier. Yes, I can just see Moses, I can see him sitting there, slowly looking around the gym for anything suspicious. And there, beside him, is a white kid whose parents were murdered less than two weeks ago. His eyes are closed, his mouth slightly open.

What's happening to me? I ask myself, but it's not like in a dream, where I have no control over what happens, and internal questions like this one go unanswered. I understand immediately what's happening to me—or at least I have a sense —and when I look around once more at everyone in the gym, I realize that everything is gray, everything is colorless, except Jeffery Snyder. He's the only one with color, the only one I can sense. I know his birthday, his America Online password, his old locker combination, and as I take a step closer to him, I know that, as he's speaking, he's thinking not about his words but about how he'll die a virgin.

He's never had a girlfriend, he's never even had the nerve to ask anyone out, even though some girls have expressed interest in him in the past. One girl in particular is Sarah Porter, who, though he was not aware of it, once had a crush on him. But Jeffery was intimated by her older brother, thinking that if John Porter found out Jeffery asked his little sister on a date then bad things would happen. So he chickened out, just like with all the other girls he once had crushes on, and in the last three years he has become addicted to looking at porn on the Internet.

I pause, seeing all of this in my mind. I can hear Jeffery speaking, continuing his speech, but his words are lost to me. All that I hear are his internal thoughts, about how his parents have just recently gotten a cable modem and how he has been spending more and more time on the computer, liking how the images and videos load faster than with the old dial-up. I see everything that Jeffery has seen, all the websites he's been to, all the pictures of big-breasted women with their legs spread open wide and long hard cocks pushed up their asses.

I take a step back, breaking the montage of pornographic images, and somehow manage to look even deeper. I see how Jeffery thinks he'll never find a girl who likes him for who he is, and that's why he'll die a virgin. He's going to Syracuse in the fall and hopes to find a girl there who will put out but figures he will, in the end, have to pay some prostitute to have sex with him. Some high-priced prostitute too, not one with diseases, he doesn't want to get sick.

I take another step back, reminding myself of what I'd done to my grandmother and her friends back at Alice's. Here is almost the same thing, only I have no control over these memories, no power at all over these deviant urges. Without thinking, I ball my hands into fists—and how I'm actually able to feel them even though I'm not really here is beyond me— and take three steps forward.

A scene materializes in my mind, a party Jeffery invited himself to over Christmas break and which he had felt totally out of place. He ended up snorting cocaine. He didn't know what to expect and wasn't even sure the crack worked right, so he tried it two more times. Everyone else just laughed and cheered him on. Then later he was upstairs and walked in on Tommy Wertham having sex with Reece Davis ... except Tommy was the only one really having sex. Reece was passed out on the bed. Tommy looked back, grunting. A huge grin spread across his face. He said *Hey Jeff, you want the sloppy seconds?* and Jeffery had stood there for just a moment, before bolting out of the room and into the bathroom down the hall, the one that reeked of bleach. He threw up before he even made it to the toilet.

As Jeffery speaks, I realize that, as he looks up from his note cards, he's searching the faces of his graduating peers. He has already spotted Reece and Tommy, and the thought of outing Tommy as the one who raped Reece has crossed his mind more than once. Just stopping mid-sentence and pointing out into the crowd, telling everyone here that Tommy raped her like she was nothing and then offered him the sloppy seconds. But Jeffery, though the thought does sound righteous, will do no such thing. He doubts Reece even knows what happened that night, and even if she does, she has probably forced herself to forget. It's her dark secret of shame, unlike Tommy who has probably told all his friends, who then went on and told their friends. Has it gotten back to Reece that it was Tommy who violated her?

Probably, Jeffery thinks, though she will never do anything about it. But what Jeffery finds most unsettling is the reason he became sick that night. It wasn't from the cocaine, or the fast food he ate earlier, or the scene he just witnessed. No, rather than all of those things, it was for a split second he had almost taken Tommy up on his offer. He couldn't believe he considered doing to Reece what he saw done on the countless porn sites he's visited over the past three years. A primal, prurient urge caused blood to surge into his penis, hardening it more than ever, and for an instant he almost nodded and said that yes, he would like the sloppy seconds.

But he couldn't do that. He'd known Reece since the fifth grade—she had even given him a Valentine's Day card that year, shaped like a boat—and for some reason it felt wrong. And, Jeffery realized, it felt even more wrong that maybe he would have gone along with it had it been anyone else but her.

This all flashes through me in the space of seconds, though really for me time has stopped. I'm in a gray world, standing next to the only person with color, the only person with life. He's a scared young man, addicted to sex even though he has never had it and thinks he never will. And why I'm looking into his life makes no sense to me, but an idea comes to mind, an idea that wants to command whatever metaphysical body I possess to continue walking forward.

But before I can do this, a girl in the chairs in front of the stage cries out. Jeffery pauses, looking up once again from his note cards, and now I'm seeing the girl through his eyes. Her name is Joyce Parsons, she was one of the cheerleaders during football season, and now she's standing up from her seat. Her arms are held out at her sides as she stares down at the floor. She screams again and tries to jump up on her seat, but her heel slips and she starts to fall. Others close by begin scream-ing. Jeffery just stands there, staring out at the crowd, out at Joyce. For the final instant I'm near him, before I'm blinked someplace else, I sense his thoughts. He can't help but wonder what he would do to Joyce Parsons if he ever found her unconscious.

———

Standing in the bleachers, now on the left side of the stage, I stare across the gym and again spot Moses and myself. Moses is still looking around the crowd for anything suspicious, and the kid next to him still has his eyes closed, his mouth open. Jeffery Snyder is still speaking on stage, and when I glance at the rows and rows of students sitting before him, I realize Joyce Parsons has yet to stand up. A few words of Jeffery Snyder's speech catch my attention and I understand that it'll be another minute or so before the girl screams. Right now he's standing there, reciting the speech he's spent hours and hours writing and rewriting, while unconsciously thinking about how he'll die a virgin. Unlike before, he's now gray, just like everyone else in the gymnasium is gray.

Everyone except the woman sitting in front of me.

Her name is Cynthia Parker and she's with her husband Ben and nine-year-old son Ricky. She should be down in the seats along with the rest of the proud parents, but her daughter Michelle gave her tickets away to a friend who had an oversized family of eleven and needed extras. Cynthia, though she claimed she was not upset, has not yet forgiven Michelle for doing such a stupid and inconsiderate thing.

Like up on stage, I look around me. Cynthia and her family are actually in the middle of this section of bleachers, so the space behind them is not empty. There is another family there, an uncle and aunt and three cousins who came all the way from Nebraska to see someone named Jimmy Guernsey get his diploma, and where I find myself standing I'm actually straddling the uncle's one knee. I want to step away to someplace where I'll have more room, but it will be next to impossible to attempt without touching someone … and here, I wonder, what will happen if I were to touch one of these people? Would they shiver, feeling a chill race through their body? Would they somehow see or sense me?

Before I can do anything though, I glance once more at Cynthia Parker. Her back is to me, so I can't see her face, but I know what she looks like. The curve of her jaw, the definition of her cheekbones, the slope of her nose. She has always considered herself an attractive woman, and even now, at forty-two, she is debating whether or not to start an affair. She's been working as an RN at St. Joseph's for nearly a decade, and has recently become infatuated with a young man named Juan. He just began working as an orderly on her floor two months ago, but she knew from the moment they first talked that there was something between them. He's over ten years her junior, but still there's an intriguing look in his dark Spanish eyes every time he talks to her, something that makes her remember her college days when she went out with her sorority sisters every weekend. And his accent—good Lord, it reminds her of Antonio Banderas in the Zorro movie. Some of the girls at work have joked with her about when she's going to go after him, but she merely laughs it off, saying she wishes. She knows the flirting between them is completely innocent, just as he knows she's married with children. Yet every time they are together she feels something there, some magnetic pull that is almost too strong to ignore.

Again, just like with Jeffery Snyder, I begin to wonder what any of this has to do with what's happening now, why Moses and I are here, when I realize something. Cynthia was one of the nurses on duty the day I was brought to the hospital, when I rode up to the third floor and walked down the hallway to Joey's room. She had been one of the many on that floor who got a glimpse of me and had wondered just what was going on. The police hadn't explained much, and all that any of them knew was that the boy had been assaulted to the point where he was very close to death. Then, when the heart monitor at the nurse's station went off, she had been one of the three nurses that rushed into the room. She had been the first nurse to grab me and try to pull me away. But she hadn't kept her mind completely on task. Not that it would have changed anything in the end, but she had been thinking about Juan,

about what he might do to her if and when he took her panties
off. Would he be gentle, she wondered, or would he be rough?
Would he bite her nipples, would he squeeze them hard?
Would he take her from behind like that one boy had that
night her sophomore year at school when she'd had too much
vodka and had gotten really horny?

These were the thoughts that went through Cynthia Parker's mind in the last few moments of Joey Cunningham's life.
She never faltered in her work, however, though she would
wonder later, after the rush had left her, if maybe things would
have turned out differently had she been concentrating more
on saving the boy. She couldn't help that her thoughts kept
returning to Juan, just like she couldn't help that she was falling
more and more out of love with her husband every day. She
didn't want to hurt him though, just as she didn't want to hurt
her children. But she had needs, she had wants, and she didn't
think it was fair that she needed to be chained down in a love-
less marriage just because it was convenient for everyone else.

She glances down at her program to remind herself who's
speaking. Jeffery Snyder, in her opinion, is the most boring
person in the world. She wants to yawn but manages to
suppress the urge. Instead she glances out over the crowd on
the gymnasium floor, the place where she should be sitting
right now. She spots Michelle at once, sitting between Daniel
Paolangeli, one of the school's football stars, and Joyce Parsons,
one of the school's many sluts—at least, this is the gossip
Cynthia's heard from other school parents. Right now it looks
like Michelle's whispering to Joyce, just as many of the other
students are doing right at this moment. Cynthia can't blame
them. If Juan was here right now, she has no doubt she would
be whispering with him as much as possible, probably place her
hand on his leg, move her finger up and down the inside of
his thigh.

A hand touches her knee, startling her enough that she

actually jumps. She looks over, sees Ben staring back at her. He gives her a curious look, as if to ask if she's okay, and then smiles. He mouths *I love you* and she smiles back, takes his hand and holds onto it. And as she does she imagines that the hand belongs to Juan, and that if she were naked in her bath right now, she would guide the middle finger of his hand inside her.

She looks up then, back at where Michelle's sitting and whispering with Joyce. A few of the students, she notices with amusement, have made messages on the tops of their mortarboards with masking tape. She can barely read them from where she sits—and again, the fact that she's way up here in the bleachers makes her angry at her daughter—but one of the boys sitting one row in front of Michelle looks like his mortarboard says CLASS COCK, though that can't possibly be right, one of the administrators would surely have yanked him from his seat if that was the case.

Then, all at once, she notices Michelle's head jerk suddenly to the left. Beside her, Joyce has begun shaking and waving her hands around like her feet are on fire. She cries out and stands, tries to jump up onto her seat but slips and falls into the row in front of her. More screams erupt from the students and Cynthia realizes the boring Jeffery Snyder has stopped his speech.

I take a mental step back, watching the ensuing chaos from this new vantage point. I focus on Moses. He's half-standing now, trying to get a better look at what's happening, and isn't even aware that beside him my body is still motionless, my eyes closed.

Something in Cynthia's mind brings me back to her, and I realize that movement has caught her attention from the corner of her eye. She looks over at where all the graduating students have entered. Sunlight pours in and she sees the shadows of two figures from outside heading toward the entrance. She can't be certain, but it looks like they're carrying something in their hands.

A split second before she realizes what it is they're carrying, she squeezes Ben's hand very tightly and—

BLINK

—I'm standing in the middle aisle, between the chairs set up on the gym floor. Up on stage, Jeffery Snyder is repeating the words of his speech I've heard two times already. I look around quickly, just like I did up on stage, seeing only gray bodies and gray faces and then, at once, I spot the one person here full of color and life. And I can't help but begin to smile, even with everything that's happening—and everything, I realize, that will.

It's Melvin Dumstorf, *the* best goddamned white free style rapper in Chemung County, the one with the dope ninja skills, and he's sitting near the middle of his row, between Markus Duncan and Sandra Dull. His arms are crossed and he's staring up at Jeff on stage like this all bores him, like he doesn't have a single care in the world, when in reality that's very much not true. Just yesterday his grandparents flew in from Massachusetts, a surprise visit as his grand-pop called it, and while it's nice having them here, their arrival has certainly complicated things.

There are five people between me and Melvin, so I'm not able to get as close as I'd like. The idea that came to me up on stage with Jeffrey Snyder—and here I glance up there, for some reason expecting to see a ghost of myself standing beside him—keeps gnawing at me, wanting me to give it a try. But here the only way it might work is walking over five people, and I still don't want to touch others if I can help it. So I just stand here, staring intently at Melvin, trying to look deep inside his mind, deep inside his soul, to understand why now, out of everyone else, I'm focused on him.

The free styling, I now see, is something that does not come naturally to Melvin, though it might seem that way to dozens of drunk and high teenagers. Ever since he became a freshman, he knew he would need something to help set him apart from everyone else, something that would make him cool, and so he chose rapping. He looked up websites, he read books, and he practiced continuously in his room with the door closed. His parents knew about his hobby but never said anything to him, though he knew he disappointed his dad. Even the juggling disappointed his dad. But, he felt, his free styling and ninja skills didn't even come close to disappointing his old man as much as his true secret would. Because ever since he turned fifteen, Melvin had begun questioning his sexual preference. He was even planning to finally come out to his parents this weekend, but now, with his grandparents here, he knows he will have to wait.

No one at school knows about him, because he hasn't told anyone. There are a few students who expressed their homosexuality over the course of the year, and while some were accepted, a few were not. Melvin was uncertain how it would be for him, and so, instead of expressing himself freely like he seems to do constantly in his raps, he decided to lay low. He knew, after nearly two years of worrying about it, that he was gay, but he wasn't sure what the next step was. Coming out to his parents was the biggest step, in his opinion, but he still wasn't ready yet. His mom would understand and accept him —he was almost one hundred percent certain on this point— but his dad was a whole different story. The news, he knew, might literally give his old man a heart attack.

He's dated girls of course, has even had sex with two of them, at parties where everyone was drunk and horny and he was the center of attention, having performed his free styling that he'd practiced again and again. He hates it when people think he rehearses, even when it's true, so at Denise's party the other night, when Chad Eason said he was rehearsing, it really pissed him off and he had, after getting that citation from the cops and finally making it home, cried himself to sleep.

It isn't that he wants to be gay, and that, he tells himself, is how he knows he is. He just doesn't feel the way toward girls that he does toward guys, though he's never even kissed one before ... though, late at night, while lying in bed, he has wondered what it would feel like. Lips are lips, a tongue is a tongue, so there really should be no difference between kissing a girl and a guy—but Melvin, after much thought, has decided this isn't true. There *is* a difference, and he very much wants to experience it.

This is what I sense Melvin Dumstorf thinking while he sits there, staring up at Jeffrey Snyder. On the outside appearing cool and relaxed and in control of the world, while on the inside falling apart. So when the first mouse skitters from under his chair and between his feet, he doesn't notice until another one follows.

Someone whispers behind him, suppresses a laugh.

Melvin glances back.

And speak of the devil, Chad Eason—my old beer-pong partner from Thursday night—is sitting there behind Melvin. He's whispering to Neil Eakins. All Melvin hears, behind Jeff's low voice booming from the speakers set up around the gym and his own worried thoughts, are the words *best prank ever* before Neil stifles a laugh. Then Chad notices Melvin looking at him and lifts his chin, says, "Yo Eminem, the show's up there."

Melvin just shakes his head. He turns his attention back up front, to where Jeff continues his speech. He's hardly been listening the entire time, only knows that the speech is the usual   we-as-graduates-must-now-face-the-real-world   theme because that's what all these speeches are always about. The mice he saw are now gone, and he begins to wonder if he really even saw them at all.

I wonder the same thing, standing where I am, I wonder why I'm here in the middle of the gymnasium like this, when Joyce screams. I glance back, right at where Joyce is trying to stand up on her seat, then past her at the open entrance at the back of the gym. The two shadows aren't there yet; they still have another couple of seconds or so before they appear. And when they do, will they be carrying what Cynthia Parker was certain they were? Staring toward the open gym doors, I can't quite see from where I am, *everything* is gray (sound, taste, touch), and as Joyce begins falling into the row of students in front of her, I connect with Melvin Dumstorf's mind one last time. Right before there's another blink and I'm gone from this spot, he thinks *What kind of prank is this?*

Only more screams answer him.

CHAPTER THIRTY-ONE

I'M STILL in the aisle between rows, only this time I'm back a couple yards from where I was standing earlier. Of course, earlier doesn't exist on whatever plane I'm on, because up on stage, Jeffery Snyder is continuing his speech like he has this entire time, and Joyce Parsons has yet to scramble up from her seat and begin crying out. The person who's not gray like everyone else this time around is named Frank Olson, sitting three people in on his side of the row.

Frank Olson, who arrived just in time to witness Jeremy and his friends finishing up as they desecrated John Porter's car Thursday night. Frank Olson, who John told to go ahead with whatever it was they had planned. Frank Olson, who is ninety-nine percent certain it was Chad's idea to pull their last great prank during graduation.

I step forward, wanting to look deeper into Frank's mind, and after a short moment of mental digging, I manage to see how this started two weeks ago.

They are all in John Porter's garage, sitting around the Firebird John has been restoring for the past couple years. John's old man has gone up to Ithaca for something and nobody else is home except John's sister, who's gotten herself knocked up but has a cute enough face that sometimes Frank thinks he'd still have relations with her, even if she is pregnant. Tyler has brought the weed and Chad has brought the beer. It's Pabst Blue Ribbon, some pretty shitty beer if there ever was any, but they're only eighteen and can't complain. How the fuck Chad manages to always get the beer is beyond Frank, but he doesn't mind putting in the cash when the time comes. So as they're all smoking and drinking and having a good time (System of a Down is playing some hardcore stuff on the stereo), someone mentions how they need to pull one final prank, something that will set them apart from all the rest of the wannabes and make them legends. Frank will never remember completely who says this, but he'll always think it was Chad.

"All right," John says. He takes a hit off the roach and passes it to Sean. "So what the fuck's your idea?"

"Graduation," says the person who is most likely Chad but might not be.

"What about graduation?"

"That's where we should do our prank. Think about it. The place will be packed. Even that old shithead governor's gonna be there. We'll have a huge audience. Whatever happens there, nobody's ever gonna forget."

"Okay," John says. "So what do you suggest we do?"

They come up with a bunch of ideas, but all of them are stoned and hardly any of them remember any of the suggestions. The thought never occurs to write them down, but the only one that sticks out later in their minds is getting snakes. Small non-poisonous snakes that they can sneak into the ceremony and then let loose at the same time. Frank even looks into it, calling around to pet stores. He finds that the snakes they want are simple milk snakes, which, the woman at the store tells him, are a part of the Colubridae family. "*Lampropeltis triangulum*," she says, her voice snotty and smug, but the price for the number of milk snakes they need is way too much for any of them to spend, and they decide to scrap the idea.

"Besides," John says a few nights later in the garage, this time with some new weed and some new beer (Keystone Light, thank God) and Tool on the stereo, "think about how much fuckin' trouble we'd get in."

"What do you think's gonna happen to us?" Tyler asks. "They're gonna suspend us?"

"No, dipshit. We'd probably get arrested. Not worth it, you ask me. Shit, I already signed up for the Marines. The last fuckin' thing I need right now is a record."

It was left at that until Denise Rowe's party Thursday night, when the shit hit the fan. Then John decided they really had nothing to lose and might as well go out with a bang, so he told Frank to get things in order.

Only snakes, apparently, were out of the question. Mice on the other hand …

Of the seven of them—Frank, Randy, Chad, Sean, Tyler, Rich, John—each has four mice hidden under their robes. The plan is to let them loose during Mike Boyd's speech. They were all set and pumped to do it until they got to school today and saw how much security was around. Rich wanted to back out, but Tyler said he'd kick the shit out of him if he backed out now, and besides, what did they have to lose, they were graduating, they might as well live it up now than regret it later.

In the end, each of them took their four mice. Sean, whose parents had raised him to be a staunch Catholic (and who now had to wear his arm in a sling after Thursday night), jokingly named his Matthew, Mark, Luke, and John. They've been keeping them in leather bags under their robes this entire time, tied to their belts. The mice make some squeaking noises, but they can barely be heard in their bags. Shanice Olivarez has looked over at Frank more than once, frowning at him when she hears the squeaking, and each time Frank just shrugs. The apprehension he felt earlier has worn off and he's set and pumped again, he's ready to do this. But then something catches his attention. John Porter, sitting two rows behind him, reaches under his own robe. He's sitting behind Joyce Parsons and whispering to her. She looks disgusted like she always does, like she's too good and wants nothing to do with him.

It's at this point I step away from Frank Olson, position myself so I can see down John Porter's row and watch exactly what he's doing. John looks at me—past me, really—at someone on the other side of the aisle. I turn just in time to see that it's Randy, the other kid I didn't know Thursday who arrived late to the party with Frank. Randy, catching John's cue, nods, begins reaching under his robe. He too looks up ahead. I follow his eyes and see Sean, who nods, then Chad, who nods, and then before I can continue to watch the progress of the signal, I turn my attention back to John Porter. He already has his leather bag out from under his robe. He leans forward, whispers something else to Joyce, who turns her head slightly and mouths what looks like *fuck off* to him. Grinning, he opens the bag, leans even closer, reaches over her shoulder, and empties the four white mice right on her lap.

For an instant Joyce does nothing but simply stare down at her lap with wide, unbelieving eyes. At the same moment, seeing this, Frank Olson wonders to himself why he's always the last to know what's going on, and he despises that John Porter always seems to forget him unless he needs something. Then, a second later, Joyce—

BLINK

—knows something is wrong here at this graduation, but he just can't put his finger on it. Alan Hoffman, who has worked at the *Star-Gazette* for three years already, has covered his share of high school graduations, and he knows that the amount of security detailed right now is much too excessive, even if Mike Boyd was once the governor of this fine state.

Alan is a short man with the beginnings of a potbelly and a camera case slung over his shoulder, a mustache that just doesn't look right on his face. He stands near the back of the gymnasium, facing the stage. He, just like Cynthia Parker, is of the opinion that Jeffery Snyder is one of the most boring speakers he's ever heard. He feels bad for the kid though, because it takes balls to get up in front of people like this, even if it is for a stupid graduation. Alan's taken two shots of him already, both of which he knows will never make the layout because who really cares about the salutatorian anyway? He wonders not for the first time, and certainly not for the last, why he's always given these boring asinine assignments, when other photographers like Sharon and Matthew get the sports events and crime scenes.

Except this, he knows, is really his fault. Matthew had been away on Tuesday, when the call came in about something out on 13 near Bridgton, but Alan was going to go to lunch and decided not to take it. Couldn't be anything, he thought, probably just some vehicle accident, and it wasn't until he came back from Subway that he found out what really happened. How that kid who had been abducted Sunday night was just found. Sharon, who even told the boss to "throw Alan a bone," had captured some really good pictures even though nothing was shown in her shots except a depression in the grass.

I glance around once more, at everything that's gray—I see Moses still scanning the crowd for anything suspicious, me still with my eyes closed—and without hesitation I follow through with the idea that had blossomed in my mind when I was first up on stage with Jeffery Snyder. I walk the four steps toward Alan Hoffman until I'm forced to walk another step *into* him. Just like I thought, the man shivers only slightly, a chill passing through his body, but he thinks nothing of it. Really, *I* think nothing of it, because now I'm seeing and feeling and thinking everything that makes Alan Hoffman the man he is. The spirit or force or whatever that is Christopher Myers has no control here, is only along for the ride.

Yes, I'm irritable because I missed out on the opportunity to get some shots of where the kid was found, but what really pissed me off was just yesterday, in the mail, I got a response from *Newsweek* that no, they're not looking for any new photographers, thank you for asking. It was really nothing more than a stupid form letter, and I was mad for nearly the entire day. Even when Shelia came home and tried to cheer me up, I hardly said more than three words to her.

And Shelia's another thing that's begun to piss me off. I've been with her for two years and still she loves her work more than she loves me, she loves those fucking retards she works with down at the home. She'll never leave Elmira, she'll never follow me if I take a job somewhere else—and this, I tell myself, is the reason I haven't even tried, knowing deep down inside it's just because I'm not good enough. Our relationship is going nowhere, has been really since we started, and we've only discussed the possibility of marriage to fill conversation. When I met her she was a virgin and said she was going to wait until she got married, but it didn't take me long before I got her to change her mind. Only four months, and while that might not be a record, I sure felt damned proud of myself and have some-times even bragged about it down at the bar with a few of my buddies. Still, the fact that I'm Shelia's first isn't enough for her to love me, and that's what really pisses me off.

Maybe I'll break up with her. Ask out Stacey in advertising that I sometimes flirt with. Yeah, that's the ticket. Fuck Shelia and those fucking retards, they can love each other as much as they want for all I care.

Pissed, determined, I decide to take some random shots of the crowd in the bleachers. There's no reason for this, it's just because I'm bored, and I manage to click off only one shot when I first hear the girl scream. It's so out of place, so unnatural for this setting, that at first I'm not even sure I heard it. I've been anticipating somebody's cell going off in the middle of the ceremony (and how this hasn't happened yet is a miracle; really, somebody should contact the fucking *Guinness Book of World Records*) but nothing like this. Then others begin screaming and shouting, too, and I look up at all of them near the front, all on their feet.

"What the hell?" I mutter. I raise the camera, sight at the twenty or more students moving frantically around, press the shutter twice. I only pause when I notice a man making his way toward where all the students entered the gym almost a half hour earlier. He's moving fast and reaching into his jacket.

"*Stop*," he shouts, pulling out a gun from inside his jacket, "*drop your weapons!*"

I see the two boys then. Both dressed in black, one wearing a trench coat, they're jogging through the open doors and—and oh fuck, they're carrying rifles. They ignore the man and continue forward into the gym. The one in front even begins to raise his rifle.

The man with the gun doesn't hesitate: he fires three times, hitting first the boy in the front and then the boy in the back before hitting the first boy again. Blood splatters from each of their chests. The second boy falls to his knees moments before the first boy does. Then they're both on the ground.

At first I don't know what to do. I just stand there, staring down at the two fallen bodies, as uniformed police officers start swarming them from all angles. Then something in the back of my mind whispers *award winning* and I think that maybe yes, I will break up with Shelia later tonight. This is, after all, my lucky day. At once I aim the camera and begin—

BLINK

—waiting in the van since eleven o'clock. Dressed in black

pants and black T-shirts (Adam's shirt has Slipknot on the front, now turned inside out), they were roasting for nearly a half hour when Martin finally pulled out his bag of hash. Usually he grins at Adam before rolling their joint, but this time he just went straight to work. The fuzz was outside but neither of them cared, and after Martin lit his and took a hit, he passed it to Adam who took two hits and then just stared out at the gym.

I'm crouched in the back of the van, actually feeling a bit vertiginous after my experience walking into Alan Hoffman. Of course I'm no longer inside, I'm out in the parking lot, but I know that Jeffery Snyder is continuing halfway through his speech, everyone inside listening to it for the first time while this would be my sixth. The van, though I can't feel it, is stifling hot, and it's messy as hell. I try not to pay too much attention to it right now (not to the mattress or the pair of rifles on top), because I understand whose van this is, and I know what's going to happen very soon. Not only that, I recognize these two from the other night at Denise Rowe's party. The one who was drenched in beer is behind the wheel. His name is Martin Luhr, but the one who has color, who has life, is Adam Grant, sitting in the passenger seat, both of his feet up and pressed against the dash. I take a step forward, trying to look deeper into Adam's mind. I'm not sure I want to step *into* him, at least not yet, not after the restriction I had in Alan Hoffman, because once I was in I wasn't able to step out until I was blinked here.

The windows of the van are down. Martin doesn't want to run the engine because he fears it might attract attention, which Adam thinks is funny considering that the outside of this black piece of shit is an eyesore everywhere it goes. So there's no A/C and they have the windows down, but not all the way.

Martin picked up the rifles last night. They're two match

rifles, EA-15 Golden Eagles with .223 caliber and twenty-inch Douglas Premium barrels. They're nearly ten years old and have their serial numbers scratched off. Martin drove all the way to Syracuse and bought them both—along with two boxes of Wolf Ammunition—for five hundred bucks from a guy who sometimes sells them heroin. (He even admitted to Adam he used the fifty bucks he had left over on a hooker he picked up on Canal Street behind the Greyhound bus station; he wanted her to fuck him and she said no way, not for that little, but he got a blowjob instead.)

That morning they had breakfast at a greasy diner in Big Flats, both ordering hotcakes and sausage links and coffee, and then stiffing the old bat of a waitress out of her tip. Adam doesn't know about Martin, but he didn't sleep very well last night. Even this morning, while they ate at their booth in silence and chain-smoked Pall Malls, he kept yawning. Then they got into the van, drove behind the Elmira-Corning Regional Airport, and silently loaded the Golden Eagles. Finally they drove here to the high school, the radio playing some kind of rock music, though if asked, Adam would be hard pressed to say what because he can't recall a single song.

They watched them out there waiting to go inside. All dressed in their fancy blue robes and talking and laughing. Even a few couples stood off to the side, holding hands, kissing. It made Martin and Adam sick. They should be there too, walking in formation with their fellow graduating peers while proud parents took snapshot after snapshot. But no, here they are instead in Martin's van (reeking of sweat and body odor and hash), which Martin more or less lives in now.

From where I'm crouched, I glance once at Martin, who's now taking a drag of the joint. He's the hard case, I realize, the stronger—and angrier—one of the two. Why he's not the one in color now I have no clue, though I wish he was, I wish I could look deep into his dark and twisted soul. Instead I can just glimpse into Adam's and see how their friendship began.

Friends since they were five, they became blood brothers the day Martin cut his hand on a rock while they were playing down near Newtown Creek. He made Adam cut his own hand too, on a black rock with a sharpened edge. They then held their hands together, so that their blood could become one. "All right," Martin said, "from this day on we're blood brothers, you got it? That means we're friends forever." Forever is a long time, but at eleven years old it was just a word with no real meaning —though a word both boys promised to live by, no matter what.

Martin's grades were never good, while Adam's were so-so. But after Martin flunked out of eleventh grade and stopped going, Adam only went for three weeks his senior year before deciding to drop out. He has no friends besides Martin, and at times outside his regular classes, like during lunch or home-room, he felt so alone.

His mom was pissed but she was already too wrapped up in her own life to worry much, what with all the gin she drinks every night and the men she brings home after working nine hours at the bar. Adam has gotten used to the loud drunks who come in and fuck his mom and then leave after they're done— only sometimes they don't leave right away, as Adam remem-bers one night waking up to a man pissing right on him in bed; he was thirteen and scared and didn't know what to do, so he started crying, which caused the man to laugh out loud. Some-times they place money on the kitchen table before leaving (almost always two or three twenty dollar bills, never anything larger than a fifty), and at first this made Adam mad until he realized that, if he got up early enough, he could take a bill from the scattered pile and his mom would never know. His dad walked out on him when he was six and who the fuck knows where he is now, for all Adam cares the bastard's dead, so it's just been him and his mom and the random guy who sticks his cock in her hole the night she brings him home.

Martin's parents, on the other hand, never split apart, though they never really cared for him much either. He was seven when he first started playing with fire and almost burned down the garage. Babysitters would never work twice after watching Martin. He always tried to pull up their skirts or touch their chests, and after a while it became known that Martin Luhr was not a kid you wanted to watch for five bucks an hour—after all, his mom was on welfare and could hardly afford to pay more, his dad was in jail half the time, so most of the families around the neighborhood felt sorry for him. For the first couple of years anyway.

It was the occasional times Martin saw and talked with his dad that gave him the idea. How this world is designed for winners and losers, and how each boy and girl is destined from the moment they are born which they're going to be.

"Martin," his dad would say, his breath reeking of tobacco and whiskey, "you're my son, which means you're a goddamn loser like me. But that's okay, it ain't so bad. It's your job to show them winners just how big of a loser you can be. Really shit on their parade, you get me? And so what if you end up going to jail once or twice. Ain't no shame in it. I tell you, sometimes I prefer it to actually finding a goddamn job."

It didn't take long for Adam to see that he was a loser too, that he would always be a loser. Nothing he could do would change that. There are winners, there are losers, and as a loser himself, Adam began to hate those that weren't like him. He began to see them differently, just as Martin did. He imagined the lives the winners would have, the wives and husbands they'd marry, the jobs they'd get, the houses they'd own and the families they'd make, the vacations they'd take during the summers to faraway places. It made him sick sometimes, and even sad.

"Come on, dude," Martin said one night, when Adam let this slip, "it really ain't so bad. Think about it. You wanna be a loser, or you wanna be nothing at all?"

The answer is simple, of course, actually very obvious. But still Adam's been having second thoughts, ever since two months ago, when they first started talking about what they could do to right the balance. How they can make those who see themselves as winners take a step down to the level of noth-ingness, if not for a few seconds, where Martin and Adam will then be on top. It's beautiful, something that has made Adam smile more than once, but still he's hesitant, still he keeps wanting to talk to Martin about this seriously, not when they're high. Martin has become determined, has become almost philosophical in the way he sometimes talks, that it scares Adam.

Which, I realize, is the reason I'm here now, why every-thing else is gray and lifeless except him. He's been scared for a while, just like he's scared right now, and maybe I can use this to my advantage. Maybe stepping into Alan Hoffman was a practice run. Maybe this time, if I attempt it again, I can gain control.

"Look at 'em," Martin said earlier, while all the graduating seniors waited outside under the warm and heavy glow of the sun. "It'd be like shooting fish in a bucket. You know what I mean?"

"Yeah," Adam said, thinking *Ain't it barrel?* By then they'd already done two hits each and were working on their third. "You wanna do it now? Just mow 'em down like they're fuckin' nothing?"

"Shit, Adam. You know the plan. We wait, take as many out as we can inside. Let their parents watch. Let them see how their goddamn precious winners quickly become nothing."

Adam, really feeling it then, started to laugh. "That's fuckin' awesome."

"Damn straight."

Martin had parked relatively close to the gym, but not too close that the fuzz would come by looking inside. Even if they did, all they would see besides the Golden Eagles and the two black boxes of Wolf Ammunition would be a mattress and some clothes, some empty Rolling Rock cans, some skin magazines that were so obscure even Adam hasn't heard of any of them.

Now, nearly a half hour later, they pass their second joint and watch the empty lawn. It's short and even, having just been mowed early this morning or late last night. The two exit doors are propped wide open. Two uniformed cops keep walking around the building, and Martin has it timed out just right. At least he says he does, Adam isn't totally sure. They don't know what's going on inside or who's speaking, and are both pissed that the ceremony was moved inside, instead of out on the football field, where they could see everything.

Finally Martin decides to quit wasting time, and says, "You ready?" Adam, holding the joint, takes one final hit. Then he just stares at his friend, his only friend in the world, for what seems a very long time. He grins and nods, passes Martin back the joint, and it's at this point I move forward, prepared to stop this any way I can. I've already seen what the end result will be but maybe I can still change it somehow, maybe I can prevent it. So I move forward and then sit *into* Adam, who shivers just once, then shakes his head. Martin has taken the joint and snubbed it out on the dash.

"The fuck you doin' man?" I say. "That's good dope."

Martin breaks out his switchblade and releases the knife. It pops up, a good six inches of stainless steel, and for a second I think that this is it, this is where Martin finally snaps and kills me. *Oh shit oh shit oh shit*, I think, but then Martin takes his hand and runs the blade across it. A thin red line of blood appears on his palm. He points the knife at me.

"Your turn."

"What the fuck?"

"Listen now. You agreed to this. You know we might not come out of this alive, and if we do, we'll end up going to jail where we'll probably die anyway. But at least we won't be nothing. Now remember when we were kids, how we became blood brothers? Okay, so gimme your hand."

I just sit there in my seat, my feet still pressed against the van's dash. I want to shake my head, I want to tell him no, I want to get the fuck out of the van and just run away. But all I can do is just sit here, like I'm paralyzed or something.

"Come on, Adam," Martin says, staring at me hard. "You know we have to do this. Besides, we gave them a chance to redeem themselves and look how they fucked it up."

That's right, we did give them a chance. It was my idea, my way of trying to talk Martin out of it. I mentioned this party I'd heard about, up at this one girl's house in Breesport, and how all the popular kids would be there, all the shitheads who were winners just because their parents were winners. I said that if we tried to go to their party and they were somehow cool and let us in, then why would we punish them? Martin didn't seem like he bought into it completely, but still we went there and didn't even make it through the front door. Some assholes out front smoking pot and drinking beer started calling us names, started pushing us around, and then one of them poured his cup of beer right on Martin's head. Yes, they had their chance and fucked it up, so really whose fault is it in the end?

I reach out my hand and squeeze my eyes tight when Martin draws the blade across my palm. There's no real pain, and for some crazy reason I'm reminded of getting a paper cut. Seconds later, though, my hand starts to tingle, the fingers going numb. Blood seeps out of the wound. We place our hands together, letting our blood become one again. I don't say anything, but this ritual thing Martin's into is kinda gay.

"I wasn't going to tell you this," Martin says. His face has gone a little pale. "But three nights ago this ... this guy showed up right outside the van. He knew my name, what we were planning on doing, everything. I thought he might try to turn us in, but he said he was proud of us. He said that if and when we made it, we could have anything we ever wanted. Any girl, any time, any way." He takes his hand away from mine, stares at it, and then wipes it on his shirt. "I thought I was crazy, but now ... now I know it was real."

I don't say anything. I *can't* say anything. For a second, I think that Martin's just fucking around with me, but I know that can't be right, because I never told him what happened. Thursday night, after we had come back from that bitch's party, I smoked a bowl and lay in bed, trying to sleep, when this guy approached me too. Out of nowhere, like he was the fucking boogeyman or something. One moment I'm alone in my room, while downstairs my mom's getting banged by whoever the fuck she brought home this time, and the next moment this guy's standing there smiling at me beside my bed. I started up at once, really freaked out, even started to say something, when the man held out his hand.

"Quiet now," he said. "I'm a friend. Normally I only observe, I enjoy the show, but I have a lot riding on you and your pal. So I'm willing to offer an incentive. If you succeed, whatever you want, whenever you want it, any way you want it." And then, standing there, the man's face started to ripple in the dark, it started to change, until he was no longer a dude, but a fucking woman. Her face was smooth and soft, her lips big. She was completely naked, her breasts large, her pussy shaved. I couldn't tell for sure because it was so dark, but her eyes kinda looked like they were black. She reached out her hand and set it down right where my dick was under the sheets, began massaging it into a full-blown boner, slow at first, but then picking up speed, until I couldn't take it anymore and I leaned my head back on the pillow, squeezed my eyes shut real tight, and just sprayed my shorts. When I opened my eyes, the woman was gone, the hand that was stroking me my own. "The fuck?" I muttered, really freaked out, but then I laughed, went and smoked some more, then fell asleep. Downstairs, my mom was still moaning, she was still getting fucked, and I promised myself that if any of her asshole boyfriends ever tried pissing on me again, I'd cut his fucking dick off.

But I didn't tell Martin any of that, because it had to just be my fried imagination. *Had* to be. But now, after my best friend just tells me the same thing ...

Martin says, "Ready?"

We waste no time getting the rifles. Each box contains twenty rounds, and as the Golden Eagles take up to thirty, we split it down the line. We figure we have enough to make a few solid kills. Hopefully if we get close enough and have enough in a line, we can take out more than one. Maybe do a hat trick or some shit, I don't know what it's called when taking out three people with just one bullet or if that's even possible. Martin pulls on his trench coat, which I think is a bit tacky, like he's trying too hard, but what the fuck, and then he slips his switchblade in one of the pockets.

For one last second I get the sudden feeling that we should stop. This is wrong. And it has nothing to do with the guy—

I'm a friend

—who might or might not have appeared out of fucking nowhere Thursday night in my room.

Thinking this now, I say, "Martin?"

He turns and looks at me, his face hard.

"What did he give you? As ... as an incentive?"

For a moment Martin just stares back at me, like he doesn't know what I'm talking about. Then he grins. "What do you think?" he says, and then he opens the door and steps out. Once again, that feeling that we should stop hits me, but I ignore it and jump outside. The air is cooler than the van and feels good on the sweat that's already on my face. Martin, holding the rifle with both hands, turns to me. "Remember what my old man told me," he says, and then starts toward the gym.

I follow a step behind. I know exactly what Martin's dad told him. It has to do with lemons. That when life gives you lemons you don't make fucking lemonade like them cheery assholes always say. No, what you do is stomp on those lemons until they're dead on the bottom of your shoe.

Nothing more than that.

Nothing more at all.

When it was over, when those three consecutive gunshots were fired, everything went silent. The world seemed to stand still for an instant. I was again in my body, I was again Christopher Myers. I realized somewhere along the line I'd held my breath. When I opened my eyes I saw everything in color, just like before. Then a second later, when the world started back up, I knew it was over and began to breathe again.

CHAPTER THIRTY-TWO

"So that's it?"

Moses placed the Metro in park, turned off the ignition. "You're talking to me now?"

"Does this mean it's over? Did we … did we beat Samael?"

It was six o'clock in the evening, the sun already sloping toward the horizon, sending a fading orange glow down on the valley just beyond The Hill.

Moses turned in his seat and stared at me for a couple moments. "What happened to you back there?"

"What do you mean?"

"Before those two kids with the guns came in, something happened to you. I could feel it. It was like … like you were sitting next to me but you weren't."

It was Dean who'd seen them coming into the gymnasium. He shouted a warning, and when it was clear that he'd be ignored, he did what he had been trained to do: shoot to kill. The first boy, Martin Luhr, had died only seconds after hitting the ground. The second boy, Adam Grant, had only been wounded and was taken away in an ambulance.

"I don't know what you're talking about."

"You're lying."

"Do you really want to fucking start with me right now?" I held his gaze, and when he didn't answer, I said, "I didn't think so. As far as I'm concerned, thirty-four people were supposed to die at that graduation. But they didn't. And now it's over."

I unclipped my seatbelt and reached for the door handle when Moses spoke.

"Christopher, there's one more thing I need to tell you."

"Let me guess—you and Joey *did* kill my parents after all."

He didn't even flinch. "I told you before we didn't."

"No, but you knew it was going to happen. You could have prevented it but decided not to. So yes, in a way, you did kill them."

I opened the door, started to get out.

Moses said, "Joey didn't pass anything on to you."

I stood frozen, one foot in the car, the other foot on the grass, staring at a red, white and blue pinwheel spinning in front of someone's trailer.

"It's important for you to understand. There are people just like Joey in the world who know things. They don't know how they know what they know, or why they do, or how to control it."

The pinwheel kept spinning and spinning, the colors mixing into one all-American shade.

"Christopher, do you understand what I'm telling you?"

My body unfroze, and I stepped fully out of the car, turned and ducked back down so I could see the man in the driver's seat.

"Moses, please don't take this the wrong way, but I don't ever want to fucking see your face again. Got it?"

I slammed the door shut before he could say anything else. Then I was walking, taking slow deep breaths, trying to forget everything that had happened today. My plan was to check on my grandmother but I wanted to stop at my own trailer first, take a shower and change out of these clothes.

As I headed down the drive, a screen door banged open and a voice called, "Christopher! Christopher, wait!"

Carol, my grandmother's friend who had only eight more months to live before dying alone in a hospital bed, rushed down the steps of her trailer. I hurried over to her, asking what was wrong.

Catching her breath, she said, "I was keeping an eye out for you."

My gaze shifted over to my grandmother's trailer. "What is it?"

"It's Lily. She was rushed to the hospital."

"What? When?"

"Almost an hour ago." She paused, her hand to her chest, taking slow breaths. "I was walking my poodle Sky, and I heard her cry out inside her trailer. She said a name—it sounded like Kevin. I knocked on her door asking what was wrong, but she never answered me. When I went inside to check on her, she was right there on the floor. She looked just like my dear husband Stanley did when he had his stroke, God rest his soul."

"She had a stroke?"

Carol shook her head. "Them ambulance people wouldn't say, but I'm sure it was a stroke. Lord, first Nancy, now Lily. I've been trying to call Dean since it happened, but I can't get a hold of him."

She told me about my note and how she'd been keeping an eye out for me. I asked her which hospital they'd taken her to, but I already knew.

"St. Joseph's," she said matter-of-factly. "Do you need directions?"

"No, I know the way." I started down the drive, toward my car.

"One more thing."

I turned back.

"Do make sure she didn't get any burns. I checked her trailer after they left to see if the oven was on, or maybe her curler, but I couldn't find what it was. I even mentioned it to the ambulance people, though they claimed they didn't smell anything. But I swear I did smell it when I first went inside. I know I did."

I was in a rush, but something made me pause, made me ask her what it was she had smelled.

"Well, when I stepped inside the trailer, the first thing I smelled was something burning. It was an awful stink. An awful, nasty stink."

CHAPTER THIRTY-THREE

They had her in a private room on the fourth floor. I sat in a chair beside her bed. The machines around it beeped steadily, the green thin lines on the monitor sloping up and down. The room had no noticeable smells, which bothered me. For some reason I felt I should at least smell disinfectant, or my grandmother's dying body on the bed.

I thought of my final words to her last night, of telling her goodnight before I went to my trailer. Did I tell her I loved her?

She wore a blue paper gown. Her chest rose and fell. Her calm and long face was pale. Behind her eyelids, the movement was slight.

Before I knew it then that chill shot through my soul and I saw her just as she came out of the bathroom in her trailer. I was there with her, standing by the Magnavox in the corner. I could hear her radio, playing light jazz; I could smell the tuna sandwich she'd made herself for lunch, the potato chips and ranch dip. I watched helpless as she walked out and saw the figure standing there before her. Its clothes were charred, as was its skin, and though I only saw the back of its head, I knew it was staring at her with the darkest eyes she'd ever seen. Memories of her youth swarmed her and she cried out a name before her heart failed her. She fell to the floor, her soft head knocking against the edge of the counter.

Blinking, I was back in the hospital room, not standing but sitting, staring at my grandmother's near-lifeless body. For a moment my mind was a complete blank. Then thoughts and shards of the past began seeping in, and I understood.

"You didn't say Kevin," I whispered. "You said Devin."

I remembered the man whom I'd thought was Lewis Shepherd tell me a fragmented history of the Beckett House, and that he said *Supposedly Reverend Beckett was involved with one of the local girls ... supposedly she was a minor.*

I remembered my first day in Bridgton, sitting beside my grandmother on her swing as she told me how she'd only been in love with two men in her entire life, and about the first she said *It was really nothing more than a hopeless crush on a man twice my age.*

And while it may have seemed like some very thin evidence, I connected the dots, I saw the link. Once again that feeling passed through me and I saw them there, back in 1953, a young Lily Thorsen going to meet with an older Devin Beckett, a man with whom she had a crush on, but a man who respected God and himself, who even respected Lily. They talked about simple things, like school and the weather, and more complex things, like God and the Bible. Lily quickly understood that while she thought she was in love, it was only a crush, and while Beckett agreed to speak with her in private about whatever she wished to talk about, he made it a rule that it would be their secret. He knew how townspeople liked to gossip and didn't want to think what would happen if word got around he'd become friends with an underage girl.

Except, of course, that secret was finally revealed, which somehow sparked a massacre that kept killing unto this day.

"Everything," I whispered. "It all comes back to you."

Whether her unconscious mind heard her me or not, she made no response. The only sounds I was left with in the cold sterilized room were the steady beeps of the machines. The steady beeps, and the slow rise and fall of her chest.

I must have dozed off. The last thing I remembered before closing my eyes was that it was a little after seven o'clock. When I awoke, my arms were crossed and I was slouched in the chair. Through the slim space between the plain curtains, I saw it was nighttime. Dean stood at the foot of Grandma's bed.

"What time is it?" I asked.

He glanced at his watch, told me a quarter after nine.

"How long have you been here?"

"Ten minutes."

He never even looked at me, instead stared down at the woman in the bed. Her face remained long and calm, there was still movement behind her eyelids, but nothing else.

"Have you talked to the nurses?" I asked.

"Yeah, I did. Heart attack." He shook his head. "They said the only things keeping her alive right now are those machines."

His face reminded me of the first five days he'd been in Lanton. Hard and cautious, his eyes cold. Only now his face was red too, and wet from tears. Because the room had no distinguishable scents, I had no problem smelling the lingering cigarette smoke coming from his direction. I imagined him smoking ever since he heard the news—on the drive over from Bridgton, flicking the ash out the window as he sped down 14, then in the parking lot, sitting in the Explorer and chain-smoking his Winstons until he was finally able to come inside. Now here he stood, in the same clothes as this afternoon, his arms at his sides, his hands flexing in and out of fists.

"I saw what you did today."

I didn't think he was going to answer me. He continued staring down at his mother. Finally he nodded. "I know you did, Chris. Everybody there did. They saw me screw up."

"Screw up? No, you were a hero. You saved lives."

Thirty-four lives, I thought but didn't say.

His eyes shifted away for the first time, stared back into my own. He looked so helpless there, so alone. Nothing like the man who'd confronted me earlier today just outside the gymnasium, the man who'd nearly called Moses Cunningham a nigger.

"When you become a cop they tell you to learn the law. To memorize it, to live it, and that's what you do. They tell you to keep the law, to enforce it, and you do that as best you can. But you know something? The only thing the law does is protects the bad guys. No matter what somebody does, there's always a technicality to get him off."

He shook his head.

"Sometimes I wonder if it's worth it in the end. That all the time and energy I spend trying to catch the bad guys and keeping the peace is even worth my time. Driving home every night I ask myself what I'm sure every cop asks himself—am I making a difference? Am I doing something that will somehow make the world a better place?"

He shrugged, wiped at his face.

"But it's not like I can complain. Hell, I'm just a deputy assigned to some sticks town, not a cop walking the beat in New York City. But today when I saw those two, instinct took over and I reacted. I shouted at them. I told them to stop, to drop their weapons, and when it became apparent that they wouldn't, when the one in front even started to raise his rifle, I knew I had no choice. I fired at them both. The one's dead. The other ... he's actually in this hospital somewhere. I think they have him on the third floor."

"Dean," I said, leaning forward in my chair. "What is it? What's wrong?"

He stared down at the bed. He actually grinned, though it was an empty grin, the grin of a defeated man.

"As it turns out, I didn't warn them that I would shoot. I shouted stop and I shouted drop your weapons, but I never gave them that warning. You probably think it's no big deal, and in reality it's not. But some lawyer came forward about an hour ago—he was actually at the graduation, some school parent—and he said he'll represent the Grant kid, and the Luhr family. Says that I could have handled the situation differently. Says both parties might still be alive. That had I done my job properly, none of this would have happened."

"But that's bullshit. Those kids were planning on shooting up the place. They wanted to kill people."

"I know that, Chris. You know that. Hell, everyone there knows that. But the thing is, with our fucked up judicial system that doesn't matter. Because there's always some technicality a lawyer will try to play. It's a game to them. He might get it past a judge and jury, he might not, but in the end it doesn't matter. He's going to drag this thing out for as long as he can to get his name in the papers, because he thinks he's doing what's right. And that's really what pisses me off. That *he's* the one who thinks he's making a difference."

I asked what this meant for him.

"This lawyer, his name's Gray, he's already talked the families into suing me, the county, even the school district. My supervisors say I don't have anything to worry about, but I can tell they aren't one hundred percent sure themselves. They know how the system works. They know how fucked up everything is. Even if I do end up coming out of this clean, it'll be months, years, before that happens. And by then I'll probably have spent all my savings and I'll be in debt thousands of dollars."

He paused, shook his head again, and muttered, "Just because I was doing my fucking job."

My uncle went back to staring down at his mother. In the silence, the only sound was the machines beeping. I glanced up at the screen, watched the green lines sloping up and down. I thought of today, of this past week, of my entire life. How it had all come to this point—my parents dead, Joey gone, two teenagers shot, and me sitting in the chair beside a woman I barely even knew.

"Dean, can I ask you something?"

He didn't even look at me when he said sure.

"Who owns Shepherd's Books?"

I knew this wasn't the right time or place for such a random question, but it was something I needed to know. Something that'd been gnawing at me ever since I read Mrs. Porter's obituary. I still couldn't believe I'd been so stupid. And though I knew it really was Gerald Alcott, I had to hear it from someone else, someone who lived here and possibly even knew the man.

The question didn't seem to faze Dean at all. Still staring ahead, he took a breath and said, "Shepherd's Books? That'd be Gerald Alcott." He paused. "Why do you ask?"

I shook my head. "Just curious."

As I went to rise from my seat, Dean cleared his throat.

"About before, what I said about you being bad luck." He spoke without looking at me. "I wish I could say I didn't mean it, that I'd just been caught up in the moment. But then I'd be lying. Because after everything that's happened since you arrived—with Mr. Cunningham and his son, with the mess today at the high school, and now Mom—I have to ask myself if any of this would have happened had you not been here. And the more I think about it, the more certain I am that somehow it all comes back to you."

"What are you saying?"

He turned his head to meet my stare. "That I want you

back in Lanton as soon as possible. That despite you being my nephew, I never want to see you again. And it's not because I dislike you—because I don't—but because every time I see you I feel like something bad is going to happen. And today just proves it."

I didn't know what to say. As much as I wanted to disagree with him, to tell him he was wrong, I simply couldn't. I couldn't, because deep within my soul I knew he was right, and it scared me. It scared me to death.

CHAPTER THIRTY-FOUR

THE GRAVEL PARKING lot was deserted. I turned off my low beams as I pulled in and parked in front of the porch. The lights were on upstairs. I expected the side door—the bookstore's entrance—to be locked and that I'd have to kick it in. It wasn't. The knob turned just fine, and then I was inside and heading past the shelves and cardboard boxes of books that still reeked of stale paper and dust.

He must have heard me on the steps, because when I opened the door he'd already gotten out of his recliner. His eyes were wide and expectant, but when he saw me they narrowed. He growled, "What the hell do you think you're doing, barging in on an old man like this? You best leave now before I call the sheriff."

I stood there and surveyed the living room. It looked just like it had the last time I was here, only those piles of old newspapers and *Life* and *Time* magazines were back on the threadbare couch. The TV was on, its sound muted.

"Sit down," I said.

"After you leave my house, I will. Now get, before I call the sheriff and have—"

"Sit down, Gerald."

This made him stop. His dry face paled, his mouth dropped open.

"What—what did you say?"

"I said sit down, Gerald."

He took a slow step back, then another, until his legs bumped against the recliner. He sat with a heavy *humph*, like nearly all the life had been punched out of him. "How ... how do you know my name?"

I shook my head and shut the door. The space between us was maybe ten feet, but it wasn't far enough. Rage caused my body to shake and the only thing I wanted to do now was take the knife that had been in my glove box, the one now in my back pocket, and stab him in the heart.

Instead I crossed my arms and said, "You have no right to ask me a fucking thing. So before you speak again, remember that I know everything there is to know about you. I know what really happened to you in 1953. I know what happened to your family and the reason behind it. And I know about Samael."

His eyes widened for just an instant, giving me my confirmation.

"Let me guess. He came to you and gave you a choice to pick and choose lives, and you chose your own."

"No." His voice trembled. "No, that's not what happened."

"Then why don't you tell me what happened, Gerald? Explain to me why seven children were burned alive in that stone house. Explain to me why those children's mothers and fathers were all murdered in their beds. Explain to me why all the firstborns are dead now except you."

"The curse—"

"Yes, I know about the fucking curse. But tell me what makes you different. Why are you still alive?"

Tears had begun to form in his eyes. He wiped at them, with no real sense of purpose, as he stared down at the throw rug.

"I—I had no choice. He came to me and asked me if I wanted to die. I—I was only a boy then, only fourteen. Dying was the last thing I wanted. So he told me to start a rumor about Reverend Beckett, about him and—"

"My grandmother."

He looked up at me and nodded slowly. "Yes, him and Lily. But Lily and I were friends. I even had a crush of my own on her and didn't want to ruin her reputation. So I kept her out of it but still spread the rumor that he was involved with a young girl. And then ... then they were all dead."

"But that doesn't answer my question. Why are you still alive?"

The tears now fell freely down his face; he had given up even trying to wipe them away. He just sat there, slumped in his chair, shaking his head. I thought briefly about the doors in his mind, how the ones that mattered had never been locked in the first place. They'd been open all his life, forcing him to remember that summer of his boyhood. Then I thought about the room just down the hall, across from the bathroom. The room that smelled of aged paper and mothballs, with all the newspapers and magazines recording tragedies. Gerald hadn't kept those simply because they were news that needed saving. He'd saved them because Samael loved bringing tragedy and chaos to the world, and each one of those pieces of news was a reminder.

"I don't know," Gerald whispered. "I swear to you, I don't. I hate myself for what I did. I hate that they all died because of that rumor I started. I hate that I've got no one, absolutely no one at all. I hate that he controls me, makes me do things I don't want to do."

I said, "Like killing my parents?" and it took everything I had at that moment not to rush across the room and cut his throat.

"Your parents?" Genuine confusion filled his face. "I ... I don't know what you're talking about."

"Joey then."

He shook his head. "I—I still don't understand—"

"Then how does he control you? What does he make you do?"

The old man was silent, staring again at the floor. The front of his shirt was damp from where he'd wiped his hands.

"You sold your soul," I said. "He owns you. You're his puppet."

"Don't you think I know that?" Freely sobbing now, his body shaking. "Don't you think I lie in bed every night regretting the decision I made? But I can't ... I can't change it now. What's done is done."

"That's bullshit. You could have said no. You could have told him to go fuck himself."

"You have no idea what you're talking about. He's not— he's not *human*. He's beyond our world. I've wanted to die for years now, I've even tried, but *he won't let me*."

"How much did he tell you? About his plan."

"His ... plan?"

"Thirty-four lives. He gave Joey a choice to save thirty-four lives for the price of one. What do you know about that?"

"I don't—I don't know anything about no thirty-four lives. But he did tell me to watch out for you."

"Why?"

Gerald only shook his head.

"Did you know he was going to visit my grandmother?"

He looked up at me. "Lily? What happened to Lily?"

"Why the hell should I tell you?"

"I—I didn't know anything about her. Why? *What's happened to her?*"

"Don't act like you care. Just tell me the truth."

"I am! I swear to you!"

"And why should I believe you, Gerald? You're a liar. And liars are right down there at the bottom of the barrel with child molesters and rapists."

"I told you, I had no choice!"

"That's bullshit. There's always a choice. So what if you're his puppet? Even a puppet can cut its own strings. When are you going to stop living in fear and just stand up to him? When are you going to be a man for once in your life?"

He said nothing and lowered his chin, stared down at his lap. Tears fell down, dampening his shirt even more. It was pathetic really, watching him cry like that, but I couldn't move from where I stood. Because I knew that if I took even one step forward, I would continue until I was right there over him, within striking distance, and with Joey's present in my back pocket, I didn't trust myself if I came that close.

"Tell me something, Gerald. When you finally die and stand before God, what are you going to say to Him? What will be your excuse for everything you've done? That you were scared, that you refused to stand up for yourself? My grandfather believed that there comes only one time in a person's life when they'll have to make a choice that directs their future. But the more I think about it, the more I think he was wrong. That time doesn't come just once. It comes all the time. So what if you make the wrong decision? It's possible to do something about it, to change your mind and try to make things right. So when every time they yawn, you have the chance to control your own fate."

He looked up at me, his eyes red. "Every time ... what yawn?"

"Churchyards," I said, and like that all my anger and rage

disappeared. I was able to move again, to take a step forward if I wanted and not try to kill him. But instead I turned, deciding it was time to leave. Right now all I wanted to do was get out of this place, away from his sad, useless old man who'd created his own personal hell.

So without a word I left, entering a hell all my own.

CHAPTER THIRTY-FIVE

HE STOOD BESIDE MY CAR, dressed in the same clothes he wore the night before his murder. The brown slacks and white shirt, his silk tie crisscrossed with red and gold. Even the same brown penny-loafers, the pair I'd gotten him for Christmas. I remembered all the cuts and gashes on his face and body, how the blood had dried to his hair. But now they were gone, like they had never been there in the first place. Everything about him was the same—the stubble on his face, the cleft in his chin, the stance of his body, and the part in his hair.

Everything was the same except for the black eyes staring back at me.

"Good evening, Christopher," he said, the voice even that of my father's.

"Samael."

The night had gone completely still. No insects, no distant traffic, not even any wind.

"What do you want?"

"Look at you. Asking me what I want. Just like your grand-father. He figured it out before I visited him. I wonder though how he would have reacted had he not known. Would he have soiled himself like some of the others? Or maybe screamed like a woman? I wonder the same about you, Christopher. I wonder how this moment in time would play out had you no clue I existed at all."

"Well, unfortunately for both of us, I do know you exist. Now what do you want?"

"It's not what I want. It's what you want."

"Let's not talk in circles, okay? This whole thing is about you."

"Is it that obvious?"

"You're a piece of shit. Innocent people died because of your, what, games?"

"Innocent?" A harsh darkness entered his voice. "Don't even begin to think you understand innocence. Innocence is once being free to roam Paradise and then have it snatched away without another chance."

"Another chance? You defied God. What makes you think you deserve another chance?"

"For the same reason you mortals do. Each and every one of you is given countless chances, all of which you take for granted. But what about me? What about the rest of my fellow brothers? Just because we followed Lucifer we will never get another chance."

I glanced at Half Creek Road. Wondered what would happen if a car or truck passed by. Would the driver see two figures facing each other almost twenty yards apart? Or would he just see me talking to an old and dented Cavalier?

"Okay," I said. "So what do you want? You want me to feel sorry for you?"

"No, Christopher. To be sorry is to show weakness, and you have proven thus far you are not weak. Even that time a year ago, when I stood in your bedroom and decided to end your life. Yes, you remember that, don't you? You woke up before I could finish the job. You fought back. So no, you are not weak. At least, not yet."

The silence of the night thickened.

"What I want is quite simple. It's what everyone before you has done. To make a choice."

"Everyone before me," I said. "Like my father?"

"No, Christopher. I decided to let him die instead."

"You decided. Like you have the power."

"You doubt my abilities?"

"What about my uncle then? What was his choice?"

Samael did not answer.

"And what if I refuse? What if I tell you to go fuck yourself instead?"

"Those are very bold words for a mortal whose fate lies in my hands."

For the first time since coming outside, I thought about the knife in my back pocket, my parents' murder weapon that Joey had given to me to use when the time was right.

"You think I know nothing about you, Christopher, but you're wrong. Do you remember our encounter at the restaurant? The question I asked? Because while it might not seem like much, it tells me a great deal about you."

"Oh really?" I slowly reached behind my back, lifted up my shirt, and gripped the handle of the knife. "Well guess what, you're wrong. Because whatever the choice is, I choose myself. Kill me instead."

"It's not that simple. The choice is for two lives, one or the other. And if you refuse to decide, both lives will perish." He tilted his head, just enough that the moon was reflected in his black dead eyes. "Now, are you ready to see just how innocent you truly are?"

CHAPTER THIRTY-SIX

DARK CLOUDS INFESTED the sky sometime during the night. By seven o'clock that Sunday morning, a light rain had begun to soak the earth surrounding Bridgton, New York. By eight, it had increased to a shower. By nine, it had begun to pour.

I took her up to Harris Hill Park, to the same spot she'd brought me to for our picnic, the spot I'd brought Moses to a few days later. The area was deserted. I parked the car facing the split-rail fence and benches and just sat there, staring out at the gray clouds and the occasional flicker of lightning. The windshield wipers were off and it took only a few seconds before I could hardly see anything at all.

"So," Sarah said after a long moment. "What's up?"

I didn't answer.

"You wanna know a secret? I've always thought I was a princess. A real princess. Just like in that Anne Hathaway movie. And that someday my long lost grandmother or grandfather would show up at my door with a tiara and a scepter or whatever else royal people carry, and then they would take me away to my own private island where I would rule over just a handful of people, mostly the servants there to keep me company."

I still said nothing, staring out the windshield.

"Okay," she said after another moment. "That was a joke. A lame joke, I know. But come on, what's this about? You show up at my door, tell me about Lily, and ask me to take a drive with you. I'm supposed to be going to church with my dad and my brother, but I say sure, okay, I can tell you really need somebody to talk to. And so then you drive us here without a speaking a word, and now here we are and you still haven't said a word. So … what's up?"

The rain battered the car. Lightning flickered.

"Chris?" she said, reaching out and placing a hand on my arm.

I jerked my arm away.

"Whoa," she said. "Take a chill pill, okay?"

I looked at her then for the first time, listening to the blood pounding away in my ears. My throat was dry, and I had to swallow before speaking.

"You told me a secret, so let me tell you one."

"Oh gosh. Please don't let this be the scene where you tell me you're a hermaphrodite."

She said it with a grin, meaning to make me laugh or smile or at least break the sudden tension between us.

"This is serious," I said.

"Okay." The grin fell off her face. "So what's your secret?"

"Three months ago I was suspended from school."

"That doesn't sound like a big secret."

"I was suspended for fighting. It happened in the cafeteria. I kicked the shit out of this kid for no apparent reason. Had they not pulled me off in time, I probably would have killed him."

Sarah was silent.

"It was my very first offense. Before that"—I smiled, almost laughed—"before that I was what you might call a model student. I got straight As, was never late to class, always turned my work in on time. I'd never had one detention."

Lightning flickered again, followed by thunder.

"The kid's name was Grant Evans. He was in my grade. We'd had a few classes together, but we weren't friends. And one day, a couple weeks after Mel got the abortion and she'd stopped speaking to me, I'd noticed something was wrong with a friend of mine. She was one of those girls who was always positive about everything, always nice. Like her smile could literally light up a room. But she wasn't smiling that day. I'd asked her what was wrong but she wouldn't look at me. And ... well, I thought she was still pissed about what me and Mel had done. I knew she didn't approve, but that had been a couple weeks ago, and since then we'd talked and ... anyway, so she wouldn't talk to me, started to turn away, and I reached out and grabbed her arm. And right then I knew. It was like ... like somehow the memory was transferred to me. I knew about the party she'd been to over the weekend, how somebody must have slipped something into her drink, and how ... how Grant Evans raped her. I saw it all in this flash, like it was nothing more than a brief memory, and my friend, she just stared at me, like she knew I now knew too. Next thing I knew she ran away, ducked into one of the bathrooms, and I turned and started walking. I found him in the cafeteria. He was sitting with his friends, laughing and joking. I grabbed him, pulled him out of his seat, and punched him in the face. He hit the ground, and I climbed on top of him and just kept punching him. And ... and before they pulled me off, I leaned down to Grant's bloody face and whispered that I knew what he'd done and that if he ever did it again I was going to kill him."

Lightning flickered again, followed by more thunder, and I blinked and looked at Sarah for the first time since I began speaking.

"He never pressed charges. His parents wanted him to but apparently he refused and then a couple months went by and my parents were murdered and I … I actually thought he had done it. That it was his revenge. But he didn't. He was just this stupid fucking kid who'd date raped a friend of mine and then got the shit beat out of him in front of all of his friends."

Sarah was turned slightly in her seat so she could watch me. She didn't speak, didn't move at all.

"So I guess my whole reason for telling you this is I'm wondering something. Do you think it's possible for people to know things they're not supposed to know?"

"Yes." Her voice was a hesitant whisper. "I do."

Now it was my turn to say nothing.

Sarah opened her mouth, closed it, opened her mouth again, and said, "Friday, after you stopped by the house to see John, you wanted me to promise you something. That I wouldn't go to graduation. You wouldn't tell me why either, just that you didn't want me to go. And … and yesterday, after everything that happened, I—I wondered to myself, did you know? And now … now I guess I have my answer. You did know, didn't you?"

I was silent.

"Chris." She started to reach out again but caught herself and didn't touch me. "How … how did you know?"

I glanced at the dashboard clock. "You're going to be late for church."

"Chris …"

Turning the ignition, the Cavalier's engine rumbling to life, I stared at the steering wheel. "I didn't know. Let's just leave it at that, okay?"

I could see her from the corner of my eye, staring at me. "Okay. But why did you bring us up here? You could have easily told me that story back on The Hill."

"I don't know," I said, placing the car in reverse and backing us out of the space.

But it was a lie. I knew. Not how exactly, or why, but I knew that if we didn't come here and stay for at least ten minutes, Sarah would die.

CHAPTER THIRTY-SEVEN

My uncle's Explorer was parked right in front of the church. It sat at an awkward angle directly before the steps leading up to the entrance.

As I pulled up behind it, Sarah glanced at me. "Lily?" she asked.

I placed the car in park, undid my seatbelt, and opened the door. "Stay here."

I stepped out into the rain and hurried up the steps to the main doors. They were both locked. I turned, started back down the steps, when the noise came from inside.

Curiosity had gotten the best of Sarah, and she was getting out of the car when the noise sounded.

I stared down at her just as she stared up at me.

She said, "Was that—"

"Get back in the car, Sarah."

"But were those—"

"Now!"

I ran back to the car, placed it in gear, and slammed on the gas as I spun the wheel.

Beside me, Sarah was hysterical. "What's—what's—what's happening? Were those—were those—were those *gunshots?*"

Tearing through the parking lot, the rain coming down even harder, lightning flickering again, I thought about my grandmother, about Joey and Moses, about my parents and everybody inside that church right now.

Right before turning onto Half Creek Road, I slammed on the brakes.

"Oh my God, oh my God, oh my God," Sarah sobbed, jerking in her seat. Her face was pale, covered in tears.

I said to her, "Can you drive?"

"Oh my God, oh my God, oh my God."

"Sarah," I shouted. "Can you drive?"

She jerked in her seat like I'd just slapped her. Staring at me, wiping at her eyes, she said, "What?"

"I need you to drive my car back to your house and call 911. Can you do that?"

She just stared back at me, her lip trembling. "My dad and my brother, they're in there."

"Sarah, can you do that?"

Slowly, so very slowly, she nodded.

"Good. Now you need to be where I am. How's the easiest way?"

She swallowed, wiped at her eyes again. "I guess … I guess I'll have to walk around."

"Do you think you can do that?"

With a little more confidence, she nodded again.

"Then do it quickly."

She had her door opened and then closed in the matter of seconds. As she hurried around the car, her right hand on her bulging belly, I leaned across the middle console and opened the glove box, reached in, and extracted Joey's present.

My door opened and I slammed the glove box shut,

concealed the knife in my jacket, and stepped back out into the rain.

"Chris," Sarah said, shaking, her hair completely soaked. "Come with me."

"Go."

"But—"

"Go!"

She got in the car.

I shut the door and stepped back and watched as she drove away, the Cavalier's engine roaring as she climbed the hill toward her house. Then I turned and sprinted back toward the church, the rain soaking me, lightning flickering again, followed by thunder, then even more thunder.

Only that wasn't thunder coming from inside the church, a distant but distinct *crack crack crack*.

I started back up the steps before I remembered that the doors were locked. I just stood there then, staring at the building. Two windows were on either side of the locked entrance. There was an exit in the back of the church, but I somehow knew it'd be locked just like the front.

I rushed to the window on the left and tried pushing it open. It wouldn't budge. I didn't bother trying the window on the right and instead ran directly to Dean's Explorer.

The passenger side door was locked, and I feared the driver's side would be as well. It wasn't. I released the trunk door and then went to the back. There was a roadside kit and a spare tire and a fire extinguisher and—

"Bingo," I said, grabbing the crowbar.

I chose the left window and shattered the glass. After sliding the crowbar around the frame to get rid of the shards, I threw it inside, gripped hold of the ledge, and lifted myself up to peek inside. Nothing. I took the knife out of my jacket pocket, tossed it inside, then grabbed the ledge again and pulled myself up and into the church's foyer.

The foyer was still deserted. The table with the coffee pots and Styrofoam cups and bagels looked picked over, while the table with the missionary pamphlets looked untouched. Nearly every hanger on the trio of coat racks was in use. At least half a dozen umbrellas leaned against the wall. A folding chair was propped between the entrance doors' handles, which meant whoever had done it was more concerned about someone trying to get in, rather than trying to get out. With nobody around, the fluorescents in the ceiling made the room much brighter, somehow less real.

The knife was on the floor by some shards of glass. I picked it up.

Now that I was inside, I could clearly hear people sobbing in the chapel. Even the sound of a baby crying.

I noticed something on the floor just in front of the chapel doors. It was a cigarette butt, its tip still lit. A thin tendril of smoke drifted toward the ceiling. I stepped on it, smashing it out with the toe of my sneaker. I didn't have to pick it up to know which brand it was.

I touched one of the door handles but paused. I tried listening for sirens, for anything outside. There was nothing at all, except the rain beating against the unbroken window.

I stared down at the knife in my hand. Joey's present to me. The thing that had been used to murder my parents. A thing which had been used for evil but which Joey had believed would eventually be used for good.

Inside came another gunshot, followed by more screams, then silence.

CHAPTER THIRTY-EIGHT

IT WAS like walking into my parents' bedroom. Only the first thing that hit me this time wasn't the smell, but rather the sight.

Random spots of blood soaked the carpet and walls. Dead bodies lay motionless on the floor and in pews. Men, women, children—no one had been denied their death, except the fortunate few who fate had been kind enough to spare. These people either lay or sat on the floor behind the pews, cowering with their heads bent, their eyes closed. Others who didn't have their eyes closed watched me, wondering just what the hell I was doing as I moved down the aisle with my arms raised.

I could smell the fear and blood around me, even the reek of defecation from those who were dead. And as I walked, I turned my head slowly to the left and to the right, looking at each murdered person, knowing who they were and how they died.

Harold and Betty Swanson, Steve and Jessica Churchill and their one-year-old daughter, Chris Thompson, Nancy and John Rohrer, Heather Maxwell, Lydia Strick, Robert Russo, Jack

Hauser, Philip and Wendy Fey, Paul Upton, Nick Daly, Bob and Jessica Wood, Dan Stilling, Jason Clarke, Dawn Bowyer and her young singer daughter Lindsay, Shawn and Lisa Gable, Reverend Peart, Tim and Murray Delaney, Emily Miller, Henry and John Porter, Gary and Natalie Wilkinson—each of them shot in the face, in the neck, in the back, in the chest.

Thirty-two people dead.

And two more to go.

I was less than twenty feet from the front of the chapel, my arms still raised, when my uncle spoke.

"Stop right there."

Dean had Moses on his knees facing the congregation. He stood behind him with a Beretta pointed at Moses's head. An empty rifle lay at my uncle's feet, what I knew had been used for most of the killing.

Moses had his eyes closed and his head bent, no doubt praying.

"I've been waiting for you, Chris. I knew you would come."

Around me people continued to sob and weep, that baby continued to cry, but I was able to filter it all out only to hear my uncle's words.

"He came to you, didn't he," I said. "He gave you this choice."

"He said … he said everything would work out. That Mom would get better. That Susie would realize we were meant for each other. That I'd never have to worry about anything another day in my life."

"He lied to you, Dean. None of that's going to happen."

"But it was Dad!" For the first time the gun pointed at Moses's head began to shake. "It was Dad, Chris. I know you won't believe me, that nobody will, but it was him. He said that if I came here and made these people suffer, then everything would be okay. He said … he said he'd be proud of me."

The gun kept shaking.

"She's dead, Chris," he whispered. "Mom's dead. She died an hour ago. And I was there. I watched her die."

In my mind I saw the green lines, sloping up and down, until they stopped and were flat.

"Then I … I came home and Dad was waiting for me. He said all I needed to do was come here and … and do this, and everything would be okay. But … but I don't think it was him, Chris."

"How so?"

"Because … because Dad's dead. He's been dead four years now. Hasn't he?"

So far his face had been blank, showing no emotion, but now it opened up like a flower, filling with fear and anger and confusion. Tears sprang to his eyes, and with his free hand he wiped them away, closing his eyes.

"It's okay, Dean." I didn't realize until then that I'd begun taking slow steps forward. Now I was less than ten feet away from them. "Just put the gun down. No one else has to die."

His eyes popped open and he stared ahead, and now that I was close enough I saw the madness in his face, the insanity that had been driven there by seeing his dead father.

"But what if he's right? What if—what if everything can work out?"

"No, it can't—"

"Dad said the nigger first"—he poked the gun's barrel at Moses's head—"then you, and everything will be better. Mom will be alive again, and Susie will come back, and we'll all be a happy family. And Dad … he'll be proud of me."

At that moment Moses opened his eyes. Stared straight up at me. Mouthed the words *It's time* and I nodded with my eyes, acknowledged that I understood. And I did too. I'd understood the moment I grabbed Joey's present from the glove box. The knife that now rested on my right arm, the handle against the inside of my elbow, the sharp tip pointed toward the ceiling. All concealed by the sleeve of my jacket.

It happened too quickly then. I was less than five feet away when Moses attempted to jump to his feet. Dean, surprised, shot him in the back, then immediately raised the gun at me. By then I'd brought my arms down, opening my right sleeve by spreading my fingers. Gravity brought the knife out, just as it had for Melvin Dumstorf, only now the blade sliced my hand, cut my fingers, and then I had a grip on the handle, I was bringing it up and shoving it into Dean's neck.

But not before he'd pulled the trigger.

This last shot was the loudest of all, yet strangely it was also the quietest. I fell to my knees, then onto my side. Dean followed suit, his entire body convulsing, blood flowing from his neck. On the floor I found myself staring at Moses. Tried saying his name. I crawled the short distance to him. He was still alive, but just barely. His mouth was moving, blood coming out of it.

"Moses."

With a shaking hand, I went to cover his wound, to keep in the blood. But the look in his eyes stopped me, the look that said there was no need, that he was already gone. His lips still continued to move slightly as he tried producing words. I couldn't hear them or even read them, so I crawled even closer, making it so my head was right by his mouth. He tried again, his voice barely audible over the wheezing coming from his throat. Then there was no more wheezing and no more words as the life finally faded from Moses Cunningham's body.

A hand touched my shoulder, but I ignored it and stared back into Moses's face. He'd said three words, I was sure of it.

"Son, just lie still," said a voice. It belonged to Harry Quinn, a fifty-three-year-old man who had lived in Bridgton his entire life. That's all I knew about him, all I could sense. He was dressed in his Sunday best, dark slacks and jacket, polished wingtips. His tie was blue, Italian silk, and some blood had been splattered near the bottom. "An ambulance has been called. It'll be here very soon."

Even though I was wounded—Dean had shot me right in the stomach—I managed to stand up. I glanced behind the man at everyone else alive. Most had gotten to their feet, while others stayed crying on the floor or in the pews. A few fled the chapel, either to call 911 or cry in private.

"Son, maybe you shouldn't stand," Harry said. His wide eyes stared at all the blood seeping through the fingers covering my stomach. "Just lie back down and wait for the ambulance. It's okay. It's all over now."

I thought of Joey, alive a week ago today. His face expectant as he stared back at me. Saying, *It all started here ... it makes sense it should end here too.*

I looked at the man and shook my head. "No," I whispered. "It's not over yet."

"What? But I don't understand. What do—"

Without a word, I turned and staggered toward the exit door in the corner. I pushed it open and stepped out into the rain. Lightning flickered, followed by the loudest roll of thunder I'd heard yet. I stood there, staring up at the gray sky, letting the drops soak me and wash everything from my shaking and dying body—all the doubt, all the fear, all the suffering.

But the pain was still there. It was like a blaring siren going off inside my head. It was like my parents' alarm clock on the morning I found them dead, never-ending, just pulsing away inside my body. Making me colder. Making me weaker. Making me understand that soon I was going to die.

But not yet. Not until I'd finished this. So I started

forward, through the rain, staggering toward the pine trees and the trail leading back to the Beckett House. And as I did, I thought of what Moses had said. Those three words he managed to whisper before he died. Confirmation for something I'd been wondering my entire life.

He does care.

CHAPTER THIRTY-NINE

EVEN WITH THE rain and the shadows cast by the trees surrounding it, the Beckett House was no more intimidating than the night I'd come down here to see Joey. Except now I knew more about its dark history, and I wondered if maybe it had started even before the giant had begun killing the children of Bridgton. If maybe these grounds were unholy, if ancient tribesmen had done sacrifices right on this spot.

But I knew that wasn't the case, at least here. Just like people, places don't need a reason to be evil. Sometimes they just are.

Someone had taken the time to drive stakes around the house and encircle it with yellow and black crime scene tape. Whether from the rain or some wild roaming animals, most of the tape had been ripped from the stakes and now lay useless in the grass and bushes.

I don't know how long I stood there, holding my stomach, staring at the entrance. Only darkness stared back. Besides the rain and the random thunder, the only other sound I heard was my own heart beating in my ears, getting weaker and weaker by the second.

I started forward.

As I neared the entrance, I expected to see my father again. Standing in the middle of the room, wearing the same clothes as last night: brown slacks and white shirt, his tie and penny-loafers. Grinning like he always did when he had a secret. Only his eyes wouldn't be the same blue as they had been in life. Of course they wouldn't.

Or maybe it would be my grandfather. I couldn't remember him too well, but I could almost picture him standing there instead, just as he'd looked near the end of his life. His body hunched over, his face full of wrinkles. Liver spots would mark his hands and forehead. I didn't know his eye color but it wouldn't matter, because just like everyone else Samael took on as a shell, his eyes would be black.

It could have been anyone—even Joey—and as I stepped into the house, I closed my eyes. Held my breath for a second or two. Finally opened them.

There was no one here. The place was completely empty, the bottles of Bud Light and cigarette butts gone, taken and marked as evidence by the police. Even the faint smell from before—alcohol and piss—was absent, instead now only the scent of rain and damp earth.

I stood there for a long time, waiting for something to happen. When nothing did, I turned back around.

And watched through the doorway as Gerald Alcott ran toward me through the trees, a rifle in his hands.

"Christopher!" he shouted, waving the rifle at me. "You gotta get outta here! Do you hear me? You gotta get. He wants to kill you."

I stepped out into the rain and stood with the house behind me. My hands hadn't yet left the wound on my stomach. I had no voice at first and just stared back at him. It obviously had been a long time since he last ran, and it appeared as if each step caused him pain. When he reached the top of the trail, he slowed his pace, catching his breath as he walked the rest of the short distance.

Lightning flickered, and for an instant I thought I saw something around the house. Something that looked like a dozen shadows spread out. Thunder quickly followed the lightning, and then I found my voice and asked a very stupid question.

"Who?"

Gerald stopped at once. Just like last night his face paled, but his eyes widened even more. His mouth opened as if he wanted to say something, but now he was the one with no voice. Then I realized while his eyes were directed at me, he was staring at something over my shoulder.

"Come now, Christopher, you're smarter than that," said a voice behind me, a voice so dark it hardly sounded human at all. "Now turn around so we can finish this."

I didn't recognize him at first. He was tall and wore a long dark robe. His brown flowing hair hid none of his face, which looked almost perfect, handsome, but cold. The only reason I knew it was Samael was because of his bottomless black eyes, which seemed to sear into my very soul. And then I remembered how my great-grandfather had described the demon so long ago. This must be what he'd looked like not just then, but since the beginning of time, before his wings had been ripped away like his chances of redemption.

"When is it going to end?" My voice was still hardly my own, and I tasted blood in the back of my throat. "You've already got your thirty-four lives. Killing me will make it thirty-five. If you kill Gerald, that's just one more. And who knows how many there were before now. When are you going to stop? Until a million lives are lost? Until everyone in the world is dead?"

"Don't make yourself out to be a martyr. It's beneath you. What do you care of life and death when it's not your own?

Thousands of people die every day. That's the thing—death is inevitable. But does that affect you? Has it ever caused you to lose sleep? Of course it hasn't, because you are just like every other mortal on this earth. You care only for yourself and no one else."

I staggered again, the pain becoming so much I hardly even felt it anymore. "That's not true. Joey cared."

"Yes, but mortals like him are few and far between. Besides, look at the result of his caring." Samael smiled. "When faced with the choice of life and death, mortals always take life. Every one is susceptible to the fear of death. They will do whatever it takes to save them and their own. But to answer your question, no I do not plan to kill everyone in the world. What good would that do? How then would I have any followers?"

"Followers? You're not …"

His smile widened even more, as he saw the understanding pass through my eyes.

"Do you know when Lucifer challenged God and was banished from Heaven, when the legions of angels followed him—do you know what I felt that day? Jealousy. I remember watching it happen and feeling an emotion that should never have even existed deep within myself. I could not understand how Lucifer had attempted such a bold act. And at the same time I could not understand why I had not tried it myself. It took centuries, almost a millennium, until I gathered enough courage to do the same thing Lucifer had done to God. Only this time, I challenged the Morning Star himself."

Samael motioned for me to look behind me. I turned.

Gerald still stood in the same place in which he'd stopped, the rifle in his hands aimed at the ground. The barrel trembled. He'd decided to take a chance and defy Samael, and now he was so scared he could do nothing more than stand frozen, not even attempt to run away.

I wasn't sure what Samael meant for me to see until the

lightning flashed again. Like before, in the instant of brilliant light, I saw shadows. Only now there were more than a dozen. Now there were hundreds of shadows, all gathered before the stone house.

But they weren't just shadows. They were something more, something my mortal eyes could not perceive in the instant the lightning lasted. Would Joey have been able to see them? Perhaps. But it didn't matter. Even without seeing them completely, I knew what they were. Angels who had once tasted the glory of Heaven but who had followed Lucifer down into the depths of Hell.

Now they were fallen angels who had followed Samael.

They were his legion.

"Every day more join my army. They know the future has already been written. That Lucifer is to lose his battle against God. Why follow me then? The answer is quite simple, Christopher. It is because I'm the wild card. I'm the thing God's omnipotent mind did not see coming. And in the end I will be more powerful than Lucifer ever was. I will challenge God like I should have done in the beginning. And do you know something, Christopher? I will *win*."

Once again that familiar feeling—a pang of ice shooting through my soul—passed through me and I sensed them all. Not hundreds or thousands, but *millions*. In every space stood an angel both fallen from Heaven and Hell, each staring toward this spot, toward their master. Toward their god, and the sacrifice he had planned.

"The giant was my first. He was my first true mortal follower. I had no influence over him. One day he just began praying to me. Can you even begin to fathom the power in that? In a mortal being choosing you over God or the Morning Star? You have absolutely no idea how empowering that felt. And then to lose that one follower, the very first, to four boys thinking they were making a difference. Suffice it to say something had to be done. Somehow they had to pay for their sins against me."

I turned back to face him. His eyes were no longer looking at me but rather out at his legion. This was a day of reckoning, a day when he not only proved his power to his followers, but to Satan and to the world. To God.

"So then this is all about power." My voice was weak. I staggered some more. "Everything that's happened. All the people that died because of what my great-grandfather and his friends did. All this is to somehow do what—prove you shouldn't be fucked with?"

"I have been patient. I have waited for others of my kind to follow me, as well as mortals all over this earth. They have all chosen to worship me. Power has nothing to do with it. God has power, but what else? *Everything.* That is what I want. Not just power, but fear and love and hate and understanding. For the longest time I have been known as a being that takes life away. Now I will also be known as a being that gives life."

This entire time he had been slowly approaching me. Now he was less than two feet away. Without warning my legs gave up their fight. I fell to my knees, my jeans soaking in the wet earth. I felt faint, so very faint, like any moment I would close my eyes and never open them again.

But Samael reached forward. He placed his hand against my stomach.

And like that, the pain began to ease. It began to decrease, becoming less and less, until it was gone.

I blinked. Looked up at him.

Samael held out his hand. I took it, and he helped me to my feet. I just stood there for a moment, not sure what to say or do. I felt fine. I felt good. I felt *great.*

Samael placed his hands on my shoulders, slowly turned me around so I could stare out at Gerald Alcott and the invisible legion of fallen demons surrounding us.

"Christopher?" Gerald's hoarse voice was small. The courage that once resided in his eyes had now been replaced by fear. "What—what's happening?"

Another feeling shot through my soul, this one sharper than ever. There was movement in the trees behind him. Branches and leaves stirred, and before I realized what was happening, it emerged. Gerald Alcott must have noticed my eyes widen, or sensed what was there himself, because he slowly turned. The rifle fell from his grasp.

The thing had been human once. Now dead and decaying, it walked upright on two large legs like it had in life. Ragged pants and a shirt covered its huge body, hiding most of its raw skin. Just how long had it been dead? Almost a hundred years, if not longer. How Samael had preserved it this long, I had no idea. But the giant still had both its eyes, though they looked milky and useless in its massive skull.

"You've been wishing to die for years now, Gerald!" Samael shouted behind me. "Now I grant you your wish."

Whether the old man heard him or not, I can't say. His back was to both of us, and he took a step back, then another, then bent to pick up the rifle he'd dropped. The dead giant moved with a strange sense of ease, covering the ground between the trees and its prey in only seconds. Somehow Gerald managed to aim and fire. The bullet struck the giant in the shoulder, but this did little to slow the beast. It continued until both its large dead hands gripped Gerald Alcott's neck.

Rain fell and lightning flashed, and I saw all the shadows near the giant and old man, I saw them all watching what now happened with admiration.

Gerald fought his hardest for the few seconds the giant allowed him to live. He was lifted in the air, his boots kicking the space just above the ground. The giant kept him there for only a moment before snapping Gerald's neck. I hoped the giant would stop there and drop the body, but it didn't. Instead it continued shaking Gerald, the dead man's arms and legs flapping with no control, and seconds later there was the sound of ripping skin as the head was separated from its neck.

I closed my eyes, forced myself to quit watching, but still I heard Gerald Alcott's body hit the wet earth. When I opened my eyes again, the giant stood before us. It held Gerald's head face out, toward me and Samael. The old man's eyes bulged in terror. His mouth was open in a silent scream, his bottom dentures crooked. Rain fell down his face, like the tears he'd shed last night in his living room.

His hands still on my shoulders, Samael whispered into my ear, "Now do you see my power? Besides healing you, that is one thing I have in common with Lucifer. But I have something else over him too, something that rivals even God."

Staring ahead at Gerald's dead bursting eyes, I asked him what he meant.

"Mercy," he said. "Mercy is something Lucifer has never been able to show. In fact, it is beyond his ability. But today I will show mercy. Because you should die here, Christopher. You should meet the same fate as Gerald. But instead I have decided to let you live. I have decided to show you mercy."

"How?" I heard myself whisper.

"It's simple, really. The trail to your left, the one leading up to the clearing beside the trailer park—I'll be waiting up there for you. If you manage to outrun my giant and reach me, and fall to your knees before me, I will show you mercy and spare your life."

His hands left my shoulders and I knew he was gone, that he was now waiting at the top of the trail. Would he really spare my life if I made it to him? I wanted to believe he wouldn't, that he was lying. But I knew he would. He had already healed me, had taken all that pain and faintness away, so I knew he had the power, and I understood that by showing me mercy, he would (in his own mind and in the minds of his legion) elevate himself next to God.

At that moment pain roared through my body. I grabbed my stomach, staggering again. I understood that the healing had only been temporary, at least for now, and that if I did as Samael wished it would be permanent. So I stood there on weak legs, gripping my wound, keeping my eyes closed because I knew what would happen when I opened them again.

When I did finally open my eyes, the giant still stood in front of me, Gerald's head still in its grasp. As lightning flashed once more, the beast dropped it to the ground. For a second it just stood there staring back at me with dark blind eyes. Then it started forward.

I turned and ran.

CHAPTER FORTY

THEY SAY the moment before you die your whole life flashes before your eyes.

That isn't the case for me as I sprint up the trail.

The distance isn't too long but yet it seems like I've been running forever. The pain still roars through me, but it's become background. I can hear the giant behind me, I can hear its unsteady breathing and its heavy feet slapping the earth, and I know that if I pause for even a second, if I lose my footing just once, it will tear me apart. That's its purpose after all, to make me suffer.

Lightning flashes and I see them all around me, on both sides of the trail. All standing there staring, all waiting for me to either slip and die or make it and live. And now that I'm closer to the clearing, making sure not to trip over rocks and vines, I see Samael at the top of the trail.

Images invade my mind again, only these are sporadic, completely random.

Joey lying in his hospital bed, the machines beeping around him, saying, *Did you ever wonder what would have happened had Adam and Eve said no to Satan?*

Moses in his RV, after having poured rum into a *Sesame Street* glass, saying, *Man acts, God reacts.*

My grandfather the day he took me out of school, in the driver's seat of his Impala as the state police were outside with guns drawn and about to take him out of the car, saying, *Know when to stop.*

And now I'm almost there, I'm almost to the top of the trail. Very soon I'll make it to Samael. I'll drop to my knees and bow before him and his legion so that he can show me mercy.

Rain pours and lightning flashes and thunder rumbles, but I ignore it all and stare forward, at Samael who stands there staring back at me. He's smiling, and I can see it in his eyes, the satisfaction, the knowledge that soon he will be raised above Satan and closer to God.

Behind me, the giant's gaining distance. How far exactly I don't know, but I know it's getting closer, and that its long legs are giving it that extra step it needs. I've got maybe thirty yards left to run and then it will all be over. A cramp is forming in my side, accompanying the pain, but I know I can ignore it, I know I can make it and fall to my knees, bow before Samael and keep my life.

He must sense it even before he sees it in my face. First his smile begins to fade, then his eyes begin to narrow. He starts shaking his head, starts opening his mouth to say something. But already it's too late. Already I've slowed my pace until there's only twenty yards between us now, maybe fifteen, and behind me the giant continues, it somehow sees me and it sees flesh to destroy so it runs with purpose.

Lightning flashes one final time, and in that instant I see the legion is no longer looking at me, waiting to see my fate. Now they're looking at Samael. His body's trembling, and his head's shaking, and I can hear his voice through the rain, I hear him as he begins screaming.

"No! No, you can't! YOU CAN'T!"

Then the world explodes in a mass of bright, intense light, and I know no more.

CHAPTER FORTY-ONE

THE CHURCH PARKING lot was deserted. I parked in the same handicapped space I'd used three weeks ago. Unlike then, James Young wasn't waiting for me at the door. Instead there was a note taped to the glass that said: *Christopher, please let yourself in.* I pushed open the door and stepped inside.

Then stopped.

From where I stood in the foyer, I could see down the hallway, into the main lobby. I could see the ladder there, a yellow A-frame. I could see the sneakers that were balanced on top.

"Christopher?" James Young called. "Is that you? Please, come here. I need … I need to tell you something."

I started forward. "Pastor Young, what are you doing?"

"Hello, Chris." A noose circled his neck, the other end wrapped around the weathered wooden beam in the ceiling. "I'm glad you came."

I took another step forward, slowly this time, for some reason afraid that if I took a wrong step the ladder would tip.

"You don't have to do this."

"But I do, Chris. I know you won't understand—that nobody ever will—but I have no choice. I … I'm a damned man. I have sinned by murdering, by lying, by believing in false idols. And then the Lord took my family away from me. But I … I didn't want to. Please, Chris, please understand that." Tears falling down his face, he spoke quickly, almost babbling. "Please, the last thing I wanted to do was hurt your folks. But I … I had to choose. My *father*, my father who's been dead for seven years, he made me choose. And I …"

"Pastor Young, please." Taking another step forward. "Don't do this."

"Stop!" he shouted. "Just answer me one question."

I stood waiting.

"Do you think … God will forgive me? That … that I'll get my redemption, my forgiveness from doing this?"

I shook my head. "Not like this."

He said, "Well, then I guess we'll see," and kicked the ladder out from under his feet.

The room they put me in was the nursery. I was surrounded by tiny chairs and tables, surrounded by friendly pictures of Jesus on the walls. In every picture he had long brown hair and a smile on his face and he had his arms open, welcoming the poor and the diseased and the whores. Welcoming everyone who was willing to come to him.

Eventually the door opened. Steve Carpenter stepped inside. He didn't say anything at first. He came toward where I was leaning against the counter in the room, where they probably changed the toddlers' diapers. Then he stopped and surveyed the room, realized there was nowhere to sit, and sighed.

"So what happened?"

"I already told the other officer."

"That's great. Now tell me."

For the past hour I'd been thinking over what had happened. About what I'd told the first officer who took my statement, and whether that statement was going to work. For some reason I wasn't surprised this was how it ended. Samael seemed to like testing men and women of God, he liked to see just how strong their faith truly was. James Young had been the one who murdered my parents, the one who painted the cross in their blood on my bedroom door because that was what his dead father had told him to do. And now James Young was dead, just like nearly everyone else in my life.

"He called me last night, wanted me to come see him again. I figured he wanted to follow up on the conversation we had last time. You know, the one we had before I went up to Bridgton. But then ... well, when I got here, he was like that." Nodding my head toward the door, indicating what was beyond the door, the hallway which led to the lobby, the lobby which had the tipped over A-frame, the body of James Young hanging by a noose.

"And that's it," Steve said. His voice betrayed the fact he didn't believe me at all. "He didn't leave a note or anything. He just killed himself like that, wanted you to find him."

"Huh," I said, more to myself than to him. "You know, that never even crossed my mind. That, you know, he wanted me to find him. But ... well, I don't know."

I fell silent then, hoping that would be enough. Steve just continued standing there, tall in his police chief's uniform, his massive arms crossed. After calling the police, I'd snagged the note taped to the entrance door and flushed it down the toilet. I knew there would be no other notes, at least in terms of the suicide, because James Young had only wanted one person to know the truth.

Steve said, "You know, this entire thing is fu—" but he quickly cut himself off, remembering where he was. "This entire thing is screwed up. All of it."

I knew he wasn't just referring to this recent matter.

"Yeah," I said. "Tell me about."

He was quiet for another moment before he uncrossed his arms and jerked a thumb at the nursery door. "Let's take a walk."

We used the exit door at the back of the church. Here the afternoon sun was bright, hardly a cloud in the sky, yet there was a breeze blowing that made it feel like a nice enough summer day. The property here sloped down toward a drainage dip, filled with rocks and littered with debris: an empty soda bottle, a torn black flip-flop, a Twizzler wrapper.

Standing in the shade of the building, Steve said, "I want to apologize. Before you left, I promised you we'd find the guy who murdered your parents. But we haven't come close. It's been almost a month now and we've turned up nothing. The state police couldn't find much either. It's embarrassing, really, and I'm sorry."

I just stared down at the drainage dip, watching the red candy wrapper shivering in the breeze.

"So anyway," Steve said, when he realized I wasn't going to answer him, "I'm also sorry that this is the first time we're talking since you got back. I mean, after what happened up there in Bridgton. I tried calling that Sunday because Dean hadn't gotten back to me, and I heard what happened. I wanted to go up there myself but couldn't. I talked to Sheriff Douglas though, and she told me what happened—about your grandmother and uncle. She said you were in the hospital. She said that you'd been shot and that ... that you'd been struck by lightning."

Lightning was the official word. There were witnesses that reported to have seen it from miles around. For the second or two it touched down on earth, satellite and radio waves had been disrupted. TVs and computers and radios blinked off at the same time before coming back on, like nothing had happened.

But I was there. I felt it. And I knew it wasn't lightning that struck.

"That's what they tell me," I said, and forced a smile. I didn't tell him anything else, though. Not about how when I woke up in the hospital it had been Tuesday. How the doctors told me I'd been in some kind of coma. How even though everyone at the church witnessed me being shot, there was no entrance or exit wound. Even the cuts on my hand were gone. I didn't tell Steve that I was released just in time for Grandma's funeral, then Dean's. That I even attended some of the others' too, like Henry and John Porter's, even Dawn and Lindsay Bowyer's. That a week later I'd gone to Ohio, to return two friends back to what they would have called home, so one could be buried next to his wife, the other's ashes spread above his mother's grave.

Steve turned to me. He wasn't wearing his hat and the breeze caused some of his gray hair to twist and turn in a kind of dance.

"So that's it," he said. "That's all you can tell me about what happened."

"Honestly?"

He nodded.

"Honestly, I can't remember much about what went on. Even at the church with Dean. I just … I can't remember."

But I was lying, and I hated myself for it. Steve had proven himself a friend throughout this entire thing, and I had no reason at all to lie to him like this. But the truth was I didn't want to tell him. I didn't want to tell him that ever since I'd awoken from that coma, my memory had improved. And not just of that one week in Bridgton, but of my entire life—every good thing said and done, every bad thing, all there in my head, ready to be picked at random. I imagined that green field of endless doors in my mind, all those doors now standing open.

Not only that, I also had better insight into other people's lives, both living and dead. I could see everything Moses and Joey had gone through. I knew everything Sarah had ever thought. Even right now, standing here with Steve, I knew about his wife, how she'd been told just five months ago that the lump in her breast was indeed cancer and that after all the tests, it appeared it was malignant.

"Well, I figured as much," Steve said. "I was hoping you could at least tell me about the old man they found by that stone house in the woods. From the reports I read, he had a rifle with one expelled shell, and his head … his head had been pulled off."

I glanced back down at the drainage dip, back at the Twizzler wrapper. "I wish I could tell you, Steve, but like I said, I just can't remember. I think … I think getting struck by that lightning screwed up something in my head."

Steve nodded like my answer was acceptable enough, just like the police up in New York had when I told them the same thing. They'd been sympathetic but had wanted answers too, answers that I knew were much too wild for them to believe. So I did what I swore I'd never do again and lied, told them I couldn't remember. After talking to the doctors they then let up on their questioning. They said it was actually a miracle that I was alive to begin with, that I'd been standing in the right spot when the lightning struck. Anywhere outside the area I was found lying unconscious and I'd be dead. I didn't believe it until I went back a few days later and saw for myself. All the grass and trees were darkened and dead except one spot, a spot that was green and full of life.

"Can you at least confirm one thing for me?" Steve asked. "I hear someone came back with you. A young pregnant girl. Supposedly she's staying with you at the house."

"Sure," I said, feeling grateful that I could finally talk about something. I told him about Sarah, how her mom had died two years ago and how her dad and brother had been killed at the church along with everyone else. "She's got no one in her life right now, the same as me. So I offered to let her stay as long as she wanted until she figured out what to do with her life."

"You know people will gossip."

"People will always gossip."

He smiled and nodded, and then his face became serious once again. "Okay, Chris, one last thing. I've read all the police reports and news articles about what happened that week in Bridgton. And I don't know what it is, call it intuition, but something tells me there's more to what took place than what you're letting on. I know you say you can't remember, and maybe that's the truth, but I think there is one thing you can tell me."

"What's that?"

"Is it over?"

I thought about it for a long moment. "I have no idea."

We stood there behind the church then, alone with the soft summer breeze and the sound of the traffic on the highway. Neither of us spoke a word. And at that moment, the silence between us was the only thing that made sense.

From where I pulled off along the road, I could see the farmhouse very clearly. I thought about all the times I'd been inside it or somewhere on the property, either in Melanie's room or in the dining room having dinner with her folks. Helping her mom wash dishes in the kitchen. Sitting with Patty and listening to one of her many knock-knock jokes. Then there were the times I'd helped Jack Murphy, with mowing the massive lawn or helping with something in the barn, and how there had been times I would look at him and think what a great man he was, how I would be proud to someday call him my father-in-law.

She was in there now with her mom and sister. I could see both of their cars, as well as Jack Murphy's pickup truck. I doubted Mel was busy sharing everything she'd seen and experienced while over in Europe. I was sure whatever pictures she'd taken were still in rolls of film, waiting to be developed. It might be a long time before they were developed, and what then? Would Mel sit down and look at each picture, try to remember what day they had been taken, how at that moment in time, while she was on the busy streets of London or Paris, her father had attempted to molest her sister? Just how did you come back from that, with the knowledge that one of your family members—your own father—had that evil inside him?

I had done too much to her already. I may not have been solely responsible for the pregnancy, but I sure as hell was for the abortion. That had been me entirely. And then I'd gone and caught her father before he did something unspeakable. Forever I would be known to Mel as the guy who forced her to have an abortion, the guy who got her father arrested. Sure, I'd saved little Patty from a worse fate, but would Mel see it like that? I wasn't sure. All I knew for certain was that I needed to talk to her, I needed to tell her I was sorry.

But not today. When, I didn't know, but not today.

By the time I arrived home it was early evening. For some reason the house looked different without the crime scene tape circling it. I noticed the grass was a bit too high and knew I'd have to mow it either tomorrow or Sunday. It felt so strange, entering back into normality, something I thought I should welcome but didn't.

Henry Porter's truck was parked in the driveway, one of the few things Sarah had kept from Bridgton that wasn't her own. I parked behind it and went inside and found her in the living room. She sat on the couch reading a trade paperback I hadn't gotten a chance yet to read myself—the same very trade paperback Moses had noticed me looking at in his RV.

She said, "So how'd it go?"

Meaning, how did things go between me and James Young, who'd called last night, asking me to stop by to talk with him.

"Can you come with me?" I asked. "I want to show you something."

We took my car. I had to help her down the steps and into the passenger seat, as she was already eight months along. Not much longer now before the due date. Not much longer until I found out whether my choice would stick.

It took ten minutes to get there. We played Coldplay the entire ride. I had to take a few back roads that weren't paved and were bordered by fields. Farms and silos dotted many of them. Finally I came to the point where the sycamore tree marked the crossing. I didn't have to worry about pulling over, because hardly anyone ever used this road.

I helped Sarah out of the car and then stood with her, facing toward the sun that had already begun to set.

"This isn't quite Harris Hill Park, I know. But it's the highest spot in Lanton. When I was younger my parents used to bring me here with the telescope they got me for my birthday. I don't know why, but I always thought that I'd be closer to the moon and stars right here than anywhere else."

She smiled at me and looked out at the horizon, at the colors the sun and clouds made together. And as she did, my eyes drifted down to her belly, and I thought about the baby inside her. I thought about the night I'd come out of Shepherd's Books to find my dead father standing beside my car.

"It's not that simple, Christopher," Samael said. *"The choice is for two lives, one or the other. And if you refuse to decide, both lives will perish. Now, are you ready to see just how innocent you truly are?"*

And as I released my grip on the knife, knowing it would be useless, Samael explained to me my choice. That the two lives involved were Sarah and her baby. That childbirth is not always an easy process and sometimes there are complications. Something may happen where the life of the baby is endangered. Or something may happen where the mother's life is the one endangered. And sometimes both lives become endangered and it's impossible to save either one.

"So I will give you the chance, Christopher. I will give you the chance to save Sarah's life, or the life of her unborn child. Both do not have to die, but one must. Which shall it be?"

"What are you thinking about?" Sarah asked.

I blinked and looked at her. "Me? Nothing."

She grinned and poked me in my side. "I don't know, Chris. Sometimes I wonder just what goes on in that head of yours. But I do want to thank you. I want to thank you for everything. My baby thanks you too."

Sarah stared back out at the horizon. It was reddish-orange, the sky above us purple. She took my hand and gave it a slight squeeze.

"It's beautiful, isn't it?"

But I didn't answer. I just stood there holding her hand. And even though we were both watching the same sunset, there was no doubt in my mind we were seeing two completely different worlds.

EPILOGUE

LIFE ISN'T FAIR.

It's an old adage, a tired cliché, but you know this to be true. You've known it all your life, ever since you were a boy.

Your parents knew it too. So did Moses and Joey. So did your grandmother and uncle.

So does Sarah.

Her baby's name is Joseph Christopher Porter. He's been born almost a year. You remember just how nervous you were when Sarah went into labor. You didn't want to go with her to the hospital. You didn't want to hold her hand. You didn't want to be there when it happened and the realization of your choice finally came to pass.

But there were no complications.

Neither Sarah's life nor the baby's was in danger.

Now the three of you share the house you once lived in with your parents. Together you make a strange but stable family. Because every time you look at Sarah and Joey, you remember the night with Samael and the choice you made. You can't help yourself.

Still, you think you make a good father—which feels strange, because there is nothing romantic between you and Sarah, you are both simply friends. You care for Joey like he's your own. When you feed him or hold him or change him, you are reminded of the baby you would have had with Mel.

When you're not at home, you're at work. When you're not at work, you're at home. This is your life now.

But at least you lived through the nightmare.

You keep telling yourself that like it's something to be proud of.

Then one morning you wake from a new nightmare. You've had others similar to this one, though each is unique in its own way. And every time you wake from one, you hope it will be the last.

You lie in bed for a long time and stare at the ceiling. When you finally do get around, shower and dress, you grab the sports bag from inside your closet. You've only used the sports bag three times before. Each time you came home, you packed it again and kept it in the closet, just in case you had another vision.

The last was over three months ago.

Downstairs you find Sarah in the kitchen. She's feeding Joey, who now sits in a high chair. The bib he's wearing shows Elmo's red face. He sees you and smiles. Applesauce drips from his chin.

Sarah notices the sports bag in your hand. Her own smile fades.

"How many?"

"Thirteen."

"Where?"

"Boise, Idaho."

She nods once and turns her attention back to Joey. Dabs the applesauce from his chin.

"How long should I tell your boss you'll be gone?"

"Two weeks."

"Will you call me when you get there?"

"I'll try."

Then you're outside in your car, sitting behind the wheel. The engine idles. The radio is off. Silence is your only friend now, silence and maybe the sports bag on the passenger seat. Besides clothes, inside it are your grandfather's Bible, the green ceramic umbrella you once gave your mother, and the plush Tasmanian Devil. You don't believe in luck, but you've taken these items with you each time before, and each time you came back alive.

Waiting in the car, you stare out the windshield at nothing in particular. This has become your ritual every time you get a new vision. Sitting in the car staring ahead like maybe you'll change your mind and go back inside, try to get on with your life.

But you haven't yet.

You doubt you ever will.

Sarah seems to understand this too, though she's never happy when it happens. The last three times she's asked you the same question when you returned, just like she will ask you when you return this time—if you return this time.

Why do you do it?

She knows the answer but asks anyway. You know why she does. It's for your benefit, not hers.

You close your eyes for a second and think of the vision you've just had. Of the thirteen faceless people in Boise, Idaho, whose lives now hang in the balance. You've got eight days before they die. And the only thing now standing between them dying and living is you.

Opening your eyes, you put the car in gear. Begin to roll down the driveway, until you're stopped right before the street. Then you think of the question Sarah will ask you, the same very question you ask yourself at this moment before continuing.

"Because I couldn't live with myself if I didn't," you whisper.

Only then do you ride off into the backwards sunset.

ABOUT THE AUTHOR

Robert Swartwood is the *USA Today* bestselling author of *The Serial Killer's Wife*, *No Shelter*, *Man of Wax*, and several other novels. He created the term "hint fiction" and is the editor of *Hint Fiction: An Anthology of Stories in 25 Words or Fewer*. He lives with his wife in Pennsylvania.